CALL ME
ZEBRA

CALL ME
ZEBRA

///////////////

Azareen
Van der Vliet Oloomi

HOUGHTON MIFFLIN HARCOURT
Boston   New York
2018

For information about permission to reproduce selections from this book, write
to trade.permissions@hmhco.com or to Permissions, Houghton Mifflin Harcourt
Publishing Company, 3 Park Avenue, 19th Floor, New York, New York 10016.

hmhco.com

Library of Congress Cataloging-in-Publication Data
Names: Van der Vliet Oloomi, Azareen, author.
Title: Call me Zebra / Azareen Van der Vliet Oloomi.
Description: Boston : Houghton Mifflin Harcourt, 2018.
Identifiers: LCCN 2017044915 (print) | LCCN 2017047825 (ebook) |
ISBN 9780544944152 (ebook) | ISBN 9780544944602 (hardcover)
Subjects: LCSH: Self-realization in women — Fiction. | BISAC:
FICTION / Literary. | FICTION / Cultural Heritage. | FICTION /
Psychological. | FICTION / General. | GSAFD: Love stories.
Classification: LCC PS3622.A58543 (ebook) | LCC PS3622.A58543 C35 2018 (print)
| DDC 813/.6—dc23
LC record available at https://lccn.loc.gov/2017044915

Illustrations by Murphy Chang
Book design by Kelly Dubeau Smydra

Printed in the United States of America
DOC 10 9 8 7 6 5 4 3 2 1

"On Exactitude in Science," copyright © 1998 by Maria Kodama; translation
copyright © 1998 by Penguin Random House LLC; from *Collected Fictions:
Volume 3* by Jorge Luis Borges, translated by Andrew Hurley. Used by permission
of Viking Books, an imprint of Penguin Publishing Group, a division of Penguin
Random House LLC. All rights reserved. The dictionary definition on page 233
is from the *Online Etymology Dictionary* © 2001–2017 by Douglas Harper.

Background research for this novel was made possible in part by support from the
Fulbright Scholar Program, a program of the United States Department of State
Bureau of Educational and Cultural Affairs, and from the Institute for Scholarship
in the Liberal Arts, College of Arts and Letters, University of Notre Dame.

For
all my dead relatives

— Zebra

However many beings there are in whatever realms of being might exist, whether they are born from an egg or born from a womb, born from the water or born from the air, whether they have form or no form, whether they have perception or no perception or neither perception nor no perception, in whatever conceivable realm of being one might conceive of beings, in the realm of complete nirvana I shall liberate them all. And though I thus liberate countless beings, not a single being is liberated.

— THE DIAMOND SUTRA

CALL ME
ZEBRA

PROLOGUE

The Story of My Ill-Fated Origins

LLITERATES, ABECEDARIANS, ELITISTS, RODENTS ALL — I will tell you this: I, Zebra, born Bibi Abbas Abbas Hosseini on a scorching August day in 1982, am a descendent of a long line of self-taught men who repeatedly abandoned their capital, Tehran, where blood has been washed with blood for a hundred years, to take refuge in Nowshahr, in the languid, damp regions of Mazandaran. There, hemmed in by the rugged green slopes of the Elborz Mountains and surrounded by ample fields of rice, cotton, and tea, my forebears pursued the life of the mind.

There, too, I was born and lived the early part of my life.

My father, Abbas Abbas Hosseini — multilingual translator of great and small works of literature, man with a thick mustache fashioned after Nietzsche's — was in charge of my education. He taught me Spanish, Italian, Catalan, Hebrew, Turkish, Arabic, English, Farsi, French, German. I was taught to know the languages of the oppressed and the oppressors because, according to my father, and to my father's father, and to his father before that, the wheels of history are always turning and there is no knowing who will be run over next. I picked up languages the way some people pick up viruses. I was armed with literature.

As a family, we possess a great deal of intelligence — a kind of superintellect — but we came into this world, one after the other, during the era when Nietzsche famously said that God is dead. We believe that death is the reason why we have always been so terribly shortchanged when it comes to luck. We are ill-fated, destined to wander in perpetual exile across a world hostile to our intelligence. In fact, possessing an agile intellect with literary overtones has only served to worsen our fate. But it is what we know and have. We are convinced that ink runs through our veins instead of blood.

My father was educated by three generations of self-taught philosophers, poets, and painters: his father, Dalir Abbas Hosseini; his grandfather, Arman Abbas Hosseini; his great-grandfather, Shams Abbas Hosseini. Our family emblem, inspired by Sumerian seals of bygone days, consists of a clay cylinder engraved with three As framed within a circle; the As stand for our most treasured roles, listed here in order of importance: Autodidacts, Anarchists, Atheists. The following motto is engraved underneath the cylinder: *In this false world, we guard our lives with our deaths.*

The motto also appears at the bottom of a still life of a mallard hung from a noose, completed by my great-great-grandfather, Shams Abbas Hosseini, in the aftermath of Iran's failed Constitutional Revolution at the turn of the twentieth century. Upon finishing the painting, he pointed at it with his cane, nearly bludgeoning the mallard's face with its tip and, his voice simultaneously crackling with disillusionment and fuming with rage, famously declared to his son, my great-grandfather, Arman Abbas Hosseini, "Death is coming, but we literati will remain as succulent as this wild duck!"

This seemingly futile moment marked the beginning of our long journey toward nothingness, into the craggy pits of this measly universe. Generation after generation, our bodies have been coated with the dust of death. Our hearts have been extinguished, our lives leveled. We are weary, as thin as rakes, hacked into pieces. But we believe our duty is to persevere against a world hell-bent on eliminating the few who dare to sprout in the collective manure of degenerate humans. That's where I come into the picture. I — astonished and amazed at the magnitude of the darkness that surrounds us — am the last in a long line of valiant thinkers.

Upon my birth, the fifth of August 1982, and on its anniversary every year thereafter, as a rite of passage, my father, Abbas Abbas Hosseini, whispered a monologue titled "A Manifesto of Historical Time and the Corrected Philosophy of Iranian History: A Hosseini Secret" into my ear. I include it here, transcribed verbatim from memory.

Ill-omened child, I present you with the long and the short of our afflicted country, Iran: Supposed Land of the Aryans.

In 550 BC, Cyrus the Great, King of the Four Corners of the World, brave and benevolent man, set out on a military campaign from the kingdom of Anshan in Parsa near the Gulf, site of the famous ruins of Persepolis, to conquer the Medes and the Lydians and the Babylonians. Darius and Xerxes the Great, his most famous successors, continued erecting the commodious empire their father had begun through the peaceful seizing of neighboring peoples. But just as facts are overtaken by other facts, all great rulers are eclipsed by their envious competitors. Search the world east to west, north to south; nowhere will you find a shortage of tyrants, all expertly trained to sniff out weak prey. Eventually, Cyrus the Great's line of ruling progeny came to an end with Alexander the Great, virile youth whose legacy was, in turn, overshadowed by a long line of new conquerors, each of whom briefly took pleasure in the rubble of dynasties past.

Every one of us in Iran is a hybrid individual best described as a residue of a composite of fallen empires. If you were to look at us collectively, you would see a voluble and troubled nation. Imagine a person with multiple heads and a corresponding number of arms and legs. How is such a person, one body composed of so many, supposed to conduct herself? She will spend a lifetime beating her heads against one another, lifting up one pair of her arms in order to strangle the head of another.

We, the people — varied, troubled, heterogeneous — have been scrambling like cockroaches across this land for centuries without receiving so much as a nod from our diverse rulers. They have never looked at us; they have only ever looked in the mirror.

What is the consequence of such disregard? An eternal return of uprisings followed by mass murder and suffocating repression. I could not say which of the two is worse. In the words of Yevgeny Zamyatin: *Revolutions are infinite.*

By the twentieth century, the Persian empire's frontiers had been hammered so far back that the demarcating boundary of our shrunken nation was bruised; it was black and blue! Every fool knows that in order to keep surviving that which expands has to contract. Just look at the human heart. My own, reduced to a stone upon the double deaths of my father and my father's father, both murdered by our so-called leaders, is plump and fleshy again; your birth has sent fresh blood rushing through its corridors.

Hear me, child: The details of the history of our nation are nothing but a useless inventory of facts unless they are used to illuminate the wretched nature of our universal condition. The core of the matter, the point of this notable monologue, is to expose the artful manipulation of historical time through the creation of false narratives rendered as truth and exercised by the world's rulers with expert precision for hundreds of years. Think of our own leaders' lies as exhibit A. Let us shuffle through them one by one.

When the century was still young, our people attempted the Constitutional Revolution but failed. In time, that failure produced the infamous Reza Shah Pahlavi, who ruled the country with thuggery and intimidation. Years later, during the Second World War, Mr. Pahlavi was sent into exile by the British, those nosy and relentless chasers of money — those thieves, if we're being honest. And what, child, do you think happened then? Pahlavi's son, Mohammad Reza Shah Pahlavi, who was greener than a tree in summer, stepped up to the throne.

Claiming to be the metaphysical descendent of the benevolent Cyrus the Great, the visionary Mohammad Reza Shah Pahlavi anointed himself the "King of Kings" and launched the White Revolution, a chain of reforms designed to yank the country's citizens into modernity by hook or by crook.

It was just a matter of time before the people rose against the King of Kings. Revolution broke out. Mohammad Reza Shah Pahlavi spilled blood, tasted it, then, like a spineless reptile, slid up the stairs of an airplane with his bejeweled queen in tow and fled, famously declaring: "Only a dictator kills his people. I am a king."

The Islamic clergy, whose graves the king had been digging for years, hijacked the revolution, and in one swift move, the monarchy was abolished. The king's absence allowed the revolutionary religious leader Ayatollah Khomeini to return to the country after a long political exile. Khomeini, former dissident, swiftly established the Islamic Republic of Iran and positioned himself as the Supreme Leader. The Grand Ayatollah proceeded to outdo the King of Kings. His line of metaphysical communication skipped over Cyrus the Great; it pierced the heavens to arrive directly at God's ear. The Supreme Leader claimed to enjoy unparalleled divine protection.

How did he employ his blessings? By digging the graves of the secularists and the intelligentsia just as the Pahlavi kings had dug the graves of dissidents, Communists, and the clergy. With one hand, God's victors eliminated their revolutionary brothers, and with the other, they shucked pistachios, drank tea, raided their victims' closets, ate cherries picked from their gardens.

Child, we, the Hosseinis, were persecuted by both sides. The King of Kings, seeing his end in sight, made no exceptions. His men garroted the old and the infirm and the young. Mothers and children are still weeping for their lost loved ones. Your great-grandfather, Arman Abbas Hosseini, was among the executed. The ruthless pigs dragged him from his deathbed when he was eighty-nine. Two days later, your grandfather, Dalir Abbas Hosseini, had a heart attack. He could not endure the thought of his father being hanged from the rafters. Before he died, he told me that he could not stop hearing the sound of his father's brittle bones crackling under the weight of his body as it hung from the noose. Until you came into this world, my only consolation was that my father, at least, had died in his own bed. You are a flame of light in these dark woods.

Like everyone else in this trifling universe, we Iranians are a sum of our sorry parts. Put our pieces together and what emerges is not a whole, clear image. Our edges are jagged, nonconforming, incoherent. Our bloodline is so long and varied, it can be traced back to the origins of the universe. How is man to make sense of his condition when the wrangle over power between conquerors old and new herds history's stories in ever more puzzling directions?

Now that you have heard the story of our cruel fate, you are ready to listen to the Hosseini Commandments, a text that has three giant heads that you must make part of your own. Why, you might ask? Because if you know the ways of man, the various conditions of his iniquitous mind, you will not be stumped by fear, guilt, avarice, grief, or remorse, and therefore, when the time comes, you will not hesitate to plumb the depths of the abyss and send out a resounding alarm to the unthinking masses, those who are willfully blind, warning them of the advancing army of the unresolved past.

FIRST COMMANDMENT: Ecce homo: This is man, destined to suffer at the hands of two-faced brethren inclined to loot the minds and bodies of friend and foe. Ill-fated child, trust nobody and love nothing except literature, the only magnanimous host there is in this decaying world. Seek refuge in it. It is through its missives alone that you will survive your death, preserve your inner freedom.

SECOND COMMANDMENT: Like a gored bull, history is charging through the world in search of fresh victims. Think! Does a gored bull run straight? No. It zigzags. It circles around itself. It is bleeding and half-blind. Be warned: The world's numbskull intellectuals, which form 99.9 percent of all intellectuals, will feed you lies. History, they will say, is linear, and time continuous. During Pahlavi's final years, these deluded intellectuals hoped that revolution would lead to democracy. What came of it but death? Your ancestors, the Hosseinis, paid for their leaders' ignorance with their lives. Do not be caught unawares. Spit the lie right back out. Aim for their heads.

THIRD COMMANDMENT: We Hosseinis — Autodidacts, Anarchists, Atheists — are expert connoisseurs of literature and therefore capable of taking a narrative apart and putting it back together faster than a wounded man can say "Ah!" This talent, passed on to you by your honorable ancestors, is your sword. Draw it anytime you need to strike stupidity in the face.

The depth of our knowledge, the precision of our tongues, and our capacity for detecting lies is unparalleled. We are the true intellectuals, the exception to the rule, the .1 percent. This is yet another source of our ill-fatedness.

We are the loneliest of the lonely. Our message falls on the deaf ears of the unthinking masses. Nevertheless, we are destined to wander the earth spreading the word of our forebears and our forebears' forebears, the Great Writers of the Past, who, like us, knew to retreat into literature in order to survive history's bloodshed and thus be in a position to share the truth of it with the world. For this we will always be persecuted: for pointing our fingers and asking, Is this a man?

Ill-fated child, when your time comes, you must dive headfirst into the swampy lagoons of our pitiful human circumstances and, after roving the depths, emerge with the slimy pearl of truth. Be warned: The truth is ugly, wretched, full of craters and holes through which rise the fumes of death. Most men, smug and cowardly, will turn their noses away from its stench. Sooner or later, you will have to engage with these men; you will have to persevere despite their private delusions and collective ignorance.

Suffice it to say that in combination with the events that unfurled during my childhood years, events charged with everything that is futile and unspeakable in this universe, my father's monologue transformed my consciousness. I had not been alive long before my mother, Bibi Khanoum, died. Her death flattened my heart into a sheet of paper. It leveled my mind. It rubbed my nose in manure. My only good fortune is that I realized early on that I am one of the wretched of this earth. But this is a matter for later.

According to my father, during the long revolutionary months prior to the establishment of the Islamic Republic of Iran, my mother — a woman with strong legs and a sweet disposition — would remind my father, Abbas Abbas Hosseini, that he had been accused by the Iranian intelligentsia of being "a passive traitor whose nose was hooked into books while others' were being rubbed in the blood of their brethren."

Bibi Khanoum, my father informed me, would say: "Don't test your luck, Abbas! People don't like to be snubbed while they're being martyred for their beliefs."

In response, my father would pace the corridor of their Tehran apartment convulsing, his moods swinging dramatically, while he spewed ad infinitum: "I am a Hosseini. I would rather die than hold my tongue! Pseudo intellectuals! Imbeciles! People have disappeared, been arrested, executed, their bodies discarded, scattered across the earth. And they still believe democracy is around the corner? The revolution is going to be hijacked. Don't they know history is full of ruptures, haphazard events, and prone to recycling its own evil phenomena?"

The following year, an ashen sky, grayer and heavier than a donkey's behind, settled over Iran. As my father predicted, the revolution was promptly seized by the Islamic leaders. And even worse, Saddam Hussein, that wide-eyed despot, came sniffing around the borders of our freshly assembled Islamic republic and proudly launched a brutal and tactless war on a fatigued and divided Iran.

A year after the war broke out, the few remaining intellectuals who hadn't been jailed or fled the country with false papers declared my father a clairvoyant truth teller. But my father — Autodidact, Anarchist, Atheist, whose character they had previously assassinated — refused to have his moment in the sun. Instead, he and my mother, Bibi Khanoum, ran for the hills. She was pregnant with me, and my father had suffered enough loss to last him a lifetime. It was winter. The journey was cold, and damp, and dangerous. It had felt interminable to them. But they survived it and took shelter in that stone house in Nowshahr, near the Caspian Sea, which was built as a sanctuary by my great-great-grandfather, Shams Abbas Hosseini, who referred to the house as either the Censorship Recovery Center or the Oasis of Books, depending on his mood.

I have been told by my father that halfway through their journey, in the middle of the rugged Elborz Mountains, which separate Tehran from the Caspian Sea, he stopped the car and got out. He looked over his shoulder at Mount Damavand, which hovers over our capital like the shiny white tooth of a gentle giant, and wept until the skin around his eyes was paper-thin: "That pig-headed Saddam is going to level our city!"

And level our city he did. But even in the midst of darkness, there is always a flicker of light. Months later, in 1982, I was born in the heart of the Oasis of Books, the library, which was designed in the shape of an egg and built around a date palm that shot to the sky through an opening in the roof. My mother leaned against the trunk of the tree and pushed. I — a gray-faced, black-eyed baby — slipped out of her loins into a room lined with dusty tomes, into a country seized by war. I immediately popped a date in my mouth to sweeten the blow. My parents looked down at me, grinning with hope.

I learned to crawl, walk, read, write, shit, and eat in that library. Even before I could read, I nurtured my brain by running my hands along the spines of all the old books and licking their soot off my fingers. After feeding on the dust of literature, I sat on the Persian rug and stared at *The Hung Mallard*, which was fixed to the wall. Once I was old enough to walk, I paced in concentric circles like a Sufi mystic, masticating dates and muttering the family motto to myself: *In this false world, we guard our lives with our deaths.*

The days passed. My education unfolded in the midst of the interminable war. My father read aloud to me from Nietzsche's oeuvre on a daily basis, usually in the mornings, and after lunch, he taught me about literature, culling paragraphs from books written by our ingenious forebears, the Great Writers of the Past: Johann Wolfgang von Goethe, Mawlānā (alias Rumi), Omar Khayyám, Sor Juana Inés de la Cruz, Dante Alighieri, Marie-Henri Beyle (alias Stendhal), Teresa of Ávila, Rainer Maria Rilke, Franz Kafka, Sādegh Hedāyat, Frederick Douglass, Francesco Petrarca, Miguel de Cervantes, Walter Benjamin, Sei Shōnagon. The list went on and on; it included religious thinkers, philosopher-poets, mystics, secularists, agnostics, atheists. Literature, as my father would say, is a nation without boundaries. It is infinite. There are no stations, no castes, no checkpoints.

At the end of each lesson, as bedtime neared, my father stiffly ordered: "Ill-fated child, assimilate and regurgitate!" In this way, he nurtured my mind. He taught me the long-lost skill of memorization. What is the purpose of memorization in the Hosseini tradition? It is twofold: not only does it restore the ritual function to literature — its orality — which harnesses literature's spontaneous ability to transform the listener's consciousness, but it also protects the archive of our troubled, ruinous humanity from being lost through the barbarism of war and the perpetual ignorance that binds our hands and feet. Count the times books have been burned in piles by the fearful and the infirm, men and women allergic to inquiry. Memorization is our only recourse against loss. We Hosseinis can reproduce the pantheon of literature instantly; we can retranscribe texts from the dark folds of our infinite minds. We are the scribes of the future.

While my father and I spent our days united in the realm of literature, my mother, Bibi Khanoum, spent her days in the kitchen. If she ever ventured out of the house, it was to find us food: rice, oranges, fish the local tribesmen had managed to wrench out of the sea. I didn't spend much time with her. She didn't agree with my father's methods. She considered them invasive and extreme for my age, but he, twenty years her senior, had the upper hand in all matters governing our family.

I remember my mother once walked into the oval library, where she had given birth to me, with her apron tied around her waist and her face moist from the kitchen steam, to scorn my father: "Abbas, you are raising this child to be a boy! How will she survive in the world? Who will marry her?"

My father reproached her: "These are times of war and you are worried about marriage?"

"And who do you suppose will feed her once we are dead?" she retorted. "A mother has to worry about her child's stomach!"

Confrontation ensued, but I don't remember anything after that. I have tried hard to remember my mother's face, the tone of her voice, the feel of her touch, but the details are out of reach. She would die not long after that argument, and the void left over by her death would push my father and me over the edge. He would fill the lacunae of our lives with literature. Over time, my mind, filled to the brim with sentences, would forsake her.

In the meantime, on the other side of the Elborz Mountains, that megalomaniac Saddam was spreading mustard gas across the frontier, shooting missiles at random targets, burying mines in the no-man's-land separating our two nations. What did the Supreme Leader of the Islamic Republic of Iran do? He sat on his newly established throne looking healthier than a fresh pear and ordered human wave attacks to blow up the mines that his nemesis, that bushy eyebrowed man-child, had buried at the front. Human wave attacks! As if it were the Great War!

Now, Rodents, let us ask: What is the purpose of a flicker of light in the midst of all that bloodshed? Easy. To illuminate the magnitude of the surrounding darkness.

At a certain point during the long war, my father started to wander about the perimeter of the house or along the seashore, night and day, holding me up as if I were a torch. He used my head, which shone like a beacon with all the enlightened literature he had inserted into it, to measure the scope of the encroaching abyss. Iran, he decided, was no longer a place to think. Not even the Caspian was safe. We had to flee. We had to go into exile. We departed: numb, astonished, bewildered.

Thus our vagabond life began. We left our home, stopping just beyond the door and looking back once. Pitiful, simpering, we waved our goodbyes to the Oasis of Books, to the orange groves and eucalyptus trees, to the rice paddies and sandy shores. Pressed together on the rear of an ass, my father, mother, and I set out across Iran's forbidding horizon toward the Turkish border. Of our earthly possessions, we took only our samovar, a rug, our books, and *The Hung Mallard*. We had packed a few provisions, the little food we had left in the house. It was the middle of summer. Other deserters had died in the rugged flanks and stony depressions of our mountains. We didn't want to be caught in a snow blizzard. We didn't want to die against an icy stone, frostbitten. We rode in silence for a long time, fearful and worn down. No one dared to ask: Will we ever set foot on these grounds again? Smell the jasmine bush? Stuff our mouths with the sweet meat of dates freshly fallen from the trees?

At first, the dirt path under our feet seemed to trot along with us — kind and concerned for our safety. But our fate took a turn for the worse. Somewhere between Khalkhal and Mount Sahand, in a long stretch of no-man's-land littered with Iraqi missiles, a poisonous black cloud billowing over the southwestern horizon, my mother, Bibi Khanoum, died. She had walked into an abandoned home in the middle of a razed village to see if the deserters had left behind any food. Just at that moment, likely when she was hovering over the kitchen table, the house collapsed. She was crushed under the weight of its stones.

I stood before that collapsed house in a state of shock. I could hear my father's voice rising and falling in the distance. He whimpered and yowled. I could hear him choking on his tears. I didn't know where we were. I covered my ears. I couldn't stand listening to him sob in that manner, like a wounded animal left to die in the dry gales of the desert. But I could still hear his sobs rising into that godless gray dome that keeps us pinned to this meager earth. The world seemed nebulous, unnavigable. I felt as though someone had taken a rolling pin to my heart, razing it and extinguishing its warmth. I felt a gaping hole bloom in my gut. Then those crucial four words of the first Hosseini Commandment, which my father had whispered to me upon my birth, trumpeted through my void: *Love nothing except literature.*

I put one foot in front of the other and walked toward my father. He was curled up near a rock. My hand hurt as I nudged him. I told him we had to unbury my mother. I told him we couldn't just leave her there to rot. When he finally looked at me, I saw that his eyes had turned into two murky puddles and that the skin of his face had drooped. To me, his features seemed to have melted; his nose was indecipherable from his cheeks, his forehead had merged with his chin. The only thing I could see clearly was his thick black mustache.

It took us a full day and night of hard labor to retrieve Bibi Khanoum's body from the wreckage. My father kneeled against her and pulled her into his arms. He rocked her and wept silently. I stood behind him and watched. Her face was flat and gray. It was covered in dust. It could have been anyone's. Once I had seen it, I couldn't unsee it. Her face had introduced a distortion in my visual field. The world, all of its parts, which, when summed up, still refused to make a whole, seemed unstable at the edges.

Hours later, breathless and confused, we buried my mother beneath a lone date palm. Our fingers were numb from clawing at the earth. We stood over her grave and cried, then we waved our good-byes the way we had waved at the stones of our village, at the jasmine bushes lining the streets, at the magnolia and citrus trees, and at the rows of eucalyptus growing wild near the sea.

As we rode away from her makeshift grave, my father brought his hand to his mustache, which was as long and limp as Nietzsche's, pulled on the tips that were stained yellow from all the tea he drank, and nervously said: "It could have been worse. At least she was buried in her homeland. There is nothing worse than dying a stranger."

At the ripe age of five, I thought to myself: Worse than strangers are estranged brethren. As we moved farther away from my mother, I felt that void — deep, dark, craggy — widen. But I said nothing. Because sometimes, as Shakespeare famously wrote, *the rest is silence.*

We continued our journey. In order not to arouse suspicion, my father designed a senseless path, full of digressions, one long detour after another. This vagabonding through the dead of night, through dark and silent fields, across terrain that was being drenched with poison gas and blood and death, turned us numb and sluggish. At times, my father seemed to have forgotten who he was or where we were. In those moments, he would look at the sky with a wide, dry mouth, and it would seem to me that even his mustache was barely hanging on to his crusty upper lip.

Every morning, the grainy light of dawn came down on our heads like a guillotine. We didn't have time to mourn. We tried to push away any emotion that arose: panic, shame, fear, despair, astonishment. We didn't know how else to carry on, how else to move through our remaining days. Sometimes, in an effort to lift our spirits, my father would speak. He would say, his voice breaking, that the lesser men on this earth are the most powerful and that we, the ill-fated, must draw from scant reservoirs, plumb the depths of our singed minds and hearts, just to find the courage to survive in this world that acts against us with such violence. Worse than violence, he would say, is the indifference of those who watch the destruction of others and remain unmoved by it. With what little conviction he could muster, he would remind me that it was our job to resist the tyranny of hate and its behavior of choice: the elimination of others.

The next time my father and I came across a leveled village, we sifted through the rubble and dug out from the debris six blackboards that had been used in the village school; we tied each pair together with a piece of old string and mournfully slipped the boards over our heads and saddled our ass with a pair. We wore them like shields. But while we continued on, our ass, in still another tragedy, died of exhaustion. By the end, the poor animal barely had the energy to keep his ears pointing at the godless heavens. My father, unusually lighthearted, stood over the animal's body and saluted him. "Good-bye, dear Rocinante!" he said, as if our ass had been Don Quixote's infamously weak horse. He knew how much I loved the trials and tribulations of that Knight of the Sad Countenance.

And so my father and I went through the lowlands and highlands of Iran's West Azerbaijan province on foot, dragging our suitcase of meager possessions along with us. We walked by night and hid by day. We were caught in the approaching winter. Our teeth chattered; our bones ached. It wouldn't be long before glistening sheets of snow would settle across the rugged landscapes that lay ahead. We ate potatoes, beets, turnips; anything my father managed to procure every now and then. We were reduced to desperation by our aimless path, which seemed to fold over itself a million times before delivering us to the border. Our bodies had metamorphosed. We were skeletal, ragged, dirty, stupid from the rough blows of our journey toward nothingness. In the rare occasions when we saw villagers moving across the landscape, ambling into the light and crossing out of it again, they pretended not to see us. It was as if we didn't exist.

One morning, as we sat huddled together at the center of a cluster of trees, my father said rather conclusively of my mother: "The whole world is a mind. Her mind has been absorbed back into the mind of the universe." I looked around. A thick mist hovered over the landscape. The whole world seemed unreal, tinged with my mother's death and the death of the Hosseinis. I thought to myself, she is everywhere; she has contaminated everything. I took comfort in this. I dragged that vaporous air into my lungs and held my breath.

Nights passed, and we marched on. The closer we came to the border, the more dead bodies we found: dissidents who had tried to flee but who had frozen to death, Saddam's victims. We were north of the front. His men must have been aiming with their rectal holes, killing anything with a pulse.

On a particularly morbid night, my father, who seemed for my sake to recover a little bit of his strength with each passing day, paused near a dead body lying face down on the ground, and mournfully said: "It's a good thing we buried your mother. We didn't leave her exposed to the merciless elements. Now, child, look around. As your great-great-grandfather, Shams Abbas Hosseini, would say, *Death is coming.* Take this chance to train that Hosseini nose of yours! It is the only way to guard your life with your death."

As I listened to him speak, I was reminded of the second Hosseini Commandment: It is our duty to remember that history's unfinished business will recycle itself. I remembered: The only way to remain one step ahead of death is to cultivate our ability to sniff the bloodthirsty past before it approaches to settle old scores.

The next time we came across a pile of bodies, I looked at the faces of the dead. My father removed their clothes and piled them onto my small frame. Snow was drifting through the air; it had stacked on the ground, a spectral glow that would soon cover those who lay there, dead and abandoned. I smelled them. They smelled of shit and vinegar and rust. The stench of history, the miasma of death, was coming up from the southern front in waves. For days, there was blood in my head. Blood in my eyes. Blood everywhere I looked.

Weeks stretched on like an interminable road. Through the coldest stretches, my father carried me on his back as if I were a load. Time moved unnervingly slow. But it was in the midst of that decay and putrefaction, and that harrowing winter we had tried so hard to avoid, that my father resumed my lessons in literature. We reclaimed our old habits. They gave us a sense of order. We felt bolstered by the architecture of words. Every day, before we rested from our night's hike, he instructed me to sit on a pile of rocks that jetted out of the brightly glazed snow, and said, "Life crushes us, grinds us to a halt, wears us down."

I listened to him through the bitter chill of the ancient howling wind. I closed my eyes and inhaled his words. I swallowed them as if they were food to my stomach. I felt nurtured by literature's web of sentences, connected through them to this strange and dark universe.

My father warned, echoing the third and final Hosseini Commandment: "Child, you must follow in the tradition of your ancestors, your forebears and your forebears' ingenious forebears, those great martyrs of thought who retreated into literature in order to survive death, in order to outwit the cruel absurdity of the world."

He always said *child* just like that; never *my child* or *sweet daughter of mine* or *my doll*. He didn't believe in the possessive. According to his logic, I was a vessel, the latest to be produced in our ill-omened bloodline, designed to receive and transmit literary signals; destined to contaminate the world with our cross-generational devotion to literature. "Remember," he would say during those dawn lessons, pacing back and forth before a pile of icy rocks, "literature reveals the lies and the hypocrisy of the world. It is the only true record. After I am gone, you will be the last remaining scribe of the future."

After a long, thoughtful pause, he would artfully say: "Repeat after me: Memorize! Regurgitate! Transmit!" In the surrounding silence of death, I would echo those words with my eyes still closed. I prepared for my ill-omened fate.

At the end of each lesson, my father instructed me to open my eyes. He pulled out a broken piece of chalk from his pocket and transcribed several verses from memory on the front of his blackboard, which he refused to remove lest someone was shooting at close range. As a result, all the verses were lopsided. He had me recite them back to him, a difficult task. No one should have to carve words on their heart, and no one should be expected to read that writing. But I did.

There were lines from Dante Alighieri, Pier Paolo Pasolini, James Baldwin, Matsuo Bashō, W.E.B. Du Bois, Mary Wollstonecraft, Khwāja Shams-ud-Dīn Muhammad Hāfez-e Shīrāzī (alias Hāfez), Katherine Mansfield, Virginia Woolf. My father's head was like the library of Babel. Each day, he transcribed different verses. I stored them all away so I could feed on their marrow during the starved days of exile that lay ahead. They were a balm to my wounds; a remedy against the brutal winds that would blow through my void, causing its craggy walls to sting. The line I remember most often goes like this: *Like desert camels of thirst dying while on their backs water bearing.* We walked hundreds of miles with that sentence scribbled on the front of my father's blackboard. We were those camels, only instead of water we carried literature's bountiful load on our backs. We were united in our struggle against hunger, the frigid air that kept us raw, the excruciating pain of my mother's sudden death.

When we arrived at one of the promontories of Mount Sahand, that comatose beast of a volcano looming over Iran's northwestern border, my father looked east toward Tehran, south toward Baghdad, and northwest toward Van, the first destination in our long journey of exile, just over the Turkish border. It was the end of winter.

There was a terrible silence as we stood there surveying the land surrounding us. I wondered if I would ever lay eyes on that land again. Then my father spat on the rocky ground, and said: "I spit on you, you bunch of patriarchal nepotists!" His face, ordinarily wafer-thin, puffed up with rage and grew red. It looked like a swelling pool of blood. I had never seen this side of him before. I felt an odd terror. The wind beat the taut sheet of my heart as if it were a drum. It hammered and beveled that sheet until it was in tatters. I felt indignation rise in wafts through the hollows. I felt my ears grow hot with fear and scorn.

We were near Lake Urmia along the Iranian-Turkish border when my father gave me the last literature lesson I would receive within the confines of our bludgeoned nation. The shallow, salty waters of the lake were full of bloated waterfowl, dead from Saddam's waves of poison gas. Greater flamingos were languidly drifting across the saline surface. My father took one look at those dead birds, and said: "According to the illustrious poet

Abū-Mansūr Qatrān al-Jili al-Azerbaijani, *Those who perished were saved from misfortune and badness, while the living are plunged in a sea of deep sadness.*" I stared ahead, thinking of my mother's flattened face. My heart folded over itself like an envelope, but I said nothing.

After that, time warped. It slowed down and sped up at random. At some point, I remember my father removing the clothes of a dead Kurdish man, who, like many other borderland Kurds, had been fighting against Saddam alongside the Iranians. My father put the man's clothes on himself and informed me of his twofold plan to avoid our being identified as Iranian deserters and intercepted by the border police. Since he had neglected to teach me Kurdish, I would have to pretend I was a deaf-mute about to go blind while he, who spoke impeccable Kurdish, would pretend to be a Kurdish father who was taking me to be seen by the only doctor in the world who had given us hope, a Berlin-educated Kurdish eye surgeon in Van. I had no idea how he had come up with all this. I had no idea what was going through his head.

"The Kurds are like us," he said. "They are the kind of unlucky men who help their ill-fated brothers. They'll help us get across the border into Van. You'll see."

But I saw nothing. He had tied a strip of black cloth, torn from the clothes of the dead man, around my eyes. I was blindfolded and mute. Like a good pickle, I was soaking in the brine of death.

The next thing I remember, my father and I were sitting in the back of an open-air truck, pressed tightly against other bodies. I could hear my father's voice over the engine. I understood nothing except the following declaration, which he repeated with childish ebullience — "Kurdistan is like Hiroshima!" It was received with feverish enthusiasm by his fake compatriots. "Kurdistan is like Hiroshima!" they repeated with warmth and complicity, clapping, sighing, and patting one another on the shoulders. The sound of their laughter rushed at my ears as if from across a great distance. I felt lonely, cut off from my father, ugly, wretched, as pitiful as a soiled manuscript forgotten in a damp trench.

But upon arriving in Van, my father removed the black band he had placed over my eyes. He held my hand, and said, with a bucolic euphoria, "We made it across the border!" I looked at Van. The city lay on the eastern shores of an emerald green lake ringed by pleated mountains, where sheets of snow were starting to melt. It was spring, but there was still a chill in the air. We had survived, each of us one of the few who hadn't been caught or killed, and the knowledge of it would estrange us from the world for good. We were perched on the edge of Van Castle, atop a steep bluff overlooking the craggy ruins of an old city. All that remained were the blunted edges of fallen homes.

"Look at the ancient city of Van," my father said, pointing at that decimated land below us. "Here, the Armenians were wrenched by history, exterminated at the hands of the Ottomans. The first Holocaust!" he muttered, pitifully pulling on the ends of his stained mustache.

I leaned over the edge of the castle. My head was still spinning from the smell of the rotting corpses in that no-man's-land, from my mother's death. I looked at the leveled city, which is known as the Pearl of the East. No bigger lie has ever been uttered. Its remains shone like copper wires in the winter sun. The *Pearl of the East*! Let those who want to lie to themselves lie to themselves, I thought. I remembered the slimy pearl of truth: remorseless, monstrous, and full of a terrible stench.

Before we continued on, my father returned the black band to my eyes, and I was plunged once more into a deep lacuna. But over time, that black band heightened my senses. Deprived of sight, I saw the immense magnitude of the darkness that surrounds us more clearly than ever before; I smelled the eternal return of the residue of history; I heard the ringing void of the long exile that lay ahead of us, first in Turkey, then in Spain, and finally in the New World; the white noise of death — the past death of my mother, the future death of my father, the death of the Kurds, of Iranians, of Armenians, of Iraqis — booming in the margins of the universe. One day, I told myself, I will emerge from the void of exile, and I will drag the stench of death out with me. After all, I am the youngest of the Hosseinis, the last in a long lineage; it is my job to exhume the buried corpse of our deadly collective history — our truth.

NEW YORK CITY

The Story of My Father's Death and
Burial and the Consequent Formation
of My Multiple Irregular Minds

AFTER LEAVING VAN, MY FATHER, ABBAS ABBAS Hosseini, and I spent years moving across the surface of the earth in search of a place to think. We were like the slugs that come out after a hard rain: ugly, weather-beaten, dispossessed, the refuse of the world. So it goes. No matter how many times you try to replant an uprooted tree, it seems always to fail to take to the soil. The exile never outruns history. Such are the consequences of being born unlucky in an inhospitable world. There is a line by Baudelaire that sums it up rather well: *Il me semble que je serais toujours bien là où je ne suis pas.* I encountered that same line, written in the words of Paul Auster, after we'd settled in the wretched New World: *It seems to me that I will always be happy in the place I am not.* It seemed just as prophetic then.

By the time we did reach that so-called New World, many years had passed since my mother's death, since our harrowing fugue from Iran — an egress that had chilled our bones and left our hands permanently cold. From that point on, I had maintained the temperature of a corpse. Under the specter of grief, we moved through Turkey, and after a series of digressions designed to renew or falsify this or that paper, we arrived in Barcelona, our destination, the City of Bombs. There, my father hoped to meet other Autodidacts, Anarchists, Atheists. But events never unfold the way one imagines they will. Barcelona, cautious, worn down by the years of oppression it was subjected to by the childish whims of General Franco — that wide-eyed despot — ultimately disappointed him, and soon we were on the road again.

At times, during our long journey, we seemed to make progress in leaps and bounds. We would move across huge chunks of this uneven universe at the speed of light, then, suddenly, breathless and exhausted, we'd be unable to proceed and would move backward again. The path we had taken would fold over itself, looping backward as if it were leading us toward some information we had been too impatient to discover the first time. We would scurry back in a panic only to discover that there was nothing there. This sense that we had forgotten something — the haunting aftereffect of an indigestible loss — had turned both of us into entirely unintelligible beings. I don't know how long we stayed in each place. I drifted in and out of the light. I was often lost to myself, and even when I wasn't, I had no idea how it was that we had come to be wherever it was we were. I still don't know. All I know is that when we finally arrived in Barcelona I was two years older than when we had first left Iran. Three years later, we were in New York City — hopeless, disoriented, famished.

More than a decade had gone by somehow. Now twenty-two, I still burn with rage, grief, and confusion at the arduous path of my past. I stood with my back to the Cloisters and looked out over the river. The Cuxa, the Bonnefont, the Saint-Guilhem, and the Trie were behind me, all having been clinically sliced from medieval French abbeys and rearranged here into an artificial whole. The Hudson was below me: green, serpentine, slithering lazily by. I sat down on a bench to take in the commanding view. The fog climbed up the sides of Fort Tryon Park. Suspended over the water, caught in the gauzy winter light, the George Washington Bridge looked like a giant mosquito net. It was a dreary, damp day.

My father was in our Inwood apartment, lying supine on his mattress, approaching death. Soon I would have to bury him, just as I had buried my mother. I would have to lower his body into the ground. I would have no one left to love. Sitting on that bench, watching the fog rise over the river, I thought to myself, years have passed since we left Iran. I sat there and yearned for the most banal things: figs, pomegranate trees, hydrangeas, date palms, birds of paradise. Then I thought, enough: There is no point in pining over a country with a thousand heads, a country that is always changing, that had become unrecognizable to us.

I got off the bench and walked up to the railing that runs along the perimeter of the park. I leaned over the edge. I could hear the river down below — swoosh, swoosh, swoosh. The moving water made the same sound the sentences written by my ingenious forebears made as they swirled around the infinite abyss of my mind. I could no longer see out; the fog was covering everything. Instead, I looked inside myself. I saw acres of consciousness decimated by the lacunae of exile. I felt indignant, downtrodden, lost.

I considered leaping into the river. I didn't want to survive my father's death. Then I thought: No. I am truculent, combative, as good as any other human at kicking around the dust piled up on this miserable earth. And if I were to kill myself off, why should I do it here? I looked around. I said, "Never." If I'm going to die, I thought, let it be among estranged brethren. As forlorn as I was, I would never leap off the edge of this New World, this land of thieves, with my back to a conglomeration of fake cloisters that have been dismantled from real French abbeys and reassembled here. As if the Old World were a mausoleum. What a laughable lack of perspective.

I marched back out of the park with new resolve. It was time to check in on my father. He hardly ever left our apartment, a fourth-floor, rat-infested, rent-controlled studio we had partitioned into two rooms with an old bookshelf. Like many other exiles, we had traveled across the world, dying and resurrecting along the way. But now, I reminded myself, as if to prepare, my father was approaching physical death — the least final but most tangible of all deaths.

I opened the door to find him talking to himself. He had grown gaunt, grim, fragile. His cheeks sagged. His hands were blue and freckled. Our vagabond life had taken a toll on him. I saw him lurching across our studio with an ashen face, leaning against this or that, mumbling from beneath his mustache into the cold air: "Exile is death's muse." I watched his curtained lips form the word *exile*. But I heard *forced separation, expulsion, the refuse of the world*. I couldn't stand to see his diminished figure.

It was time to drag him out of the house. Perhaps an outing would revive his spirits. The next morning, I took him to Brighton Beach, where the waters are as dark and oily as the Caspian. The fog had lifted, but there was a bitter chill. It was the middle of winter. The beach was deserted. Lead-colored waves were scraping the metallic underbelly of the sky. Scattered across the shore, between briny patches of sea foam, were piles of seaweed and dead fish rotting in the wind and sand. Those fish activated my father's trauma. Dead animals often brought on his rage. He staggered over and weakly pointed his cane at those limbless vertebrates, then wailed that the sea had heaved out all those scaly, gilled creatures in the same way we had been forced to flee our bludgeoned country and that now we all had been left to die on the fringes of the New World. As I watched his fury unfold, I realized more clearly than ever that we could have been living anywhere: in a hut in Cambodia, a houseboat docked in the canals of Amsterdam, a tent made of coconut hair in India, a prison at the bottom of a snow-capped mountain in Tibet. Our address would always be the same: the Nation of Exiles, neither here nor there. With him gone, I would be alone in that boundless nation, aimless and adrift. I felt an intense dread approach from far off. Then I pushed away the thought and all the feelings it had the power to exhume. I refocused on my mustached father.

In honor of the Hosseini family tradition, I had brought a stack of books with me to the beach. When my father was done airing his frustrations, I helped him down to the sand. He could no longer read. His eyes were too weak. He suffered from advanced macular degeneration. So he sat there, hunched over, mouth downturned, cheeks puffy, sulking while I read out loud to him. I took turns cracking each book open to a random page as if it were an oracle. There were certain sentences that delivered an electric pulse and momentarily brought him back to life. It worked like a charm. There was no denying it: There are units of language that have a mysterious aura about them, a metaphysical force. Encouraged, I got to my feet and walked in circles around my father like an old peripatetic Greek. Better yet, like an old Sufi mystic, the way I had walked in that oval library as a child.

My father slapped his knee with enthusiasm. The pink tip of his tongue protruded through his lips; it grazed the ends of his mustache. He was content. The man had persevered for my sake through that nauseating no-man's-land, through the toxic fumes of war. The least I could do now was continue reading despite the brutal winter chill and the fact that my feet kept sinking into the sand, causing my knees to buckle. So I opened the books one after the other and recited ominous sentences in a prophetic tone.

In a clipped voice, I repeated the following: *Things are going to be spoiled by those who are already rotting.* Dalí. One of my favorites. A man with a tongue as sharp as a rigger brush who wasn't afraid to use it. I could tell my father was happy because he dug the end of his cane into the sand like a child, making little holes. His eyes moved inquisitively from side to side, and beneath them, his mustache looked as if it were about to levitate. I felt useful, invigorated, blithe. When I was sure I had committed the lines to memory, I sat back down. We shared the view of the Atlantic under that gunmetal sky a moment longer. Then we got on the subway and rode back to Inwood.

You could say I am the AAA's most militant member. I have a tattoo of our family seal on my left forearm: three *As* enclosed in a circle. In deep black ink, our family motto appears beneath the seal: *In this false world, we guard our lives with our deaths.* Upon my father's passing, I will be the only Hosseini left, the last in a long lineage. My inheritance of their intellectual prowess will be complete. I don't take the charge lightly. I have always been schooled by my father just as he was schooled by his. But, truth be told, the tutorials with my father had ended long ago. I could no longer study with him because he was nearly blind and, as a result, extremely impatient. He struggled to access his mind. I watched, bewildered by his helplessness. It was like watching a toothless dog gnaw on a bone, resolute despite his inadequate resources. For a time, fearful of betraying our family's long tradition, I remained mentorless. Guruless. I worked on my mind alone. I prepared for the desolation that lay ahead. Once my father was gone, I would be leading a life with no railing to lean on. A life with no foothold. But we had not come all this way just to surrender to this unscrupulous New World. No. I had no other recourse but to continue fortifying my mind — which he had worked so hard to arm with languages and literature — by stuffing it with even more texts.

Over the years, I had received an endless stream of mail from this or that recruiting university offering me a variety of scholarships. I have no idea how the universities got my name or address, perhaps through the tortured process of acquiring our residency papers. No matter. I rejected all their offers. I was certain that this mail was just another way for the New World to shed its white guilt while simultaneously exploiting Iran's ousted intelligentsia. This is perfectly in keeping with American foreign policy, in my humble opinion, which seems to subscribe to the following mission: Interfere with and profit from far-flung governments at the peril of their citizens, and once those poor, unfortunate souls have been dispatched to the Four Corners of the World, in exile and on their knees, offer a scattering of them asylum and a compensatory education. But the buck stops here! I, an ill-fated member of this infested universe, a Hosseini descendent, would never give in to such effacement. I would never eradicate my difference.

Nevertheless, I didn't want to remain mentorless forever. So I made an exception to my boycott of American institutes of so-called higher learning: José Emilio Morales, reluctant Professor of Romance Languages and Literatures at New York University; Chilean exile (kicked in the rear by that madman Pinochet); fervent Communist (though he has learned to keep his politics to himself — he has mouths to feed in Chile); and ex-confidant of the deceased poet Pablo Neruda.

I will never forget the first time I saw Morales. He was walking around this congested and surreal island — the self-proclaimed center of the world — with a copy of Neruda's *Tercera Residencia* tucked into a pouch he had sewn into his suit jacket. Every fifteen minutes, he pulled the book out of his jacket, flipped it open to a random page, and breathed in one or two lines. I followed him all the way to Washington Square Park, where he walked the perimeter. At first he kept his arms clasped behind his back and his head hanging, pensive; then he lifted his arms up in front of his face, holding Neruda's book in his hands. I couldn't believe my eyes. Search the world over and you won't find another man like him.

He is a physically unique specimen. He has white hair; an unruly salt-and-pepper beard that grows in uneven patches; a round, oily nose; and small gray eyes that appear distorted due to the thickness of his reading glasses, which are held in place by the greasy end of his stubby nose. Like me, he is not attractive. Like me, he has an inward-looking gaze that suggests that at any moment he might sink into himself and disappear, vanishing from the earth entirely. But unlike me, the man is fixated on the color red. He wears red slacks, a red button-down, a red tweed suit jacket, red socks. The only contrast comes from his shoes, which are brown.

I kept my eye on Morales for months. I didn't want to approach him right away. I was afraid he would startle if I came on too suddenly. Every afternoon, during my father's long naps, I set out to watch him walk the perimeter of the park with his head in Neruda's book. He read with one eye, and with the other, he navigated the dogs, the hippies with their guitars, the skateboarders, the wealthy Lower West Siders with their fingerless gloves and frothing lattes. He never bumped into another person. He never tripped over a cable or the stumpy roots of a tree. One day, when the moment was ripe, I followed him all the way to his office at NYU. When he got to the door, he finally turned around, and as though he had eyes in the back of his head, he asked, in a surprisingly unguarded voice: "What do you want?"

I told him I was in need of a mentor, and then I provided him with a few basic coordinates of my life. I exposed the nature of my relationship to books. I told him that my ill-fated ancestors and I had survived death through our intimate engagement with literature. Then, I thought to myself, *engagement* is too mild a word, so I replaced it with *refuge*. I said: "We, the ill-fated, have taken refuge in literature." But this description also failed to communicate a sufficient level of intensity. With a hint of violence, I added: "Hear me! We have pitched our tattered tents in the dark forests of literature!"

At this, Morales invited me into his office, which was long and rectangular and had a small boxy window overlooking an interior quad where a few sad trees that barely got enough sun were clawing the air. Without bothering to look at the floor, Morales stepped over a few rows of the books he had laid out on the floor in alphabetical order and sat down in the leather chair behind his desk. He leaned forward and rested his weight on his elbows. He said, "If you can cite the following lines of verse, I will take you on informally." He leaned back and a wide grin spread across his face. He looked like an old dried flower, that white face with all the red cloth blooming around it. He said, "They can't fire me if I do. They've tried many times to eradicate my presence from this campus. Communism is still treated as a crime in this country. Every year they ask me to sign a paper that says, *I, José Emilio Morales, am not a Communist.* I have never signed it, but still I wear red every day to get back at them for that piece of paper."

He reached up and turned on a dusty lamp. In a melodious tone full of drama and melancholy, he recited: *"Oh pit of debris, ferocious cave of the shipwrecked."* He closed his eyes. Behind those thick glasses, his lids looked like raw dough. *"In you the wars and the flights accumulated."*

Every evening after watching Morales walk the perimeter of the park, I had returned home to read Neruda, the poet who moves through the subterranean channels of the human heart with expert precision. And so I said, "Easy breezy. 'A Song of Despair,' the honorable and deceased Pablo Neruda circa 1924."

"Ah," he said, "you have pitched your tent in the same dark forests as I have."

That's life. You travel the world over, aimless, friendless, adrift. Then suddenly you find another rodent who shares the sorrows of your juiced organs. I felt as though he had ironed out the wrinkled sheet of my heart.

We agreed to hold weekly meetings in his office. I reveled in our encounters. I looked forward to them, and for their duration, I could feel an electric charge coursing through my void. At our first official meeting, I informed Morales that in order to honor my father, Abbas Abbas Hosseini, a man whose mind was as vast as the library of Babel, I intended to compose a manifesto titled "A Philosophy of Totality: The Matrix of Literature."

"Methodology?" he asked, removing his glasses and rubbing his eyes.

"Memorization," I offered.

He nodded respectfully.

I informed Morales that I wanted my mind to become so elastic it would be capable of containing all of literature; once internalized, the maxims, diatribes, and verses written by the Great Writers of the Past, my ingenious forebears, would begin to mingle spontaneously with one another in the decimated fields of my consciousness and produce unexpected but truthful associations that I planned to record in the manifesto for the good of my fellow vermin. Memorization, I declared, is the Hosseini way. I told him that we have combated the potential loss of will to power, a natural consequence of war and our lifelong ill-fatedness, by reciting lines from the vast web of literature. Memorization, I insisted, is how we have kept our minds engaged, decolonized; it is how we have kept ourselves from giving in. We, I told him, employing a conclusive tone, are the scribes of the future. We are the guardians of the archive of literature.

Though he agreed to test my memorization skills during our weekly meetings, he was quick to follow up with a countercondition. If we were going to work together, he said, employing an edifying tone, he needed to know that I understood and would abide by one thing.

"What thing?" I asked.

He answered with the following: *There is no such thing as reading; there is only rereading.* As cool as a cucumber, he relayed his expectation that I should read every book several times at different hours and in different settings, and that I should recite quotes in the original language as well as the English translation. I agreed. It was a brilliant idea. I would be dispatching different parts of my mind — each language I had learned was housed in a subsector of the same quadrant — to metabolize texts. In other words, I would approach each text from multiple angles, employing the sum of all my disparate parts.

All winter, I studied under his guidance; I read more than I had ever read before. I matured my Spanish, Italian, Catalan — languages over which Morales had an impeccable command. I worked my way through the canon, then through the avant-garde. I read this and then that. I underlined, scrutinized, read again. I skipped over certain things to make way for others. I read various translations of the classics. I combed through every line multiple times. Each time, as Morales had implied, the line appeared differently. It made a different sound, produced a different meaning, stirred awake this or that buried self.

I reported all of this to Morales during our weekly meetings, which he spent awkwardly pacing through his overflowing office in his Communist uniform, hands clasped behind his back, head hanging as he stepped over stacked columns of books, empty boxes, unopened mail. Every once in a while, he paused to push his glasses up the bridge of his nose.

If I really impressed him with my pronunciation and memorization skills, he would say, "Brava, brava!" and gently tap my head with his spent copy of *Tercera Residencia.* Under the shadow of that book, I recited the works of Jorge Luis Borges, Octavio Paz, Clarice Lispector, Cristina Peri Rossi, Alejo Carpentier, María Luisa Bombal, Miguel de Cervantes, Dante Alighieri, Francesco Petrarca, Josep Pla, Mercè Rodoreda, J. V. Foix, Quim Monzó, Salvador Espriu. The list went on and on until the names blurred together.

On a particularly blustery day in January, while I was headed toward

Morales's office for my weekly recitation, a girl with a nose piercing and a purple Mohawk and pale green eyes that looked out from their sockets with a mixture of pride and disgust stopped me near Washington Square Park.

"Not so fast," she said, raising her gloved hand as if I had been trying to avoid her.

I stopped. She was tall and thin, all angles, no curves, as sharp as a whip. She looked like a futurist statue. Even as she stood still, she gave the appearance of being in motion, as if she were headed someplace more important, where things stood a chance of being resolved. She was wearing a studded dog collar, and the metal bits kept catching the bright winter light, nearly blinding me. She had deliberately cut holes in each layer of her outfit. She wore black surfaces all the way down, leading me to conclude that it was her sole purpose in life to expose the depth of the darkness that surrounds us, to signal the infinite and stratified nature of the abyss. I immediately liked her.

She pulled a book out of her bag and knocked me over the head with it in the same way Morales would knock me over the head with his copy of Neruda's saddest poems. I never knew which good-bye between my father and me would be our last, and these whacks, delivered from the realm of literature, drew me out of the fog that settled over me each time I left our apartment. I examined her face. I understood immediately: She, too, had been an informal pupil of his. There were many of us. Morales was using official means to nurture the dissident tendencies of his unofficial advisees, who had flocked to him like moths to a light. No wonder the university was trying to fire him.

"I studied with Morales for a while," she spat out. "And it's true, there is no one like him." She paused thoughtfully and turned her nose to the sky. Then she added, "But he never gave me this." She handed me the book she had pulled out of her bag. "This is a book one anarchist woman gives to another. Read it. It will make you feel a lot better about all of this shit."

I looked at the book. It was *Don Quixote* by Kathy Acker. I had never heard of her before, and I felt my heart quicken with excitement at the thought of discovering this radical woman's sentences. The cover was a glossy gray blue, and it featured a photograph of the author. In the picture, she has her back to the camera. Her shoulders are bare, exposing a flower tattoo that extends across her upper back. The photograph appears to have been ripped to pieces and then fit together along the edges of the seams. I took these fissures to be indicative of what lay between the covers. I was stunned by the beauty of the composition. By the time I looked back up, the girl had begun walking away. I stood there and watched her; her Mohawk made an incision in the sky, tearing the godless heavens asunder.

I sat in the park at the foot of the commemorative statue of Giuseppe Garibaldi. I saluted the short, bearded "father of fathers" drawing his sword and, under his aura of resolve, prepared to inhabit Acker's sentences. I took pleasure in lifting the book to my nose. I picked up mild tones of sage, black olives, nicotine. I noticed wine stains on the spine. The pages were brittle, yellow. I opened the book three times at random. In the Hosseini tradition, I consulted it as if it were an oracle.

I read: *Isolation is a political tool.*

Then: *I have left behind all that I know, so I go into the room of my death.*

And finally: *I travelled all over the world, looking for trouble.*

As I closed the book, I thought to myself, these three prophecies will come to mean something very soon.

Morales didn't have a dearth of official students. I often bumped into a particularly banal pair of them on my way to his office. Alice and Tomaso were a feckless duo with broad, plain foreheads. They wore overalls and thick old-man glasses (it was unclear to me why they dressed alike), and they called themselves the New Poets. They walked around fluffing their feathers and boasting about having been admitted to the master of fine arts in poetry program. A couple of amateurs. While they struggled to compose a single verse a month, I read and wrote until my fingers were bruised.

I wanted nothing to do with them, but they were clingy, wide-eyed, curious types with spongy cheeks and large ears; the kind of undiscerning, overprivileged humans who ask inane questions and then listen to the answers with their mouths ajar.

That afternoon, I was particularly loath to talk to them. My hand was burning from holding Acker's book. I wanted to get through my meeting with Morales as quickly as possible so I could return to my apartment, where my father would likely be reclining on his mattress, and read the book cover to cover.

The New Poets beckoned as we crossed paths in the hallway. "A minute of small talk?"

Small talk! Their diction was as terrible as their breath. I had had it with them. I told them that I would never use the term *small talk*, let alone engage in it as an activity. I considered speaking to be a grand waste of time unless its purpose was to get the big unsaid truths out in the open. I declared: "I have no time for small talk! While you two expose yourselves to the detrimental effects of a formal education — reduced self-knowledge, submission to authority, covert institutional indoctrination in linear time — I am employing unorthodox methods of learning in order to facilitate grand associative leaps, heightened cognition, and transcendental intellectualism, because with my father's death fast approaching" — I bore into them with my eyes — "it is my duty, as the last remaining member of the Autodidacts, Anarchists, and Atheists, to make a major philosophical intervention aimed at correcting the skewed and pitifully narrow perception of the world's pseudo intellectuals and heretics, your erroneous brethren!" The words came out with such ease, with such deliberate organization, that I realized they had been sitting on the tip of my tongue awaiting their turn to manifest.

The New Poets stood with their backs against the wall, looking mystified and confused. They gawked at me as if I were an exotic animal they were seeing for the first time, a wildly frustrated creature pacing inside a cage. I could see saliva pooling in their open mouths. Throughout my monologue — let's call it what it was, an intervention — they were nodding at me with so much fervor I thought their heads had come loose. When they finally got it together, they asked me if I wanted to go eat a taco with them.

"A taco?" I asked. There was smoke coming out of my ears.

"A taco!" they implored in unison, as if they were twins.

There was no use in repeating myself. That pair wouldn't be able to see themselves clearly if I held a mirror up to their tongues.

"I don't eat tacos," I said, and they dropped the subject.

///////////

The events of that drafty day marked a turning point in my thinking. The intervention I had spontaneously offered to the New Poets, the way those words had glided out of my mouth, *grand associative leaps, heightened cognition, transcendental intellectualism,* helped me to realize that I was on the cusp of a revelation. By funneling extreme amounts of literature into my mind, I had engineered it to make a Grand Leap in Consciousness. All that was left to do was to push things over the edge, the way our exodus, in combination with my mother's untimely death, had shoved my father and me over the threshold of sense.

I did this by reading even more intensely than before, with a passion bordering on madness — madness contained, the irrational in the palm of my hand — and with what I had identified through my studies as the Paranoiac-Critical approach of Dalí; a *spontaneous method of irrational knowledge* that allowed me to carve ever more *delirious associative pathways* within and among texts and therefore to expedite the plan I had been hatching all along: a vast constellation of literary networks I could inhabit during the period of grief that awaited me due to the rapid decline of my father's health. In other words, due to his imminent death.

The night of my encounter with the New Poets, while my father was fast asleep, snoring through his mustache, I walked in concentric circles honing my plan. I said out loud to no one, "In contradistinction to the New Poets — literary attachés to the master of fine arts in poetry, a pair of disengaged numbskulls who lazily read with their eyes — I, outsider and literary terrorist in training, read not with my eyes but with my consciousness, scanning the stratified layers embedded in each text like an archaeologist in an excavation site!"

The next morning, I found my father in a fit. He was in a horrifyingly bad mood. It was obvious why. We both could see that my plan to compose a manifesto and his approaching death — his disintegration and eventual reabsorption into the mind of the universe — were inversely related. He pushed his glass of tea over the edge of the dining table with the end of his cane. It shattered, and I had to clean up after him. I looked around. The apartment was in a terrible state: dirty, disorderly, its corners patched with cobwebs that matched my father's white-haired armpits. "This," I said somberly, "is a Room of Broken Heirlooms." At that, he fixed his eyes on me. His gaze was loaded with helplessness and rage. I watched him try to take in the circumstances of our lives, but he couldn't. A barrier had gone up, and he was stuck on the other side of it looking as lost and bewildered as I had felt as a child. I nearly wept as I looked back at him. I turned away to conceal my pain.

The apartment was scattered with objects — most of them rusty, damaged — that we had either carried with us across that no-man's-land, that miasma of death, or accumulated during our subsequent exodus through the Mediterranean in search of intellectual freedom. A vain search that turned up nothing, because no matter where you go, knot-brained idiots outnumber honest and straightforward men.

I stood near the dining-room table, dustpan in hand. I examined the objects of our lives: a rust-stained samovar, a hand-woven rug that looked like it had been bludgeoned, an old suitcase shaped like a chest, *The Hung Mallard* (our most prized possession), and a book of poems by Hāfez, which was lying on the floor near my father's La-Z-Boy. He was sitting in that armchair now, slumped over, nervously tugging on his mustache. He had staggered over to it with his cane, grunting along the way, while I swept up the shattered glass.

My father often consulted Hāfez's poems. In what turned out to be the final weeks of his life, these poetic consultations confirmed for him a fact he had firmly come to believe and that seemed to have revised his thinking up to that point: Our future had been sealed off, we had been permanently barred from it, and we would never have access, not now, not ever, to Life, Liberty, and the pursuit of Happiness; we, to put it shortly and sweetly, belonged to the cast of the living dead and there was no point in our continuing on.

"No point! You hear me?" He spattered so loudly that his voice carried across the room. He was breaking down inside. He had given up his sword.

I walked into the kitchen, stunned. I removed the lid from the garbage and got rid of the shattered glass. My father, annoyed at my lack of response, got up and lurched across the rug to the window that looked out onto the street. I came back out of the kitchen and watched as he struggled to open the window. He kept pointing at the glass, at the people on the street below. He was repulsed by their dress, their manners, their way of being in the world. He banged his cane against the sill. The framework came loose. He stuck his cane out, pointed it at a passerby, and announced: "I spit on my life!"

Then he wheeled his head around, slipped his cane out of the crack in the window, and pointed it directly at me. He said: "You should know: The final hour is always approaching." His hands were shaking. His cane was bouncing up and down. I noticed his mustache was wet. The tips were so long that they were getting caught in his mouth. I took this as evidence of a bad mood gone sour.

That night, before my father went to bed, he reached into his pocket and retrieved an image of Mohammad Reza Shah Pahlavi's face, a cutout from an old rial banknote. When I was a child, he had made me a mobile out of those cutouts; he would twirl the mobile around and I would see the king's shadowy face redoubled on the ceiling and the walls. I remembered him telling me: "Look, the Ruler of the Aryans ate the ground!" Or, with a chorus of defiant laughter, applauding his own sarcasm: "If we who have mingled with the Arabs, Turks, Mongols, and Greeks for hundreds of years are Aryans, then the Spanish are pure-blooded Iberians!"

Now, as if the King of Kings were still alive, my father looked at me from across the room and let out: "Ha! The man thinks his sweat is as white as milk!" He was holding the king's face up to the light. His mind had unreeled.

He seemed to be working his way backward across his life, which was ending in the most unfortunate place: exile's cold claw. As I observed him, I felt a sharp pain in my chest. This pain, I believe, derived from the sudden and unexpected loosening of the screws that kept the lid on my past tightly shut. I was faced with the prospect of having to open that lid in order to fit my father in the same container I had relegated not only my mother to but also the senseless phenomena that had accumulated during the course of my ill-fated life. I was sure those forgotten fragments of memory, sharpened into spears on the jagged cliffs of time, would inevitably slip out and stab me in the gut. I had no doubt that upon my father's death I would enter a labyrinth of grief so complex that I may never find the exit.

That fateful day finally arrived. In April, while the cherry trees were blossoming and the sky was a cloudless blue, my father died. His heart stopped.

I came home from my weekly meeting with Morales and found my father sitting in his La-Z-Boy, dead, his cane resting across his lap, his mouth open, his tongue sunk back, his mustache flat and lifeless. I felt as though my heart had been put through the shredder. I heaved and wailed, but I couldn't shed any tears. I had gone dry, like that no-man's-land we had traversed. My eyes stung and my gut burned. I bit my lips until they bled. I gnawed on my fingers. I attacked myself the way animals do when they are in distress. Sometime later, somnambulant, comatose, I walked over to my father and caressed his face. I closed his eyes. Then I went into the kitchen and poured some tea. I didn't know what to do with myself. There was a small radio balanced on the windowsill that led out to the fire escape. I had never turned it on, but I did then. There is a first time for everything, after all. I leaned against the sink and listened to the voice coming through. It said, "The long siege." We were right in the middle of the reckless chaos of the Bush years.

I retreated from the kitchen and again looked at my dead father. There was a white hue to his skin. I couldn't stand to see him that way. I looked around. There was a notebook I hadn't noticed before on the dinner table. My father had left me a present, a leather-bound notebook with a note on it that said: "Ill-fated child, last of the Hosseinis! Add to history's pile of ruins the uselessness of our suffering."

I grabbed the notebook and went back into the kitchen. I leaned against the sink. I opened the tap. I watched the water run down the drain. I looked out the window. The New World. There it was, shamelessly conducting its business while halfway around the globe whole towns, cities, and villages were being razed to the ground. Then I thought, what does that word — new — mean anyway? I had never seen anything new in my life. All I had seen was the anxiety of people wanting to say something new. The New Poets! The New World! I examined the word. I filled a glass and took a drink of water. I turned off the tap. "New!" I turned the word over on my tongue. "New!" I laughed. I laughed with repulsion, with hatred. The sky changed colors. Yellow to ochre to rust. I don't know how much time went by. Soon it was evening. In the street, the neon lights of the shops came on. Their green glare glided across the walls. I felt as if I were standing at the bottom of the sea. For a brief second, I remembered the wrinkled surface of the Mediterranean, how it shone like treated leather in the muted light of dusk. Fragments of the past were already pushing their way up to the surface in spontaneous fits and bursts. The Mediterranean, that green sea, that Sea of Sunken Hopes, appeared like a photograph, a surface without depth. I laughed. I laughed until I had no idea what I was laughing at. I laughed until there were tears coming out of my eyes and ears. Brackish waters rose through the craggy walls of my void. It stung so hard, I thought my organs had been set on fire. Then I called 911.

The police and paramedics came and went. I told them they were not allowed to move my father from the La-Z-Boy because I, his only surviving family member, was in the middle of a funereal ritual.

The paramedics leaned over his pale body. They tried to resuscitate him despite the obvious signs of death. I wanted to speak out, to stop them from touching him, but my voice had drowned.

Finally, I murmured, "He is not returning. He has gone back to the beginning, to the space before his birth. His mind is in the process of being reabsorbed into the mind of the universe."

They hardly heard me. They pumped his chest. They shocked it. They gave him mouth-to-mouth. Nothing. Finally, they gave up and pronounced his time of death, then proceeded to walk around, investigating the scene with sinister grins, clearly hoping to uncover a crime.

"Look all you want," I said, exasperated, my voice thin. "My father died when it was time for him to die."

They pretended not to hear me. I tried to raise my voice a notch, but a thinner voice emerged, a babble incomprehensible even to me. I was standing there watching myself dissolve. I couldn't tell where I ended, where the room began.

Eventually, one of the police officers came up to me. He was tall and imposing, and had a flat face. He looked like he had been attacked with a pan. There were three of them altogether. Two men and one woman.

"What do you do?" the flat-faced officer asked, and my mother's face swam up the back channels of my mind. I pushed it away.

I heard myself say, rather matter-of-factly, "I am composing a manifesto."

His face distended, as if someone had gone over it with a roller. Thoughts were galloping around my mind, colliding into one another. I took a step back and corrected myself. I told him it was more complicated than that.

"What do you mean?"

I leaned against the bookshelf near my dead father. I drew several deep breaths. Then, as coolly as I could, I explained to the officer that I was preparing my mind to produce a manifesto and that once I had sufficiently primed my mind with literature the manifesto would come to me as if it were my second voice. I would just have to transcribe that voice into my notebook as faithfully as possible. I pointed at my notebook, which was on the table. I picked it up and sniffed its pages. They smelled musty, old. I looked over at my father's face. He looked thinner than he had been an hour before. He was already shrinking, shedding parts of himself, beginning to disappear.

I looked at the officer again. He had brandished a pen and a notepad from his pocket, and was jotting a few things down. I saw him carve a question mark into the paper. He was making such a tight fist with his hand that the ball of his pen nearly tore through the sheet.

"Are you a graduate student?" he asked, looking up at me. His eyes were narrow and blue, barely a contrast against his veiny white skin.

"Exactly," I lied, letting myself off the hook, because my mother's face had returned to occupy its proper place next to my father's, and with my parents' dead faces illuminated by the feeble light of my mind, I felt I was going to faint.

Before the policemen and the paramedics had arrived, I'd extended the La-Z-Boy by pulling on the lever and managed to straighten and then bend my father's limbs. I wanted to avoid the worst of rigor mortis. After that, I pulled all of Nietzsche's books off the shelves and laid them on the floor in a circle around my dead father. The police officers were examining those old tomes now. I told them that I planned to walk around my father's body all night, picking the books up one by one and reading several passages from each book out loud. He had read to me through the deepest recesses of our lives. Now it was my turn to read to him, to siphon literature into the hollow left over by his absence.

I said to myself, "Walking is the best medicine!"

The policeman with the flat face looked at me with the suspicious gaze of a passport controller. He looked like a man whose head is full of questions.

Before he could form his words, I said, bitterly, "Don't ask me. I plead the Fifth!"

A terrible silence fell.

I wanted to push him over. I added, "Keep on bombing Iraq and invading Afghanistan, strangling the region, and there will be more of us here!"

His flat face grew red. It looked like a plate that had been rubbed with the blood of a rare steak.

"Get a grip!" he ordered.

I wasn't sure if he was talking to himself or me.

"A grip?" I echoed. Inwardly, I thought that, like my mother, my father will soon be swallowed up by the earth; there are no ledges in the abyss of grief.

I walked over to my father and placed my hand against his forehead. His body was growing colder by the minute. I combed his mustache with my fingers. I pressed my hand against his cheek. Again, I felt dizzy, as if someone were draining my blood. My legs grew weak.

The other two police officers, who had been mute until then, came over. The woman had brown hair and thick, straight eyebrows that sat over her round eyes like dashes. Her partner, a short, bald, squat man with glasses and arms as long as his legs, walked around with hunched shoulders, emanating a kind of resigned kindness. He looked like a man who had taken a few beatings in the neck.

"Do you have a cemetery plot?" he asked, his voice gentle and reserved. "Have you called the morgue?"

"Yes and yes," I lied, steadying myself against my father's body. Once I had regained my strength, I said, "Your flat-faced partner over here is looking at me with such sadistic appetite, you'd think I was a pig about to be butchered."

He apologized on his partner's behalf.

"We'll get out of your way," he said.

The female officer was so wide that she looked like she had swallowed a helium balloon. She floated across the room and took the other two with her.

I closed the door behind them. I was alone with my father. I could finally breathe. My mind freshly oxygenated, I did what I had to do. I walked in a circle and wept through the night, shuddering and incredulous. Even so, I read to him until the crack of dawn. When I came across his favorite verses, I managed to stay calm long enough to kneel and whisper them in his ear. By morning, my face was dirty, streaked with tears. Tracks of salt sliced my cheeks in half. I caught my reflection in the window. My hair was a tangled mess. I had never seen anything so ugly. I thought to myself, I am one of the wretched of this pungent, futile earth. Far off in the distance, the half-moon, which had risen through the night, faded; it turned a translucent white. The lights that had come on in a sequence along the empty road, a necklace of pearls that illuminated the ghostly street through the night, died down. Instantly, my image vanished from the window's reflective surface.

I went to the bathroom and washed my face, then headed out to the neighborhood café, which had free Wi-Fi, and searched eBay for a cheap cemetery plot. There was a man in Westchester County selling a grave his father had purchased before moving away; he had left the plot behind. His son, who said his name was Kevin, had taken several photographs. The grass was overgrown. The stones in the adjacent lots were falling over. There were a few fake flowers scattered across the lawn, blown here and there by the wind. In one of the photos, Kevin, wearing a white polo shirt and slacks with a cell phone clipped onto his belt, was lying down on the site of what would have been his father's future tomb with his arms on his chest. He looked as good as dead. I told him my father was much thinner than he was; in fact, he was emaciated, but judging from Kevin's graveyard portrait, about the same length. Kevin confirmed that it was the perfect size for an adult male, and I bought the plot then and there.

The next day, I took my dead father for a ride on the Metro-North in our chest-shaped suitcase. It took hours to fold his knees into his chest so he would fit. But I persevered. It was how he would have wanted it: transported in the memorabilia of the past.

He weighed next to nothing. Even so, we both arrived at the funeral home a few pounds thinner.

///////////

I sat in the funeral home for hours, waiting. Eventually, the man who prepared my father's body for burial and wrapped him in a white sheet — a reserved, thin man with polished cheeks — came out to offer his condolences. He disappeared through a door and then reappeared a moment later and offered me a glass of water. It was so quiet, I could have heard a pin drop. The man stood there, hovering over me while I drank the water. I wanted him to go away, but he continued to stand there in silence. He seemed to expect me to say something, to explain the circumstances of my father's knotted body. I began to lay bare the various nodes of my ill-fated life. I found myself saying that I intended to reverse our exile — "Our forced retreat from the past," I said with emphasis — by retracing our jerky, incoherent journey across the Mediterranean, street by street, in a backward manner. As soon as I heard myself say the words, I realized I had been nurturing the idea since the start of my father's decline, the onset of his blindness.

It became clear to me then and there that my father's missive to record the *uselessness of our suffering* would become, over the course of the following months, an unstoppable impulse. An impulse that would require everything of me. I, alone in the world and without family, am a person of little consequence. But, I thought inwardly, let the story of the Hosseinis, which is also my story, the story I inherited and through which I must slog, be a resounding alarm to the rest of humanity, the 99.9 percent of anti-intellectual rodents who scamper about this earth indifferent to the pain of others. I'm not talking about a mild heartache. No. I'm talking about the kind of pain that eviscerates, the kind that levels your life, that leaves you barely holding on. I reached for my notebook. "This notebook is my only hope," I told the gentleman who had prepared my father's body. "Everything rests on it. I am willing to extend my life, which is itself a death, in order to put these words in the record."

The man stood there, nodding along and smiling warmly.

I said, "I intend to dive into the lacunae of exile. In other words, just like my father and my mother, I am going to become nothingness, fade into the white noise of death — only I will do so by physically retracing the ill-fated steps of our journey from Iran through the Mediterranean to the U.S.A."

His eyes widened, but he kept nodding.

"The U.S.A.," I said, letting out a chuckle. "The Unanimous Station of Apathy, a station where the selfish and the greedy readily set up shop with the intent of exploiting the vulnerable!"

The funeral director looked at me with that polished countenance of his.

I said, "Just so the message is clear" — at this, he looked like I had slapped him in the face with a dirty dish towel — "I intend to prolong this ridiculous habit of living just long enough to examine the landscapes we traversed during our long and brutal exodus. After that, there is no knowing what I will do."

Once his initial surprise had passed, the funeral director did his best to normalize the situation. He stood there and continued to smile kindly while he searched the ground at his feet. But his unresponsiveness failed to soothe me; it only fueled my anger. I raised my notebook to my nose and sniffed it, then I took another sip of my water.

"Soon," I said, swallowing, "this notebook will smell like ink, like the blood of literature, the blood that runs through all Hosseini veins."

The man took a respectful step back. He stood there with his hands clasped, his head bent humbly. He was still staring at the gray carpet beneath his feet. I took another sip. His mouth finally opened. His tongue had started working again.

"I understand," he said humbly. He raised his head and looked past me at a man who was walking across the room carrying an arrangement of roses, lilies, and white hyacinth.

I got up and walked over to the chest-shaped suitcase, which I had parked near the door. Naturally, my dead father was no longer in it, but the pungent odor of his corpse had been absorbed into the leather and wood. The scent of his death made me dizzy, but I carried on. I had to persist in the face of dread. It was the valiant thing to do. I pulled out a few of our favorite books: *The Divine Comedy*, *Don Quixote*, *The Odyssey*. I walked back over to the man with the polished face and asked him if he could give the books to the undertakers to put in my father's casket before sealing it. I wanted him to have access in death to the tattered pages from which he had so often read to me in life. I could see the man wasn't pleased with my request, but again he nodded and said he understood.

"And who do I give the epitaph for the tombstone to?" I asked, shoving the old tomes under his arm.

"I can take care of that for you," he said.

I handed him a piece of paper. It read: *Like desert camels of thirst dying while on their backs water bearing.* The man read the note. He looked up from the page, and asked: "This is what you want on his tombstone?"

"Exactly," I said. "And make sure the engraving is poorly done. I'd like the words to be lopsided, as if they were written hastily and upside down during times of war, between bouts of carnage, detonations, and bombings." As I spoke, the bony knobs of my knees ached the way they had hurt when we walked across that no-man's-land with those blackboards hanging over our chests and backs to protect us from the imprudent blows of history.

The man who had been carrying the flowers was now walking back across the room. This time he was holding a blown-up photograph of one of the world's other recently deceased, a man with glasses, a tiny nose that looked like it had been chopped off, and white hair.

After that, I don't know what happened. At some point, hours later, I was standing out in the cemetery under a cluster of trees looking at the plot I had seen on eBay. It had since been dug up. It was a moist black hole. I was dazed, holding my notebook, watching as my father was slipped into the mud of the earth. Again, I had the feeling that someone was draining my blood. I yielded to the dizziness until I was at the point of delirium, until I felt myself double, triple, quadruple. I thought to myself, I am among the loneliest of this pitiful world; all the other Hosseinis are dead.

My void widened in order to contain my increasingly voluminous loneliness. In response, my consciousness stretched and spun. Just then, like a bolt of lightning, a magnificent thought struck my mind. It occurred to me that I would need a new name for my journey of exile, one that referred to my multiple selves. I declared inwardly: I, the last of the Hosseinis, will continue to live so that this scattered collective of selves can fill my notebook with literature; in other words, my manifesto — composed of literary fragments systematically organized into a vast matrix, with each portion reflecting a disparate self — is my only vindication, my final line of defense.

At that critical moment, the light came down through the trees in the cemetery and fell across my father's casket so that it appeared striped. The image was charged with an electric force, and for a brief moment, my inner and outer worlds were in perfect alignment. I felt as though the fate of my future self were tied up with that image of my father's casket wrapped in alternating bands of light and darkness. It formed a kind of chiaroscuro composed of shadowy, inky bands laced with contrasting stripes as white as paper. That's when the word appeared in my head: *zebra*.

I let it sit for a moment. I watched the undertakers — three men dressed in black, all of them strangers — sow my father into the earth, thinking, as I did, that the juxtaposing stripes of light and darkness were sending a message to me, a message that consisted of that very word, *zebra*, which had spontaneously manifested itself much as the truth does. The truth, which is odder than one expects.

I turned the word over on my tongue; I muttered it to myself. I examined it. Zebra: an animal striped black-and-white like a prisoner of war; an animal that rejects all binaries, that represents ink on paper. A martyr of thought. That was it. I had arrived at my new name. To the funeral director's astonishment, I declared out loud, "Call me Zebra!"

The funeral director leaned his polished face over to look behind the trees, his eyes searching for a zebra grazing in the grass. But unbeknownst to him, I was the zebra; the zebra was I. I gave him a broad, happy smile. He shrank, like any man would, because that smile was the smile of a conqueror.

That night, after returning the empty suitcase to my studio, I set out again despite feeling exhausted. I went out on a peripatetic walk in honor of my father. I walked around New York for hours, thinking of him, of the long lineage of autodidacts I had descended from, of the relentless machinery of terror that is history, of its wheels that never stop turning. I thought of the dim light cast by my perpetual exile, of the way we had been gored by history, and felt sadness set in, and a mild sense of vertigo. I sat down on a bench. I comforted myself with the thought that all conquerors are secretly melancholy. For a moment, I felt my sadness lift. In that brief reprieve, my new name — Zebra — echoed in my ears. Then the sediment of grief settled again in the craggy pits of my void. A man walked by with his dog. A woman dragged a suitcase on wheels past me. The sky was growing steadily darker. After a while, I got up. I stopped at a deli and bought a scalding cup of black tea. The Pakistani man at the cash register counted out the money I handed him with robotic movements. I examined the mechanical aspect of his gestures. He, too, seemed divorced from his environment, but while I was scrutinizing the gap between myself and the world to the point of dizziness, he was simply detached. I left, drank my tea, walked. Hours later, run-down, drained, I got on the subway.

Underground, the air was stale and damp. The train pulled into the station, and I got on. It was a busy time of night. At every station, the doors pumped open and more people piled in. A few of them looked at me with an odious glare, and when they eventually got up to leave, I felt the residue of their hostility resonating through the orange color of their abandoned seats. I looked around. There were women with eyeliner running down their tired faces; men in suits with hunched shoulders, their shoes freshly shined; families carrying bags of fruits and vegetables; Orthodox men in fur hats hiding their faces behind newspapers. I felt like I was being squashed between the bodies of the other commuters. I couldn't breathe. I tried to suck in air. The back of my throat was burning. For a second, I had the distinct sensation that the train was headed to a mass grave, that the whole city was a graveyard full of discharged energy and waste. Then the subway doors pumped open, and still more people piled in. When my stop was finally announced, I got up, and pushed past the crowd of bodies. I climbed the urine-and-grease-stained stairs and walked north toward our building.

Inside the apartment, I struck the odious bulb that burned in the center of the room. The bulb didn't shatter; it swayed from side to side like a pendulum until it lost momentum and went still. A cacophony of emotions cycled through me: rage, grief, numbness, amazement, shock, guilt. Every time I heard a noise, I asked: "Who's there?" But there was no one. My father was gone. Exhausted and at the edge of despair, I draped myself over the La-Z-Boy. Hours later I was possessed by a strange euphoria. I got up and began walking through the apartment in ever-expanding concentric circles. I thought long and hard. I consolidated my thoughts from the funeral. The circle — prehistoric, divine, natural god of geometry, responsible for the ever-increasing speed of human travel. According to the Greeks, the smoothest, most perfect of forms. Innate. Embedded in the earth, manifest like death in the body. I dragged my hand against the wall of the Room of Broken Heirlooms, across the boundary of the circle. *What path leads to freedom?* I asked. *Any vein in your body,* I answered, thinking of the great philosophers of the past. I felt relieved for my father. As it turned out, death was the only liberty there was. I wanted to taste that liberty. I wanted to be wrapped, like my parents, in the silky folds of death.

But as the sun was coming up, I was struck by another bolt of lightning. A Hosseini Commandment. That literature, magnanimous host, does not treat life and death as if they were two antagonistic blocks. It is courageous enough to dissolve the barrier, and therefore, it is liberty in life. It was then that Acker's words trumpeted through my void. I whispered them to myself: *I travelled all over the world, looking for trouble.* Trouble! What a wonderful word, originating from the Latin *turbidus*, meaning opaque, milky, turbulent. I muttered the word again: "Trouble!" Then I thought of the Provençal word *trobar* — to find, to invent — origin of the word *troubadour*, a medieval lyric poet. In other words, I, a modern literary inventor, was going to walk the void of my multiple exiles causing trouble, discombobulating the world.

I sat back down on the La-Z-Boy. I thought: If Ulysses can set off on a Grand Tour of the Mediterranean, Don Quixote on a Grand Tour of Literature, and Dante the Pilgrim on a Grand Tour of Human Nature, then it stands to reason that I, Zebra, can do all three at once. Done and dusted. I was going to use the papers I had secured through the inky sweat of my father — my American passport — to embark on a GRAND TOUR OF EXILE.

Just one obstacle remained: I, a penniless rodent, did not possess the funds to backflip into the void of exile. But I had a meeting with Morales in a few days. I had prepared myself to relay the truth: that my father had died and that I needed money — roughly ten thousand dollars — to fund the Grand Tour of Exile. I barely had any savings. My father, who had found erratic work as a translator, had left behind enough money for me to pay a few months of rent, basic utilities, and food if I ate nothing but mint-and-onion soup.

When the day came, Morales offered his condolences, and then he reprimanded me: "The Grand Tour makes exile sound like a delight!"

I felt irate. "Am I so worthless that I am barred from taking pleasure in my own suffering?" I rejoined.

He said nothing for a while. He leaned forward and put his elbows on the desk. His eyes had pooled over. I could see his pupils swimming behind the thick lenses of his glasses. When he finally spoke, his tone was unusually reflective.

He said: "Compose your manifesto and we'll talk again. In the meantime, I'll pull some resources together so you can be on your way."

I stood up and bowed respectfully, like a warrior, like a soldier of death. I stepped out of his office thinking only of those lines he had recited so many months earlier and of the prophetic nature of literature I had been attuned to since birth: *Oh pit of debris, ferocious cave of the shipwrecked. In you the wars and the flights accumulated.*

I spent the following weeks feverishly composing my manifesto. I barely left the apartment, and to save money, I began rationing the little food I had left in the refrigerator. I grew as light-headed as a Sufi mystic. There were days I survived on a single date. As I chewed the sweetmeat, I thought of the date palm I was born under. The thought was sufficiently loaded with the weight of loss that it caused me to feel full instantaneously.

On one such day, as I stood near the kitchen window, I noticed there was more room in my mind for my thoughts to move around than there had been before. Something had shifted. Pathways that weren't available to me before had suddenly appeared. It occurred to me that, before being absorbed by the mind of the universe, my father's mind must have lingered. It had to have traversed the atmosphere. Then I remembered Pythagoras's theory of the transmigration of souls, which supposes that the soul — or, as the Hosseinis believed, the mind — decomposes in death and continues its journey through the world.

In a clipped tone, I said the words: "Metempsychosis. Palingenesia." Indeed, I thought to myself, that's what had happened: More than likely, I had absorbed my father's mind before the mind of the universe could get to him. In other words, I had beat the universe to it. I felt soothed by this notion, comforted. The sting of loneliness subsided a little. As a result, I was thinking with the brain capacity of two minds, each of them multilingual, extremely literary, and shattered by their shared and perpetual exile; which is to say that each mind contained multiple minds inside of it, many of which, by virtue of having come into existence under different cultural and linguistic parameters, had different intentions, objectives, and patterns of thought. I thought to myself, I am a person with a myriad of unsettled minds all operating at once, a kind of irregular genius. Not unlike the many-headed country of my birth and origin: Persia, Pars, Iran.

After that, my thoughts became lucid, electric, charged. I decided to spend the day advancing my manifesto by simultaneously reading Cervantes's and Acker's *Don Quixote*, along with Borges's "Pierre Menard, Author of the *Quixote*." I would read the texts concomitantly by going back and forth between them with my many minds, metaphysically superimposing the texts and blurring the lines between them. Reading these works in concert would allow me to significantly increase the speed with which I built the constellation of literary networks that I had come to refer to collectively as the Matrix of Literature, an infinite cosmos created through the Paranoiac-Critical method of spontaneous association. To the rows and rows of tomes, I announced: "A many-headed reading experience!" and got to it.

Within a matter of hours, I arrived at the following conclusion: Kathy Acker's *Don Quixote* and Borges's "Pierre Menard, Author of the *Quixote*" are distorted duplicates of the original *Don Quixote* by Miguel de Cervantes, which is itself a duplicate of other texts, a giant literary womb in which the chivalric tales of times past are gestating, preparing to be born again. I was struck then by a thought of epic proportions: Texts have been leaping across eras for centuries in order to cross-contaminate one another.

Without effort, I declared: "Literature is so self-aware that it knows how to perpetuate itself like a disease. Every text is a mutant and a doppelgänger!" This discovery drew another into the light: that we, the Hosseinis, have been operating like literature for centuries. In other words, each of us is a distorted duplicate of the other. My father fit inside me the way his father and his father's father had fit inside him — a *mise en abyme* of Hosseinis.

This was the tip of the iceberg. I was just getting started. The voice of my manifesto, woven together from my plethora of minds, had appeared.

I needed to give it some air. I grabbed my father's cane and left the apartment.

Outside, I made a series of left turns and ended up on a street I hadn't walked on before. The street was undergoing repairs. The asphalt had been overturned, and there was a ditch in the center. I peered into that abysmal wound in the center of the street. The sun was baking the sidewalks, the building facades, my head. A pregnant woman walked by. With a great deal of complicity, I announced to her, "Literature is pregnant with itself, too! It's constantly having triplets!" She stopped, looked at me pleadingly, then hid her face behind her hair, hugged her belly, scurried away. I watched her leave and wished someone was there to take my photograph, the first portrait of Zebra. But I didn't have a camera. So I took a mental photograph of myself instead and imagined that the following caption, simultaneously inspired by my family motto and Blanchot's transcendent words, was written beneath it: *Death is nothingness and nothingness is the essence of literature.* So, I thought, weaving together my various thoughts, if liberty = death and death = nothingness and nothingness = literature, then it follows that literature = liberty, death, nothingness. I was headed in the right direction. I was going to disappear into literature.

I climbed out of the hole and walked up Broadway. I stepped over a half-eaten chicken thigh and a slice of pizza that had been discarded on the road. I walked past a group of old men chattering loudly and playing bridge on the sidewalk. I walked past the neighborhood grocery store. Through the shop's glass wall, I saw rows of Bustelo coffee cans stacked on top of one another, piles of plantains, loads of polished vegetables. I pressed my face against the glass. I gawked at that food for a few solemn moments. All the produce looked unreal. Then I walked away, gripped by a strange euphoria, utterly convinced that I had absorbed my father.

That night, as I lay awake beneath *The Hung Mallard*, I made tremendous progress. A single but epic thought kept belting around my many minds: that I had metabolized a critical mass of books, that I had read enough to conclude once and for all that literature is duplicitous, and that texts give a false impression of being closed systems capable of operating independently of one another when, in fact, they secretly reside in a mutable and ghostly environment, a dynamic matrix where they disappear inside one another, mirror each other in a series of replicas. I watched the blue light of the moon glide across the hung mallard's beak. Books, I realized, are connected to one another via nearly invisible superhighways of language, the way stars are interrelated via light and dust, the debris of the universe.

Finally, I fell asleep. But in the early hours of the morning, as the dewy light of dawn was rolling in and the city was starting to come to life again, I startled awake. I bolted straight up. Literature, I mouthed, reciting as if from a script, has evolved over time through a process of borrowing, repetition, plagiarism. I was edging toward wakefulness. Every book, I whispered into the retreating night, is a distorted duplicate of another book, the ghost of a false original, which, like the seed of the universe and my dead ancestors, is nowhere and everywhere at once. I made a mental note to go to the library in search of proof before revealing my findings to Morales. Then I went back to sleep. I had earned myself a few good hours.

The next day at the campus library, I walked through the damp corridors of books until I was dizzy. Hours later, exhausted, dehydrated, starved, my legs shaking beneath my head, which was becoming progressively more detached from my body, I reached for a book at random and found what I was looking for — proof, in a book by none other than the deft and mystical Blanchot: *The world and the book eternally and infinitely send back their reflected images. This indefinite power of mirroring, this sparkling and limitless multiplication — which is the labyrinth of light and nothing else besides — will then be all that we will find, dizzily, at the bottom of our desire to understand.* A few passages later I found a summary — Blanchot via Borges: *The book is, in principle, the world and the world is the book.*

"Yes!" I declared, and petted the shelves with exaggerated tenderness. I felt satiated. The librarian had her eye on me. She was a plump middle-aged woman I deplored. Her head kept popping up between the aisles. I hated her fleshy cheeks. I walked faster, wove in and out of the corridors of books in order to lose her. I was looking for a pen. A minute later, I stole one from a sleeping freshman, who had likely been pulling an all-nighter and had left his supplies sprawled across the table. Pen in hand, I returned to the book to register my revelation. I crossed out both quotes, the Blanchot and his paraphrasing of Borges. Neither of them went far enough, which is no surprise. One is always alone in putting the nail in the coffin.

I wrote: *Literature, with its cunning and duplicitous nature, aware of itself, in possession of a supraconsciousness, is the only true thing in the world; it exposes man's denial of reality's shattering pluralism.* I slipped the book under my shirt, prepared to steal it even though I had a library card. A minute later, the librarian showed up behind me.

"Young woman, you are done for the day!" she announced, and kicked me out for writing in the library books and, as usual, for having entered with Morales's card, which he had duplicated for me. As she closed the door behind me, I told her that her lavender smell made me wretch.

I had succeeded in stealing the book. It was mine. Only its trace would remain in the library system. I walked over to the dying rose garden adjacent to Morales's office and wove my way between the sickly plants. It was evening. The next day, I would have my final meeting with Morales. I was eager to know if he had procured the money for my journey. I walked farther toward the hedges bordering the garden. I slid from bush to bush thinking about "A Philosophy of Totality: The Matrix of Literature." Then I leaned against a young tree. My thoughts branched out, took on horrifying proportions. The exile, I thought, whose identity is shattered with each progressive displacement from her homeland, also unmasks reality's dizzying multiplicity. I looked at the bushes. Variations on a theme. What's more, I realized, is that those among us who have not had to seek refuge in a land of hostile strangers, who have not been persecuted or strangled by the crushing hand of grief, maintain the privilege of deluding themselves into believing in a coherent and linear reality; in other words, metaphysically speaking, they think they are immortal! As if parts of their lives, whole blocks of consciousness, couldn't suddenly die or become extinguished only to have to rise from the ashes of death like a phoenix. I walked up to a rose and punched it in the face. A few petals floated down to the gravel and caught a sinister beam of light coming off the moon. I had never felt more awake.

The time of my meeting with Morales had arrived. I told him about my revelations. I told him about the web of literature. I recited my manifesto from memory. I opened my mouth and a voice emerged. It was the voice of my other self, the voice of Zebra. I said, "By going on the Grand Tour of Exile, I plan to prove that literature is an incarnated phenomenon; I, an exile and a Hosseini, am the embodiment of literature." I informed him that my multiple selves and the archipelago of quotes that made up the Matrix of Literature *eternally and infinitely send back their reflected images* and that I would be collecting still more fragments by the Great Writers of the Past, and therefore more selves, throughout my journey. Morales looked at me, remote, philosophical. I told him that I would record the tour in my notebook and that by revisiting the origins of each of the multiple selves my knobby, incoherent exile had produced — selves I had no conscious memory of — I would give birth to literary duplicates and distribute between them the pain of the erasure that the so-called original version of myself had endured.

Morales stood up from his desk, removed his heavily framed glasses and set them on the table. He hadn't shaved in days, and without his glasses on, I could see how much he had aged over the course of that long year. There were more white hairs growing on his cheeks, at the nape of his neck, and in his sideburns. Even his red suit looked pale, more of a salmon pink. I gave him the book I had stolen from the library and instructed him to open it to the earmarked page. I had added more notes to the margins of the page overnight. He put his glasses back on. They sat crookedly on his face.

"The Final Exit," he said, reading my notes back to me, humming, rocking back and forth on his heels. He adjusted his glasses.

"Yes," I said. "I am preparing for a Final Exit from the New World and its lineup of fakes who refuse to acknowledge the warped nature of reality!"

We both laughed. Then Morales paced his office with his head hanging, eyes searching the ground, thinking. Finally, he looked up, and said, "It's time for you to go. Be on your way. I have made a few arrangements."

He handed me an envelope. It contained ten thousand dollars. It was money the university had given him over the years to fund a research assistant, but he had never found a worthwhile candidate. He explained this in his usual matter-of-fact tone. He also added that a certain Ludovico Bembo, whose contact information he had enclosed, would pick me up on the other side of the pond so long as I communicated my arrangements. I thanked him. I knew that I would never see Morales again.

//////////

That week, I drained what little money we had in our bank account ($80.56), gave my notice, purchased a plane ticket (depleting a full tenth of my reserves), went to my father's grave, and said my final good-byes. I grabbed the old chest-shaped suitcase and began to pile into it the residue of the past, my broken heirlooms. I grabbed the samovar and shoved it into the suitcase. I removed *The Hung Mallard* from the wall, took a knife to the canvas, and separated it from the frame. I rolled it up and put it in the suitcase. I thought of my dead relatives, the Autodidacts, Anarchists, and Atheists, of how they had retreated into the deep web of literature in order to survive their deaths while all around the world was being shattered, blasted into a million shards, its parts repeatedly, unceasingly added to history's pile of ruins. I rolled up the bludgeoned rug. I put the leatherbound notebook and my most cherished books, those old tomes lining the walls of the apartment, into the suitcase. By the time I was done packing, the chest was so heavy I could barely pick it up. It weighed as much as my ill-fated past — a burden I had to shoulder in order to do what my father had asked me to do since birth: to sound out the Hosseini alarm, to leap into the pitiful abyss of our human condition and rove the depths in search of the slimy pearl of truth.

A few days later, at dawn, the hour of false hope, I, Zebra, left New York City forever. I got on the A line and headed to JFK. I looked around at the empty orange seats. Soon they would be filled. History, I thought, according to my father's logic, which was now also my own, has a way of choosing new victims. Metaphysically speaking, I wondered, where do the world's exiles, its living dead, reside? I thought of Dante's triangular purgatory, and the answer came to me immediately: in the Pyramid of Exile, an elastic funnel in which the refuse of the world can be piled.

I closed my eyes. I saw an infinite stack of ill-fated corpses. In the devastation, I captured a memory of the future: I was wearing a gas mask, standing alone under a crescent moon in a gloomy, ashen landscape. I breathed in. I breathed out. I watched the glass panel over my eyes fog up, then clear. I was bruised and wounded, standing inside a hologram of the future, my future, which was composed of quotes from literature's past. I could smell the rubber of the gas mask. I was holding a telephone in my hand, then setting it down to transcribe words on a typewriter. Then the image transformed, and I was standing on a cobbled sidewalk in a remote town somewhere in the Mediterranean. Or, I wondered, was I in the no-man's-land of my childhood? There were dead bodies scattered everywhere. Windows and shutters of the houses were drawn. There was dried blood on the faces of the dead. Even through the gas mask, I could smell oil, vinegar, rotting corpses. The only people on the street were a group of undertakers wearing masks. They were lifting the bodies into cars, into wheelbarrows, onto horses, carrying them out to the graves in distant fields. A line from Calvino floated through my mind: *And you know that in the long journey ahead of you, when to keep awake against the camel's swaying or the junk's rocking, you start summoning up your memories one by one, your wolf will have become another wolf, your sister a different sister, your battles other battles.* I opened my eyes. The image resolved itself. Each thing, I thought, replicates itself to compose the wretched eternal return of life. I felt as though I had been trapped in a terrible nightmare.

As the train lurched forward, I realized that my fate had been sealed. I felt more clearly than ever that my vindication, my survival, depended on training, through the literature of the void, to stand against my opponents — nonexiles — those fakes who increase their own longevity by hastening the exile's death, borrowing time and well-being against our increasingly dwindling resources. In the waning darkness, as I set off on my Grand Tour of Exile, I registered the message: I had become a literary terrorist, a Knight — no! — an armed Dame of the Void.

BARCELONA

The Story of How I Leapt into the
Void of Exile and Became Entangled with
Ludo Bembo, the Embalmer of Words

THE BOEING 747 RUMBLED DOWN THE RUNWAY AND took off into a misty gray sky. The plane was buffeted by strong crosswinds. It spat and skidded its way through a mass of clouds. Once we were airborne, a flight attendant emerged in the feeble, dimmed light of the cabin. She came down the aisle in a superhero pose, legs spread wide for balance, both arms up against the overhead luggage compartments. It was clear she was expecting severe turbulence. With a shrill voice, she announced, "Seat belts!" She leaned over my neighbor — a middle-aged woman with a moist, round face, who was already fast asleep — to make sure she had strapped herself into her seat.

There was something austere and unforgiving about the flight attendant's features: the drooping corners of her thin and forbidding mouth; her eyebrows, which were narrowed into blades; her square chin; her face, which reminded me of the corpse-strewn deserts of that no-man's-land I had traversed so long ago with my mustached father. That land that drew everything toward itself and returned nothing, the land where my mother was buried. I looked through the window. The sky was as white as the sheet my father had been wrapped in before he was slipped into his casket. It occurred to me: There is no longer any "we" to speak of. I am alone.

At that precise moment, an alarming noise originated from the right engine. It lasted a few seconds. Long enough to cause a great deal of uneasy shuffling in the cabin. Everyone was agitated, everyone except my neighbor, who was still sleeping. People were looking out the window at that measureless white sky and then turning away from it to scrutinize one another, the plane. Some flailed their arms. Others sat rigidly, holding their breath. I could see steam coming out of their mouths and ears. The steam of war, I thought, and stuck my neck out to study the anxious faces of the passengers. What if someone is sitting here with bombs strapped to their person or with explosives stuffed in their shoes? Someone who is eager to die, to take everyone else down with them.

I shrank into my seat. The captain came on the intercom and hopelessly announced: "Be advised, we are going through a storm." I heard a wave of whispers spread through the cabin. It was unbearably hot. People were muttering in different languages, crying, holding hands with their neighbors. This was the other 99.9 percent, the world's numbskulls, its sheltered amateurs. I had enclosed myself in a plane with them. I thought of Rousseau. *"What about me,"* I murmured. *"Cut off from them and from everything else, what am I?"*

I sat there contemplating the question for a while. *What am I?* I considered my options: a brute, a pitiable creature, nothing. Then I heard my father answer from a faraway place: "The .1 percent," he grunted. If he were alive, he would have taken me by the scruff of the neck, and said: *Child! Enfant! Get a grip on your death!*

The swift communiqué from my father galvanized my spirit. I felt as fit as a fiddle. I removed the in-flight magazine from the seat pocket in front of me. As the plane rocked and rolled through the sky, I skimmed glossy picture after glossy picture. I looked at infinity pools, light-flooded hospitals, fluorescent images of brains, ornately plated molecular foods, biodegradable coffins. My father's coffin was made out of the cheapest materials. Papier-mâché, cardboard, recycled paper — how should I know? I felt a sharp sting in my void at the thought of his body being buried in that misshapen New World. I looked at my neighbor. Was she dead? Her chest was rising and falling. So she was alive but sleeping, as unmoved as a stone.

I inspected the 99.9 percent. I met the gaze of a bald, bearded man who was sitting across the aisle and had the dignified look of a Renaissance man. His hand was shaking. He was nervous. He stroked his beard; it was heavily perfumed. I got a waft of lavender, sage, mint. I felt sorry for him. I thought, this man deserves to know the truth. The truth about life. His beard is asking for it. Besides, why should I keep my wisdom, hard-earned in the trenches of literature, to myself when I could be providing him with ground-breaking perspective?

I echoed my father. "Life," I said to the man, "is brutal, savage; it will wear you down." After a brief pause, I came into my own. "You could be struck by the whip of uncertainty at any moment" — he stroked his beard again (his mouth had fallen open and I could see his lips were thin and chapped) — "and what can a two-legged rodent like you do in the midst of all that uncertainty except rise above the flotsam and jetsam?"

He had square yellow teeth. He pointed at himself, and weakly asked: "Are you speaking to me?"

"No," I lied, smiling softly at him. It was a hopeless cause trying to help him. I leaned into my neighbor, and announced across the aisle: "I am speaking to that other bearded man."

He looked around. There was no other bearded man. I watched him through the corner of my eye. I gave him a second and then I raised my voice. "Give it up!"

I watched his pupils dilate.

"Give what up?" he asked desperately.

But I didn't respond. I was through with him.

The plane got blasted by a series of strong winds. After a brief rush of adrenaline, I suddenly felt defeated, morose, sullen. The hunchbacked and uncertain piece of metal we were enclosed in was being propelled across the sky by a listless pilot. I calculated that it had a 50 percent chance of making it across the Atlantic Ocean. I reached down into my bag and retrieved my notebook. I petted its musty pages. I sniffed the leather binding. So what if the plane doesn't make it? Why worry about it when we, like everyone who has died before us and who will die after us, will be buried in the indifferent landscapes of history; will turn to ash, residue, into poor fodder for someone else's plants? I looked at the Renaissance man again. He was anxiously stroking his facial hair. I inhaled the dusty herb perfume of his beard. He looked pale. The blood had drained from his face. His pupils were still dilated.

A moment later, we hit a vacuum. The plane dropped a few thousand feet. I belched. In that abysmal drop, I heard myself say: "Descend into the Matrix of Literature, which is infinite, elastic, as mysterious as the universe." I looked out the window to see if that false New World was still visible, but I couldn't see anything. We were enveloped in a dense white mass. We were too high up in the air. I thought to myself, what use is there in looking one last time at a land where people plot their lives in advance of the future, as if history will never come knocking with its cruel claw on their door?

The plane began regaining elevation. The copilot came on the intercom. "Our apologies for the unexpected plunge," he said. "One more storm to cross. We've weathered worse. Nothing to worry about here."

His voice failed to inspire confidence.

The plane drifted across the sky laterally. We were rolling through another cloud mass, and it seemed the pilots' strategy was to let the aircraft ride the waves. We hit a bump in the sky. I nearly jumped out of my seat. The plane skidded, then righted itself. There was a deafening sound overhead. The engines started wheezing, a brutal screeching noise. I looked around: supplicating human faces. Impossible: my neighbor, still asleep while everyone else, after a brief reprieve, was sighing, shifting, pleading with their personal god. In the theater of my mind, I imagined my neighbor in conversation with me. My neighbor, who was grinding her teeth, whose saliva was trickling out of the corner of her pink mouth.

I said to her, "I, Zebra, am primed to expose death's movements, to illuminate the way ruin moves among us in plain sight."

"How so?" I heard her ask.

"Because I live my life in the Matrix of Literature."

My neighbor winced and nearly slid out of her seat. She must have drugged herself.

"Should I go on?" I asked. But before I could, I was interrupted.

The flight attendant burst into the cabin and came running up the aisle. She landed in her jump seat. I heard her clear her throat. I leaned over my neighbor and looked down the aisle. The attendant sat facing us, her captive passengers. I watched her flick three imaginary specks of dust off her pencil skirt with the back of her hand — whoosh, whoosh, whoosh. She crossed her legs, strapped herself in. Military precision, hers.

My neighbor shifted in her seat. For the first time, I took in the details of her face. She had rosy cheeks and a flat, oily nose and wispy hair, which she had coiled up on the crown of her head. Her head was tilted to one side, and there was a peanut stuck in the crease of her double chin. I studied her hands. She was holding an open bag of trail mix. I helped myself to a peanut, to some chocolate. The copilot came on again and announced that there would be more turbulence ahead.

He said: "Keep calm and pilot on!" He laughed vigorously at himself.

My mind was suddenly flooded with incongruous memories of Dante the Pilgrim. Easy to be calm about life, I thought, but not so easy to shuttle between life and death, between the persistence of memory and oblivion, like a lost pilgrim, an exile, neither here nor there. At least the pilgrim was *midway through the journey of our life* when he found himself banished into the dark forests of exile far from everyone. I was not even halfway through mine when its infrastructure, meager to begin with, was extinguished in a two-pronged blow. I felt the toxic fumes of my parents' deaths rise through my void. I could barely keep down my stomach.

The engines picked up speed. Out in the distance, the clouds were beginning to break up. This was the last stretch before the wide-open sky. I could hear the motors revving furiously beneath the wings, which were trembling and folding upward. My palms began to sweat. I dried my hands on the bony knobs of my knees. If we crashed, who would die first? I didn't have my neighbor's padding. Suddenly, everything went still and silent, as though the plane were hovering in the sky without power and was about to drop. The flight attendant was still strapped in her jump seat. She stared ahead with glassy, unperturbed eyes. She looked like a mannequin. The plane tilted sharply to one side.

"Brace!" the mannequin yelled. There was a burst of wind.

A food cart that had been stowed away broke free and rolled down the aisle. A man's hairy hands fanned out to catch it. The way his hands launched out from the peripheries in desperation reminded me of my father's flailing his arms as he recited lines of literature, and then of the distorted bodies of the men and women that Dante, the exiled poet-pilgrim, had to witness as he worked his way down the spiral of hell into the icy core of the universe. I thought of sharing all of this with my neighbor. I wanted to tell her that my exile had evacuated all meaning from my life, left me with nothing, with no choice but to pursue that nothing, that nothingness of death that, as it turns out, is the essence and privilege of literature. I reached for my notebook and again sniffed its pages. I recited to myself: *The straight way was lost.*

"Lost," I said out loud, and clicked my tongue.

"Listen to this," I said, turning to my neighbor. "*I came to myself in a dark wood / for the straight way was lost.* Dante, circa 1320. And now listen to this: *In a village of La Mancha the name of which I have no desire to recall.* Cervantes, 1605." The opening lines of those two books had begun to form a kind of slogan for my journey. Reciting them had helped to settle my stomach.

"Do you see the connection?" I asked. Then I said, making a dramatic gesture, "You see, these books were conceived at the site of a rupture, a trauma; they are about loss of identity, about death!"

My neighbor stirred in her seat. Her head dropped again to the opposite side, and she momentarily opened her eyes. I leaned over to pry. Her eyes were gray blue. She began to snore more loudly. I was close enough to her face that I could smell her malodorous breath. I imagined forest insects crawling out of that bird's nest on her head.

"Never mind," I said, and sat back.

I turned away from her and looked out the window. The sky was clear. We had made it to the other side. We had arrived at the golden blue sky I had seen in the distance. We had arrived at what only a moment ago had been the future, and in its soft atmosphere, the plane glided with ease. I looked back at the darkness that was now behind us. I saluted the abyss of my past and thought of the exile that had repeated throughout my life like a bad joke, like a wretched eternal return that had leveled my psyche and left in its wake a void through which I could hear the wind whistle.

The pilot said, "We have a few hours left until we land in Barcelona."

Barcelona. I pictured General Franco's face: the puffy, childlike cheeks; the distant, austere look in his eyes; his squared mustache; his chin always held high as if he were proudly surveying the spoils of his labor — the look of an adult harboring an angry, tormented inner child. I remembered my father saying that we, like the Catalans, had survived — no, thrived — under the sign of death, under the threat of erasure. That's why we had fled to Barcelona: because the Catalans, according to my father, were our brethren, and Barcelona — the City of Bombs, the Rose of Fire, the Manchester of the Mediterranean — was the home port of the AAA. I got a whiff of my father. He smelled like bergamot, cardamom, and eucalyptus. Just then, a large cascading cloud rolled over the wings of the plane to a great and striking effect. It reminded me of Nietzsche's mustache and my father. I watched as it glided over the plane. I remembered reading Dalí's words. *That mustache is a Wagnerian mustache, the mustache of a depressive!* He hated Nietzsche's mustache.

The cloud quickly disappeared. I pictured Dalí's paintings, his hyperreal renditions of the Catalan landscape, and immediately remembered walking along the white shores of Catalonia with my father, climbing to the top of a huge granite cliff out of which cork trees and marine pines emerged like horns. The Mediterranean Sea lay slack and purple below, and black birds darted through the sky at dusk like missiles. I remembered being pushed along the coast by the tramontana, that great wind that left in its wake a polished, limpid, unornamented sky. I wanted to have that emptiness — that flat periwinkle expanse rinsed clean by the hand of the tramontana — hanging over my head every day. That void was the same void I had experienced when my father had placed the black band of blindness over my eyes as we were crossing into Turkey. I wanted to inhabit literature beneath that sky that represented the nothingness of my ill-fated life, the void of exile.

The flight attendant got up and reached for the intercom. She fixed her glassy eyes on us, and announced, icy, cold, metallic, "You are now free to move about the cabin."

Free. I parsed that word — *free* — on my tongue. I remembered the mathematical principle I had devised in the weeks following my father's burial: liberty = death = nothingness = literature. I wanted to stamp my neighbor's body with that formula. I wanted to impart an education to her. Others should stand to benefit from the knowledge arriving to me in spontaneous droves from the Matrix of Literature. What good are the ill-fated if we do not open our fellow men's eyes to their willful blindness? I retrieved a red pen from my belongings and traced the formula in a circle on her hand. It looked like ringworm.

On that first evening in Barcelona, I met Ludovico Bembo. He came to pick me up at the airport, thanks to Morales — Chilean exile, Communist who had redistributed university money to fund the Grand Tour of Exile, beloved literary guru with a knobby forehead who had called in favors on my behalf.

According to Morales, Ludovico Bembo, who went by Ludo, was a runaway philologist from Italy and the literary protégé of an old friend of his who had warned Ludo Bembo to get out from underneath the shadow of Berlusconi as quickly as possible because — according to her logic, which was not unlike my father's — a country run by a buffoon is no longer a place to think. Before departing, I'd also conducted my own investigation into Ludo Bembo and discovered that he was a man of exceptional literary pedigree. He was a descendent of none other than Pietro Bembo, the famous sixteenth-century literary scholar, poet, Petrarch connoisseur, and member of the Knights Hospitaller. Pietro Bembo's father, Bernardo Bembo, had erected a tomb to Dante Alighieri in Ravenna, a city that I discovered was referred to by the mighty Russian symbolist Alexander Blok as *the realm of death*, and by the wild Oscar Wilde as the city *where Dante sleeps, where Byron loved to dwell*. From all of this, I'd deduced that, like me, Ludo Bembo was part of the .1 percent.

As I walked through the airport, I imagined Ludo Bembo standing in the dusk air beneath a row of palms at the curb, sniffing the brackish Barcelona air. I thought to myself that even though Ludo Bembo, an expatriated Italian living in Catalonia, is among the world's unfortunate he isn't as unlucky as I am. I was thinking of the Pyramid of Exile, which I had conceived of upon exiting the New World. I located myself somewhere in the middle of the pyramid, sandwiched between an infinite number of sorrowful rodents who are pressed together in the craggy plateaus beneath me and the more fortunate ones like Ludo Bembo, who occupy the upper echelons.

"Is that your final assessment?" I posed to myself.

"Yes, Ludo Bembo belongs in the upper echelons of the Pyramid of Exile," I replied, "because unlike me, who has been betrayed repeatedly by the treacherous hands of history, Ludo Bembo has only been pushed in a westward direction once, leaving him a hop, skip, and a jump away from his hometown of Florence. I have had to travel in punctuated movements from East to West with such dizzying frequency that I remember nothing. No, not nothing," I corrected. "Nothing except the shards of memory that shoot up at random from the swampy lagoons of my mind to pierce the surface of my consciousness with fresh wounds."

Moments later, while hovering over the carousel at the baggage claim, I felt my father's mind spinning inside my own. He was cobbling together sentences. He was funneling information to me from beyond the grave. I heard his voice, thin, wispy: *The ruins of the world are hiding in plain sight,* he whispered. *Future exiles are perpetually manufactured in the factory of war.* Just then, the chest-shaped suitcase that I had used to transport my dead father to his grave tumbled down the chute and landed on the shiny black conveyor belt. It looked like an abandoned body bag. I leaned over it, eager to reclaim the sorry remains of my past, but then something came over me, a kind of melancholy bemusement, and I stepped back to regard it affectionately as it whizzed around on the moving belt. I watched it spin. A bitter scent rose from my suitcase in wafts; it was the putrid odor of my father's death. Each time I inhaled it, it burned my nose and caused my void to swell.

The carousel finally stopped spinning. The motors died down. I heard the stupid laugh of a child. I looked down. The laugh was being directed at me by a little girl in a pink dress. "This is a coffin!" I exclaimed to her, winking. She retreated behind her mother, who was standing next to her, and looked at me with a fixed and fearful eye.

I removed my suitcase from the carousel and dragged it across the floor. The automated doors pumped open. I heard them say: "Zebra, your father may be dead, your mother may be buried under a lone date palm in no-man's-land, your ass may be rotting in the desert, but don't forget that you have inherited a passport through the inky sweat of your father. Know your privilege. Welcome to the Grand Tour of Exile!"

Outside, Ludo Bembo, a multilingual man who spoke English with native fluency, was standing at the curb just as I had imagined he would be. He looked alert, at the ready, like a man who is always at his post. He was holding a sign that read: *Here to reclaim José Emilio Morales's friend.* I searched his face. He was surprisingly good-looking. He had curly hair, round glasses, a Roman nose that reminded me of the flank of a mountain, a charming gap between his front teeth (he was smiling), and like the true and pedigreed gentleman he was, he had a pipe and a silk handkerchief tucked into the breast pocket of his suit jacket. I examined his aura. It had an antique veneer. It was the aura of a man whose energy field has been fattened with the residue of his literary ancestors, the Bembos.

He waved at me. I observed his hands. They were delicate, feminine, nimble. I imagined him running those hands over my legs. I imagined telling him the truth about my existence: that I, Zebra, alias Dame of the Void, am in worse condition than Dante the Pilgrim, because I have never encountered the straight way; my life has been crooked from the start, and that overexposure to grief has flattened my heart into a sheet of paper. It would have been an honest introduction. But something utterly strange came out of my mouth instead. My words were misshapen by a kind of nervous affliction. "Have you ever possessed me?" I asked, pointing at his sign.

He craned his neck over it. "Possessed you?" he echoed. Then he looked at me, and his pupils instinctively narrowed. He stepped back toward his car, a banged-up two-door 1980s Fiat. I heard him clear his throat. He adjusted his glasses on the bridge of his nose. Then he gathered himself and reached out to shake my hand.

"I'm Ludovico Bembo. You can call me Ludo. It's a pleasure to meet you," he said, employing a formal professorial tone. He leaned in and gave me two kisses.

In the space between our faces, I saw an infinite number of miniature Bembos. Those tiny men opened their mouths, and said, *To wish is little; we must long with the utmost eagerness to gain our end.* I recognized the quote. Ovid through Petrarch. I stepped forward. I was channeling Ludo's points of reference.

"Technically speaking," I said, pointing again at his sign, "you can only reclaim something if you've claimed it once before."

A miserable pause ensued.

In that gloomy silence, I searched his face. His expression was equal parts intrigued and guarded. I could see the wheels of his mind spinning. I considered telling him that our ancestors — his and mine — have been mingling in the Matrix of Literature since time immemorial and that, metaphysically speaking, he and I cohabit the Pyramid of Exile where he, in his privileged position relative to mine, is afforded a great deal of oxygen as well as the good graces of those below him, like me, who shoulder his weight. At this, I pictured my mother buried under the stone house that had come down on her head, and I heard her words echo across a great distance. *Who will marry her? Who will feed her once we are dead?* I nearly said, *We have all the necessary ingredients for an arranged marriage!* But before I had a chance to speak, Ludo plowed ahead with that linear, bureaucratic mind of his.

"Did you get any sleep on the plane?" he asked. He maneuvered around me and crossed to the back of the car, his gestures confident, calculated, precise.

"The plane?" I huffed. I was annoyed by how quickly he had engineered a change in topic. I pictured the stifling sky we had flown through. I said: "I flew here on the back of an ass!"

He let out a short rudimentary laugh, and in that laugh, I diagnosed the dryness of his character. A terrifying seriousness that lifted my spirits because it confirmed his relation to the Bembos, a somber bunch of poets. People shuttled past us on either side. A second later, a swallow fell through the sky. It hit a palm on the opposite side of the road and landed on the ground. It was dead.

"Did you see that?" I said to Ludo. He was fussing with the trunk of his car.

"Birds die all the time," he said, with the dull indifference of an administrator.

I looked up at the sky. It was dusk. The dead swallow's verminous friends appeared, a hovering black mass checking out the scene of death. A moment later, the birds gave up, disappeared. They left a streak of ink across the sky. The streak read: *Like Sancho Panza to Don Quixote, so too Ludo Bembo to Zebra*. I laughed with childish ebullience. I was giddy, weary, and worn-down from the trials and tribulations of my Final Exit and, at the same time, astonished, amazed that I had managed to get away from that wretched New World that had claimed my father's life. My eyes misted over. Ludo cast me a circumspect look over the trunk of his car. I crossed behind the Fiat. I was eager to pose my question again, to return to the subject of his signage. "Have you e-ver po-ssessed me?" I asked.

Ludo leaned against the trunk. His mouth looked like a sealed envelope. I wanted to open that envelope. I said, "Ludo Bembo, I, Zebra, beg of you: Speak now or forever hold your peace!"

His mouth opened. "That's not the name I was given," he said tersely. His cheeks puffed out a little, like a fish's gills.

"Don't worry," I said. "I recently acquired a new name." I felt versions of my former self diffuse through my void. It was a terrible sensation. I scurried up to him to distract myself. "Now tell me: Have you ever possessed me?"

He stuck his head in the trunk. A weary little voice spilled out from inside that cavernous void: "It was just a sign!" he mumbled tiredly. He sounded as if someone had removed his lungs.

"If it's just a sign, then why not play a little?"

His head reemerged. My commitment to reinvigorating him was producing moderate results.

"To the best of my knowledge, I, Ludo Bembo, have never claimed you before this moment." His tone, though firm, revealed undercurrents of exhaustion; it was as if he had been called to the witness stand in a court of law.

I laughed. A second later, a smile broke across his face. It was a jagged, uncertain smile, but it was a smile nonetheless. He was coming along.

"So you stand corrected?" I asked.

"Sure," he said, and plunged that curly head of his back into the trunk. I watched him push a car jack and some books aside to make room for my suitcase.

Security officers in neon vests were waving their hands at waist level, trying to get us to move along. I was standing directly behind Ludo. I was looking at his ass. It looked like a bowl of fruit. I heard him murmur something into the Fiat. One of the security guards approached us. A red-faced man with a goatee and a gash for a mouth. He ordered us to get going. Ludo nodded apologetically. Then he bent over my suitcase to pick it up.

"Ready?" he asked.

"Yes, but be careful," I replied, pointing at my suitcase. "This here is the corpse of my past."

I saw his face fall a little.

A moment later, we found ourselves in the car, enveloped in a dismal silence. I considered explaining myself. I considered telling Ludo Bembo that the *corpse of my past* is a metonym for my *library of books*, but it occurred to me that if I did the mood, after briefly trending upward, would most certainly wilt even further than the dire straits it was currently in. So I sat there quietly instead. I watched Ludo Bembo stuff his pipe, and roll the window down. He leaned his head back and sucked, then blew the smoke out of his mouth and nose. His eyes looked soft, sensual; his lips moist. Then he sat up, pushed the gearshift into first, and we drove off.

I watched the airport retreat into the darkness through the car's side mirror. When I looked up, I saw the flank of Montjuïc. My father and I had hiked that flank. I remembered his telling me that Catalonia's thinkers had been shot and tossed over the side by Franco's men; they had been kicked into an abandoned stone quarry and left to rot in the wind and the rain. I should have known then and there that the flank was a sign of the twists and turns ahead of me and Ludo Bembo.

We maneuvered around a series of roundabouts and merged onto the highway. We drove past factories, metal-processing plants, strips of freeway. The sky was darkening by degrees. Again, I could feel my father's mind spinning within my own. He whispered: *The exile is the cannibal of history.* I let out a dark and labored laugh.

"What's so funny?" Ludo asked, drawing on the end of his pipe with his sublime wet lips.

I considered telling him about the lines of literature that had become slogans for my Grand Tour of Exile. I considered telling him that I was laughing at the fate of the exile because, in order to survive, the exile must carve out a future that is neither discontinuous from the past nor a false replica of it, which is, of course, an impossible task because in this dissociative world of radical ruptures there are only two options made available: the amnesia of Don Quixote or the passionate yearning and nostalgia of Dante the Pilgrim. I considered telling him that the exile's options are total forgetfulness or a complete collapse into the claw of history, both of which lead to discontent and to a self-perpetuating cycle of violence. But after all that thinking, I didn't say anything; I wasn't sure Ludo Bembo would understand. I sat there watching him look at the road through his glasses, those round silver-rimmed spectacles of his until, prompted by a glance he cast in my direction, I finally lied. Or rather I provided him with a red herring. I said: "*With mirth and laughter let old wrinkles come.* Shakespeare's golden words."

"So you are laughing in order to age well?"

"Yes," I retorted. "Like a good pickle!"

He let out a generic grunt.

We looked at each other, and even though his lips were wet, he managed to let out a dry, stiff smile, a Bembo smile, which I recognized from the various portraits I'd seen of his bearded ancestors. I decided to reward him for his effort.

"If you must know, I'm laughing because I've devised a terrific theory."

"What's that?"

"The Theory of the Pyramid of Exile."

Ludo pushed his glasses up the bridge of his nose. His expression was one of quiet contemplation. "Go on."

"Think of Ravenna," I said. "Think of Dante buried there in exile. Forgotten. Abandoned. Banished. He lives at the bottom of the pyramid. Not in its catacombs, which are reserved for those even less fortunate than Dante, but at the bottom nevertheless. But you," I said, "live somewhere at the top of the pyramid. As a man in voluntary exile, you have access to the most oxygen. You are at the peak of a mountain, filling your lungs with pure oxygenated air, unaware that each time you take a step you are stomping on the heads of those less fortunate than you. I am one of those," I said. "I live in the middle of the pyramid. There is a sea of refugees beneath me. The pyramid constantly gets fed with fresh blood."

"The upper echelons?" he retorted. "Not bad." He seemed pleased with himself.

We made a series of ninety-degree turns and maneuvered around octagonal chamfered blocks until he located the address I had given him: Carrer de Girona, 37. I was renting a room from a certain Quim Monzó. We were in the somber grid of L'Eixample, a neighborhood designed by Ildefons Cerdà, a whiskered man obsessed with geometric lines. I looked through the window at the rectangular nineteenth-century buildings with their delicate ironwork balconies, floor-to-ceiling windows sealed with wooden shutters, and high angular foreheads evoking alertness, intelligence, equanimity.

"So this is it," Ludo said, pulling into an empty spot beneath a row of plane trees. He turned on the overhead light, wrote his number down on a piece of paper, and handed it to me. "I teach at the university most days, but there's always someone who can cover for me." He put his hand on my leg. I let it sit there. I felt heat radiate out from his palm. I felt his cardboard rigidity give way to longing, to a deep tenderness; how easily one person can become laced with another. Then he lifted his hand and tucked my hair behind my ear. I was convinced my lecture had turned him around, rehabilitated his tone. So I barreled on.

"I'd like to know where you live. You already know where I will be living, which gives you an unfair advantage. But before you answer," I said, putting my hand up to stop him, "I'd like to acknowledge that this is a ludicrous, one-dimensional, earthbound question. No one really occupies a concrete, singular position in space, which is what the question erroneously implies. *Where do you live?*" I huffed mockingly. "We should really be asking *in what places do you tend to lead your multiple lives* or *what is the geography of your inner world* because, as much as we would like to divide life along categorical lines, interior and exterior, we can't, because each of those surfaces is composed of other intersecting surfaces, which means that life, generally speaking, is a confused and blurred experience. Let's return to Dante for a moment. Think of the first verse of *The Divine Comedy: The straight way was lost.* Blurred and lost."

As cool as a cucumber, he said, "I live in Girona. You're welcome to come and see for yourself if the roads are straight or crooked."

"Finally," I said, "a thorough answer." I didn't tell him I had been to Girona long ago with my father. I just applauded him for having found his stride.

He looked like a frog had jumped down his throat. I looked around distractedly. There were cars parked alongside the curbs, small delivery trucks double-parked on the corners, bikes and scooters between the pruned plane trees on the sidewalks. I saw a few people drunkenly stumble out of a café. Night was spreading its dark wings, stroking Barcelona to sleep. I turned back to Ludo.

"So you came all the way to Barcelona from Girona just to pick me up?" I asked.

"We pass our favors forward here. It seems my mentor owed your mentor a favor."

"How long do you pass them forward for?"

"Generations," he said.

"Then I suppose this is as good a moment as any to tell you that all of my relatives are dead. With the exception of Morales, I have no contacts left in this vast and ghastly universe."

I thought of my suitcase. When I had pulled my father out of the chest, his mustache had been bent out of shape. I'd had to flatten it into place by putting my hand over his mouth while using the other to tug on the long bristly ends of his mustache. As I remembered this, I felt a sudden tightness in my chest. It was as if the edges of my paper heart were being folded and torn at the seams.

"Well," Ludo said callously, as I sat there remembering the trials and tribulations of my dead father's mustache. "It's a good thing you can always procreate."

I pressed my hand against my chest to dull the ache and pushed the memory aside. Then I told him that I don't believe in procreation, that I would never do anything to perpetuate this worthless race of humans. "But I do believe in sex for the sake of sex, and should we have it, I plan to be on top since, metaphysically speaking, I'm already carrying your burden on my shoulders."

He flushed and looked away. It was clear I would have to spoon-feed the man. I got out of the car. There was nothing left to say or do after that. I slammed the door. Then I pressed my face against the window to look at Ludo Bembo again. He looked offended. His features — nose, mouth, eyes, eyebrows — had drifted together and formed a knot in the center of his face. I walked around the car and knocked on his window.

He rolled the window down. I could tell he was annoyed by my sudden leap out of the car, but with an amicable reserve, he said, "Let me take care of your suitcase."

A proper gentleman. He got out. He pulled my suitcase out of the trunk and put it down on the ground. Then he leaned in and gave me two kisses. That was the first time I saw myself in his eyes. I was standing in the dark center of his pupils, looking out at myself, my notebook in hand. I waved at my reflection. Ludo Bembo waved in response. I saw my image as if from across a great distance. I was standing there alone in the midst of ruins.

During my last weeks in the so-called New World, I had done so much more than mentally compose my manifesto. I had made arrangements and phone calls, searched for a place to stay, ran errands that required a great deal of effort. I had found the apartment I was subletting from the previously mentioned Quim Monzó online. His advertisement read: *Recently retired literature professor rents room in very desirable neighborhood of*

L'Eixample. Dada fanatic. Proud owner of a pet cockatoo. Not to be mistaken with the writer Quim Monzó.

As it so happens, I had met the writer Quim Monzó months before at the Cervantes Institute in New York. Quim Monzó, the writer, is a master of irony, literary joker par excellence. This other Quim Monzó, former literature professor, had instructed me to pick up the keys to his apartment from the grocer near his building. He had gone to Greece to say his good-byes to the archipelago. He had written to me in an e-mail: *Off to salute one last time that cradle of civilization, which is once again in the process of collapsing.*

I located the grocer easily. The yellow streetlights illuminated the dust on the shop's glass door. I pushed it open and stepped in. Quim Monzó had assured me that the grocer was a reliable man, a trustworthy type he considered to be an extension of himself, since he, the grocer, had been the grocer for as long Quim Monzó could remember, and he, Quim Monzó, had lived above the grocer's store for as long as the grocer could remember. In fact, before the grocer had become the grocer, he had been the previous grocer's son. Quim Monzó had gone on for so long about the grocer, and repeated the word so often, that I had begun to think it was a code for something else or, at the very least, that the grocer would turn out to be an indicator of certain mystifying events, a possibility that quickly confirmed itself almost as soon as I was on the other side of that dusty glass door.

I left my suitcase in the entryway and, in my best Catalan, told the grocer — a stout, bald man with a bulbous red nose — that I was there to pick up Quim Monzó's keys. The grocer retrieved the keys from a rusty register and handed them to me. The exchange took less than a minute. He didn't ask any questions. He just grunted and dismissed me with a wave of the hand. His fingers were thick and black. There were walnut shells piled on the counter. The lights in the glass display cases were off; the cheese and the meats were spoiling in the darkness. The grocer's physiology — thick, heavy, rooted — confirmed Quim Monzó's narrative that he, the grocer, was a fixture in the neighborhood, that he was born on that block and would die on that block.

The grocer's cat, which until now had remained hidden, jumped up on the counter and knocked over the pile of walnut shells. The grocer lifted his blackened hand to pet it on the head, and almost immediately, I thought of Schrödinger's cat. It occurred to me that we are all living in that sealed box of Schrödinger's. At any given moment, any one of us could be dead.

Bells I hadn't heard before rang. How long had I been standing here for? I had lost track. I started to pile rice into a clear bag. I looked at the grocer. In contradistinction to him, I thought, I was a body that, through its haphazard intention of folding the path of exile back over itself, had registered, in the path's senseless progressions, the meaningless course of human affairs, *that mixture of error and violence that is history*; I was a body without a home. I looked down at my hand grasping the metal handle of the scoop. The skin on my hand was cracked, exposing ancient violence embedded in matter. My body, due to exile, was undergoing a steady process of erasure; soon it would be annulled, negated by my perpetual homelessness. My writing hand, I thought, looking down at it and thinking again of Blanchot, is a *sick hand*.

The grocer was still petting his cat, which was licking its paw. I walked across the store toward a stack of onions. I picked one up. It looked like a shimmering globe. Morales's ancient mineral voice echoed in my ear: *Catalan literature will speak to you*. It had spoken to him, a Chilean exile. It had spoken to my father, too; I remembered him feverishly pacing around his translations of Catalan authors, and saying: "Barcelona is the world's literary frontier!" I tossed the onion up in the air and watched it spin. Right before I caught it, I said in Catalan: "According to Mallarmé, *everything in the world exists in order to end up as a book!*"

Just then, I stumbled over my chest-shaped suitcase — my father's first grave, his pregrave — and landed in the open bags of rice. For a moment, right before I fell, the grocer's store acquired larger dimensions; it appeared to have doubled in size. I was a speck of dust in the infinite, dizzying whole. A dark smile spread across my face. The grocer came around and stood over me. I saw my reflection in his eyes. I was horrified. I had a miserable, scrawny, skeletal frame. The grocer continued to stand there. He looked stupefied, like a fish that's been shocked out of the water. Then he opened his thin, chapped mouth.

"Balls!" he croaked perversely, in his native tongue. He blinked and my image vanished.

As he walked away, I leaned back into the merchandise and made a mental note: Specimen demonstrates resistance toward literature. I let out a ghastly laugh. He didn't bother to turn around.

I got up and paid for the rice and a single shimmering onion. As I counted out the euros I owed the grocer, I thought to myself, I am regressing through the forests of exile. I have come here to excavate my grief, to resurrect the memories I have buried in the deep crater of my life. I thought, I am in Barcelona, the least Spanish of Spanish cities. I have arrived in Catalonia, but I am also in Spain, a country with a bizarre tendency to cast history into the pit of erasure with one hand and with the other retrieve what shards of facts and memories can be salvaged from that very same pit, to restore them, so to speak, once they have been deranged by the passage of time. Spain, I argued inwardly, a country that is engaged in both the business of oblivion and of restoring historical memory, as if memories were like pieces of old furniture that could be restored to their original dimensions. *Spain that is extremist to the point of death*, Dalí had said. A reproduction of his painting *The Persistence of Memory* was hanging over the counter. There it was: time swollen. Limp, fleshy clocks clinging to nature in a dilated landscape of rocks: the past, the present, and the future leveled into a single undifferentiated plane. Beneath that warped temporal field, the grocer had started to go about his business again, moving between the aisles of vegetables, stoic, unaware, having, after a brief moment of concern, completely forgotten about me.

I made my way to Quim Monzó's building. I rode the elevator to the third floor, exited, identified his door. "Quim Monzó," I said, thinking of that other Quim Monzó, the writer I had met in the New World, as I fiddled with the key to retrieve it from the lock. I liked saying his name. The hard consonants, the *q*, *m*, and *z*, are exquisitely balanced by the sharp vowels, the *o*, *i*, and *u*. What could be better? I nudged the door with my foot. It was whispering its owner's name as I was saying the writer's: Quim Monzó, Quim Monzó. The two names, uttered by me and the door, enhanced each other.

The apartment was engulfed in darkness. I felt a sense of uneasy anticipation, of uncertainty, as I walked across the threshold. It seemed infinite, an elastic architecture that had the capacity to expand beneath my feet irrespective of the direction I walked in. I could make a series of left turns or walk straight, and the rest of the apartment would appear with its subtle, nearly imperceptible surfaces. I dragged my hand along the wall in search of a light switch but found nothing. I stepped into the darkness. I pulled my suitcase in behind me. Suddenly, I remembered what Quim Monzó the writer had said to me so many months earlier during his lecture in that false New World. I remembered his dark eyes, his uneven gray hair, his eyebrows' inquisitive arc. Morales, who had been hosting him, had put me in charge of providing him with water. I'd handed him a bottle and asked him if he needed anything else, at which point he leaned in. His eyes looked like two drops of oil. He put his hand on my shoulder.

"Yes," he said. "I would like a noose."

I tore a napkin and rolled it into a noose. Just then, the New Poets walked into the room. Their hair was so greasy that it looked like it had been licked. As usual, they were wearing their overalls. They looked like a pair of dejected farmers. Overalls! As if intelligence could be harvested. True intelligence, I had thought to myself as I watched them — not the cerebral kind, but the kind that is born in the irrational mind of the heart — is earned through a degree of suffering the New Poets would never experience. For the sake of their health and the health of those who had swallowed the myth of the *new*, my ancestors and I had been adrift in the deserts of the world, inhaling toxins, stepping over charred corpses, pulling our ass this way and that. And what had they ever done for us? I felt livid. They were pink and plump. I could feel my blood coursing through my legs. I wanted to walk over and smack them across the head, but I stopped myself because ignorance cannot be slapped out of anyone.

I handed Quim Monzó the noose.

"A good luck charm," I said.

Quim Monzó was delighted. He slipped the noose into his breast pocket. Halfway through his talk, he retrieved it, held it up to the light, looked through the ring as though it were a monocle, and said, "Love is just lust dressed up in a bow tie!"

I happened to be carrying a book by Badiou that day. I opened it at random, as if it were an oracle, according to the Hosseini tradition, and read: *Love is no more than an imaginary canvas painted over the reality of sex.*

A second later, the interviewer, a Catalan translator, asked Quim Monzó about Josep Pla, a writer also known as the Memory Man whose books I had been consulting that very morning. This double coincidence emboldened me. I felt as though I were descending the craggy, interwoven slopes of literature. The farther down I went, the more aware I became of the lie of reality, the treachery of this illusory world that, according to Josep Pla, is *the sewer where we all slog.* I looked at the New Poets and mouthed at them, "Unlike you, who are just a pair of amateurs, I navigate the labyrinthine corridors of literature with the speedy diligence of a dirty old rat in a maze!"

But that was months ago, long before my father's death. Now I was alone, staring into the darkness of this other Quim Monzó's apartment. I slid my hand across the surface of the wall, still in search of a light switch. I thought of the pile of ill-fated corpses. I thought, I am a stranger wherever I happen to go, a pitiable migrant with no one to hang on to. I thought of my mother. I imagined her rummaging through the house for food before its stones came down on her head. The tenses in my life were being radically demolished. The past was projecting itself into the future, becoming the future, while the future, I realized, had been sending signals all along to the present, which was now the past. Time itself was becoming literature. I dragged my hand along a different wall. Finally, I found the switch. The foyer lit up like a stage.

As I moved through the apartment, my breath was labored and shallow. Still, I could smell damp feathers, barley, cheese, and rotting vegetables. I remembered Quim Monzó's bird. Quim Monzó had told me the bird's name was Taüt, and I tried calling for it as I walked around. "Taüt," I said a few times, each time louder than the last. There was no answer. I headed to the kitchen. I sucked in little patches of air. I turned on all the lights along the way. I watched the darkness retreat. The walls, sound and stable, came into view. In the kitchen, there was a string of chili peppers hanging from a nail in the wall and a container of coffee beans that had been left on the counter. I opened the fridge. Inside, I found a half-empty jar of mayo, three cloves of garlic, a package of *jamón*, manchego cheese, and an old baguette. I broke off a piece of the bread and chewed on it. I thought to myself, *There is not a thing that is more positive than bread.* Dostoyevsky. I walked through the rest of the apartment. The furniture was old and heavy, indicating a long genealogy of owners. In the living room, a recamier and a chesterfield were separated by a wooden coffee table (too heavy to move even an inch). Lined against the walls, like a moat surrounding the central decor, were twelve armchairs with cabriole legs and splats that finished off in palmettes. There was something worn and patient about the chairs, as though they had recently served to cup the shocked bodies of mourners after a funeral. In the corner, resting on a broken Corinthian-style column, was a telephone in the shape of a lobster tail. I pictured Quim Monzó speaking through that tail. I remembered his Dadaist inclinations. The chairs, I concluded, may have been arranged for a séance or a group session of automatic writing inspired by hypnosis.

I moved on to other surfaces. A long table sliced the dining room in half. I detected ghostly water rings and wine stains on the wood, sugary red bumps that prompted me to look through the pantry for a bottle, which I quickly found: a middle-of-the-road reserve rioja from 2009. I sat on one of the dining chairs, uncorked the bottle, and drank half of it at once. A line piped into my head: *I lost the empty feeling and began to be happy and to make plans.* Hemingway. I drank some more wine. I snapped off another piece of the baguette. I felt drunk, queasy. I said, "Rigor mortis," out loud to no one. I felt a sharp pang in my chest. I got up and opened the window. I opened the molded shutters. The wind had picked up. There was a mild fall chill. I leaned my head out. Catalan flags of independence, marked with their four red stripes of blood, were hanging from the iron terrace of the building across the street, being dealt remorseless blows by the wind.

Once my breathing had steadied, I sealed the window and resumed my tour. I walked down the narrow bleak hallway and opened all the doors. The first two gave way easily, but I had to force the third door open; it was as withholding as Ludo Bembo. I banged on it. I kicked. I side-slammed the door. Finally, it jerked open. I fell across the threshold into a room devoted entirely to the bird. A small square window carved into the back wall let in a dim trickle of light from an interior courtyard. Perching branches had been screwed into the walls. In the bleak light, the branches blurred into scissors, blades, spades, swords. The room looked like a fake forest. Plastic ivy plants hung from the ceiling in woven baskets. The bird had chewed through the straw. A tall wide cage rested on a gilded stand in the center of the room. It was empty. The bird was nowhere to be found. I lingered in the room. I looked through the window at the darkening bands of the universe. A thick canopy of clouds veiled the stars.

I felt exhausted, drained, confused. I had the distinct sensation of being in multiple places at once. I retreated from the bird's room and moved methodically down the hallway. I felt my eyes close against my will. I forced them open again. The final door led to the bedroom. An oversize mattress was nestled in a wooden bed frame with dramatic turned posts that looked like obelisks. "Taüt," I called out one last time, and pictured the bird emerging from the mouth of a mysterious tunnel to greet or attack me.

I dragged in my suitcase of books and set it down next to the bed. I flung myself on the mattress. I turned away from my suitcase to avoid inhaling the fetid odor of my father's death. My head spun with little patches of memories. I remembered that Quim Monzó had sent me a photograph of the bird as an attachment in one of his e-mails. In the photograph, the cockatoo is perched on the arm of a swivel wall lamp in the living room, his crown and right tarsus raised, his toes tense and spread wide as though he were simultaneously saluting and warning the cameraman to halt. The bird had cast a stubborn and furtive glance at the camera, wickedly aware that his picture was being taken. I had never seen anything like it. Then I remembered the bird's date of birth: January 1, 2000. So that bird, wherever he was, had been born the same day that the odd parade of the twenty-first century began, which so far had been a century of haphazard bombings, of revenge killings, of undeserved misery, of terror without reprieve, of death. It wasn't the Great War, but it was the end of the world as we know it all over again. I heard my father's voice boom across my void. He said, *It is always the final hour*. My heart, that soiled and wrinkled piece of paper, folded over itself like an envelope.

I smelled my hands, sniffed them like an animal seeking comfort in the porousness of the earth. They smelled like dirt and onions. I said to myself obtusely: "You are in Barcelona; the Grand Tour of Exile has begun!" I started laughing hysterically, laughing at the thought of my body being tied to the bedposts and sacrificed in the night. I fell asleep with my clothes still on, my lips stained with wine, a stale chunk of bread in the palm of my hand. If I had seen myself from above, say from a helicopter after an air raid, I would have mistaken my body for a corpse.

///////////

That night I dreamt I was walking through a tunnel illuminated by a garish light. I was thirsty, weary, famished. But I kept putting one foot in front of the other. I was afraid that if I didn't keep on walking I would vanish into thin air. I persisted, and the tunnel deposited me in front of an ugly building devoid of character, a funereal administrative building constructed of slabs of concrete that were covered in smog stains. The facade was interrupted only by a series of windows, all covered in protective metal bars casting geometric shadows across the glass. I peeled the double doors of the entrance open and stepped into a rectangular waiting room. There were people sitting on wooden benches — all of them dressed in black, as stiff as mannequins — waving forms like fans to circulate the stale air. When I examined their faces more closely, I realized that my forebears, Dalir Abbas Hosseini, Arman Abbas Hosseini, and Shams Abbas Hosseini, were all there, along with my mother and father. I couldn't believe my eyes. A stain of blood spread across my paper heart. It rolled and flapped as if it were being dragged through the streets and valleys of the world by a violent gale. I lunged forward. I wanted nothing more than to embrace them, but as soon as I arrived at where they had been sitting, they were gone. They had vanished. That sheet of paper, heavy with blood, sank into my void and faded into oblivion.

In their absence, a security guard appeared. He was large and had terrible breath.

"Death certificate?" he asked.

"Yes," I replied, as I anxiously scanned the room. There was a wall of windows at the rear of the building, and beyond them, I could see date palms and eucalyptus trees planted in rows; a thin layer of fog had settled over the fertile paths winding between the trees. I thought I heard the Caspian Sea gurgling in the distance.

"Look around all you want," the security guard said. "There is no one here. We are all alone in our final hour."

"But I belong with them!" I moaned, looking again at the place where my family had been and then beyond, through the windows, at the trees.

The security guard hooked his plump arm around mine and walked me to a separate room where a secretary sat at her desk. She was wearing orange lipstick, and she moved her mouth like a fish sucking in little puffs of air. She handed me a number and instructed me to sit down. I took a seat.

"Where am I?" I asked the secretary. "Iran?" I protested. "Islamic Republic of Iran? Van? Ankara? Istanbul?"

She told me to keep my mouth shut.

Just then, a set of speakers, which were hanging precariously from wires over our heads, announced my name. "Zebra!" a mechanical voice declared.

I looked at the secretary. She was busy filing her nails.

"Come here," she hissed, fixing her glassy blue eyes on me. I approached her desk. She informed me that I had to report upstairs.

I went up a flight of stairs and stepped into an elevator. It jerked up. The doors opened onto a dim and drab hallway. There were water stains on the walls. I could see the second door at the end, which the secretary had instructed me to knock on, but it appeared to recede every time I tried to move closer to it. The hallway was elastic; it was extending with my every step, an infinite corridor. Exhausted, I leaned against the wall, drenched in sweat. After some time, a second security guard appeared. He looked like the first one's twin.

"Visa paperwork," he demanded.

"But I'm dead."

"You need a visa in order to get a death certificate," he said.

"A visa?" I whined with astonishment. Inwardly, I tried to enumerate how many visas and passports we had filed for over the years. A light came on overhead. It didn't do the security guard any favors. He had a fleshy mouth. I could see the black roots of his fallen teeth, and he had combed a few remaining strands of greasy hair over his balding scalp.

"I've had enough of visas!" I intoned fiercely, and watched his confidence retreat.

He stood there motionless, guarding the corridor despite his obviously waning confidence. There was a long interval of silence during which I shuttled up and down the hallway. I felt small and helpless, as though I were walking on a suspension bridge and on either side of me there was a door to nowhere. I was an exile in the cosmic corridors of the universe. I don't know how much time went by. Years, decades. The security guard grew old. His hair grew white. He slouched down into his chair and fell asleep. Finally, I was able to get past him. But I, too, was older. I walked up to the door and turned the knob.

The door opened onto a network of caves. There were shadows drifting across the stone walls. I walked from hollow to hollow. Each cavity had been assigned a letter — A through Z — as if the caves composed an abecedarium. I wove my way through the alphabet. I came to the letter Z. "Z for Zebra!" I sighed. After Z, there was nothing: the void, pure and simple.

A slender man with round glasses appeared. He was sitting on a rock at the end of the cave. I told him, "I'm here to collect my death certificate."

The man nodded his head and removed his glasses. His eyes were muddy, bloodshot. They looked like they were about to run down his face.

"What are you doing in this pit of sorrow?" he asked. A thick fog rose around him and obscured his features.

"I need my death certificate! I am the last of the Hosseinis, all of whom are in this building," I explained, nearly weeping. He ignored my pleas. I spoke again, but my voice, thin and desperate, was barely audible. The man scribbled something on a piece of paper and handed it to me. I read: *Raphèl maì amècche zabì almi.* I recognized the line. Spoken with icy breath by Nimrod, the founder of the Tower of Babel, in Dante's hell. I had never felt more alone or more exhausted. I thought of the origin of different languages, of the confusion and miscommunication that ensued thereafter among humans. I thought to myself, I speak so many languages and yet I am understood by no one. I have been deserted, abandoned. I am companionless despite my ability to operate a plurality of systems. Then the fog grew more viscous.

I woke up in a terrible confusion, covered in sweat. At first, I wasn't sure where I was or how long I had slept. I got out of bed and walked through the apartment. A grainy light was filtering through the window at the end of the corridor, revealing a lead-colored sky. I looked at my reflection in the glass. I couldn't remember how old I was. I might have been any age. I was young and old at the same time. I looked down at the street where Ludo Bembo had dropped me off. It looked ghostly, deserted. Suddenly, I was struck by the gravity of the situation: I was adrift in the world, alone with my notebook. Who was I retracing my past for? Even if I recovered its shattered bits, even if my disparate selves appeared in my notebook, witnesses to life's reckless blows, there would be no one to share it with. I looked around. The apartment was flooded with a feeble light. I walked into the kitchen and took a drink of water. I grabbed a knife. I grabbed my notebook. I carved the title of my manifesto into the leather binding: *A Philosophy of Totality: The Matrix of Literature.* The telephone started to ring. I let it ring on and on. I wondered if it was Ludo Bembo. Or maybe it was Quim Monzó calling from Greece. I looked around for Taüt, but the bird was nowhere to be found.

I went back to bed. Immediately, I fell into another dream. I was swimming in a sea of ink. I climbed onto a rock. My chest-shaped suitcase was bobbing along near the rocks with its lid open. It contained a map of the Mediterranean. I wondered if my father was lying beneath that map, but as soon as I craned my neck to look, the chest sank to the bottom of the inky sea. I looked up at the sky. It was dark. There were books suspended like stars in the air. Ink was dripping off the books into the sea. I sat there perched on the rock until the sun came up, until I was drenched with the blood of literature.

In the morning, on the edge of wakefulness, before I opened my eyes, I thought to myself that books, like the catacombs of the world, contain the ruins of humanity. I turned that word — *humanity* — on my tongue. It repulsed me.

During that first week in Barcelona, I couldn't bring myself to leave the apartment. I felt more directionless than I ever had. My thoughts spun and staggered, contaminated by the shadowy sheen of my dreams. I was afraid that if I went walking through the city I would get dragged along a current of human bodies and, eventually exhausted and uncertain of my gait, fall over and get stepped on by a remorseless stampede of feet. Who would peel me out of the city's grooves and gutters? No one, I concluded. So I stayed within the confines of Quim Monzó's apartment and, true to the inky principles of the Hosseinis, reinforced my mind by training in literature.

A week went by during which I slept by day and read by night. I worked on my notebook. I saw no one. No grocer, no Ludo Bembo. I never saw the bird. I kept strict library hours: four-hour segments during which I, formal steward of death, trained in nothingness through intense reading and contemplation. In between segments, I paused to search for the bird. I looked under the bed, under the cushions, in the kitchen cabinets. He was nowhere to be found. I continued to read. I read in order to drag the Catalan portion of my mind out of the mud; with it, certain aspects of my father's mind came along. I gained access to his Catalan literary consciousness, that part of his mind that came into being during our years in Barcelona.

By the week's end, my manifesto had evolved. I devised from Salvador Dalí's Paranoiac-Critical approach an Irrational-Pragmatic methodology that consisted of entering and being consumed by the void of exile in a systematic manner in order to produce writing. My methodology involved writing in five-minute segments with a black band over my eyes. Each time I did this, I experienced déjà vu. I saw the faces of my family, the Hosseinis, as I had seen them in my dream. They would appear before me, composed and full of a strange light, before fading into the surrounding darkness, leaving me alone in the eerie stillness of night. The band, torn from one of Quim Monzó's shirts, was a tribute to the black band my father had placed over my eyes before we crossed into Turkey while each of the five minutes was a salutation to the most influential members of the Hosseini lineage, starting with me and going as far back as my great-great-grandfather, Shams Abbas Hosseini. I wrote for five minutes and rested for five minutes. During the pauses, I received signals from the Matrix of Literature regarding the next segment of writing. I made more than a few entries in my notebook.

In a matter of days, I read all the books in Quim Monzó's library that I remembered to have been a part of my father's Catalan oeuvre. I selected the writers that my father had translated during our first months in Catalonia under the shadow of my mother's, Bibi Khanoum's, untimely death that, I now concluded, had pushed my father further into the abyss of literature. In his grief — well disguised as it was due to the fact that we, the ill-fated, have to swallow our bitterness to survive — my father had nevertheless absorbed my mother in the same way that I had absorbed him. This thought ushered in a welcome companion insight: Since I had absorbed my father, I had also absorbed the traces of Bibi Khanoum that had already been absorbed by him. I welcomed the residue of my mother into my consciousness. I saluted her. "Ah, the transmigration of minds!" I repeated into the darkness of the night. It was strange and exhilarating to be in the presence of her residue; an odd euphoria swept over me, a feeling of mild mania. I felt as though time had not elapsed and yet, somehow, everything was different.

Time was a riddle not meant to be solved, I concluded, as I walked into the bedroom and sat bolt upright on the bed. I was flooded with emotions: I thought to myself that the act of swallowing our bitterness and absorbing one another upon death had increased our wretchedness. I pitied myself. I had inherited the stinking pile of rubbish, the unspoken emotions, everything that had ever been discarded by generations of Hosseinis; their unmetabolized pain was rotting in the ever-widening pits of my void. No wonder I didn't often feel hunger. At that realization, a single question looped through the ghostly chambers of my many minds: When I die, who will absorb me? There was no one left. I was the last of the lineage. I sobbed uncontrollably. I wept until I gagged on my tears. I wiped my face with the sheets.

By dawn, at the edge of despair, I had moved from the bed to the red recamier. I thought, what remedy do I have but to resort to literature? The sun, round and orange, rose into the sky. It looked like a ball of fire. I stared at it through the window. I sat in quiet contemplation. Hours later, in a somewhat more pragmatic state of mind, I remembered that some of my father's translations — not the ones we had lived off of, but the ones belonging to his private collection — consisted of transcriptions, of copying a text word by word just as a medieval scribe would have done in the days of yore. My father had never explained the theory behind his transcriptions to me, but with my mind sufficiently primed to receive spontaneous signals from the Matrix of Literature, I instantly deduced his logic. Obvious was the fact that the practice of transcription had served as an additional tool for his memorization, ensuring his position as a scribe of the future. The more striking revelation, however, was the following: Had my father not gone nearly blind and thus continued his practice, the Art of Transcription would have led him to a very desirable state, a kind of nirvana, which men of a lesser constitution could only reach through the use of opium. It was midday. The sun's rays pierced through the window and stained everything with a copper tinge. My thoughts, nurtured by the rusty fall light, spread into a complex web. Due to the inevitability of human error inherent in the manual reproduction of texts, which guarantees that each version produced is minutely different from its predecessor, the practitioner is able to recognize life's infinite multiplicity, its capacity for perpetuating and recycling itself. In turn, I concluded, this recognition allows the practitioner to take comfort in two basic facts: (1) the interconnected fabric of humanity (we have all been erroneously reproduced by others; we are degenerate copies of one another), and (2) the nothingness of being (despite being connected to a million other strands of life individuals can expire suddenly without warning, not to mention that, more often than not, the people one is connected to fail to help us move along our path because they are too busy avoiding their own wretchedness, pulling rank, grasping for power at the cost of others and to their own detriment). I had expanded upon the Hosseini Commandments by culling wisdom from the abyss. My manifesto had grown wings!

Over the course of the following nights, I managed to reread most of the authors my father had transcribed during our Catalan years. I filled pages and pages of my notebook with transcriptions from each of the following writers, all of whom, in one way or another, had been touched by exile: Josep Pla (a man of immense candor), Salvador Espriu (a man in possession of a labyrinthine mind with a great propensity toward codes), Mercè Rodoreda (a genius of the double-edged sentence, apparently blunt but actually emotionally cutting), Miguel de Unamuno (a man with an encyclopedic sensibility), Federico García Lorca (a lyric erotic) and his friend Salvador Dalí (eccentric, hyperrealist, provocateur, whose work I can never get enough of), Joan Maragall (a Hellenistic bore who became an antianarchist halfway through his life, but one I am inclined to forgive for his splendid translations of Nietzsche from the French; the man didn't speak a lick of German), and Montserrat Roig (eloquent, graceful, master of embedded dialogue, highly attuned to the ways in which architecture absorbs historical grief).

When I was done with my list, I closed my notebook. It was the middle of night. I ran my sick hand over the engraved title. I paced the corridor. Immediately, I heard: *Forgetfulness is the only revenge and the only forgiveness.* Ah, Borges. I laughed at his maxim. Because, contrary to his missive, I was experiencing a loss of forgetfulness. I was regressing through the chain of selves produced by exile and, in doing so, was recovering patches of memories, of feeling, none of them exact, all of them falsified due to the patina of time. I was in the mood for conclusions. There must have been a full moon causing the tides of my mind to rise to unprecedented heights. I looked through the window at the end of the corridor. There it was, hovering over L'Eixample, a wide silver disc. I raised my grief antennas. I concluded the following: I had retraced the words my father had transcribed during our time in Catalonia; soon I would have to retrace the paths we had walked together. I would have to leave the apartment.

I stood in the corridor a while longer and thought of our long walk of exodus through that putrid no-man's-land, and for a moment, my feet hurt, the bony knobs of my knees ached. I remembered the bitter cold, the frozen terrain, the spectral snow of those final days. My father had been dragging our suitcase along while carrying me, his ragged coat drawn over our backs. Fatigued, breathless, he put me down on a glistening icy rock, and I remembered looking up at him and seeing my own reflection in his eyes. We were undernourished, skeletal, a pair of living dead. Our lips were blue. Our eyes bulged out of their sockets.

I sat on the red recamier and watched the moon's glow fade behind a traveling herd of clouds. I closed my eyes. For better or worse, I thought to myself, I am approaching my *own buried past.* And that's when I realized: I had returned to Barcelona to set off on a series of walks — no, not walks, Pilgrimages of Exile — during which I *would conduct myself as a man digging, unafraid to return again and again to the same matter.* I realized the enormity of the task and nearly succumbed to panic. I drew in little breaths. I calmed myself by thinking of how literature's interconnected network of sentences would chaperone me into a great silence, into the void at the center of my life, into the dark folds of the universe. "Ah, Benjamin, martyr of thought," I murmured as I retreated to the bedroom and put my notebook on the nightstand. For the first time in a week, I went to sleep at night. My job was done.

The next morning, however, my plans were delayed due, in some measure, to the fact that the bird had finally made his debut. I looked at him. What a mongrel. He was pecking at the piece of bread I had left in the bed my first day in the apartment. The bedroom was engulfed in darkness. There were no windows. I had barely eaten. The last person I had interacted with was the grocer. I hadn't gone outside since Ludo Bembo had dropped me off. I felt trapped, unreal, far away from the world. I examined the walls. I could have died, or disappeared, or been absorbed by the objects in the room. No one would notice my absence. No one, I reconsidered, but Quim Monzó's bird.

Without light, it appeared as though the surfaces surrounding the bird, which was white, marked the edges of a black hole. I reached out and turned on the table lamp. The ceiling came into view. It sagged in the middle. It reminded me of the droopy sacks of yogurt I had seen hanging from village trees and swinging in the rancid wind of that decimated no-man's-land. I ran my hand across the bird's back. It occurred to me that if the room was a black hole then my hand and the bird were on the edge of an event horizon, a precipice of sorts. "Oh, the ecstasy of darkness," I said out loud to no one.

The bird turned his head and peered at me through his right eye. He looked haggard. What did I look like? For all I knew, my face was a void — a symbol of the very abyss of exile that had summoned me. I hadn't looked in the mirror since I had arrived in Barcelona. There was a high probability that I had been reduced to nothing more than a sick hand. A hand that knows nothing other than my notebook. I laughed helplessly at the idea.

I stroked the bird. Some of his feathers were bent upward and grainy to the touch. I remembered his tyrannical look in the photograph, his claws grasping the air, his rigid stance.

"Here, here," I said to the bird, as I stroked it. "I come in peace."

My words echoed back: *I come in pieces.* With the suddenness of a revolving door, Taüt cocked his head to the side and snapped his beak open and bit my finger. I let out a shrill scream. There was a drop of blood on his beak. I could see the drop glistening in the dull light of the lamp. I remembered the stain of blood spreading across the flattened sheet of my heart in my dream. I backed away from the bird. Taüt retreated. He knocked his feathered head back and gargled as he retreated across the bed. Then he stopped and pressed his talons into the sheets. He spread his wings and shimmied from side to side.

"Taüt!" the bird screeched in an impatient voice, before gathering himself and exiting the room.

I wondered if the apartment was diseased. I wondered if Quim Monzó, the retired literature professor, had gone to Greece to disabuse himself of the idea of order; perhaps he was engaging in some kind of entropy tourism, a tour of the authentic disorder of life.

The darkness quietly tugged at the objects in the room, reeling them discreetly into its hollow sphere while the weak light of the table lamp pushed meekly against it. I felt myself begin to unreel. It occurred to me that the apartment, cluttered and potentially diseased, was, in fact, a hospital. I slipped out from between the humid sheets and ambled down the corridor. I wanted to confront the rest of the apartment. No, not confront, I corrected as I walked out of the bedroom; I wanted to extract information from it. I walked past my chest-shaped suitcase full of books and heirlooms. I got a whiff of my father's death. I walked down the corridor, the corridor of exile — the long dark corridor of my mind. As I paced, it occurred to me that before walking through Barcelona I had to commit to the nonsense of the apartment, the nonsense of the bird, which was no different from the nonsense of the world, nonsense that people deny because their consciousness has been reduced through the falsification of history to a singular dimension. The falsification of history! The words gave me a distinct pleasure.

I entered the kitchen in a mild state of hilarity, made coffee, poured it into a dusty cup, carried it to the window. The Catalan flags hanging from the buildings on the other side of the street looked limp, defeated. The four vertical red stripes looked rusty, like dried blood. The street was largely deserted. It was still early in the morning. There was a radio perched near the window. I turned it on. I heard, "The whole world is a potential front. We are all foot soldiers." I turned it off. A plump woman in an apron appeared in a window on the opposite side of the street. She leaned out and began to beat her flag with a broomstick. Patches of dust lifted off into the dense air. The bells sounded out; their peal receded into the enormous distance.

I got up and moved to the red recamier. In the living room, I noticed a Swiss cuckoo clock I hadn't seen before; the pendulum was swinging, making a rhythmic clicking sound. The rooms of the apartment had begun to reveal their true colors over the course of the past week, coming forward with all they had initially withheld. It was like being inside Velázquez's *Las Meninas*. There was a mirror on the wall opposite the window.

In it, I saw the attenuated reflection of the pendulum, the curved end of the recamier, the bronze studs lining the velvet seams, the wooden shutters beyond the window, and blue strips of sky through the louvers. The clouds had moved on. The sun was shining.

I ran my hand across the red velvet cushions on the recamier. There were cigarette burns in the fabric. The crusted edges reminded me of the mouth of a volcano. I thought of Mount Sahand. "That comatose beast!" I said out loud, and laughed. I felt time slow down, come to a halt. Everywhere I looked, I saw holes, depressions, ditches. In the shadowy yolk-colored light, the objects of the apartment seemed to be acquiring density, pulling me toward them. Again, I had the sensation that the apartment was a black hole. Quim Monzó, whoever he was, had taken his leap. I had to take mine: the leap into the void, into the nothingness of exile. I was preparing myself to walk the streets of Barcelona, a stranger once again. Or worse than a stranger, I thought, a restranger, a double alien ready to approach her buried past.

Just then, it occurred to me that I could think of the Matrix of Literature as a black hole: an abyss with no boundaries, an elastic void that consumes everything and from which nothing but a faint residue radiates back out into the world — a nonplace where time collapses, becomes imaginary, and therefore, finally, truthful. It occurred to me that if the matrix is an elastic void capable of digesting the whole then its structure is analog to the future, which, much like a black hole, is a vast, open nothingness capable of containing everything that approaches it. I said to myself: "Literature is the residue of the past radiating back out into the world." Then I examined the thought from a different angle: The past, I concluded, contains within it a trace of the future. That trace acts as a conveyor belt through which certain images can be experienced as visions in advance of their time.

I looked at the three black encrustations on the red fabric of the recamier and imagined steam rising from the mouth of a volcano. The apartment, I realized, was nourishing me. It had been doing so all along. With all its accumulated clutter, it was signaling to me that until now I had been floating around the matrix. Until now, I had been metabolizing literature. But, as I watched the steam rise into the air, it occurred to me: What if literature metabolized *me?* I imagined being regurgitated by the matrix, my body radiating back out into the world as the residue of literature and spreading across the surfaces of the Old World, which was itself an after-image, a residue. I felt incredibly pleased with myself. I felt delighted with the irrational symmetry of my plan. I realized that I must be receiving private communiqués from the Matrix of Literature: signals of genius, signals of Dalínian proportions. I, Zebra, was exactly where I wanted to be: in the land of oblivion and the land of persistence, on the precipice of the future and about to enter the past. I was on the verge of becoming more Zebra than I ever had been before.

I walked up to the window at the end of the corridor and opened it. Fresh air streamed into the apartment. It smelled like sardines and salted cod; it flowed sweetly through the wooden gaps in the shutters. The streets were coming to life. There were people walking on the sidewalk. I could see their limbs moving through the louvers. They seemed tiny and far away. An electric current traveled down my spine. As I inhaled the warm, brackish air, I said to myself, "Something horrible is going to happen." I had the distinct feeling, a premonition, that the cruel events that were working their way into the fabric of the world — political suicides, spontaneous bombings — would soon accumulate into an undeniable critical mass; there would be no turning away from the stain of horror. "Not even love will save us," I whispered into the sealed shutters. Love! What is love when it can't save us from the wrenching severance of death?

For a moment, I saw myself as a child in my father's arms. I felt a tickle in my mind. My father was pressing his mustached mouth against my void. I heard him whisper: *Read to me from your notebook!* He must have known my notebook was in a great state, pregnant with citations, *in stato interessante*, as they say in Italy. As I thought this, I realized that I had not heard a peep from Ludo Bembo. This lack of contact confirmed to me that he was, in fact, a part of the .1 percent; it proved his literary nature was underscored by an innate suspicion of others. Were it otherwise, I concluded, he already would have showed up at Quim Monzó's door. And yet there was a part of me that wished he had. A part of me I could only acknowledge in brief segments, that had been yearning for Ludo to interrupt the brutal progression of my mourning, the miserable state of linking together a wretched sequence of thoughts and memories.

My father slumped down into a chair inside the vaulted maze of our double mind and tapped his cane on the floor. He was growing impatient. "Read to me!" he echoed. I retrieved my notebook and consulted it at random in accordance with the Hosseini practice of bibliomancy. I read from a list of transcribed quotes and maxims extemporaneous to my father's Catalan oeuvre. I announced: *Those Unconscionable Maps no longer satisfied, and the Cartographers Guilds struck a Map of the Empire whose size was that of the Empire.* Borges. I walked in concentric circles reciting the sentence. This seemed to soothe my father. Soon, he was replaced within my void by words. It was as if the words *Unconscionable Maps* were sitting on the chair he had vacated, cross-legged, regal, polite.

With my father folded again into the obscure sheets of memory, I walked into the kitchen to get a glass of water. There was that ghoulish bird. He was walking across the counters. I stared at him in dumb astonishment. He kept sticking his beak into this and that, spilling coffee grounds, peeling cloves of garlic. The next time I looked down at my notebook, my eyes fell on the following transcription: *Someday that mustache of yours will poke a hole in the world!* From my father's oeuvre! A joke Josep Pla had often repeated to Dalí. I crossed out the word *mustache* and replaced it with the word *beak*. Certain sentences are extraordinarily accommodating. "Someday that beak of yours will poke a hole in the world!" I warned Taüt. The bird cringed forward in response and plunged his head into a bowl of sugar Quim Monzó had left near the stove.

I took a step back. Considered from the Paranoiac-Critical perspective of Dalí, whose presence had manifested serendipitously, Taüt's seemingly insignificant gesture began to yield meaning. After retreating from the bowl, the bird turned his plumed head and looked at me with impish resolve. I noticed a soft depression on the surface of the white crystals. In my mind's eye, this cavity in the sugar bowl immediately positioned itself alongside the other indentations that had surfaced in Quim Monzó's apartment. I reviewed each instance — craters in the recamier, the black hole that had insinuated itself in the morning, the bedroom ceiling that had the appearance of a sinkhole — and concluded that, reflected upon together, this procession of hollows intimated the following: that Taüt was no ordinary bird; no, he was a real-life manifestation of Unamuno's *pájaro sabio*, the famous origami bird through which Unamuno, a life-long paper folder (producer of reverse folds, pleats, and sinks), had ironically expressed Plato's views on love and politics. Unamuno, who had suffered two blows of exile for refusing to allow ideology to interfere with intellectual life. In other words, a Hosseini hero.

"Poor Unamuno!" my father deployed from the cave of our double mind. "Tortured by the simpleminded Franco for possessing a tragic sense of life!" His voice echoed as if it were emerging from an ancient grotto.

"Poor Unamuno," I answered my father in agreement, "whose famous lines express the importance of contemplating nothingness, an activity relegated to the world's misunderstood and disenfranchised, and the very wheel that animates the Grand Tour of Exile!" Then I told my father, "Listen to this one: *The deepest problem: the immortality of the crab.*"

My father pounded his cane against the walls of my void as he laughed. My paper heart crinkled in response. The sound of his laughter was a balm to my wounds.

I felt as though I had been admitted into a world of sublime parallels and auspicious coincidences. I stood there, leaning against the kitchen counter, daydreaming, thinking about the immortality of the crab until the church bells struck eleven. Two ones, I thought. It was the hour of the double, of duality. Under the retreating peal of the bells, Unamuno multiplied, acquiring a second self in addition to his first.

"Take that, General Franco," I said, with great pride. "You who will always remain locked in your grave for lack of imagination, for not allowing your mind to fold over itself and fan open like flowers toward the sun, for being a degenerate nonreader, for neglecting to cultivate your consciousness and, consequently, for being incapable of surviving death. You," I barreled on, "will suffocate in your grave while Unamuno, like all the other honest writers of our senseless world, will double and triple and quadruple at the hand of future writers who echo his tragic sense of life and who will plagiarize his words, therefore inserting his legacy again and again into the world."

After a moment's pause, I yelled out: "*Una-muno, una-mano!*"

With a definitive air, I raised my sick hand and gave the *pájaro sabio* a pat on the head. The bird winked at me. He was still walking across the counters.

"Aha," I wrote in my notebook. "At last, the bird and I are on the same page."

I sealed my notebook and stood in the kitchen with my eyes closed. I raised my grief receptors, which allow me to receive infinite amounts of data from the most recondite reservoirs of the matrix. I received the following message from the benevolent Rousseau: *It's time to go for a solitary walk.*

"Yes," I intoned. "A Pilgrimage of Exile!" It was time. The walk took form in my mind. I considered its shape. I decided that my first walk through Barcelona should consist of an Architectural Pilgrimage of Fragmentation. Away with the sourpuss seriousness of L'Eixample! Exile had shattered my identity and caused me to suffer a grief of dizzying proportions. I needed to lay my eyes on mercurial buildings, vertiginous structures. It was the only way to trigger memories and feelings I had long repressed, severed from my consciousness. I wanted those shards of forgetfulness to pierce through the manure of my mind and rise to the surface.

"Where should I begin?" I asked myself, opening my eyes and walking over to the recamier.

"At Antoni Gaudí's famous Park Güell," I answered.

I visualized the park: an upward slope speckled with coastal brush and petrified stone, with paths as knotted as sheep's intestines.

"No one," I concluded, "can deny that the roads in Gaudí's park mimic the dead-end roads on which the homeless exile walks, triggering the multiple parts of herself to resurface like shrapnel absorbed during a long remorseless war. In other words," I said, watching Taüt, who was busy walking in figure eights on the living-room floor, shaking the sugar crystals off his wings, "it would be more honest if Antoni Gaudí's Park Güell were renamed the Metaphysical Garden of Exile!"

It occurred to me that everything that goes up must come down. If I were to hike up to the Metaphysical Garden of Exile, I would then be obliged by the laws of physics to descend to the city's opposite point — the port — and, once there, officially salute the Mediterranean, that Sea of

Sunken Hopes. I realized, almost instantly, that the main road connecting the Metaphysical Garden of Exile to the Sea of Sunken Hopes is the legendary Passeig de Gràcia, a section of which is, incidentally, also known as the Block of Discordance. What could be more complete? I smiled vaguely. I felt as though I had stepped from shadow into light.

I thought of Walser, committed walker and authorial sage, and declared: "It is time to leave Quim Monzó's *room of ghosts.*" I washed my face, got dressed, grabbed my notebook, tucked a pen behind my ear, and opened the door. Immediately, I heard a voice, in a jubilant tone: "So you never said. Where are you headed with that suitcase?"

It was Ludo Bembo. I could hardly believe it. He had finally found his way. I felt as if the tension, built up over the course of those long nights, was being released at once, causing me to stagger and feel giddy in his presence. He was standing on the other side of the threshold wearing a linen vest over a white shirt with his sleeves rolled up. He had the same mildly apprehensive expression on his face he'd had when he picked me up at the airport, but he had switched his tune. Now his timidity — if it was timidity — stood in sharp contrast to the seductive robustness of his question.

"Well?" he went on.

"Morocco," I joked. I told him that if he hadn't picked me up I would have arranged for a donkey to meet me at the airport. "I would have ridden that animal across the deserts of Spain and, upon arriving at the port city of Tarifa — famished, as thin as a rake — I would have pushed the donkey, which would be dead by then, into the water and used it as a raft to get across the channel to North Africa." I told him that, like a true explorer of the literary abyss and not unlike the nauseated Roquentin, I would have sat on the dead ass's belly and dangled my feet in the clear water, allowing the currents to transport me hither and thither.

"Who's Roquentin?" Ludo retorted, looking down at his feet. His shoes were made of braided leather.

"Who's Roquentin!" I repeated disdainfully. "And you call yourself a literary scholar."

Mildly exasperated, he protested, "I'm a philologist!"

"And why wouldn't a philologist know about Roquentin, beloved bearer of Sartre's cross?"

"Because I spend my days working on dictionaries," he whined.

"Ah," I said. "So you are in the business of embalming words!"

This seemed to relax him.

"You're very funny," he said, undeterred, leaning casually against the frame of the door.

I leaned against the door, too. We were so close we could easily have kissed each other on the lips. Two .1 percenters. With a little training, I thought to myself, I can turn Ludo Bembo into a literary terrorist. The very thought of his company filled my lungs with purified air.

"Ludo Bembo," I said, remote, philosophical, and in a silky tone. "You should know: *Nothing is funnier than unhappiness.*"

To my surprise, he let out a gleeful laugh. He seemed to have grown more resilient, more open, since I'd last seen him. Where, I wondered, was this Ludo Bembo before? This Ludo who was — in contradistinction to the anxious, reserved edition who had met me at the airport — calm, supple, curious.

We stood there in the hallway staring at each other. An old woman carrying a basket of freshly cut asparagus, whose gaze betrayed an artless candor, staggered up the stairs. Once she was out of view, Ludo volunteered: "I was in town yesterday and spent the night. I . . . I thought I would check in on you before heading back to Girona."

"What did you do all night? Did you take a solitary walk?" I teased, thinking of Rousseau's orders.

"No," he intoned, looking away. "I spent the night at a friend's house."

I detected a hint of sexual melancholy in his voice, and his hair looked tousled. He obviously had slept with someone. I leaned in and sniffed him. He smelled like ferns. He stepped away from the frame and nervously reached for his pipe, which he had tucked into the breast pocket of his vest.

He asked me if I would be interested in getting a bite to eat at the Boqueria. He told me it was the Fiesta de la Mercè. I remembered the celebrations. There would be fireworks, a procession, neighborhood teenagers dressed up as devils running around with pitchforks and playing with fire. I agreed to meet but told him I had to run a few errands first.

"What errands?" he challenged.

"I am going on an Architectural Pilgrimage of Fragmentation," I offered matter-of-factly. "But I can meet you in the afternoon when I'm done."

He looked at me with a seriousness and a sensuality that implied *soon we will be wrapped around each other in bed.* He held my gaze for what felt like a long time, then teased: "Do you even eat?" He crossed his arms and tilted his head. His curls fell across his face.

I felt my corporeality evaporate. My mind clouded over. I saw myself double: I was standing outside that ruined house that had come down on my mother, and at the same time an older version of myself was leaning against the frame of a stranger's door in Barcelona speaking to Ludo Bembo while wondering if my mother had found anything she could have eaten — fried liver abandoned on the stove, a bowl of walnuts, dried mulberries — before that house came down on her head. I felt my void clench.

Without realizing it, I mumbled: "I prefer not to eat."

"We'll have to fix that," he said. "We'll have to show you how to eat like a true Mediterranean."

A sweet, cool draft blew through the door. I remembered that with each stone we had lifted off my mother's body my father had recited Marx's famous words, *Change the world*, followed by Rilke's, which echoed not only Marx's but also Nietzsche's, illuminating a triangular pattern in the matrix: *You must change your life.* Change! I chewed on the word. I looked Ludo Bembo up and down. The word secreted a mild anxiety. Was there room for him in the Grand Tour of Exile? I was afraid he would derail me from my objectives. More than anything else in the world, I felt the need to record the uselessness of my family's suffering in my notebook. That obligation to share our story, to sound it out as an alarm, had been assigned to me by my dead father and was so exhaustive that it competed with every rudimentary need: food, sleep, the company of others. And yet I was in a divided frame of mind. I knew I was also afraid that without another person anchoring me to this trifling universe I would fade into the ether entirely, vanish into nothingness.

Ludo reached out and squeezed my hand.

"That's my sick hand!" I told him, trying to squash my desire. But, like a phoenix, it rose its dusty head once more.

We walked out into the yolky light of midday. Before we each went our own way, we agreed to meet in the afternoon at the side entrance of the Boqueria between the vegetable stalls. I watched Ludo retreat through the brutal grid of L'Eixample. Then I walked to a corner newsstand, which was run by a middle-aged woman with a fleshy face and kind eyes. I bought the paper. I checked to see if there was news of the Grand Tour of Exile. Perhaps Morales had dispatched a press release. I stood there and leafed through every page. Nothing. Not a word. There was news of a homicide-suicide, of stranded boats loaded with refugees adrift in that great green sea, of kings and queens, of politicians and their wives.

"Tourist?" the owner exclaimed, nosily craning her head out of the newsstand's opening, gesturing at the carefully arranged rows of trinkets, guidebooks, and maps of the city.

"No," I exclaimed impatiently in Catalan. "A returning exile!"

She reeled her head back into the enclosure of the newsstand.

I picked up a map of Barcelona and slid it between my fingers. It was a pocket-size laminated map that folded conveniently over itself. Where would the Spaniards be, I thought, without Unamuno, the man who had introduced them to the art of paper folding? I purchased it. Then, thinking of Borges's words, I asked the fleshy-faced woman if, in her opinion, the map I had bought was conscionable or unconscionable. She pretended not to hear me, so I repeated the question. "Conscionable or unconscionable?" I posed. But her phone rang before she could respond, and she walked to the back of the newsstand to pick it up.

"Una nena, una nena!" I heard her exclaim a second later. A girl had been born. She had popped her veiny blue head into this woman's life.

I folded the newspaper and tucked it into my notebook. Then I opened the map. I searched for the street I was standing on. Carrer de Girona. When I found the street, I pointed at it and simultaneously tapped my foot against the ground in order to indicate to the various intersecting surfaces of the city that I, Zebra, Dame of the Void, was as receptive as an antenna, ready to channel information; that my double mind, which contained multiple subminds, each motored by a different language, was a fertile ground for receiving signals from the palimpsest of time that is, it goes without saying, contained within the Matrix of Literature. The first private communiqué I received kindly suggested I pass the map along to someone else with the following note: "Consider yourself warned: This map, like all maps, is a lie. Literature is the only true form of cartography in the world."

I transcribed the message onto the map's borders and then walked to the grocer's. As soon as the grocer saw me, his face took on the disgruntled expression of a pug.

"I come bearing gifts," I said.

No sooner had I spoken than the grocer's face slackened and turned red as if it had been grilled and deboned. I put the map on the counter and told him that enclosed in the map is a message from the Matrix of Literature, indeed from the illustrious Borges, one of the matrix's greatest masterminds, and that he, the grocer, a primitive, miserly, and nonliterary man, should consider himself lucky that I had chosen him as the recipient. "Open the map and read what I have transcribed in the margins," I ordered.

After a moment's hesitation, he opened the map. I watched him work the laminated edges with his gnarled walnut-stained fingers. He spread the map across the glass counter and examined it under the yellow glow of a dusty overhead light. He studied the map for a moment, then, like a man lost at sea, he mumbled to himself: "'Consider yourself warned: This map, like all maps, is a lie. Literature is the only true form of cartography in the world.'"

"Excellent," I said. "Message transmitted."

The grocer looked bewildered, as though he had been slapped. I ignored the peaks and valleys of his facial expressions. There were things he needed to reflect on in order to transcend his ignorant state. To butter him up, I pointed at his poster of Dalí's *The Persistence of Memory* and complimented him on his choice of art. After that, I told him that he would be a fool to ignore Borges's message, since Borges had a great deal to teach us about the labyrinthine nature of both voluntary and involuntary memory, not to mention historical versus private memory, themes that greatly concerned Freud as well — I was speaking with the voice of my manifesto — the man who dared to ask: *Where does a thought go when it is forgotten?*

That did it. I had pushed the grocer over the edge. In a resentful nasal tone, he told me that it was clear to him that I suffered from certain incorrigible limitations and that I should get out before he was tempted to throw produce at me. He said this last part while looking sorrowfully at his pile of black walnuts. I wondered what those walnuts symbolized for him. His cat appeared with its orange stripes and its tail in the air, and this seemed to calm him, at least momentarily.

I took advantage of that brief caesura to stroke my notebook. I lifted it and smelled the musty sheets. Then, in the gentlest of tones, I said to the grocer: "My dear grocer, no one is spared. Someday you, too, will join the world's unlucky, the world's foot soldiers, the bearers of grief. And when that day arrives, you will finally understand that *a book is a counselor, a multitude of counselors*, and you will think back on me fondly."

Naturally, nothing more was said. A thick silence enveloped me as I walked out of the store. Before I left, I looked back at the grocer and his cat through the glass door. He was a changed man. He and his cat both seemed resigned, aware of their smallness, of their powerlessness in the grand scheme of life. But that awareness of the dark side would soon start working on their behalf; because once trespassed, darkness begins to yield to its survivors — to the unlucky lucky — the secret revenge of laughter. I stopped to look one last time through the glass door. I could no longer tell where the grocer ended and the cat began.

The church bells let out a single stroke. I waited until the peal faded into the distance, then set off on the Architectural Pilgrimage of Fragmentation.

I walked across Avinguda Diagonal toward Park Güell. Tourists flocked past me on the boisterous, broad street. A man in an old blue Volvo honked at a woman on a scooter; she cut him off and whizzed on. Her head was enclosed in a red helmet. She looked like a giant beating heart moving unprotected through the street.

Rather suddenly, my thoughts came together like the angled points of a star. It occurred to me that a book is only a good counselor if it calls up the wounded zones of our consciousness — in other words, if the act of reading it wounds us. I thought about how the word *star* is only one letter different from the word *scar*, and this thought reinforced my conclusion that Baudelaire, that beloved dandy, had not taken his rebellion against the bourgeoisie, those who cling to security at the expense of the vulnerable, far enough. No. Because in order for a book to be a good counselor, I persevered, it must be negotiating a danger zone; there must be a transgression, a leap, a move beyond a prohibition. I went underground, got on the metro. "A good book," I said to myself, "is cannibalistic. An object that calls up the ghosts of our past in order to reflect the haunting instability of our future world."

The metro doors closed. The train moved along the tracks. Immediately, a woman's amplified voice emanated from somewhere in the crowd. "Who is the enemy?" she asked. Someone answered, "The adversaries are everywhere." Another voice said, "We are confronted with a case of leaderless resistance." I looked around. A group of wiry teenagers were leaning against the doors gloomily. Everything else was just a sea of heads. I couldn't tell where the voices were coming from.

There, in that nonplace, in the city's gutters and underground corridors, the dark rooms of grief I carried within me were suddenly called up, the insurmountable loss, the irreparable wound that had led me to retrace my life's journey in punctuated movements from West to East. I was there revisiting the dark events or, rather, the senseless phenomena that had conspired to destroy me. I was trying to recover a fraction of what had been lost from my memory. I closed my eyes. I felt like a ghost. I felt as if, with my presence alone, I were sounding out a warning of doom and gloom.

"Who am I?" I asked aloud.

I heard: "Another corpse in the ill-fated pile."

An hour later, slightly nauseated, I was standing beneath an ashen sky in the Metaphysical Garden of Exile. A storm was gathering. Another hour and the rain would be pouring down. The sensation I had in the metro lingered as I walked through the park. I slipped through a hedge and lumbered around the aloe and palms. I walked through the Portico of the Washerwoman; I could feel the wind moving through the gaps between the columns of the arcade, sifting through the branches of the trees, rushing through the coastal brush. It sounded like the park was sighing.

"What am I doing in Barcelona?" I asked myself. There was no one else around.

I answered, "I am leaping into the void of exile in order to stain my notebook with the inky residue of the past.

"And who will read your notebook?" I asked.

"Nobody," I answered despairingly, and carried on beneath the parade of clouds.

I walked through the park as a shadow, a ghost, already dead and yet still alive. I stood on the terrace with serpentine benches, looking out over Barcelona, and from that vantage point, I could sense a slight shift in the air, in the landscape of my mind. For a second, I considered leaping off the overlook. I considered killing myself, going, like a good book, toward my own disappearance. I looked out at the sea, slack and purple in the distance; at the cranes hovering over the spires of La Sagrada Familia; at the domes and turrets of the city; the slick blue glass and reddish hues of the Torre Agbar; the clay tower of the warden's house in the park; and the fronds of palm trees in between. I thought to myself, yes, indeed, I will leap off the terrace and, as Borges said, *my tomb will be the unfathomable air.*

I looked backward and forward at the fundamental fatality of my life, its senselessness and lack of reason, the swamp air of my childhood, and remembered that right before his death my father had raised his hand and grazed the yellow tips of his mustache with his leathery fingers. Then he'd tapped his temple with his index finger, and weakly said: "This, up here, is the only liberty you will ever have. Guard it with your life, your death."

I stared out at the city's skyline. Barcelona was emitting a low hum. I looked at the Sea of Sunken Hopes, at its infinite horizons and mists. Even from that impossible distance, I could hear the waves breaking against the shore — the sea swelling and retreating — and for a moment, I had the impression that Barcelona was free of thresholds, as if its perimeters were melting into the sea, the Old and the New Worlds blending together. In my mind's eye, I could see the statue of Christopher Columbus standing by the shore at the end of that long promenade, La Rambla: his face proud, his finger pointing at the myth of the new.

There it was again, that terrible word: *new.* New! Scoffing at the word immediately made me feel better. I had survived my duel with the unthinking masses dining on the artifice of the so-called New World. I thought of its companion term: *now.* I denounced them both. *"I would sooner believe in nothing, sooner in the devil, than in the now,"* I said out loud to no one, echoing Nietzsche's words. The ill-fateds' *now* had been and would continue to be leveled by history's remorseless blows; it had been beaten out of our repertoire of tenses.

Just then, I noticed a girl with a broad forehead and a sharp chin standing next to me. She was wearing a blue dress with a passenger pigeon printed on the skirt. She had the most unexceptional face. She was American.

She turned to me, and asked: "Were you speaking to me? I didn't hear what you said."

"No," I said abruptly.

I examined her dress. I hated its whimsical flair. Then I thought: Why shouldn't I speak to her? Why should I keep my thoughts to myself when the world perpetuates itself by torturing exiles, immigrants, refugees? It is my duty as a lucky-unlucky to take revenge on the world by contaminating it with my thoughts and my suffering, which are one and the same thing. She was looking at the sprawling view of Barcelona, at the blue surface of the sea, which looked like hammered leather with the wind pressing into the water, causing depressions, waves, foamy peaks and valleys.

"Actually, I *was* speaking to you," I said.

She turned to face me again with that plain, broad forehead of hers.

"You," I said, "are at liberty to turn your nose away from the cadavers of history, to protect your stupidity and your innocence" — her smooth cheeks flushed and her blue eyes went round — "but I could never do the same."

She took a step back.

"Even if I wanted to turn away from the miasma of death," I added, stepping toward her, "I couldn't because I have been ghettoed in the Pyramid of Exile for the benefit of people like you."

"You don't know anything about me," she said. She was on the verge of tears.

"I know what I know," I said. "And I also know when I see what I know."

I stopped paying attention to her. I reviewed my words: *I know what I know and I also know when I see what I know.* It was the most brilliant declaration I had made all day. More brilliant than the educational intervention I had offered the grocer.

I watched her walk away; her skirt billowed in the wind. After that, I walked to a remote corner of the park, found a moist patch of earth, and dug a hole in the ground. I scribbled that wretched word — *new* — on a piece of paper and buried it in the hole. I sniffed my fingers. I remembered the smell of the earth where my father and I had dug my mother's grave. It was acidic, poisonous, dry. Then I remembered the moist, grassy smell of the hole into which the undertakers had lowered my father's casket. The Hosseinis — all dead except me — were scattered across the world. The next time I looked up, I saw the Angel of History hovering above the city, mouth agape, batting its wings. There it was: history appearing before my eyes *as a single catastrophe*. I thought, the Matrix of Literature is a center-less swarm of interconnected books that tirelessly mirror back to us the pile of ruins that is humanity.

I kept on walking. I walked past a performer wearing a leopard-print shirt and a pair of purple leotards. He had long brown hair, a terrible wide mouth, and his eyes were hidden behind white-rimmed sunglasses. He was playing an electric guitar. A few people were gathered around, looking at him with begrudging grimaces.

I carried on. I walked away from the park through the Nature Square and the Austria Gardens with its non-native plants. I weaved my way through the Doric-inspired columns of the hypostyle room, past the famous statue of the dragon spewing water, walked down a flight of stairs that looked like the long train of a bride's dress in the dusk air, past the famous shimmering salamander. Before I left, I looked back at the Metaphysical Garden of Exile and realized that the architecture of the park was a mirror image of the infrastructure of my life: everything a bit off, disorienting, misshapen. I spotted a group of tourists near the park gates, heads down in their laminated maps. It occurred to me that in opposition to them I, whose ancestors are buried here, there, and everywhere, our dust scattered across the Four Corners of the World, am destined to remain lost. Their Achilles' heel — an aversion to gaps and fissures — is my greatest strength.

I made my way to the Block of Discordance. Certain names were coming back to me, certain facts about the city. L'Eixample, that political project, I remembered again, was designed by the utopist Ildefons Cerdà. It occurred to me that Cerdà must have organized information in his mind as sterilely as he'd designed the neighborhood's square clinical blocks, by archiving thoughts and memories into specific containers in order to avoid any risk of cross-contamination. The same way corpses are buried in times of so-called health: in individual caskets rather than piles. A middle-aged woman with a bell-shaped haircut was standing at the corner searching through her purse; she looked distraught, as if she were peering into an abyss. She kept plunging her hand deeper and deeper into her purse. Her face looked as if it were about to fall off. I walked up to her, and said, adopting an ironic tone: "It seems to me you stand to benefit from the legacy of Ildefons Cerdà: enemy of the old, anticannibal, a man eager to purify the world from the clutter of the past. Anyone who walks the streets of L'Eixample will immediately experience linear thought patterns because Cerdà has modernized the city by flattening it into a singular surface. Go on!" I encouraged. "Walk through L'Eixample! Simplicity awaits you! It is a field of answers!" I looked at her purse. It was brown and shiny. It looked like a clam. She sealed that clam and scurried off with great haste.

At the intersection with Carrer de Girona, it suddenly occurred to me that in contraposition to Ildefons Cerdà, Quim Monzó lived on the plane of antiquity, accumulating rubbish from the past that he had to grapple with day and night. I concluded that his apartment, littered with objects, represented a sustained rebellion against the rigidity of the built environment in which he lived. I felt a surge of affection for that retired literary critic.

The Architectural Pilgrimage of Fragmentation had oxygenated my mind. I walked down Passeig de Gràcia. There it was: Casa Milà, that vertiginous building designed by the very same Antoni Gaudí who had designed Park Güell. I stood on the street gawking at its undulating facade, at the spiraling figures of rock that emerge from its curved roof, which resemble medieval knights and soldiers wearing gas masks. I thought to myself: According to Benjamin, martyr of thought, we must always be prepared to confront *the adversities of outer life which sometimes come from all sides, like wolves*, the brutal winds of the future through which the dust of the past will come blowing back. My solitary walks, I reiterated to myself, are designed to resurrect the past. In other words, I am a Flâneur of Death, walking through the city, examining the palimpsest of time.

Farther down the Block of Discordance is the Casa Amatller, designed by the hairy-chinned Josep Puig i Cadafalch. I inspected the floral and neo-Gothic motifs, the stained glass windows, the intricate tile work, the ochre shutters, the peach and white and red tones, the Arab- and Sephardic-inspired asymmetrical wooden doors engraved with a star-shaped design, and again I thought of that word — *star* — and how it is only one letter different from the word *scar*, and I cried a little. An old banner, faint, weather-beaten, barely legible, hung from the terrace of the building: BUSH NO GUERRA NO SADDAM NO. The banner looked abandoned, a relic of the past. After briefly protesting the war in Iraq, the rest of the world had moved on while hundreds of lives continued to be eviscerated every day. Those who survive the long war, I thought, will carry on with their hearts extinguished. Like me, they will spend the rest of their days gawking at the world as if they were already dead.

I stood there, alone, reflecting. My father, who had been quiet for some time, sounded out his old warning: *Child, there is nothing worse than dying a stranger.* It occurred to me that my father's maxim will remain true as long as the world is full of Cerdàs and that the Casa Amatller, which had belonged to a chocolatier, a man who knew how to find pleasure in life, is a rare disruption in the pragmatic and utilitarian project of a global society that is always lying to itself, trying to outrun the past. I felt a deep calm wash over me as I continued to meditate on the building because, despite containing a plethora of decorative elements, despite drawing on so many architectural styles at once — Romanesque, Gothic, Flemish, Nordic, Catalan, Arabic, Sephardic — the Casa Amatller exudes an air of serenity. Then I thought, no, not *despite* but *because.* Because, by virtue of containing various architectural traditions, the Casa Amatller offers us a view of the infinite dizzying pluralism of life; it is a material manifestation of both the interconnected fabric of being and also of the *nothingness that contains everything.* Not unlike my father's transcriptions. Satisfied, I moved down to Casa Batlló — Gaudí's House of Bones, which is to say his House of Death — weeping and laughing in turns.

A gaggle of tourists stood in front of the building, lifting their sunglasses to look up at the House of Bones. The fractured mosaics of the building's facade were shimmering in the light of the afternoon. The scaled blue roof and the range of colors — aquamarine to gold — and the undulating facade, its smooth ribbed stone interrupted only by oval windows, gave the building the impression of being both fish and sea, animal and element. I felt my body turn inside out. The House of Bones looked like the ridged surface of a beach after the waves have receded and left their imprint on the sand and, simultaneously, like a brilliant undiscovered fish. The tourists moved on. The awe the vertiginous architecture had awakened in them sank below the surface so blithe indifference and automatism could rise again.

"Procession of fakes!" I yelled after them. They were all the same person. It was as though they had read a manual on travel etiquette in order to blend in with one another, in order to form a Free-Floating Nation of Tourists: a thoughtless mass drifting along a grid.

I felt a sudden urge to follow them like a detective. What they lent and denied their attention to, I decided, was a barometer for measuring universal levels of alienation from death, and therefore, I carried on, from literature.

I pursued them all the way to La Rambla. People strutted between the rows of plane trees. They observed the living statues. I sounded out their gait: *taa-taa, taa-taa*. I sat down on a bench and kept an eye on my specimens. They congregated around a bloody heap. I got up to look. They were taking pictures.

An overthrown trash can, with its contents spilled out — beer bottles, an old bouquet of flowers splattered with blood, food wrappers, pages of a torn and tarnished book — came into view. Gradually, a man, his limbs curled over the severed frame of a bicycle, materialized. His head was missing. He had been decapitated. The bloody stump had rolled away. The tourists I had followed were holding their phones at arm's length. They were taking selfies. Like apparitions in a nightmare, their nylon lips were spreading into synthetic smiles while in the background a living statue was miming death.

The idea that the world had been duplicated in the virtual plane left me somber and repulsed; I hated that the virtual dimension had been linked to its physical counterpart to form a single continuum and that people had started to move between the two — the physical world and its hologram, the Internet — with the same ease they would exit a highway only to reenter it on the other side of the overpass. I watched the tourists post their photos online and marvel at their image, at their fake selves smiling back at them from the virtual plane. It was as if they needed to duplicate their image in order to affirm: I exist, I exist, I exist. I was bored to death with them.

I drifted down La Rambla. Saplings had sprouted on the lower branches of the plane trees, but beneath the fresh leaves, the sycamores' trunks looked sickly; a hairy white fungus had invaded the bark. I wondered if it was an infestation, if the bottom halves of the trees were diseased. I wanted to return to my cave, where I could descend beneath the world's duplicitous facade, slip beneath its mask, its surface currents, and there, in quiet solitude, boldly look through literature into the eye of the lie of life. But instead I walked to the Boqueria.

It was time to meet Ludo Bembo.

When I arrived at the vegetable stalls near the Boqueria, Ludo Bembo was already there. He had his back to me, and he was kissing another woman. It was late enough in the day for the vegetable sellers to have abandoned their stalls, leaving behind a few wilted eggplants, some cardboard boxes, overripe bananas. I sat on one of the boxes and watched. As soon as Ludo moved his head, the woman's face came into view. She was a few years older than I was, closer in age to Ludo, and her skin was in the pink of health. She had large bright eyes and long, curly chestnut-colored hair that fanned open behind her neck. Her lips were tightly sealed. Ludo had his arms up and he was pushing her back. He was exuding discomfort. He managed to detach himself. From this, I deduced that the kiss they'd exchanged wasn't inviting or sensual; it was dry and apologetic and final.

I looked the woman up and down. She looked arrogant. She held her chin up and cast him a glacial gaze. She was wearing black heels, tight jeans, and a red button-down shirt that signaled a punitive character, a rigid kind of sexuality. Her outfit was a warning. That shirt, in conjunction with her scrupulous, cold gaze, seemed to say: *I will draw your blood.* I felt sorry for Ludo Bembo. What was he — a man with a poetic past and predisposed to a lyrical future — doing with that Tentacle of Ice?

The situation was pitiful. It was clear that Ludo was in the process of dismissing her; or, rather, given her demanding demeanor, he was in the process of gently removing himself from her presence. She was the woman he had slept with the night before. I was sure of it. I imagined her spreading her long legs to receive him. I imagined him climbing on top of her. I briefly wondered if he had yanked her hair before climaxing, and then I ambled into the market, confident that from now on Ludo Bembo would be entangled with me.

To kill time until Ludo was freed, I walked between the stalls. Only a few vendors remained open. I paused here and there to inspect the food on display: squid (black, glossy, covered in ink), minuscule sand dabs, red shrimp, rock lobsters (their claws limp), eels (displayed on piles of shaved ice), salted cod (whole, diced, cut into strips), sardines, monkfish (cross-eyed, with flat, stupid heads), barnacles, anchovies, trout, crayfish, oysters, clams, mussels, prawns, wine and cava, piles of almonds, walnuts, cashews, bins full of candy, rows of gummies designed like fruit (watermelons, cherries, slices of melon). I hadn't eaten anything substantial in days. I felt weak, drained, worthless. And then I heard my name.

It was Ludo Bembo. He had come into the market to look for me. He arrived panting, breathless. His curls were bouncing on his head. He said, "I saw you walk in."

"Are you returning from the March on Rome?" I posed, with a brute manner.

His eyes went blank.

"I wasn't alive back then," he said a bit stiffly, once he had recovered from his shock. He paused for a second to catch his breath. "And besides, I'm not a fascist; that's a very offensive thing for you to be implying," he intoned, drawing his shoulders back. He was carrying a messenger bag. It looked heavy. He swapped the bag to his opposite shoulder. His muscles tensed, and I realized that, despite his thin frame, he was robust, firm in his manners, developed in the right places. A man who knew how to desire and be desired.

A pigeon fluttered down from the rafters and landed between our feet. I thought it looked like Mussolini — it was pink and black, and had nervous little eyes — but I didn't say a thing. I bit my tongue. Ludo was looking down at the bird affectionately. I made a mental note: Ludo Bembo refuses to discuss fascism but is willing to smile at the Mussolini bird. Then I remembered his indifference toward the dead swallow that had dropped out of the sky at the airport and concluded that he wasn't so much apathetic toward birds but rather uneasy around the subject of death. Perhaps, I reflected, when it came to death, he would always look like a tide had dragged him out of the shallows; he would always struggle to keep his head above water. His inadequacy in the face of the abyss, I deduced, must have subconsciously contributed to his attraction to me, Dame of the Void. A dark chuckle squeezed out from between my lips, and Ludo looked at me, simultaneously captivated and perturbed. He had no idea what was headed his way.

"What's in there?" I asked, pointing at his bag, smiling, offering him an olive branch.

"In here? Notebooks, documents. I was in the archives." He gave a sigh. "It's so poorly organized. It's exhausting being in there."

I imagined the Tentacle of Ice wrapping herself around him. I couldn't contain myself any longer.

"Are you referring to your friend's vaginal archives?"

"What?" I watched his eyebrows float to the center of his face, then drift apart again. The words had just poured out of my mouth. To my surprise, he caught on rather quickly. "Oh," he said. "No, don't worry about her."

"I don't worry about anyone," I said curtly, cutting him off.

We made our way to one of the food stalls and sat at the counter. Ludo ordered for the both of us while I looked through the glass display case at a row of tourists sitting at the opposite counter. I felt a palpable hatred toward them, those stupid tourists with their white-gloved inspection of the most marketable qualities of another nation, another culture, their experience purified of the painful clutter of the past, of the horrifying traces of the accretion of history. While I pasted onto my face the same vacuous grin I witnessed on theirs, Ludo ordered wine, squid, poached eggs.

"What's wrong with your face?" he asked.

"You mean their faces," I said, pointing my fork at the tourists.

"Mimicry is the greatest form of flattery," he offered. There it was again: that edifying tone of his. "If you don't like them, I suggest you pretend they don't exist."

"Mimicry," I corrected in breathy stabs, "is mockery."

He reached for my hand. With his other, he lifted his wineglass.

"Cheers," he said, trying to redirect my attention. He took a sip. Then he sat there looking pensive, thoughtfully gazing at the tourists I had pointed out.

I drank as rapidly as I could. I needed to move the image of those tourists, who roam freely in green pastures while the rest of us are enclosed in the Pyramid of Exile, into the pile of ruins that is the past. Never mind that I was sitting right next to them, shoveling the same food into my mouth, looking just like them. What distinguished me was invisible, abstract. It was the feeling of nothingness that I carried with me wherever I went, a void I was convinced they had never experienced and that I, in contradistinction to them, had carried for so long that it had consumed my life. The only way I knew I was alive was by watching the pile of ruin grow, the rubbish attract rubbish until the garbage of my life was insurmountable. I felt a sharp ache in my void. I was anxious it was going to burst. I didn't say any of this to Ludo. I ate, nodded, thanked him, said how good everything was.

Encouraged, Ludo ordered more food and drinks. Beer-battered pork cheeks, black rice cooked in squid ink, crisp white wine. And when we were done with the meal, he ordered ratafia.

"Taste this," he said. "It's a delicacy."

I tasted it.

"What do you think?" he asked with boyish charm.

I told him the ratafia smelled like wet soil, limestone, clay, volcanic rock, freshly cut grass, worms, a brackish wind coming down through a mountain pass, dusty herbs, heaps of licorice. He ran his hand up along my arm and tucked a strand of hair behind my ear. "You're so beautiful," he said.

"Don't lie," I said. "Besides, even if I were beautiful, it would not be by any merit of my own."

"You have a great nose," he said.

"It's true. I have a great nose," I said. Then, to avoid saying what I wanted to tell him, that my nose is so sublime it can smell spilled blood from as far away as the deep past, I asked: "Do you like living in Girona?"

"People around here like to say it's the Florence of Catalonia. But I wouldn't go so far. The Spaniards are known for exaggerating."

"Where I come from," I informed him, leaning in and whispering warmly in his ear, "we have a saying about people who exaggerate. We say: Those who haven't seen see poorly."

"Exactly. Brava. They are narrow, provincial, out of touch," Ludo said sympathetically, sipping at the black liquor. "Where do you come from?"

"You saw my flight details. New York."

"No, before that."

"I hail from the land of Cyrus, King of Kings!" I announced.

"You mean Iran?" he asked, laughing.

The tourists paid and left. I watched them make their way to the door and disappear into the dark folds of the sky. Afternoon had given way to evening. In their absence, I felt I could breathe again. I started to speak in aphorisms, in riddles. I explained that it's not just when a country hasn't seen much that there's a problem; if a country has seen too much, it stops seeing clearly as well. I told him there is a delicate balance. Ludo, who hails from a fallen empire himself, nodded along knowingly, his face blooming like a daffodil in the sun.

"If the balance is disturbed — if one does not see enough, or one sees too much — then, according to your beloved compatriot Calvino, *the eye does not see things but images of things that mean other things.*"

"Do you mistake things for other things?" he posed.

"When I see a palm tree," I said, feeling my void tighten in response, "what I see is my mother's ashen face and her lifeless corpse." I watched his features drift apart. I could see his tongue working that adorable gap between his front teeth.

"Aren't corpses lifeless by definition?" he posed awkwardly, narrowing his eyes.

"Not initially. Life leaves the body over a long period of time, slowly, quietly, with grace. It lingers in the atmosphere until it is absorbed by the mind of the universe. In the case of my father, however, I intercepted the mind of the universe," I said, smiling vaguely. I could see Ludo's wheels spinning. "Did the Bembos pass down only a fraction of their knowledge to you?" I asked.

"The Bembos? What do you mean, a fraction?"

"All I'm saying is that your naiveté concerning death is incongruous with your literary past. But then again, I've learned that in life anything is possible!"

"My past?" Ludo asked tersely. He had taken offense.

"All I know is that you're a Bembo," I said, lifting an oyster off the plate and offering it to him. It worked. He took the ridged shell and delicately sucked the brackish muscle into his mouth.

Every once in a while, the cooks, who were wearing black uniforms that made them look like undertakers, wiped their brows with a piece of oil-soaked cloth. Then they fussed with the pans, turned up the flames, re-moved sardines from the oven, boiled crabs, threw calamari into the fire.

A vague memory of my mother, Bibi Khanoum, resurfaced. I felt weary again and noxious. I saw her standing in the kitchen of the Oasis of Books wearing a blue apron. There was a dead sturgeon at her feet. She kneeled on the floor and sliced into the fish in order to retrieve the eggs. Blood curdled around the drain; I watched it get absorbed into the pipes and gutters. My nose stung with the sharp smell. I tried to look at my mother's face, but her head was bent over the sturgeon and I couldn't see it. I felt a nudge. It was Ludo. He had a follow-up question.

"What do you mean, intercepted?" he asked.

I sniffed the liquor, and the herbal notes helped to resettle my stomach. Then I explained to him that instead of the universe absorbing my father upon his death I had absorbed him through metempsychosis. In other words, I beat the universe to it. Then I added: "I've recently discovered that I've also absorbed traces of my mother through my father, who had absorbed her previously."

Ludo leaned back in his chair. He looked like a frustrated accountant who keeps adding the same numbers and getting different results.

"What brought on this realization?" he inquired.

I told him that after my mother's untimely death, while living in Barcelona, my father had entered a period of heightened literary awareness. That, in addition to pursuing his usual work as a translator, he began to practice the Art of Transcription. My thoughts swam around the murky waters of my mind like fish in an aquarium. "Under the specter of grief," I explained to Ludo, "my father, a very innovative man — a man with a fantastic mustache, I should add — devoted himself to the manual reproduction of texts, like a monk in a monastery." I went on to tell him that recalling this apparently insignificant fact, which until now I had erased from memory, allowed me to connect the dots. I said, "I've entered a period of supreme literary activity since absorbing my father; so it's only logical to conclude that my father's heightened literary awareness in the years after my mother's death is indicative of the fact that he had absorbed her. And thus it only follows that I've now absorbed traces of her through him."

Ludo's pupils had dilated. I leaned in. He smelled like orange blossoms, eucalyptus, figs sliced open and soaked in honey; the scents of my youth came back to me with a dizzying pull. I landed a kiss on his cheek. His worries melted away in an instant.

I slipped him a small piece of paper on which I had written a message expressly for him. I told him, "This formula, extracted from reading Blanchot, allowed my ancestors to survive their disastrous fate for generations. Literature holds the key to transcendence, to metaphysically surviving one's death. Here it is." I pushed the note along the counter. He leaned over to look.

Life + Death = Totality
Totality = Unreality of the Whole

The corners of his mouth curled up as he tucked the note in his pocket. He looked enchanted, and I wondered if a new space had opened in him, a dark room to which he could retreat to acknowledge his own wretchedness.

"You should come to Girona," he said. "I live with some great people. You would like it there. You can see the Pyrenees from our apartment. In the evenings, the flanks of the mountains look purple. I've never seen anything like it. And then there's Bernadette, Agatha, Fernando. Well, Bernadette will be leaving soon. At least I hope she will. She's a nervous type, chaste, pulls the blinds down at sunset and slips into these fluffy pink pajamas, and then she seals herself in her room and prays to the pope or the Virgin Mary. If she leaves her room and I'm there, she walks along the walls like a crab. I'm surprised she doesn't try to grab the wall to save herself from falling. You've got to see it with your own eyes!" He laughed, though his laugh wasn't malicious. It was full of bewilderment at the mysteries of life.

We sat there and got progressively drunker. I told him that, as a child, I once tied myself to a tree and pretended I was a cow. I exclaimed, "The most insipid hours of my life!"

"What made you want to do that?" he asked.

I thought of *The Hung Mallard*. I heard my father echo the voice of my great-great-grandfather, Shams Abbas Hosseini: *We will remain as succulent as that duck.* I shared this with Ludo. *The Hung Mallard*, I told him, was a symbolic portrait of our collective family destiny. I told him that by tying myself to a tree I had tapped into deep reservoirs of grief that allowed me to understand from an early age what it means to live in a state of captivity, the reason I am now able to exert my will to power from within the Pyramid of Exile.

Ludo smiled kindly. I saw his reflection on the glass counter. His eyes looked darker and his hair had a red sheen. He had an attentive look on his face. He was listening. I wondered if our ancestors in the poetic dimension had oiled the gears of our conversation. Then he leaned in and planted a soft kiss on my neck.

"What's the strangest thing you did as a child?" I asked.

For a second, he looked remote, as if he were excavating the ruins of memory. Then he told me that when he was a child his parents had owned a house in the Tuscan countryside, that he used to go walking through the fields, writing out the alphabet on the rocks in chalk. "I felt as if I were inventing language!" he said with a nostalgic whisper.

"That's the strangest thing you did?" I asked.

"Yes. Is there a problem with that?"

"It seems mild."

He didn't say a word. He just sat there with his muzzle in his plate like a sad dog, then he folded and unfolded his napkin. I considered slipping him another note, one that said: "In case you didn't know, silence is a weapon!" But before I had a chance, he had paid and his mood seemed to have lightened a bit. He put his hand on my leg, and said, "Let's go. They're closing up here. We wouldn't want to keep the cooks waiting. Besides, you need to get out of your head and have some fun."

I should have known then and there. A fake philologist. A thought murderer. The din of those words echoed in my ear: "Get out of your head. Have some fun."

We stepped into the evening. We were slogging through the world together, pushing through the crowds on La Rambla, heading into the narrow enclosures of the Gothic Quarter, pausing at the Plaça Reial. The world seemed smaller, darker. I felt my mood plunge. I looked up through the buildings on the perimeter of the *plaça* toward the rectangle of sky above; it looked like a wounded sheet of paper. The crowd was swelling. With each passing moment, there was less air. I was feeling my way through masses of thoughts, through various facets of mind. I thought I heard a donkey braying in the distance. I thought I heard a house collapse. I thought I smelled the rotting of corpses. I imagined the sky splitting open, ink spilling through it.

Ludo was keeping close. There were beads of sweat running down his neck, which was long and delicate, like a swan's. My thoughts doubled over themselves. What, I wondered, am I doing with this man when I am bereft of everyone I have ever loved? When I can't endure any more loss? I feared that the blanket of grief would lift momentarily in his company only to come crashing down with added force. After all, I had loved my mother and father, and what had that led to but pain? More people spilled into the *plaça*. Ludo put his arm around my shoulders, drawing me close. His lips grazed my hair. I searched the ground at my feet. The stone floor was silver, polished; it gleamed like the surface of the moon. My thoughts folded over themselves, yanked me this way and that. I thought, I have no one left to love, no firm foothold in the universe. I let him draw me into his embrace. The fronds of the palms flapped in the breeze. The lampposts had been decorated with ribbons, garlands, festoons, fake flowers. Fireworks spilled through the sky, and for a brief moment, it seemed like there was something beyond the darkness — a flicker of light.

Ludo leaned in, and said in a grave tone: "Brace yourself. Soon there will be fire everywhere."

I noticed the crowd was emptying out of the *plaça*. Very few people were left, and those who remained lingered at the edges, standing under this or that door frame. Voices ricocheted off the stone walls of the buildings. I heard someone say, "Viva la Mercè!" Then came the deafening sound of drums, and the streets were lit up with flames.

A pack of devils spinning firecrackers came running toward us, followed by dragons spewing fire. As the devils lurked down the streets, their serrated red tails dragged along the pavement like snakes. I stood beneath the black sheet of the night sky and felt time increase its velocity, buckle under its own brute force, and come to a sudden halt. Time assumed the rigidity of death. Then, instantly, it was resurrected and pierced space with its triumphant speed once more. A sign of the apocalypse. I looked around. The city had taken on definite overtones of unreality: Opaque screens of smoke rose from the asphalt, then thinned out into the atmosphere. In the distance, beyond the shimmering veils, ordinary people dressed in

plain street clothes ducked into the corridors of fire and then emerged un-
harmed at the other end, as if they were already dead.

We walked through the world's ashes and ghosts, through curtains of
smoke and tunnels of heat that extended like veins across the horizon. I
felt a gust of wind. I turned around. A procession of papier-mâché kings
and queens built to dizzying heights streamed past us, followed by mythical beasts and smaller statues with giant protruding heads. The human
statues were holding pig bladders and knives in their rigid pink hands.
Artificial rays of light, beamed from a mysterious source, danced on their
broad, happy foreheads, on their disproportionate teeth, which were as
large as the keys of a piano. The giants twirled down the street. They vanished into the urban horizon, and the lights searched the emptiness left in
their wake.

I felt disoriented. Time itself had become warped, the atmosphere
distorted. I wondered, who is the hunter? Where is the prey? The wind
thickened. I could see feet covered in canvas shoes sticking out from beneath the extravagant costumes of the giants. People had crawled into
their hollow shapes. Sacks of blood bounced in the wind, Catalan flags
flapped and rolled, rising threads of smoke shrank into white commas,
into gaseous bubbles, into incandescent spiders that crawled up the mono-
lith of the black sky. Suddenly, a dull thud. Something slammed against
the back of my head. I looked around. A solitary she-devil with a sly, impish smile waved her pitchfork at me. I stood motionless, gazing at her spin-
dly legs, her great tufts of red hair, her pale eyebrows, her glittering eyes. I
screamed, but my voice thinned out like smoke.

Ludo grabbed my hand and pulled me along. He kept leaning over to
speak to me, but I heard nothing. The path curved, a sinister bend, and we
were suddenly standing in front of the Casa Batlló. It was as if the city had
folded over itself, cut out its unwanted parts, and left only its crown jewels
standing together on a single reduced surface.

In the dim light of the night, the undulating surface of the House of
Death glittered and swelled as if it were made of clipped waves, suscep-
tible to the moods of the moon. Mercurial beads slid down the skeletal architecture. I felt exasperated, drained, confused. I thought of Taüt. I wondered how long I had been out of the house. I couldn't remember. I had
the sensation I was seeing the world through a convex glass and that on

the other side of the distorted panel the crowds were marching on, going about their business, unaware of my displaced gaze. Police cars came and went.

Before I knew it, we were standing in the lobby of Quim Monzó's building. Ludo was coming along with me. I warned him. "I live with a bird that has the aura of a death maker." But there was no deterring him. Yet again, I felt ambushed by my thoughts. I wondered if by letting Ludo into the dark folds of my life, he, too, would die like everyone else. The lobby turned red and then white with the passing light of a police car. I turned around to look at him. He was staring vacantly at the stairs, and as the unflattering light slid over his face, he looked ghostly pale.

In the foyer of the apartment, I felt Ludo take a step toward me. It was dark enough that I couldn't see him, but I could feel his moist breath on my neck. My limbs, my hips, my waist — they all felt heavy. He continued to stand there, mute, immobile, breathing on my face.

He was a force to be reckoned with, detached and rigid, a rational man who clings to realism one moment and is gleefully attentive, his words tinged with absurdity, the next. Who knows what goes on in other people's heads? There was an enigmatic quality to Ludo that drew me in, an attraction I couldn't negate.

Suddenly, I wanted nothing more than for him to come closer, press his palms against my pelvis, push me back against the wall, lift me onto a table, unbutton my jeans. I wanted him to slide his hands under my shirt, cup my breasts, and say something lyrical consistent with the fact that our ancestors had led their lives according to the laws of literature, under the sign of poetry. I wanted him to say: "Ah, a pair of perfect pomegranates. The fruit of the earth!"

I was about to take his hands to my breasts and say "Repeat after me" when he leaned in and kissed me with a surge of passion I hadn't expected. I felt utterly dispersed and fully embodied at once. I felt as if parts of me had been scattered on different surfaces of the globe and, at the same time, as if Ludo Bembo had siphoned lead into my body, pinning me to the ground. When he pulled away at the end of the kiss, I was stunned. I was afraid of being drawn into the hot vortex of sexual passion, of being wrenched away from the Matrix of Literature. I felt the doubts that had cycled through my head rise to the surface, a doleful loop that played on repeat. So I turned on the lights, and said, for no reason, "Do you know what Silenus replied to King Midas?"

"I have no idea," he said, slightly vexed, waving his hand impatiently.

I could tell he wanted to keep kissing. Reel in, push away, I thought; it's the only way to protect myself and simultaneously protect him, by keeping his death from advancing due to contact with my ill-omened fate. He was looking around to see which way the bedroom was so he could lead me to it smoothly. I carried on with my lecture.

"It will serve you to know that Silenus replied: *What is the best of all is utterly beyond your reach: not to be born, not to be, to be nothing. But the second best for you is — to die soon.*"

His mind stopped in its tracks.

"Are you telling me I'm unworthy of life right before we have sex?"

He removed his glasses and rubbed his face. His eyes, which were deeply set, seemed to have sunk farther into his head. He looked tired. Now, standing apart from me, his stubborn reserve, which had gone up in flames when we kissed, had returned.

"I implied no such thing," I said. My thoughts were colliding into and contradicting one another. I felt them cross-pollinating in my head and added a little white lie, a cliché to smooth things over. "Besides," I said, "sex is a way of dying; so if you think about it, I am giving you the opportunity to walk through the double gates of sex and death."

"No small thing," he said stiffly, making an effort.

"Exactly, Mr. Bembo. You are on the right path," I exclaimed, to reward him. Then, in a lower register, I offered a more adequate closing statement: "So put that in your pipe and smoke it. The double gates of sex and death!"

But he was so hard by then that he couldn't hear me. I could see his penis bulging through his pants. There was no use in trying to discuss literature under those circumstances. I let myself go. I walked up to him and unbuttoned his vest. One button at a time, I felt him soften under my fingers.

"Careful," he said. "My pipe."

Ludo Bembo, I concluded, was the kind of man who regularly polishes his shoes, who irons his shirts. I reached up and pulled his pipe out from his breast pocket. He moaned. He was already losing himself. I bit his lip. It tasted like strawberries dipped in honey and had the aroma of dry herbs and tobacco. And then there was that gap between his teeth, that gap that signaled the void. I could have sucked on his lips for hours, but instead I gently inserted his pipe into his mouth, and said, "*C'est ne pas une pipe!*"

He tilted his head back and smiled before removing the pipe from his mouth and setting it down on the armchair behind us.

When he came back, I moved my hands down to his pants. He swung his head around and kissed my neck, bit my shoulder, nibbled on my ear.

I noticed something strange. A sensation I had never experienced before during any other erotic encounter: The tips of my fingers were hurting. I had no idea what this meant. Electricity coursing through my sick hand?

He pushed me down the corridor. He kept grabbing my hips from behind and pressing himself against me.

"Here," I said. "This door." And we went in.

We lay down on the bed and undressed each other. Ludo looked up at the bedposts. There was a glimmer of light in his gaze.

"Do you want me to tie you to the bed?" I offered.

"No, no," he whined. "Please, don't. You'll just start preaching about death."

I told him he had understood more than he let on, that now I had solid proof that he was a descendent of the Bembos.

"What's all this about my being a descendent of the Bembos? Of course I'm a descendent of the Bembos."

"Exactly," I said, before offering to nibble on his penis.

"Nibble?"

"To begin with."

And so I nibbled, and he swelled in my mouth. I pulled away and told him that his penis had a very well-defined head.

"That's nice," he said.

Then he slipped his fingers inside me, went down on me, reemerged, stroked his penis, and then took my hand to it so I would stroke it for him. He slipped inside me and let out little noises as if he were in pain, and I thought I heard him say, "There is something about you, a darkness that scares me," but by the time he had pulled away from me — leaving me wanting more because I had not yet come — he had switched his tune. "Your vagina," he said, "is like a tunnel of light. It feels so good." He kissed me gently on the edge of my mouth. "Did you come?" he asked, pleased with himself.

"No," I said dryly. "You'll have to carry on."

His face, which had become flush, went pale again.

Just then, Taüt, that impish bird, walked in. His sulfur crest was raised. He looked disheveled. The plumes on his wings were sticking up. He crossed the tiled floor with a pigeon-toed walk he had not displayed until now. I wondered where he had been. Maybe there was a hole in the ground he had dug with his beak, some place he liked to hide at random.

"This," I lied with stale breath, "is my bird."

My mouth was bitter and hot from all the alcohol we'd had. I needed water. I went into the kitchen and came back with two glasses filled to the brim. I spilled the water on Ludo when I got back on the bed. He let out a screech. The cold liquid was running down his loins.

"That takes care of that," I said. "Now you don't have to take a shower."

"Right," he said. His voice was uncertain.

The bird was still there, scrutinizing the situation on the bed, the steamy entanglement that he may or may not have witnessed.

"Was that bird in your suitcase?" Ludo asked mechanically.

I had forgotten he had picked me up at the airport. It's a good thing lies are naturally elastic, I thought.

"Yes," I said. "This bird is one portion of the corpse of my past. He was lodged in there with everything else."

As I spoke these words, Taüt raised his right talon and saluted Ludo. Then he turned around and shimmied back out the door.

"Una-muno, una-mano," I ululated nonchalantly, as I watched the bird retreat. Ludo leaned over and his hair brushed against my cheek.

"Shouldn't we get back on track?" he asked, sitting with his back against one of the bedposts and his ankles crossed. His penis, having completed its business, had shrunk back and was lying limply on his balls.

I made a face at him. I parted my lips and turned the corners of my mouth down and squinted sadly. I said, "If your penis were a person, this is what it would look like." I held that face for a while. I could see Ludo's eyes moving from side to side, metabolizing the information he had just received. "And if my vagina were a person?" I asked, extending an invitation for him to dramatize my reproductive organ in return.

"I suppose your vagina would be running down the sidewalk throwing its arms up in the air, helplessly distressed," he offered.

"You think I have a stressed vagina?"

"And the pubic hairs would be sticking out, particularly at the top, above your clitoris."

"That's not how I see it at all."

My vagina, I explained to him, would be gliding down the sidewalk, saying *blup-blup blup-blup*, like a fish in an aquarium.

Taüt came running back down the corridor. He went past the bedroom door at top speed, squawking as if he were being assassinated.

"What is that bird doing?" Ludo asked, running his fingers along my back, trying to pull me into his arms.

I swatted his hand away because just then I'd received a signal of magnificent proportions from the Matrix of Literature. Words by Unamuno, the man himself. It was as if he were standing next to the bed with his hatted head and pointy bearded chin, commanding me through his thin dry lips to inform Ludo Bembo, who at that very moment was asking me what he could do to help me come, to give it up because it is a known fact that *love is a battle* and that as a result he and I will only experience a simultaneous orgasm when *the heavy pestle of sorrow has ground down our hearts by crushing them in a mortar of mutual suffering.*

"According to whom?" he challenged.

The bird crossed in front of the door again. He was rushing to and fro. He had tucked his crest back to render himself more aerodynamic.

"The lofty Unamuno," I said, smiling widely. That bird, with his aura of death, was transmitting signals to me from the Matrix of Literature. It couldn't be more obvious. I watched him go. From the end of the corridor, I heard the bird echo, "Una-muno, una-mano."

Ludo reached for his underwear — a pair of white briefs — and wiped the remaining come off his penis.

"I can do better than Unamuno," he said, folding his underwear and placing it near the edge of the bed.

"Of course you can. It seems that when it comes to sex the man knows his literature." I chortled.

I could see his mind was spinning. His penis was starting to raise its tired head again. It was bouncing up and down. "You don't believe me?" he said. My heart skipped a beat. I felt both an intense urge to get rid of him, as if the fumes of my void were rising to my throat to choke me, and, strangely, a fear of him being gone. But regardless of how I felt, it seemed he had come to stay. I was both wary of and comforted by his stubborn resolve. He was a buttery, sentimental man hiding behind a severe mask. A romantic, I thought, when Ludo Bembo suddenly ordered me to lie back and spread my legs.

"Very well," I said.

I don't know what he did next, but I came again and again. That sensation of pain in the tips of my fingers returned. I felt as if my life were slipping away, colliding with his and then dissolving. It was, to my surprise, a little bit like dying and being resurrected. It was like bursting into a thousand fragments, each part of myself a plane of perception, a plateau with a view. As he worked on me, massaging my labia, licking my clitoris, images of the ruins of my past, as flat as photographs, reeled through my mind. I saw the black waters of the Caspian crashing against the calcified walls of the houses it had swallowed over the years; abandoned watermelon rinds sticking out of the sand on the shore like grotesque white smiles; men in camouflage patrolling the coast in tiny boats; sickly palms; rows and rows of dusty tomes; my father's tea-stained mustache; the blue domes of Istanbul backlit by a copper sun; the Mediterranean, slack and purple at dawn, hemmed in by cliffs and coves of pink granite against which the Sea of Sunken Hopes was railing; and then, finally, the Room of Broken Heirlooms. These images belonged to selves I had once known intimately but whose identities, dispersed by the violent onslaughts of exile, had grown unfamiliar to me. In my mind's eye, I saw a lineup of those other selves. They looked wanting, distressed, lost. They fixed their gaze on me, and I felt the parched sheet of my heart roll shut, a scroll I couldn't read. I had nothing to give. *"The second best is to die soon,"* I murmured, as I came one last time, right before Ludo pulled his face away from my vagina. The images faded. They sank into oblivion.

"We are sorry little heaps of flesh and bone," I said, catching my breath.

He wiped my hair out of my face, and said, "Look, here's your bird again."

Indeed, there was Taüt, staring at us through the frame of the door.
"And that corridor out there," I added, "is the corridor of exile."
At that, silence resumed its show.

It's a well-known fact that sex ends in emptiness. When we are done climaxing, the void yawns wider than ever and allows us to peer for a moment into the silky black depths of the abyss. Arthur Schopenhauer knew
this. So did Pascal. And I, Zebra, a privileged member of the ill-fated community of intellectuals that inhabits the Matrix of Literature, cling to this
truth as a spider to its web and, therefore, much like the above-mentioned
figures, am not only a defender of committing one's life to aesthetic contemplation in lieu of dumbly searching for love but am also repulsed by
the notion of perpetuating the human species, which is decisively worthless.

I wrote my thoughts on this subject down in my notebook and recited
them aloud each morning to remind myself not to become disarmed by
Ludo's presence. Even so, following that first encounter, we spent a lov-
ers' weekend at the apartment. And then Monday came and Ludo stayed.
He remained at the apartment with me all week, going out only for brief
excursions to buy bread, cheese, coffee. But one night, Ludo let loose the
word *love* in relation to me while he was orgasming—whether he was
aware of his speech act or not I cannot say. The next morning, after consulting my notebook, I warned him never to use that word in my presence again. He fell silent, looked away, collapsed into himself. He dipped
a croissant rather halfheartedly into his coffee, stuffed it into his mouth,
and, with a muffled voice, said, "Who said anything about love?"

I raised my hackles.

"You did," I answered curtly. "But if it's more comfortable for you to lie
to yourself, go ahead, be my guest."

There was an awkward pause during which Ludo sat at the table pout-
ing, sniffling, pushing his glasses up the bridge of his nose, looking down
into his coffee mug. The side of him that was half man—petty, clingy,
overly concerned with the ethics of earthly conduct, stiffening when things
didn't go his way, exhibiting a sense of pride when things did (prime example: celebrating his ability to facilitate my orgasms with a triumphal grin),
and, last but not least, possessing a considerable predisposition to clut-

tered thinking that I attributed to the sum of the aforementioned parts — had taken over. I was beginning to realize that he, despite inhabiting the Pyramid of Exile, had no idea what it means to be squashed by history; ground down to the atomic level; reduced to dust; pulverized; flattened to a singular surface; rendered as thin as paper, two-dimensional; and drained of any real power while those who have only been grazed by the incendiary flares of history strut about full of themselves, their hearts pumping with fresh oxygenated blood. Not to mention history's victors, those boisterous few who ignite the flames without considering who will be broiled, who will be braised, what the gravitational pull of the leftover negative space, the nothingness, will be; a black hole that will draw more death to itself, a bottomless pit that survivors will want to leap into in order to join the dead members of their family and resuscitate the past.

I couldn't stand watching Ludo Bembo sit there offended, as if I had slighted him. I told him as much. "You have no idea what it means to be slighted!"

His lips were trembling. He looked as though he might start crying.

He said, "I went down to get us croissants, and you haven't touched a single one."

I couldn't believe it. He was offended because I hadn't eaten? I ripped off the end of a croissant and ate it. Then I asked him if he considered himself a friend of Sancho Panza, who was also always worried about funneling food down his esophagus. Ludo's jaw dropped. I ripped off another piece of the croissant and affectionately put it in his mouth.

"To each his own," I said. "But let it be known that I align myself with Don Quixote, the Knight of the Sad Countenance, for whom food is anathema because he, like me, feeds on the flesh of language."

Ludo was sitting there in his underwear, his elbows resting on the table, his shoulders hunched over, his hair disheveled, his glasses dirty, the piece of croissant I had stuck in his mouth hanging out like the severed claw of a boiled crab.

"Why don't you chew?" I insisted.

He spat the bread out.

"You are impossible," he said, before succumbing to a string of Italian mutters. I heard something about the Madonna and then the word *intrattabile*, followed by its distant cousin *inquietare* and then *mamma mia*, *mamma mia, mamma mia.* He said the word *mamma* so many times with such profound desperation and melancholy that I began to wonder if his mother, like mine, was dead.

I followed him into the kitchen. It was clear that I needed to break things down for him, that he needed me to reconstruct the story of my destruction, to pick myself up one speck of dust at a time and glue myself together in order to showcase for him the origins and terms of my modus operandi. So I shoved my tattoo in his face and told him that I — the final member of the AAA — am antilove. I also informed him that I am a body composed of various dispersed particles of dirt and that because people walk on dirt all the time I am constantly being stepped on and, thus, further pulverized. There is nothing I can do about my ill-fatedness, I informed him, except to retreat into the Matrix of Literature; there, I said, my mind can roam free and become extremely refined, a supraconsciousness.

"So you see now why I don't accept the use of the word *love?*"

A long miserable pause ensued. I assumed he was formulating an appropriate response. As it turns out, I was wrong.

"Why are you staring at me?" Ludo finally said.

"Because I am waiting for you to display curiosity."

"Curiosity? After that lecture?"

"There is such a thing as a follow-up question."

"To your declaration of antilove?"

"Yes."

"Would you like to outline the conditions under which we are allowed to relate to each other?"

"I could ask you the same thing. Would you like to impose your love on me?"

"Impose?" he huffed, and set his mug down angrily.

I couldn't believe it. The man had been drained of empathy. How was I going to drill through his dense brain?

"Let's go over this again," I said.

"Again?"

"Time is more linear than we think," I lied. "And the only way we can come to an understanding is by returning to the ground zero of our argument and reliving the whole thing over again even though during the reconstruction process we will come across minor blind spots — nothing drastic, but holes nonetheless, small deaths we will have to account for later."

He looked at me, as mute as a cow.

I decided to barrel on: "It's the job of the few who cherish a distrust of love and who are aware, as Pascal famously warned, that *faking love turns you into the lover* — or as the gentle-spirited Pessoa put it, that *love is a thought* — to make sure that the other weaker members of the human race are perpetually reminded that love is a senseless fabrication designed to disinherit us from ourselves, because once the loved one dies, one is left confused and disoriented with nowhere to go, like a rat in a maze. While you are loving someone, you are subject to false feelings of permanence, but love can't keep anyone alive; therefore, it is deceitful, impermanent. So you see, my sentimental Ludo, love is a useless emotion that accomplishes little more than putting two people on a violent collision course from which they will never recover."

I felt a chill go down my spine. My hands were shaking. I could see that being exposed without warning to the toxic fumes of my life was causing Ludo to retreat. He was growing increasingly frustrated and angry. Is he going to leave, I wondered, and never return? Another disappearance to add to the inventory?

"I've had it," he said, and stomped out of the kitchen. He was muttering, "Impossible, impossible."

I followed him down the corridor. Taüt was at my heels again.

"Why do you repeat everything twice?" I asked desperately.

He said nothing at first. Then he turned around, bore into me with his eyes, and said: "Because it is the Italian way!"

"The Bembo way?"

There was steam coming out of his ears. He got dressed in a hurry and went out on a walk without brushing his teeth or washing his face. I told myself that he would be back. A man like Ludo Bembo doesn't stay out for long if he hasn't properly groomed himself. And besides that, there was the addictive nature of the sex we'd been having, which I knew would have him back at my door in a matter of hours.

I leaned out the window at the end of the corridor and saw him marching down the gray sidewalk. He looked so stiff that I thought he was made of cardboard. I told him as much.

"Any stiffer, Ludo Bembo, and people will mistake you for a fake! Part of the 99.9 percent!"

But he didn't hear me. He had turned the corner by then. I stood at the window feeling empty. I was reeling from the startling crescendo of our fight. I looked around. I was alone again, far from everyone. I sat on the recamier and caressed the three crusty crevices. The clock struck noon. A moment later, my father, whom I had thought of less and less over the course of the week, was stirring inside me. His mustache had grown. Hair grows even after a person has died. It's innately insistent, just like the ever-mutating, multiplying self. His mustache, with its frayed broomlike ends, was dragging on the floor of my void, sweeping the abyss. He wielded his cane to tap the base of my mind, and said, *Child, take the wisdom of your ancestors one step further. Complete Pessoa's sentence. If he writes "love is a thought," then finish his verse by writing "love is a thought not worth having."* Then he retreated again into the deep dark folds of the void. In my mind's eye, I saw him sink slowly, as if he were being sucked into a pool of quicksand. His mustache floated on the surface for a moment — long, white, illuminated by a ray of light. Then it, too, disappeared into the darkness. And Taüt was nowhere to be found.

Ludo's absence lasted considerably longer than I'd expected. While I waited for his return, I paced the corridor with this or that book in hand. After an hour, I had devised a system. I went through Quim Monzó's shelves and picked up books by authors whose last names began with a *B*. This I did as a twofold tribute to Ludo Bembo, whose last initial needless to say is a *B*, and who, it appeared, was a man in the habit of saying certain key words twice; therefore, *B*, being the second letter in the alphabet, was doubly resonant for him because it complemented his linguistic tic beautifully.

At first, I consulted the authors I had chosen — Borges, Barthes, Beckett, Blanchot — recklessly, with a haphazard air. Whenever it struck me to read a sentence, I opened the book at hand to a random page and read one. I didn't pause to extract from each line whatever mystical message was embedded within its grammar. I had to make up for lost time. During the days I had spent with Ludo, I hadn't consulted the Matrix of Literature. I hadn't advanced the Grand Tour of Exile. I had betrayed the Hosseinis by allowing myself to be derailed by lust. But now that I had committed the deed, it was my duty to extract from the obscure folds of literature whatever information I could find regarding Ludo Bembo. To ask: What is his role in my miserly, ill-fated life?

I continued pacing until eventually fate, or reason, or a breeze carrying with it the sweaty scent of Nietzsche — the perfume of action — stopped me in my tracks and forced me to reconsider. I realized that my plan was in need of further geometry. It was lacking in structure.

After a moment's reflection, I concluded that I should consult a book only at the completion of the second length of the hallway, the twentieth, the two hundredth, and the two thousandth. If I wasn't consistent in my tribute to the "double," then the books would refuse to yield the information I needed in order to understand Ludo Bembo. They would become reserved, withholding, mute — frigid texts, like the ones that passive readers pick up so casually. They would no longer operate as oracles.

As soon as my approach had taken on the correct mathematical dimensions, the messages started to arrive with generosity, with pleasure, with a kind of jouissance that proved to me that the text itself desired me, that a two-way street existed between me and my chosen books, an open conduit, a clear and lucid channel of communication — proof that literature, as my father had taught me, is the only magnanimous host, the most charitable company, and evidence that despite my erotic digression I was achieving my goal of abolishing all boundaries between myself and the infinite, centerless labyrinth of mirrors that is the Matrix of Literature. After completing the hundredth length of the corridor, I paused to reflect and concluded that Ludo Bembo — despite his rude lack of understanding, his powerful ignorance — played a decisive role in advancing the Grand Tour of Exile and was therefore also influential in the advancement of my notebook, which, as a mirror and record, was in the process of carving out its own corner in the gossamer of the cosmos.

But what Ludo Bembo would come to symbolize, I hadn't the faintest idea. For now, though, I was comforted by the notion that he would be back and that we would annihilate each other through hot passion once more. Comforted? I considered this and again felt suspicion raise its wary head. I felt my void swell. It was unbearably painful. My moods were cycling. To distract myself, I continued to pace the corridor. I wanted to arrive at two hundred so I could consult the oracle of literature once more.

The two-hundredth length afforded the following gift from Beckett, that lone wolf of language: *What remains of all that misery?* As I read Beckett's words out loud, Taüt appeared at my heels. The bird paced with me like a loyal dog the rest of the way. I had to slow down significantly in order for the little beast to keep up.

The consultation after the two-hundred-twentieth length revealed Borges, whose mind is a mirror image of the matrix itself: *Fate is partial to repetitions, variations, symmetries.* My suspicion that Ludo would return was consolidated. At the two-hundred-twenty-second length, weak from exhaustion, I let my gaze fall on the following quote by Barthes, playful antisystematizer: *Mad I cannot be, sane I do not deign to be, neurotic I am.*

Daylight was waning. The vast darkness of night was approaching. I looked down at the ground. The bird, I noticed, was looking more haggard than ever. I wondered if he had absorbed my father. If somehow the fumes of my father's death had seeped out of my pores and gone into the bird. I felt as if my lungs were filling with water. I collapsed on the red recamier. I needed to cry. No. *Cry* was too mild a word. I needed to sob. I needed to wail. But I couldn't. My eyes burned from the dry sting of arid tears. Eventually, I slept. I awoke right before dawn, those early hours when the light is soft and silver and tinged with a faint yellow by the emerging sun. There was a knock on the door. It was Ludo Bembo. The water drained out of my lungs. I could breathe again. I stared at that curly head of his through the keyhole. He was holding a stack of books in his hand. For a moment, hopeful, I thought he had gone out to study, to open himself up through reading to the redundant nature of the universe. But then I suddenly remembered the Tentacle of Ice, that vampire woman, and felt myself clam up with distaste. I wondered if he had gone to sleep with her in order to lighten his load, discharge himself of any built-up sexual tensions, and if the books were just a cover for the time he had spent with her. I knocked back to let him know I was on the other side of the door.

"So you're there," he said tenderly and somewhat desperately.

"Were you with the Tentacle of Ice?" I inquired with rehearsed detachment.

"Who?" he whined.

A liar and a bore.

"That icy lady with the long curls and the sexy shoes you were kissing at the market."

"You saw that?"

"You know I saw that. This is the second time I've caught you lying to yourself. In a short span of time, too."

We exchanged all this through the thick wooden door. Our voices were muffled, distant. "I was at the library," he exclaimed. "Then I saw my friend Fausta. She's a rare-book dealer."

"Fausta, as in the female version of Faust, related to Goethe?" I asked with intrigue.

"You can look at it that way if you want," he murmured into the wood.

He begged me to open the door. Through the keyhole, I could see contempt in his eyes but also foreboding, helplessness, fatigue — a man reeling from sexual withdrawal. I told him I was reluctant. I told him that I had perceived a few things in his absence. For one, that he was a man with a dual nature. In other words, that there were two versions of himself encapsulated within a single body, but that rather than acknowledging his multiple selves, as I had, he was forcing one self to hide self-consciously within the other because he refused to be at ease with the contradictions of his character. This, I warned him, would be his greatest downfall. This refusal to be multiple. If he insisted on switching masks, from rigid to tender, cold to passionate, he would forever give the false impression of being a fake even though he was one of my own, an ill-fated man sorrowfully living out his days in exile. Why else would he be attracted to me? After that, I told him it was clear he had some healing to do. The ill-fated, I lectured him, gain their power by being subtle, bold, detached, messy; in other words, by being many things at once. I assured him that even though he had a long way to go before he could accept his own fragmentation I was sure he would get there through diligence and hard work. I told him I would be willing to help him along. All of this came out of my mouth so naturally, and with such warmth, that I could see the positive effects it had on him. He was listening attentively on the other side of the door. He had his ear pressed up against the seam, and he kept nodding. I could see his curls bouncing up and down. I warned him to step away; I was about to open up.

We collapsed into each other almost immediately. It was the best sex we'd had yet. I experienced, simultaneous with his, a long sweet spasm that took me beyond the limits of my body and then brought me back again. When he had finished, he muttered something through his lingering ecstasy.

"God," he said. "Oh God, that was so good."

I had no choice but to issue a second warning. I made sure to be gentle. I said the bare minimum. I quoted Stendhal through Nietzsche.

"God's only excuse is that he does not exist."

"It's just a figure of speech," he said.

Over the next few weeks, Ludo came over with increasing frequency and always stayed the night. He often cancelled his classes or sent someone — I don't know who — to cover his lectures for him. Most likely the Tentacle of Ice. Judging from the brief but telling exchange I had witnessed between them at the market, she was desperate for his attention. After all, she had ornamented herself as if she were a Christmas tree. It seemed to me she was perfectly capable of driving sixty miles to stand before his pale-faced students and lecture on the etymology of words in order to ingratiate herself with him, Ludo Bembo, singular man whose head is, according to my diagnostics, subdivided into containers designed to avoid all manner of cross-contamination between thoughts, feelings, impulses; a man in possession of terrifying amounts of self-control; a man who, paradoxical to his inherent interest in literature, invests a great deal of his psychic energy in negating the void. A man like Ildefons Cerdà.

But still, I thought to myself, he was drawn to me in order to become multiple and to pasture, as the ill-fated do, on contradiction, pessimism, pain. He was drawn to someone who, like him, had gone through the ringer of exile. One of the many who munch on manure, where the earth's darkest humors lie; who are loud, messy, content to live in contradiction, both alive and dead, composed of a thousand shimmering fragments and as slender as a ghost at the same time. Those who haunt their hunters.

So, under the sign of contradiction, subject to the push and pull of the rational and the erratic, Ludo Bembo and I continued our amorous routine. I became accustomed to his habits. He stirred sugar into his coffee for a standard five minutes until all the granules had dissolved. He chased his meals with fine liquor. Grappa. Ratafia. Limoncello. Cognac if he was in a nostalgic mood. He shaved daily. He set his hair, one curl at a time. He ironed his clothes. He scrubbed behind his ears. He smoked his pipe after sex, like a gentleman of the Old World. He knew how to light and stoke a fire. He knew how to make refined pastries. And on top of all this, he had a habit of moving his penis from one thigh to the other after sex. This balancing act lasted for a few minutes. One night, while we were lying in bed, I asked him to explain his motivations. Unlike Ludo, who believed we could ride the currents of our affair without obstacle into the future, I felt sporadically suffocated by his presence. If I didn't have the necessary room for my thoughts to roam around in the Matrix of Literature (something I could not exercise in his presence), those very thoughts, which were wretched and soaked through and through with the fumes of death that plagued my void, threatened to poison me from the inside out. I needed to open a valve and let the stench out. So one night I confronted him. I provoked him into giving me space.

"Why do you shift your penis from thigh to thigh?" I asked.

"Because I believe in the Renaissance ideal," he retorted. He went on to tell me that the body should always be in equilibrium, the right side a mirror image of the left — the head, shoulders, waist, and hips always in proportion. "If I tucked my penis only to the left, like most ignorant men do," he said in a whimsical tone, "my right side would be deprived of its presence."

I listened attentively. It was clear he was mocking me. I wouldn't stand for it.

"I have good news and bad news," I said, after a loaded pause. "Which do you want to hear first?"

"Good news?" he said with an uncertain air. He pushed his glasses up the bridge of his nose and sniffled.

"You have a benevolent and tender mouth" — at this, he licked his lips and smiled — "and, to a certain extent, an unruffled spirit."

He leaned in and kissed me. His mouth was definitely tender.

"And the bad?"

"The bad news," I delivered nonchalantly, "is that you lack imagination; your mind is as stiff as a stick. There is no need to make up anecdotes with cerebral undertones just to please me. I would prefer it if you were forthcoming about your motives regarding the placement of your penis, which are surely more limited than the explanation you offered implies, an explanation I refuse to fall for because, as you very well know, Dr. Bembo"— I had never referred to him as Dr. Bembo before, so I had no choice but to raise my voice a notch —"people don't acquire a sense of the absurd overnight. If they did, you and I would experience more harmony."

I could hear his anxious breathing. He sounded like a dog hyperventilating.

"Unless they are tortured and you, Dr. Bembo, have spent the night having sex, not suffering!"

He pulled away from me, crossed his arms, and looked up at the ceiling. He was sulking. There it was, that long muzzle, his signature pout. His posture was ungainly, droopy headed, sheepish. He refused to look at me.

"Silence is a weapon of mass destruction," I said.

"Mass? There's only one of you," he spewed angrily.

"Only one of me!" I huffed, sitting upright. It was clear he didn't know me at all. "What about my father, and the residue of my mother contained by my father, all of which I carry within me?"

His face dropped. It was longer than ever. It looked as elastic as dough. His eyes were tearing up.

"Nothing I say will ever please you!" he whined childishly.

I let out a dismissive grunt and almost immediately his face contracted; it hardened again. He clenched his jaw. He looked as stiff as a mummy. I took in a deep breath. I told myself to stay as fresh as lettuce, as calm as a sailboat on a smooth lake. In this way, I found my composure.

I coaxed: "Ludo Bembo, allow me to explain." I could no longer remember what the original trigger of our argument had been, but I proceeded nonetheless. "Your realism and cold logic, your pedantry, need reinventing." The mummy turned its neck and looked at me with the fixed round pupils of an assassin. "But even more urgently," I continued, despite his horrifying gaze, "I suggest you edit your approach to matters of love because it's becoming difficult to understand how, despite my gentle reminders that *love is a deadly poison*, you remain stubbornly prone to sentimentality and clinginess." I suddenly remembered the origin of our conflict, his false mimicry, which greatly facilitated the delivery of a final blow: "To pretending we are like-minded!"

The mummy flew into a rage. He broke out of his cast, regained mobility, got up, dressed. "Not this again!" he yelled. With a defiant gaze, he marched out of the bedroom. Ribbons of unraveled linen dragged on the floor. I followed him out to the foyer.

"I'll be back!" he threatened, before slamming the front door.

I considered the closed door solemnly. I was alone again and could devote myself to the miserly progression of my thoughts. I called out for the bird. Nothing happened. Taüt had disappeared again and with him my only hope of sharing a convivial moment. I was alone among Quim Monzó's mute objects. I looked around. Each time I did this, it was as if I were seeing the apartment anew. I noticed a bronze statue of a bull that was tucked behind a stack of dusty books in a neglected corner of the foyer. The bull was preparing to charge: nostrils flared, head nobly bowed, horns alerting the heavens to the sacrifice ahead. Man, animal, insect, I concluded: We all know the ecstasy and perturbation involved in gorging and being gorged.

I scanned the room in the opposite direction. On the book shelves lining the corridor, I caught sight of three miniature reproductions of a toilet bowl. A quick inspection revealed that one of the bowls was filled with small turds of poop, the other with urine, the last with vomit. Together, I thought, the bowls and the bull indicated that life is hardly worth enduring on the one hand, and on the other, that Quim Monzó's apartment was asking for an inspection. I made a note to take inventory of his disparate collection of Dadaist objects in order to extract once and for all from this humble abode everything I was destined to extract. I had come to believe that each of Quim Monzó's objects was triggering an insight I was meant to record, calling up something old and stale within me that I, in loving memory of my mother and father and their mothers and fathers, whose asses were gorged by the horns of history and who were left with no sustenance but their own bodily fluids, had to transcribe in my notebook.

I walked over to the recamier and lay down. I caressed the three cigarette burns. I thought of myself, of the parts of me that are dead, like my mother long dead and my father, newly so. I cried a little. A few meager tears pooled in my eyes. There was a pressure in my chest, as if a paperweight had been laid on my heart, pinning it down against the elements. I filled each crevasse in the recamier with a little water. This is how lakes are formed, with the tears of the world. I thought of Lake Urmia and its dead waterfowl. I thought of Mohammad Reza Shah Pahlavi, self-proclaimed King of Kings, of his wife draped over a velvet fainting chair, wrapped in a silk robe, clad in jewels. I said: "Decadence, the fraternal twin of decay." I heard my father clapping in my void. But just as quickly as he appeared, he was gone.

With an air of despondency, I thought on. Not even Ludo Bembo, I considered inwardly, who thrusts his member into me with fiery passion, who drinks from my vagina as if it were a well of water, and from whose lips the word *love* leaps as easily as frogs from a pond, can endure the consequences of my company. An ill-fated who laughs with the hysteria of unresolved pain. I felt a chill go through the negative space where my father had been. I felt my energy drain. I thought: I am ugly, unlovable, worthless, inadequate. No one has ears large enough or patient enough to listen to an ill-omened person tell the story of their survival, of what it means to be crushed at the bottom of the Pyramid of Exile. I would have to bear the weight of my past alone.

This earth, stuffed to the brim with blood and corpses and hay, is like a self-cleaning oven. The buried don't remain buried for long. They turn into flowers, fertilize our food. They nurture us even as we are haunted by them. In other words, what goes up must come down, and what goes down will eventually reemerge and begin its upward climb once more.

It wasn't long before I was wishing Ludo Bembo would return or that Taüt would reappear. There was no use waiting for them draped on the recamier. As the deaf masses of the supposed New World say, I was feeling blue.

I tried to get over it. I thought to myself, it's time for another Pilgrimage of Exile. If you're feeling blue in Barcelona, what could be better than to go to the Picasso Museum and witness the gradual reduction of the chromatic range of that genius's paintings, from vivid yellows, greens, and reds to the saddest of blues in his aptly named Blue Period? With the resolve of a bull, I got dressed, washed my face, and charged through the door. I received a signal from the Matrix of Literature: *He who seeks to approach his own buried past must conduct himself like a man digging.* Ah, Walter Benjamin, again reminding me of my mission. I walked through the city with a singular intention: to investigate the pain of my past by metabolizing art and architecture. To gaze at the city would not take matters far enough; I had to drill into its most symbolic elements. I had to digest its parts. I named the walk the Pilgrimage of Remorseless Excavation and went on my way.

I walked through the gray maze of gas lamps, gnarled stone, and menacing gargoyles in the Gothic Quarter, and continued east. It was November. The sky was pale blue and garnished with patches of ashen clouds. In the distance, a tepid sun was shining, too weak to cut through the misty sea breeze sweeping the streets. There was a mild autumn storm brewing. The kind that would soon have the sea spitting rotten logs and purple jellyfish onto the city's wet golden coast.

I passed the row of soot-covered buildings near the Jaume I metro stop on Via Laietana. I felt something moving around in my gut. My father. I remembered. During our stay in Barcelona, whenever we walked along Via Laietana, he would stop to lift the tips of his mustache and spit on the old police headquarters where General Franco had ordered one man after another to come in for interrogations, likely leaving my fellow ill-omened peers on the roof to wet themselves like leeches in the rain. I cursed that foolish mime of Hitler and their mutual thirst for blood. "Bah!" I declared to the building. "General Franco, even your mustache was a coward's mustache! You couldn't grow enough hair to reach the ends of your putrid mouth." This was enough to settle my stomach, to please my father.

I turned onto a crooked arterial alley and immediately the light was sucked out of the street. I had reached the narrow cobbled streets of La Ribera, the old merchant quarter. Inside those labyrinthine streets, the world seemed to have been reduced to a miniature cardboard stage. I wanted to hold the neighborhood in the palm of my hand. I wanted to turn it around like a Rubik's Cube.

I arrived at a small opening in the street. I could see the sky again. It looked wounded; it was tinged with purple and the clouds were the color of lead. I was standing in front of Santa Maria del Mar. I peeled open the church's carved wooden doors and ventured into the darkness within.

There was something about the church that reminded me of Ludo. The exterior was ornamented with statues and floral motifs, tender, dignified, carefully groomed. But inside, a dark, cold, austere silence engulfed me.

The interior, with the exception of a few stained glass windows, was spare and somber. Man and building, I decided — each had a second face: rigid one moment and poetic, even sentimental, the next.

I paced around the nave, breathing in the heavily incensed air. I avoided looking at the image of Christ pinned to the cross. If I did, my father would wage war from inside me. He would lash out against my bowels. He would say, addressing himself to the man's pitifully hanging head, "Living is a sacrifice. Get over it!"

Instead, I proceeded systematically with my thoughts. I kept my eyes on the ground. The church and Ludo Bembo, I resolved as I admired the skulls carved into the tombs underfoot, were doppelgängers. Yes, indeed. There was no denying it: Ludo was the human equivalent of a medieval Catalan building — his external self freely gave out tender, lyrical gestures while inside he hid a severe, rational, withholding second self. In other words, Ludo Bembo, I concluded, digging my heels into the dirt and the dust, is a wounded person who keeps his wound a secret even from himself. The fastest way to become your own worst enemy. I made a mental note to tell him as much.

"A wound," I recited in advance, "is meant to be looked at, examined. Otherwise, Ludo Bembo, it will fester, wreak havoc, strip the walls of your stomach as if it were acid. Ask any doctor, no matter how mediocre. He will tell you the same."

There was a tour guide leaning against the cold, damp stone walls of the nave. He nodded along in agreement. He was watching over a group of pale, plump Russians who were whispering things to one another near the altar and taking pictures. I ignored him.

By the time I walked into the Picasso Museum's ample courtyard, another fact had become clear: Unlike Ludo, I was a Gaudí — a disruptive, colorful mosaic composed of shattered bits of tile and glass. A whole that doesn't correspond to the sum of its parts. If I wasn't transcendent, I would be vain. With this thought in mind, I, a collage in my own right, entered the museum.

I went about my business. I stood before this or that painting. I walked into the galleries featuring Picasso's Blue Period. I needed to look at something more blue than blue or else I would start crying. I could feel the water level rising in my lungs again. I looked at several paintings of Barcelona's rooftops. But Barcelona's rooftops, I reasoned, are beige, red, orange, ochre. Picasso, who was from Málaga, painted Barcelona's mood at dusk in his studio in Paris, where he lived during his famous Blue Period; which is to say, he was painting Barcelona at a double remove. Even a fool knows that a place is not the same thing as its interpretation through the falsifying prisms of memory, but this alone, I concluded, does not explain Picasso's so-called Blue Period. I was sure these rooftop paintings weren't merely a rendition of Barcelona as he recalled it — apparently intimate, seductive, full of melancholia and longing, and yet confidently resolved — but rather a result of an emotional deficiency he later corrected. The sweetest of thoughts, I reflected, arrive like the wind on the heels of doves.

Why had Picasso's affect flattened? Why had he suddenly become a monochromatic man? Because he wasn't able, at first, to navigate the multiple selves he had acquired by retreating first from Málaga to Barcelona and then from Franco's oppressive Spain to an electric Paris. Take one look at the bold, broad, colorful lines of Picasso's reproductions of Velázquez's *Las Meninas*, at his depiction of the Infanta Maria Theresa, with her disproportionately large and heavily distorted face — that dwarf forebear of the cold-blooded Bourbon, Philip V, who sacked the Catalans during the terrible War of Spanish Succession, paving the way for General Franco's systematic suffocation of what was left of them — take one look at the series' geometrical fragmentation, at the crooked forms that fold over themselves, at the cruel hooks that hang from the ceiling in the painting's foreground, at the weblike rendition of Velázquez's sober meditation on the vanishing point — which is just another word for the infinite nature of the space-time continuum famously referred to by Nietzsche as the eternal return — and my argument regarding Picasso's progression as a man and an artist quickly gains ground: He had to learn to hold the wound of multiplicity, of fragmentation, the wobbly curvature that Gaudí had mastered so early due to his prolonged solitude, his misanthropy, and his understanding of the hostile beauty of nature. But! But! But! I rocked back and forth on my feet with excitement. Picasso wasn't able to open himself up to the entropy of pluralism until he was pushed over the edge by that childish monster General Franco. His reproductions of *Las Meninas* are from after the Civil War. His Blue Period from before. Case in point.

Suddenly, for reasons I couldn't understand, I wasn't feeling well. I had a mild but distinct vertigo. My father was whispering something from inside my cavernous void. His voice was thinner than ever. I stuck my fingers in my ears to block out the sound of the other museumgoers. I turned toward my inner ear. In a wispy voice, my father said: "*Ecce Homo, Ecce Homo.*" He was making a request. *Ecce Homo*, the most reproduced painting in history and the title of one of Nietzsche's greatest works, not to mention the opening words of the first Hosseini Commandment! I worked my way back through the galleries to Picasso's *Ecce Homo*. The bald, short, beer-bellied Picasso had portrayed himself at the center, in the place of Christ, and had surrounded his figure with people from the art world and several hairy, voluptuous, coquettish women who were parting their labia with their hands as if their folds were theater curtains. My father laughed. He beat his cane on the ground of my void several times. He caressed his mustache with affection. His eyes rolled in their sockets. I had to walk away just to calm him down.

I hadn't made it far when I remembered something that stopped me in my tracks. My father had paused near a pile of stones in that ashen no-man's-land to tell me: "Child, every event has a precedent. Look here at Picasso's *The Dream and Lie of Franco.*" I remembered our country's ashes were being scattered by the wind all around us. I remembered there was a frigid bite to the wind and the sky was black and low. I remembered how weak I felt, how much my feet hurt. My father had tried to carry me on his back through the most difficult passages, but he, too, was weary from our long march. He pulled out a miniature reproduction of Picasso's paintings from our suitcase, which he had dragged along with us. His hands were cracked and his fingers were trembling. "Picasso's famous *Guernica* has its origin in these postcard-size drawings. In order to understand the future, you must blow yourself backward into the past. Then you will finally come to know history's evil nature: that the past and the future are a mirror image of each other and that the present is history itself." He had spread the drawings across the jagged rocks. I leaned over to look at them under the feeble light of the moon. I saw an image of Franco being gored by a bull. Another of Franco with a large penis. Yet another of Franco on a pig and wielding a spear. Finally, Franco feeding on a rotting horse. I read Picasso's words written beneath the images: *evil-omened polyp.* "Take these images in," my father ordered, "so you will know the past of where we are headed." It was almost dawn. We could barely carry on. We hadn't eaten in days. We huddled together against the rocks in the brutal cold and waited for the approaching daylight to wane.

I walked out of the museum in tears. The floodgates had opened. I sat on the staircase leading down to the internal courtyard. There were palms growing in terra-cotta vases. The sky was darker, the air colder. A security guard walked up to me. He had blue eyes and a thin face, a pronounced jaw and blackened teeth that were broken and had sharp reptilian edges.

"What's wrong?" he asked in Catalan. He sat next to me. There was a knowing kindness in his voice. He was a guardian of art.

I told him the truth. "I'm crying because of Franco's evil and pompous penis and the many ways in which it sabotaged, with its dimpled little head, an entire nation of people."

The security guard laughed a painful laugh. He said, "You don't have hair on your tongue!"

"It's true," I confirmed. "I'm a straight shooter."

I explained to him a very complicated thing, a thing not everyone would have the capacity to grasp. I told him that I speak directly because in order to stay alive I must always work to make up for the time I've lost due to the fact that, as an ill-fated citizen of this negligible world, I am subjected to being constantly attacked by history and that I have been trained by my literary-minded ancestors to combat the dulling effects of the psychic and emotional wounds caused by these violent attacks with verbal efficiency. Language is my sword, I told him. I may be gored by history, but I hack away at its horns with the ethereal sword of literature. I don't win. But I'm able to keep myself at ground zero. I survive in order to leave testimony.

"I understand better than I can express," he said. "We Catalans respect directness. We are not like the gold-loving yet provincial Spanish who weave a web so tangled that even the Argentines, who live near the South Pole, thousands of kilometers from here, have gotten tangled in it."

He removed a silk handkerchief adorned with the Catalan flag of independence from his pocket. He offered it to me to wipe my tears. I dabbed my face with those four vertical stripes of blood.

I told him that where I come from, when we are shocked by something someone says, we register our surprise by saying, *I grew hairs on my tongue.*

Then I said: "See, my friend, the world is so much more interconnected than we are willing to admit. If someone without hair on their tongue from your home speaks to someone from mine, they immediately grow hairs on theirs!"

We both laughed a great deal at this. Then I walked home again, having safely swallowed my tears. Oh, the guard of art and I, I thought to myself, *we are like fingernail and flesh,* an expression my father and I had adopted when we were in Catalonia long ago and that I chose to adopt again now.

In order to sink deeper into the past, in order to drill into my forgetfulness so that my buried memories could resurface, I walked to Parc de la Ciutadella. I had walked there many times with my father. It was a walk of victory. The Catalans had thrown down the fort Philip V had built during the War of Spanish Secession. Philip V had launched cannons against the Catalans, aiming with his rectal hole. He had leveled the neighborhood of El Born, razed it to the ground, and driven its inhabitants under its fallen stones like ants and cockroaches in a gelid draft. Centuries later, the Catalans had reclaimed the space and turned it into a magnificent garden — Parc de la Ciutadella — a field of sensorial pleasure. I sat on a bench. I looked around. I contemplated. To attain joie de vivre, I concluded, one has to dig through the palimpsest of grief; there is no way around it. I looked up from the shady paths hugging the palm trees and magnolias, and saw the silhouette of the Temple Expiatori del Sagrat Cor sitting on the summit of Tibidabo in the distance. The sky was the color of ink, with indigo threads running through it. Beneath that sky, Tibidabo looked as soft and plush as a crib. I got up and walked to the Cascada, with its monumental waterfall and pond. A few geese were languidly drifting across the pond's mint-colored waters. When they approached the waterfall, they circled around with knowing eyes and came back again, taking in a 360-degree view of their surroundings. It occurred to me as I watched them that they had it better than anyone. They were always surveying their space, keeping an eye on things. It was clear I had to do the same. I had to embark on a Pilgrimage of Perspective.

I realized if I traveled to the city's highest vantage points — Montjuïc, Tibidabo, the Christopher Columbus monument, Park Güell, this or that rooftop — I could, in fact, turn Barcelona around in the palm of my hand as if it were a Rubik's Cube. I walked back to the port and rode the last cable car up Montjuïc. From there, I looked at the city's rooftops, at the wretched statue of Christopher Columbus, at the spires of the cathedral, at the darkening glass of the cone of Torre Agbar, at Tibidabo and the angled Sagrat Cor facing out at the sea. Further west, there were the hills of Montseny that looked like sculpted black mist. I had already gone up to Park Güell. The only other peak I could make it to before the day's end was an unpleasant one, to say the least. I had to face the devil himself. No. Worse. I had to go up his rear end.

Why had I come to such a fecund conclusion? Because the view had allowed me to gain insight into the fact that the New and the Old Worlds formed a single unbroken fabric stitched together willy-nilly by the bloodstained hands of white imperialists. After all, Christopher Columbus had returned to the Port of Barcelona after traveling the high seas to what, from his paltry point of view, was the "unknown." So, I concluded, it is my duty to train my nose to detect an approaching assailant from as far away as the back of the beyond by sniffing the stench of Christopher Columbus's rear end. I — a living dead — whose heart had been flattened into a sheet of paper due to excess grief, a sheet that had turned as brittle as ice through overexposure to the biting draft of history, needed all the lead time I could get. I needed all the advantage I could cultivate.

I walked down the flank of Montjuïc and over to the port. I went inside the Christopher Columbus monument, paid four euros — money well spent — and rode the elevator to the top. I stood in the round, anus-shaped room, and looked out at the pudgy-faced explorer's crooked finger, which was supposedly pointing at the so-called New World. By the time I turned around to look at the city, night had fallen. It was too dark. Nothing more could be seen. It was as if the light had permanently gone out of the universe. It had been beaten back by the hand of violence.

As I took the elevator back down, I remembered my father's words. "Child," he had said to me. "You must mourn your mother's death through literature. If we, the ill-fated, begin to cry, we risk drowning in our own tears. What will we have achieved then? Life is bitter, time remorseless, and people remain civilized only so long as their own needs aren't threatened. Not a second longer. They will suck the marrow out of your bones if you let them." I remembered, too, that at the sound of those words my small body had ached with the sting of hollowness. I felt the needle of betrayal prick at my void. As a remedy, I whispered the great poet Pitarra's words, which were later repeated by the novelist Roig, both of whom my father had translated and transcribed. I said: *"Al fossar de les moreres no s'hi enterra cap traïdor!"* There are no traitors buried in the Grave of the Mulberries! On September 11, 1989, the year we had arrived in Barcelona, Pitarra's quote had been inscribed into a concave metal memorial in an empty square in La Ribera. At the top of the slender, curved memorial, a single flame burns night and day in honor of the Catalan heroes who fell on September 11, 1714, when Barcelona was besieged during the War of Spanish Succession. I thought of other September elevenths, of the thread of violence that connects us all: September 11, 1697 (the ruthless Battle of Zenta, which precipitated the collapse of the Ottoman Empire); September 11, 1973 (the dark date of the U.S.-backed Chilean coup d'état, which led to the rise of the bloody dictator Pinochet — at that, I saluted Morales); and, finally, September 11, 2001 (the al-Qaeda attack on the United States, which gave the squint-eyed, red-faced Bush an opening to launch another reckless war in the greater region of my ill-fated birth, one more in a string of inconclusive wars that barrel on with no end in sight). Every year on September 11, so many parts of the world are in mourning, proof of the interconnected fabric of being, which, as the Hosseinis well know, is fast brought into relief through the violence that plagues our pitiful species. By the time I was done recounting all those infamous dates, I was nearly in tears. I tilted my head back and reabsorbed those brackish waters. Have my organs eroded? I wondered. The elevator doors opened. I exited the monument, and before I knew it, I was immersed in the city again, walking its streets with no perspective whatsoever.

A few days later, Ludo Bembo returned. When he asked me what I had been up to, I told him, without an ounce of resentment, that I had spent my days reading, walking, transcribing my father's transcriptions, filling the pages of my notebook with the blood of literature, and then convalescing, sometimes alone, and sometimes in the company of that groggy, volatile bird, Taüt. I also told him that I had tried to get in touch with Quim Monzó, which was only half true. I had made an unresolved attempt at tracking the man down. To what end, I don't know. I suppose I had a vague feeling that my time in his stuffed dwelling was running out, that things were coming to a head.

I had unearthed what I had come to unearth in Barcelona. After all, by mourning my father's death, I had discovered the residue of my mother. I had used my consciousness to unreel the yarn of time. This experience signaled to me that the void and its characteristic emptiness had been there all along — a latent condition — which had, upon my parents' deaths, suddenly become manifest. So I had sunk as deep as I could into the portion of the void of exile that corresponded to Barcelona, the City of Bombs, the Rose of Fire. Where, I wondered, as I looked Ludo up and down, was I going to go next?

"That's excellent news," Ludo said with a distracted air. He was sitting across from me, drumming his fingers on the dining table. What part of what I had shared was excellent? I wondered, scrutinizing him up and down. There was something different about him. He was leaning back in his chair very casually. He looked older, more self-possessed, consolidated in a way I hadn't seen before. He was wearing a short-sleeve button-down shirt beneath his cardigan. I could see the crease of the sleeve under the wool every time he flexed his arms. Until then, he had always worn full-length sleeves. Anything else he considered improper. This sudden change was a red flag. No doubt about it. And, in fact, there was not just one but two red flags: to begin with, his typically rigid and outmoded choice in fashion and, to end with, the fact that he had suddenly broken that very same dress code. I moved from the dining-room table to the recamier to get a better look at him. I took note of the fact that he had zoned out halfway through my answer and of the carefree body language he had adopted — clear signs that he was, and continued to be, a compartmentalized man, a man whose head had been subdivided into casket-size boxes. In fact, I thought, intellectually speaking, he had regressed. A man living in exile, but who is afraid to walk to the edge of the abyss and peer into it, runs the risk of playing into the hand of the imperialists and the colonizers because he is cut off from his wounds and his ill-fated peers. How can a man like that be trusted? But, perhaps, I considered, that is not it. Perhaps, though it might not have appeared this way at first glance, his mannerisms may very well have been subconsciously designed to protect him from acknowledging the inherent pitfalls of our dynamic, the fight that had caused him to storm out of the apartment like a disheveled mummy. This denial, I considered, feeling yanked around by my thoughts, was productive in its own way because it allowed us to continue servicing our respective crotches. As it turned out, my suspicion of his foul nature was muddled by my desire for the warmth of his embrace, the curve of his penis. I stood there staring at him, confused by my mind's chaotic clutter.

"Why are you looking at me like that?" Ludo asked, brushing a few stray curls out of his face.

"Like what?" I posed, leaning back into the recamier and petting the three famous crevices, digging my fingers into the charred holes.

"Like what? You're sitting all the way across the room and staring at me squint-eyed!"

Was this his way of making peace after our fight? If he was going to appear and disappear at random, throwing salt into the Hosseini-shaped wounds carved in my heart by my ancestors' deaths, then I had no choice but to push him away. Finally, I thought, a burst of clarity.

"Squint-eyed? This is nothing," I said. "Boy, do I have a story for you! You should have seen the woman I saw at the post office the other day. She was incredibly short and fat. Actually, scratch that. She was rotund — that's a better word — so much so that her arms were floating laterally because there was a mass of flesh holding them up. And she had a tiny pink purse that she had managed to hook onto her arm; it stuck to her as if it had been glued. When her number was called, she slipped off the waiting room chair and rolled to the window. She was like a wheel that had been fixed with a purse!"

"What does that have to do with anything?" he pressed.

"You don't think it's funny?" I asked.

"It is, but I don't see the connection."

"Laugh and I'll tell you."

He forced himself to laugh. A weak chitter emerged from his lips. I'd been hoping for something more committed, but I let it go.

"The connection," I declared, employing a diplomatic tone, "is that those are both examples of bodies in distress: I'm squint-eyed; the lady at the post office is rotund."

He seemed pleased enough with my answer. Or fed up and ready to change the subject. I couldn't tell. When he asked me what I had been doing at the post office, I told him I was weighing my notebook. He didn't show any interest. It had become impossible to get a read on him.

As they famously say, delivery is key; there is no use laying facts at an opponent's feet as if they deserved the red-carpet treatment. Ludo Bembo certainly didn't. Not after disappearing on me only to reappear without explanation days later. And who knows what he'd been doing in between. Lecturing at the university in Girona or screwing the Tentacle of Ice.

Sooner or later, I reasoned, an opportunity will come along that will allow me to employ the information I've gathered against him — the mental notes I'd been taking, the conclusions I'd come to during my walk — to my greatest advantage. I wouldn't want to waste all the thinking I had done. Given the enormous sums of stupidity that afflict humankind, no one can deny that thinking is meant to be treated like a rare precious stone, guarded, pampered, secured in a vault. To be used with maximum discretion.

One other thing was clear: Ludo Bembo was no black-toothed, blue-eyed, skeletal art guard who had been through the ringer and had acquired, as a result of his extreme suffering, both empathy and a sense of humor. He was a Bembo who had defected, breaking away from his ancestors, whose sweat and tears are still watering the fertile trenches of literature. He was a man who pretended to be working in the service of the Matrix of Literature but was nothing more than an amateur. Why had fate brought us together? Because, I suddenly decided, it was my job to get him back in line.

I got up, walked across the room, and gave him a kiss on the lips. This was designed to disarm him. He grabbed my arm and pulled me onto his lap. We had sex then and there.

Halfway through, he said, "I like it when you ride my dick like that."

I rode him harder. At some point, I have no idea why, I felt myself fuse with Don Quixote. I was riding Rocinante — that meek, skeletal horse of his — across the Castilian plains. I saw giant windmills in the distance. The blades were cutting the air the way history had chopped up my ancestors. I felt a fierce need to attack those windmills.

"Faster, Rocinante!" I cried out.

This energized Ludo. He cupped my ass and lifted me up and down as fast as he could. As soon as we were done, he asked: "Are you saying I need to gain weight?"

"No," I said, slightly out of breath.

"Then why did you call me Rocinante? That horse was all bones!"

"Never mind," I said. "Don't worry about it."

Ludo leaned his head onto my shoulder. I could feel his moist breath on my neck. I patted him on the head. I said: "You've made progress. You've acknowledged that life is less truthful than literature."

He tried to say something, but I pressed his head against my chest and put my hand over his mouth to muffle the noises. Silly fool. He thought I was teasing him, so he playfully bit my finger.

After that, Ludo and I proceeded in relative peace. One could even say, as the Flauberts and Prousts of the world would, that we spent days of trust, of joy, of profound companionship. Days without a cloud in sight. We had sex. We laughed over Quim Monzó's assortment of trinkets. We teased the bird by hiding from him every time he made an appearance. Ludo cooked. I ate my heart out. I stuffed my void with his food.

Friday came and Ludo decided that we needed to get some air. A weekend in the great outdoors would give me a chance to ventilate my thoughts, a chance, he said, to build intimacy, to take my parents for a walk. I said nothing. I was in no mood to discuss my parents. Ever since my visit to the museum, my father had been less and less present. His absence — his manifest emptiness — was less felt. He wasn't pressing his face against my void as often as he had been, and each time he did, he seemed slightly more decomposed than the last: His nails had begun to fall; his mustache, though longer, was thinning; his muscles and tissues were degenerating, leaving his dry skin clinging to his bones. He was in the process of disappearing. Ludo's presence seemed to accelerate my father's decay. I wondered if he was punishing me. I wondered if I hadn't looked at *Ecce Homo* long enough when he'd asked me to. So I agreed to go with Ludo on a long drive up the coast. I told him that I was only motivated to do so because the brackish air of the sea would do my father some good. I could tell he had taken offense at that, but he said nothing. He swallowed his hurt feelings as if they were a pill.

We drove up the rugged winding hills of the Costa Brava all weekend.

Once we were out of the city, the road curved through mountains densely packed with pine, cork trees, aloe, cacti, eucalyptus. Near the French border, the wild jagged coastline gave way to the harsh mountainous regions of the Parc Natural del Cap de Creus, Dalí's stomping ground. We arrived just before sundown and went up through the park all the way to the lighthouse. A soft beam of light was slowly circumnavigating the surrounding waters of the Mediterranean. Underfoot, the terrain was sharp, beige, black; full of holes, slits, craters. It looked like it had been sliced and hammered. We sat inside a rock that had been hollowed out by the waves. It was like a hammock made of stone. It was December. The winter sun was halfway down the sky. In the restaurant near the lighthouse, families were sitting down to order fresh fish, squid, octopus, sea urchins.

Ludo said, "If you lean over the edge, you might be able to see the Cova de s'Infern."

I didn't think anything of it. I leaned over to look at the Cave of Hell, a slanted slit in the rock that made the shadowy waters on the other side look like molten silver. By the time we got up to leave, the rocky, wind-battered plateau was backlit by a static orange-peel sky that gave me the impression of walking on the moon. I told Ludo as much.

"I suppose so," he said in his usual humorless manner.

I turned back to look at the sea again. Below us, the Mediterranean, with its morbid, languorous temperament, looked vast, infinite, intimidating.

We drove back down the coast. We stopped at the Cala de la Fosca because Ludo wanted to look at the famous castle that sits on the edge of the beach's brass-colored cliffs. I walked along the shore barefoot. Ludo pushed his way up the cliff to the castle. He stopped at this or that rock to wave forcefully in my direction and yell that I was missing out or to chastise me for not exerting sufficient physical effort, for neglecting to capitalize on the complicity and happiness that our drive up and down the coast promised to offer. I yelled back to Ludo that only goats are meant to hike up such a steep cliff and that, besides, my feet had gone numb from wading in the cold winter water.

"It's not that steep," he yelled.

I ignored him. He looked smaller the farther up the cliff he hiked.

Overhead, the sky was white, as thin as glass, about to vanish. Ludo disappeared behind a wall of pines, and I waited for my father to stir. Nothing happened. I looked for dead fish. I found one at the opposite end of the bay from the castle — a sea bass — that had been tangled up in driftwood and kelp. It had been pecked at by seagulls; it smelled like death. I crouched down and sniffed it, hoping to trigger my father's presence, to get his blood to move the way it had on those last days of his life when I would take him to Brighton Beach and he would dig his cane into the sand and morosely move his eyes from side to side, furious at his looming death in the so-called New World but resigned to it nonetheless. I needed confirmation that he was still there. That he hadn't turned his back on me. What would I do if I was left with no one other than Ludo, a faulty descendent of the Bembos? But nothing worked. My void remained hollow, empty. I was about to faint from the rotten smell of the dead fish when I heard Ludo's voice. He was right behind me. I turned to look at him. He had a rabbity grin on his face. He was standing there with his arms at his waists.

"I'm going to take you out to dinner," he said. "You don't have to eat that."

"What's it to you?" I asked, getting up from the sand.

In the interim, the sky had darkened. It was a deep navy blue, and a few hazy stars had appeared. The water was lapping gently against the shore. It was no longer olive-colored, vintage green; it looked black and viscous. We were the only two people on the beach.

"Nothing," he said. He took my face in his hands. Then, with all the sweetness in the world, he said, "What am I going to do with you?"

A moment earlier, he'd had me perilously leaning over the edge of a cliff to look at the Cave of Hell. Now he was all tenderness. I couldn't make heads or tails of it.

"I'm not an object," I informed him tersely. "I'm not a bronze statue you need to decide where best to display!"

"A bronze statue?"

"Whatever! What I'm saying is, I'm not an impulse purchase!"

"I didn't say you were," he said. Then he added, "We're having a great time. Let's not get started."

"Fine," I said, mentally going over my notes.

He had it coming. He was asking for it.

Ludo was always concerned with his stomach. Earlier in the day, on our way up to the Cap de Creus, we had stopped at the beaches and marshlands of Roses. We had eaten cheese-and-pork sandwiches, walked along the shore, jumped from metallic salt-corroded rock to rock. We had picked flowers in the hills.

The next day, we drove farther south to have lunch in Sant Feliu de Guixols. We stopped to eat at the Nou Casino la Constancia, a neomedieval building with arabesque features. The building had a romantic flair about it, but the waiters were slow, rude, indifferent. Their white shirts were stained, their black vests unbuttoned. They were making inconclusive efforts at resurrecting the charm of the Old World.

I never paid for our meals. I couldn't bring myself to spend the little money I had left in the world on anything other than shelter and mint-and-onion soup. So Ludo fed me, bought me beach towels, sweaters, hiking shoes. I didn't care.

That night, we drove back north to have dinner in L'Escala, a fishing village famous for its anchovies. The beach was dotted with tiny black boats, which had been laid to rest upside down on the shore. We sat on the sand and looked out at the sea. Ludo lit up his pipe. The smoke lifted into the night sky in slow, steady streams. There was a thin mist hovering over the water. Everything looked black, blue, white; the edges of the landscape shone with a metallic tinge. The moon emerged momentarily and then disappeared behind thick clouds, exhausting all light from the sky. We barely spoke. Or rather, we spoke only of banal things: his friends, Tuscan wine, his dreams of owning an olive grove. I said next to nothing. It was the only way to guarantee peaceful conversation. No one wants to have their nose rubbed in manure. No one wants to be accountable to the truth. I was alone in my efforts. Alone even when I was in Ludo's company because, like everyone else, he refused to acknowledge his own hurt.

We had dinner in a café near the water. We ate fish-head soup, black rice cooked in large shallow clay dishes, cod baked with garlic, olives, tomato. We drank a flask of wine. Ludo told me about a friend of his who had lost his mind because he had gone foraging for mushrooms and had accidentally eaten a poisonous one.

"What does he do now?" I asked.

"He wanders. His mother takes care of him," he said, and that was that.

The waiter brought me a fruity cocktail with a decorative umbrella and a beer for Ludo. I removed the decorative umbrella and tucked it behind Ludo's ear.

"This isn't Hawaii," he said.

"The world is a lot more contaminated than you think," I answered, and then I got up and left.

I walked out onto the beach. I grabbed a stick and carved the following lines from Nietzsche's *Ecce Homo* into the sand: *Why do I know a few more things? Why am I so clever altogether?* I was hoping to bring my father back. Nothing. And what's more? There was Ludo again, standing behind me.

"What are you doing?" he asked scornfully. "We were still eating."

With that black sky behind him and the mist that was hovering over the water, he looked like Nosferatu: elongated in all the wrong ways.

"I am being one with Nietzsche," I answered.

"So you can't be one with me, but you can be one with Nietzsche?" he challenged.

"I couldn't have said it better myself," I answered in a mellowing tone.

That's when he lost it.

He pointed out that my features had a mercurial quality about them that put him ill at ease. "Your expression changes in a flash from grave introspection to childish mischief, or from a callous indifference to anguish," he said, as if he were reading from a book or, even worse, my notebook. "Sometimes," he said, "you look as if you were suddenly being skinned alive. What is wrong with you?"

"Why do you sound like a text?" I inquired.

"A text?" he mocked.

What had happened to Ludo's silence on all matters regarding my ill-fatedness? Ludo's literary disengagement? I considered the possibility that there were multiple versions of the same Ludo Bembo, two physical versions of the same man, each version inclined to duality, making four Ludo Bembos altogether. He seemed to have become me. He was speaking the way I would have spoken to him had I ever had the opportunity to share the mental notes I had made as a result of all my tireless thinking. I asked him to sit down on one of the boats. I even wiped off the sand to make sure he would be comfortable. He sat down with a hopeful expression on his face. I started mildly. I explained to him that most of our issues originated, on the one hand, as a result of his insistence on pursuing pleasure, on his own self-love, which he had confused with love for me, and on the other hand, from his apparent ignorance of the poetic and philosophical efforts exerted by his ancestors, the Bembos, efforts that he was recklessly throwing into the wind by living as if life were a loyal dog that walked at his heels.

It was at that moment that my father returned. His head emerged in my void. Seconds later, it sank back down in the deep dark folds of the abyss. I was devastated. I looked down at the sand. For a moment, I wasn't sure where I was. I had the impression the sand was lifting, peeling off the ground to blind me. I looked around to see if there were bombs falling, if there were corpses splayed in the corners of the landscape. I could hear Ludo murmuring something about how I was coldhearted, how I acted as if I had overcome my need for affection, for the company of my fellow humans.

Without looking up at him, I said: "I haven't touched rock bottom yet. If you think this is hard, wait till I get to the bottom of the abyss. I still have tenderness. The window opens now and again."

This left him speechless. We said nothing to each other for the rest of the evening. We drove back to Barcelona. I didn't think he was going to come up to Quim Monzó's apartment with me. But he did. He even stayed over. He fell asleep with a hopeful grin on his face. I stayed up the whole night. What, I wondered, thinking back on Ludo's words, would happen to me if I let go of him and my father didn't return? What would I do if there wasn't even a single thread connecting me to this cruel and trifling universe? I spent hours searching his face, staring at that hopeful grin. Perhaps, I thought, there was a way forward, an opening at the bottom of the abyss through which I could climb back into the world.

At dawn, I got out of bed. While Ludo continued to sleep, I paced the corridor reading my notebook. Reading was my only remedy, my only recourse; it was the only tool I had for navigating the void. Taüt was perched on the arm of the swivel wall lamp. He was sleeping. His sulfur-crested head was tucked into his plumed back. He looked fluffier and squatter than ever.

I walked past the room where Ludo's naked body lay stretched out between the four tall bedposts. He was clinging to my pillow, and the whiteness of his skin next to the red of the sheets made him look like an octopus wrapped around the rocky protrusion of a coral reef. Who is he? I wondered again. How is it that he has come into my life? I couldn't ask the question enough.

I carried on down the corridor. I looked into the bird's room to see if it had eaten. I always made sure to pour fresh seeds into his cage bowls. But, as usual, the bird, fellow steward of death, hadn't eaten a thing.

I returned to the living room.

There was a gauzy light coming through the windows. I set my notebook down on the coffee table. The next time I opened it, I read: *Love is a divine architect who, according to Plato, came down to the world so that everything in the universe might be linked together.* I recognized the handwriting. It was Ludo's. So, I concluded, he had interfered with my notebook. The moon was shining through the windows with a borrowed light. I thought back to the red flags. I had been right to be wary of him. What could be more manipulative than to invade another with love?

I had to avenge myself. I went in search of Ludo's books, the ones he had brought back with him after his supposed visit to the rare-book dealer, his friend Fausta. He had left them in the corner of the kitchen. Those poor forgotten books — all of them historical dictionaries — sitting on the kitchen counter as if they were steaks waiting to be seasoned. On a napkin, I penned a citation from the diaries of Josep Pla, who I had thought of upon entering Quim Monzó's apartment for the first time, an author who defends the banal, who is straightforward, whose mind is a machine full of extremely sensible sentences, all of which he wrote several times over, because he revised his diary for so many years that eventually he was plagiarizing himself, citing and falsifying himself until there were so many Josep Plas that the original one could no longer be found; he was a man of unapologetic contradictions, a literary hero, and the best choice for retaliating against Ludo Bembo's interference in my notebook. Here is the citation I wrote on the napkin, transcribed verbatim: *When one's heart hasn't turned to stone, one cannot kill off vanity, the painful longing to be heard, flattered, loved, cherished, et cetera. Our vain heart leads us to do the most absurd things and embark on lunatic initiatives: to interfere in other people's lives, to catechize them in one way or another — in a word* (and this I underlined for emphasis), *to invade their solitude.*

While I was leafing through the first dictionary to insert the napkin, I found something far worse that the sentimental verse Ludo had copied into my notebook. Embedded in its frail yellow pages was a folio that was, believe it or not, more manipulative than the quote about the divine nature of love. The folio, too, was in Ludo's handwriting. He had crafted his letters to look as elegant and poised as the font of a medieval manuscript. His *f* looked like a flamingo, his *s* like a swan, his *m* like an orangutan. He had conducted an in-depth analysis of the history of the word *inquietare.*

The word leapt off the page and slapped me in the face. Why that word in particular? *Inquietare,* I repeated to myself, mentally archiving its various unsettling definitions as I returned to the recamier: to disturb someone (gravely); to block or alienate someone; to diminish their peace and quiet.

The pair of red flags, which had initially been waved in my face by the rupture in Ludo Bembo's dress code, were twice validated. What more proof of his caprice did I need?

I considered eliminating him from my life. After all, I had spent most of my days on this ghastly universe in grave solitude. Why should I cling to another — a non-Hosseini — now? I walked into the bathroom. I felt a fool for having let him into my life. I looked at my face in the mirror. I couldn't remember how old I was: twenty-two, twenty-three, twenty-five. I could have been any age. I was young and old at the same time. Then I saw my mother's flattened face, wounded and bruised, looking back at me. I felt lonelier than ever. I reached out to touch her face, to soothe her. But her image vanished from the mirror's reflective surface. "What am I going to do about Ludo?" I murmured into the still air. I felt as though, without him, I risked turning into dust, into ashes that would be scattered about the world by the gale of history. He was the only person, other than my mother and father and Morales, who had known me, and as a result, my fate had become inextricably linked to his. There was no getting rid of him. Even if I tried, I would fail. I had grown accustomed to him. I even needed his stubborn resolve. Without it, there was nothing anchoring me to the world.

I went to the living room and sat on the recamier, a trail of images running through my head. That dry and sordid no-man's-land, my father and I and our ass, a trio of lamentable figures. I thought to myself, exile begins long before the exiled person is banished from her country. One is first expelled psychologically, emotionally, intellectually; physical exile is the final blow. My father and his father and his father's father had all been condemned to death. What for? For being thinkers. I got a whiff of the Caspian. It smelled like oil, watermelon, moist soil, rusted beams, a forest of eucalyptus. I thought of Dante the Pilgrim, of the words of warning he had received: You will know *how hard a path it is for one who goes ascending and descending others' stairs.*

That death sentence, I thought, hangs over my head. Perhaps it is best to finish things off, conclude the long trial once and for all. My thoughts had regressed. They folded over themselves and spun a tangled web. I got off the recamier and paced the corridor — the real corridor of the apartment and the symbolic corridor of my exile. The apartment seemed different again. Certain objects I hadn't noticed before stood out in unnatural relief against the background chaos, the most striking of which was a desk globe, its surface wiped clear. The globe was devoid of land and water masses; the representation of the world had either eroded or been scraped off, leaving a pure white surface, as though the universal clock had been set back to the beginning of the beginning. Or rather, I thought, correcting my thinking, the desk globe represented a nonplace where time did not exist, or if it did, its fabric was undifferentiated — the past, present, and future had folded over one another, rendering their boundaries indivisible, unclear.

The ghost globe, I concluded, was a sign of my unbecoming. I grabbed the globe and carried it with me into the bathroom. I contemplated its pure surface. I again felt as though I were standing on the event horizon of a black hole. I thought of the black band my father had placed over my eyes. I looked at myself in the mirror one last time. My hair was long and knotted. I could see lines beginning to form on my forehead. My skin was pale. My eyes looked bruised. I was exhausted.

The ghost globe, I realized, had been my cue to begin the process of unbuilding, of becoming residue, the nothingness that is everything. The bathroom was inviting me to be a patient, to take some pills, to draw a bath. It was inviting me to reenter the womb, blast past the singularity of my birth, to *un*become, to undo the pain of the losses I had endured so that, like the phoenix, I could be reborn ad infinitum in humanity's pile of ruins.

I remembered telling the funeral director that my father had gone back to the beginning, to a space before his birth.

I opened the medicine cabinet. The top row was lined with bottles of pills. One of the bottles was unlabeled. I unscrewed the cap; inside, there were tiny star-shaped pills. "*Star* is only one letter away from *scar*," I exclaimed, letting out an incredulous gasp. There it was: the past in the future, Nietzsche's eternal return.

I dug one of the stars out with my finger. I swallowed it. I swallowed my past. I said out loud to no one, "I am a cannibal." I turned the tap and listened to the sound of water run through the faucet into the tub. I swallowed a few more pills. I felt time begin to dissolve. I leaned over the tub and looked again at my face; it appeared deformed in the rising water. I scooped up the water and swallowed it. I drank my face. The water had a thick metallic taste; it was like swallowing milk mixed with blood. I sat on the edge of the bath until I heard a buzzing in the margins of the universe. Matter was disintegrating. Time was going limp. I peeled off my clothes. I got into the tub.

I was ready to die in order to begin again. "The sole objective and purpose of Zebra," I said out loud to no one as I immersed myself in the water, "is to reemerge from the womb as a constantly regenerating residue of the collective data of the infinite archive of literature, to spread across the web of the Old World, which forbids the accumulation of a center, is complex, stratified, simultaneous, a continent as ungraspable as totality itself . . . unreal, Irrational-Pragmatic, multiple . . ." I was becoming formless.

The room began to disappear. The tiles began to drift apart from one another. Time was breaking down. I sank farther into the water. I thought of Dante. I thought of the ice at the core of the universe. I thought of the frozen lake of our hearts. I was approaching expulsion. I laughed. It was the laugh of the darkness of birth. I felt time buckle and go limp. The water turned cold and dense. I saw myself become compressed. I saw myself become other. I saw myself become more Zebra. I faded into the ethereal distance. I felt myself become nothingness.

Sometime later, hours, days, minutes, Ludo came bursting into the bathroom.

It was morning.

"What are you doing in there?" he asked.

I heard everything he said twice. I leaned over to look at him. There were two of him. Two Ludo Bembos, like I had thought there were. I felt a sense of hysteria bubbling up inside me. Who was Ludo Bembo? Where were my father, my mother, my homeland? Who was I?

I heard Ludo say, "You look feverish."

He kneeled on the floor and put his hand on my forehead. He looked at me with concerned eyes.

I heard myself answer. "I'm not an idiot. You don't need to repeat everything!"

He looked hurt, confused, angry, and despairing all at once. "I don't know why I even bother," he muttered. I felt stabbed by those words twice.

I saw both Ludo Bembos rub their eyes. The pair looked far away, as if I were looking at them from the wrong end of a telescope. They were both as white as milk. They looked like long boiled noodles. I wanted to stab him back.

I said, "You pair of linguini need to get out of my hair!"

The pair raised their heads and looked at me with an inscrutable expression. Severity, repulsion, pain — I couldn't tell.

"Fine. I'm leaving," he said matter-of-factly, washing his hands and drying them on the towel. He was doing his utmost to resist getting dragged into the vortex of my wounds. His whole body went rigid, cold. "I can't skip any more classes," he said without looking at me. "I'm teaching in the afternoon."

For a brief moment, I felt myself resurface: the two Ludo Bembos consolidated. There was only one of him. I didn't want him to leave, but I couldn't bring myself to tell him as much. Instead, I asked him for his address. He said he would leave it for me on the dining-room table on his way out. I lifted my arm out of the tub and waved it.

"Good-bye," I said. "When we see each other again, it will be under different terms. Love is a two-way street, but until now I didn't have your address." I heard my words echo.

"Okay," he said. "Very well." His tone was exasperated, conflicted, both final and full of yearning.

I waved my arm again, hoping he would reach for my hand and drag me out of the tub. Instead, he caressed my hair as if I were a scrawny dog he had tried to save from drowning in a dreary lake, a dog that would soon return to the frothy, putrid waters, incapable of learning a lesson. After that, he left. I sat in the bath, soaking, consoling myself with the fact that he had no idea that I had used the word *love* instead of the word *interference*. He had interfered with my notebook, my life. Now I would interfere with his.

I fell asleep in the tub. The next day, I awoke to the sound of footsteps in the stairway. My fingernails were blue. My hands were pruned. I looked like a newborn: shriveled, slimy, reduced. I was shivering. My temperature had dropped dramatically. The water level had gone down, as though my body had absorbed the liquid or it had begun to evaporate. I looked at the rectangular cross section of the world beyond the window. Daylight was beginning to wane. I listened to the echo of the footsteps. Whoever was outside the front door was walking indecisively up and down the stairway.

My mind and body were slowly reconnecting. I stood up. The water slid off me like a wave in the ocean. I felt the sudden onset of vertigo. I managed to step out of the tub, to bend down and drain the water. My fingers were unstable, and it was hard to work the stopper. I couldn't feel my hands. I wrapped a towel around myself and walked down the corridor. When I got to the door, I looked through the keyhole. There was no one there. No Ludo Bembo. I looked again through the keyhole. No sign of life.

"Taüt," I called out, as if we had been lifelong friends. I retreated to the bedroom. The bird, that chimeric little monster, appeared immediately, like a starving dog. He didn't fly. He walked across the floor to the edge of the bed. The bird climbed the sheets using his beak and talons. He hopped from the mattress onto the headboard. He remained perched there, staring ahead with glazed eyes. I looked at him. I said to that wretched bird: "Undoing oneself involves unweaving the delicate web of time."

The bird opened his dark beak. I peered into that Beak of Darkness and remembered being at the cemetery watching the undertakers lower my father's casket into the ground. I remembered looking at my mother's blue hand, swollen and bruised. Then the image resolved itself. The devastation vanished.

In a wild impulse, I got up. I opened my suitcase and turned its contents over onto the bed. The pungent scent of my father's death spread through the room and contaminated the air. *The Hung Mallard* rolled underneath the bed. The books, thrust out of my portable library, piled up like Roman bricks at various intervals across the surface of the mattress. I took a step back to observe the design from a distance. I rocked back and forth on my feet. I held my breath. The obelisk-like posts, combined with the books, created the distinct impression that the bed was an abandoned city, timeless, a literary ruin. I walked around the bed as wild as an animal. A horseshoe emerged: a big capital *U*, the *U* of Ulysses. I cupped my chin with the palm of my hand. If I had a mustache, I would have stroked it. I imagined Dalí's mustache standing on its ends like the blades of an open pair of scissors. I gaped at the design. *U*, the *U* of Ulysses. I sucked in little patches of air. I oxygenated my mind in portions. A secret was being revealed to me about the genealogy and fate of literature: Literature was not dead despite what some have claimed, nor was it on its way to being dead. No, far from being dead, literature is the site of death itself. I looked at the archipelago of books on the bed. Literature is where the ruins of humanity are piled. And if literature is a retainer for death, how can it die? I asked. "Because death," I cried, "is immortal." I tossed the empty suitcase on the floor. I threw myself on my back onto the bed. I felt a sense of bliss wash over me. I felt myself begin to fade. I was on the verge of radiating back out of the matrix. I was everywhere and nowhere at once: lying in the shade of an umbrella pine in Pompeii, curled up in the navel of civilization, on a literary vessel, in a submarine about to plunge into the past.

I drifted off to sleep. In the dream, I was floating across the inky waters of the Atlantic Ocean on a mattress filled with books. I was bobbing along the waves, approaching a woolly black storm on the horizon. I didn't feel fear. The only thing that gnawed at me were pangs of hunger. I was starving. The horizon was fixed in space; it wouldn't recede and the swell was growing. I was approaching the storm at a perpetually increasing speed. I looked at my city of books and resolved to eat them. I opened them one by one. I ripped out page after page. There were too many pages. There wasn't enough time. I realized I would drown before I could stuff all that language into my mouth. I had to be more discerning. It occurred to me that the best thing to do, given the circumstances, would be to eat only the sentences I loved and loathed the most, and chuck the neutral ones into the sea. I leafed through my books. I tore out individual sentences. With a steady hand, I dropped them into my mouth. They slipped down my throat as easily as fresh oysters. I felt an intense pleasure. I was ready to glide toward my death. I opened Benjamin's *Illuminations* and quickly worked my way to "Unpacking My Library." It seemed appropriate. I ate *Only in extinction is the collector comprehended.* I was ready to devour the next sentence, to eat Benjamin quoting Hegel, to consume an infinitely receding sequence of quotes. My plan kept evolving. I envisioned building an epic book of light and dark passions from the sentences I had ingested. I was sure that my archived language would survive my bodily death, be absorbed by a kindred channel of consciousness — just as I had absorbed my father and the part of my mother my father had absorbed upon her untimely death — and fan back out into the world. I began to eat *Only when it is dark does the owl of Minerva*, but I was interrupted — Taüt, gentler than usual but steady in his ways, was peering into my mouth, grazing my lips with his feathers.

When I woke up, my head was pounding. My head, it seemed, was wrapped in cloth or plastic. My vision was shrouded, slightly muddled. I could see the contours of things, the angles of the room, the sharp spearlike ends of the bedposts, the sagging ceiling that was hanging there like a sack of yogurt. The books I had thrown onto the bed were still there. Some of them had been opened. Certain verses had been underlined. The edges of the covers had been chewed. It was clear: I had been feeding on literature.

There were other objects on the bed: a typewriter with a fresh spool of ribbon and paper that had been fed into the platen. In big bold letters, at the top of the page, I had typed the word DICTÉE. I had been transcribing. I had been cloning texts, creating fake doubles like a monk, like a scribe in a monastery. I removed the paper from the typewriter. It read:

IN THE WORDS OF JOSEP PLA, WRITER OF DEATH, PERMANENT INHABITANT OF INTERNAL EXILE:
I've asked for nothing and dominated nobody, but I have defended myself with every noble and ignoble weapon there is when people have tried to dominate me or force me to take a step in their direction. I only ever wanted to get on with my life. The laws of the state increasingly encroach on us and the day may come when we have to fill in a form in order to grow a mustache.

Then again:

IN THE WORDS OF JOSEP PLA, WRITER OF DEATH, PERMANENT INHABITANT OF INTERNAL EXILE:
I've asked for nothing and dominated nobody, but I have defended myself with every noble and ignoble weapon there is when people have tried to dominate me or force me to take a step in their direction. I only ever wanted to get on with my life. The laws of the state increasingly encroach on us and the day may come when we have to fill in a form in order to grow a mustache.

I leaned over the Remington. There were bullet holes in it. It was bruised and beaten. It was from the war. Its consciousness had been violated in the trenches. It suddenly occurred to me: I had tried to kill myself.

I was returning to consciousness in portions, in shards; I was seeing things in segments. I slowly realized that there was a hose hanging from the center of my face. I tried to utter the word — hose — but the sound of my voice was muffled by whatever contraption I had wrapped around my head. The edges of matter, like the contours of reality, had frayed. I concentrated on the hose. I followed that plastic pipe with my eyes. It wasn't easy. My senses were obstructed; I couldn't see clearly. Space had turned into a collage, something I could experience only in discrete sections. And

I, with all that industrial wreckage hanging off my face, was like a figure in a painting. I had fused with the apartment. I was completely Dada.

I walked into the bathroom and looked in the mirror. I was wearing a gas mask. My hair was sticking out between the clasps that buckled at the back of my head. I stared at the filter cartridge over my mouth through the two oval glass windows of the mask. I thought of the bestiality of war, of the machinations of history. "Who is spared?" I asked. "No one," I heard myself mutter in response.

I unclasped the gas mask. It smelled musty, old; it was caked with dirt. I looked like a warrior. The mask left red marks on my cheeks and forehead. I looked at the replication of the bathroom in the mirror: the blue tiles, the edges of the tub, all those mute surfaces were doubled, their silence amplified just as I had been doubled, had died and been resurrected in literature's echo chamber, had been regurgitated from the Matrix of Literature as residue.

I washed my face. I groomed myself. The mind, I thought inwardly, is a complex energy field capable of receiving information; it is subtle, porous. A sponge designed to soak up the dark waters of literature, all that spilled blood. I brushed my hair, then I set the brush down on the sink. I looked at myself. I had become more Zebra than ever before, as troubling as literature, as disquieting as language itself.

GIRONA

The Story of the Creation of the
Miniature Museum and My Cohabitation
with Ludo Bembo

WEEKS LATER, ON A WET JANUARY AFTERNOON, I left Quim Monzó's apartment for the last time.

It had been raining the whole day, and Barcelona was covered in a thick purple haze. The trees planted along the boulevards swayed as the wind plucked their leaves and carried them out of view into the dark veil of water coming down through the sky and rising from the ground in clouds of vapor. I was on my way to the train station when a strong flash of lightning forced me to hide underneath a doorway. Taüt was sitting on my shoulder. I had stolen the bird. I had left Quim Monzó with a false replica I had purchased, a wooden cockatoo I fastened to the swivel wall lamp where Taüt regularly perched. The real-life Taüt was breathing hard. His beak was ajar, and he kept blinking or anxiously nibbling on my ear, and his feathers were upright. He had a ghastly look. He looked objectionable. I told him as much. He seemed to take offense; he immediately grasped onto my ear with his right talon, carving his nails into my skin. In my mind's eye, I saw my ear peeling off the side of my face and blowing into the distance, like the leaves being scattered here and there.

"If you don't stop"—I cast Taüt a scornful look—"I'm going to have to shove you into the Mobile Art Gallery." The bird squinted, aware that he might drown in the putrid odor of my father's death.

Before leaving, I had converted my chest-shaped suitcase into a miniature museum. In order to fill the space of my father's absence, I had turned the fumes of our past into art, stuffed that sarcophagus with objects. In addition to my books, and my father's, the miniature museum contained objects from the Room of Broken Heirlooms and from the apartment of Quim Monzó, objects that, like my mother and father and me, had been violently severed from their context.

I said in vain to Taüt, "I have been stripped of home and hearth. If I was deprived of these objects, which conjure for me the many origins and stages of my ill-fatedness, what else would I have left in the world?" The bird said nothing. He merely clawed at my ear.

There was no one around. The city looked like it had been abandoned. I felt as though I were standing outside the world looking in. The events of the last few weeks had left me feeling stranger than ever before: as raw as a newborn and, simultaneously, ancient, decrepit, weatherworn. I looked around. Lined shoulder to shoulder on the sidewalk, the facades of L'Eixample's buildings reminded me of soldiers at the end of a long, hard war. I scanned the empty street. I had the vague impression that the city's potential had been violently truncated, as if I were looking at an afterimage of a distant and brutalized Barcelona, a ghostly projection of the city's composite past: Franco's Barcelona, the Barcelona of the Civil War, the Barcelona of the Tragic Week, the Barcelona of the War of Spanish Succession, of the Reapers' War. How many times had this city reinvented herself? How many times had she died and been resurrected? How many times had she been exiled from herself? The city seemed haunted by the ghosts of her own past. And yet, like the Hosseinis, she had persevered.

I was drenched. The wind was blowing sheets of rain left and right. I pressed my back against the doorway and saw my reflection in the first-floor windows. I looked like a fugitive. A fugitive attached to a stubborn and volatile bird whose beak hung ajar. I let my mouth drop open, too. Steam came rising out of it. I took a long, hard look at myself standing there with Taüt. Flattened onto the surface of the window, the bird and I seemed to be looking back at ourselves in disbelief from behind the smoky veneer of an old photograph.

Finally, the rain diminished and then ceased. A pale winter sun emerged, casting its mild light on the window. Taüt and I disappeared from view. The street started to fill up again. People moved about briskly, hoping to avoid the next downpour. I resumed my walk to the train station, sliding past lottery vendors, street sweepers, businessmen in slim black suits and pressed white shirts, middle-aged women in boxy colorful outfits that made them look like gifts waiting to be unwrapped; there were office clerks, cocktail waiters in double-breasted suits, teenagers wearing puffy down coats and shoes made of foam and rubber that looked good enough for walking on the moon, whose depressed, acne-pocked skin reminded me of the craters in the red recamier in Quim Monzó's living room. These people had places to go, loved ones who would be angry, or worried, or disappointed if they failed to arrive. Next to them, I felt like a feral animal, untethered and unstitched. I felt the sweetness and the bitterness of my solitude in my mouth. As I watched them, it occurred to me that if I'm going to be condemned to death in life I should at least have a thinking chair. I wished I had stolen the red recamier, too.

On the train, I thought of Ludo Bembo. Ever since he had walked out and left me soaking in the tub, as wrinkled as a prune, I had been planning to show up at his house unannounced. He had abandoned me in a moment of need, thickening my distrust of humanity; he had poured salt into my Hosseini-shaped wounds. In an hour, I would be at his door in Girona. I would be able to impose myself on his life just as he had imposed himself on mine by interfering with my notebook.

I closed my eyes and assessed the sum of the thoughts I'd had in the weeks since Ludo had abandoned me. I remembered that for a few days I had considered my imposition on his home and hearth an artistic performance of what one of André Breton's translators refers to as *the love of the irrational and the irrational of love*. I had consulted one of Breton's books at random while pacing Quim Monzó's corridor and his words had detached themselves from the page and hovered over the book in three dimensions, an occurrence that lent them a prophetic quality. Breton's words had soon positioned themselves alongside my father's: *Love nothing except literature.* Words taken from the First Hosseini Commandment.

The two phrases, stationed in my mind as opponents and prepared to engage in conflict — one steering me toward Ludo and the other away — had provoked in me a serene sadness that was almost blissful, joyous. The more I considered my options, the more intoxicated and elated I became. It was in that state that I deduced the following: By showing up at Ludo's house unannounced and — how shall I put it? — prepared to move in, I was going to teach him a lesson. What lesson? The following: If love is irrational and if one loves the irrational, then it follows that one

— i.e., Ludo Bembo — loves *love;* and when one loves *love*, one risks turning into a steamroller, a psychic murderer of one's lover — i.e., me, the object of Ludo's love. By moving to Girona and imposing myself on Ludo, I was going to demonstrate the damaging effects of love, its fundamental intrusiveness, and would thus be engaging with Breton's missive and, simultaneously and rather paradoxically, would also be proving the inherent wisdom of the First Hosseini Commandment. In doing so, I would be establishing a complex truce between the two sides of my brain. By using literature to expose the lie of love, its false pretense of unconditional generosity and kindness, I would be proving yet again that literature is the only magnanimous host in this piddling universe, and as if that were not enough, I would be doing so in Ludo's presence, which I was loath to admit I had missed.

I felt a few pangs of hunger. Before leaving Barcelona, I had counted the money Morales had given me. It was halfway gone. As a result, my food rations had become even more meager than before. To distract myself, I opened my eyes and looked at the Mobile Art Gallery. I took inventory: the typewriter, the telephone, the gas mask, the bronze statue of the bull, the miniature plastic reproductions of the toilets, the ghost globe. To my view, I hadn't stolen any of Quim Monzó's objects. I had merely reappropriated them. I had given them new life by turning them into art objects. Quim Monzó, Dadaist though he is, hadn't taken things far enough. It was I, to whom the world had offered nothing, who, by creating a box in a valise in the Duchampian spirit, had taken the literary critic's belongings to their logical conclusions.

I had spent hours designing the interior of the suitcase. I had attached a retractable wooden cross to the inside of the lid and fastened *The Hung Mallard* to it. Now, when I opened the lid and extended the cross, the painting would unfold and hang over the rest of the objects with a great deal of somber ceremony; the Hosseini mantra — *in this false world, we guard our lives with our deaths* — hovered ominously over the objects in the gallery.

I had built shelves for the miniature reproductions of the toilets, the bronze bull, the ghost globe. I arranged my portable library at the bottom of the valise. I squeezed in our rusty samovar and our rug. On top of the rug, I fitted the typewriter, telephone, and gas mask. Inside the valise, these last three objects, ordinarily pitiable due to the abuses inflicted upon them during the world wars, had suddenly taken on the dignified, grave look of art.

The train carried on. We went past raked fields of wheat, vineyards, poles, towers. I sat there with the composure of a mannequin and reviewed the Mobile Art Gallery's function with surgical precision. I had built two foldout tables that I could secure to each side of the chest. I pictured myself sitting at the desk with the typewriter, practicing the Irrational-Pragmatic methodology by transcribing five sentences, one for each member of the Hosseini lineage (including me), before moving over to the telephone on the opposite desk; there I would pick up the receiver and listen to the silence at the other end for a corresponding number of minutes. This silence, I decided, which was loud enough to hear, was the white noise left over after the devastation of exiles the world over, those of us whose fates have been bludgeoned by failed constitutional movements, world wars, dictatorships, coup d'états, and counterrevolutions. In other words, by coupling the Irrational-Pragmatic methodology with the Art of Transcription, I had caused a live Dadaist performance to be born. What would Quim Monzó have to say about that? I wondered smugly.

One evening, while I was sitting on Quim Monzó's red recamier in the smoky light of dusk, I had raised my grief antennas and received the following message from the Matrix of Literature: Since I have a more refined sense than most for the virtues of literature in relation *to the total problem of life*, it is my job to expose the macabre state of the world to its tired and tried posers through a series of performative transcriptions designed to put the uselessness of our suffering on display, to expose the only truth that exists: the truth of literature, an ugly truth disguised in the form of a beautiful lie. It is my job, I considered, to warn the world that we have not yet hit rock bottom; that we, members of the twenty-first century, the supposed *moderns*, are on the cusp of a profound and prolonged senselessness, a senselessness that will be even more senseless than its senseless predecessors. No one will be spared. There will be war everywhere, a sporadic, remorseless war that will appear and disappear at random, a war that will spread to the Four Corners of the World. At this thought, I rose from the red recamier and announced: "Squirmy little rodents, if one of us is ill-fated, sooner or later we will all be ill-fated. Bah! The *war to end all wars* is the biggest lie we have ever been fed." I sat back down.

After my epiphany, I affixed wheels and a handle to my chest-shaped suitcase. That way, I could easily transport the Mobile Art Gallery. There would be no place out of reach. If I was going to sound out a warning, I would have to do it without bias. Its message was meant for everyone; it didn't matter how remote a village a person lived in. They deserved to know the truth, and the Mobile Art Gallery was capable of delivering that truth anywhere, anytime. My notebook, though filled to the brim, was not enough. What about the illiterates and abecedarians of the world? Who would sound out the Hosseini alarm to them? I needed a visual representation of my notebook, a three-dimensional sculpture that would drag the ghosts of our past into the present and ask: Why is the present, which is history itself, not being addressed?

The train was beginning to slow down. I looked out the window. We were pulling into the station in Girona. Soon, I would see Ludo again. I felt as though a hundred horses were galloping across the flat fields of my heart. The train came to a stop on the elevated tracks, and the doors pumped open. I got off and stepped into the powdery light on the platform. There I was: a ghost of my former self, a double alien in Girona, a stranger once again. Taüt pressed his talons into my shoulder. He held on tightly.

I left the station. It was raining, and I stood for a while under the awning of a nearby store. There were blue buses idling in the parking lot, rings of smoke rising from their exhaust pipes only to be pushed back down to the ground by the dense, moist air. I turned around to look at the station's facade. A giant round clock, flat and cream-colored with two thick, rigid arms, hovered at the top. With its fascist severity, the clock brought to mind Franco's moronic face, as indifferent and withholding as the moon.

I felt something move inside me. It was my father. He was making an appearance after a prolonged caesura. I felt renewed by his presence, emboldened. He had always liked Girona. I remembered him spitting with excitement: "Catalonia is Spain's literary and political frontier, and its capital, Barcelona, is famous for attracting and producing thinkers, writers, artists. Barcelona is the Manchester of the Mediterranean, the City of Bombs, the Rose of Fire. But Girona . . . Girona is a hothouse and exporter of exiles!"

It was true. Sandwiched between France and Barcelona, Girona had been the corridor through which exiles had come and gone from Catalonia for centuries.

"Verily!" I said to my father with a bucolic glee, delighted to see him now, caressing his mustache. He rolled its ends around his finger and tickled me.

"Moronic fascist! Moronic clock!" he exclaimed, gagging with laughter.

Despite my father's sporadic entries, I had observed a disturbing pattern: He had become more desultory with every passing day. He was aging in his death. He was decomposing. There were pieces of his nails and hairballs and flakes of dead skin on the floor of my void. He kicked them up every time he made an appearance, causing parts of his body to blow about my inner deserts as recklessly as tumbleweeds in the wind. He seemed to be running out of breath more quickly than before. Seeing him come undone, I felt as though I, too, could suddenly evaporate, dissolve into nothingness, become an echo of the past. My sick hand ached.

"Father?" I inquired in vain. But there was no answer. He had submerged himself in my void once more.

I began advancing through Girona without him, crestfallen and glum. The interlocking network of streets returned to me in segments, block by block. I didn't have an umbrella, so I hugged the sides of buildings as I made my way. Taüt moved to my right shoulder, the side protected from the rain. By the time I had made my way to the Pont de Pedra — an arched stone bridge that hangs over the Onyar River and marks the center of the Old Quarter — the rain had ceased and a diaphanous glow filled the evening sky.

I stood on the bridge for a moment and stared at the still, moss green waters of the river. The rain had kicked up soot and dirt. The water looked dreary, a metaphor of doom and gloom. A line of Dalí's piped into my mind: *I have never denied my fertile and elastic imagination the most rigorous means of investigation.*

I emitted a pained laugh. "The most rigorous means of investigation!" I repeated.

My mind, I considered, is even more centerless and elastic than Dalí's. My mind is as supple and resilient as the Matrix of Literature, which, by nature of being a working cartography of the literature of the void, is itself infinite. How am I supposed to carry around a mind like that? I thought. A mind that never stops stretching? A mind that contains all of literature?

I looked straight ahead into the vanishing point of the landscape that stretched before me. There were more bridges farther up the river and colorful buildings crowding the embankment. Their windows resembled a row of eyes, and the iron railings of their terraces protruded like swollen mouths. They stared back at me dumbly, each one a different color — salmon, mother-of-pearl, mint, toast, olive, white, mustard, pistachio, red, muted orange.

Rain clouds moved quickly overhead, and the glow of the sky diminished. A grainy evening light emerged. I navigated the darkling streets. I went deeper into the Old Quarter. I walked up stone-paved plazas, through cobbled alleyways. The distant hum of conversation flowed out from the doors and windows of dimly lit restaurants and spread across the deserted streets. Everyone was eating, drinking, carrying on with their lives. My reflection in the glass superimposed itself on their figures: I looked sordid, miserable, ragged. The skin around my eyes and mouth was tight, my lips were as thin as a razor. I was livid with envy. The people on the other side of the glass were living the good life, feasting on pleasure and bliss while Taüt and I — and the Mobile Art Gallery, corpse of my past turned future — walked along utterly invisible.

I continued on. I passed recessed wooden doors affixed with rusty knockers shaped like gargoyles, barred windows, gas lanterns, and metal rings previously used to tie horses. I thought of our dead ass, of its ashes scattered across that no-man's-land, and felt my envy calcify. I looked up. The sky was a long, solitary black strip, as narrow as the road. This was the kind of street, I thought, where the sun would go to die. It would plunge itself headfirst into this frigid narrow path. What did Ludo Bembo think, I wondered, as I dragged my body through that ghostly tunnel; that I was just going to lie down and die? Or lick my wounds out of view like a wild animal under a bush? That I was unable to speak, to resist, to react, to push back against the injustices the world and its subjects, including him, had assailed on me?

It was true that I, as a middle-ranking member of the Pyramid of Exile, hadn't had the willpower to shape my own life — a life that had been subjected to an infinite number of independent variables — let alone exert myself as a force upon the lives of others. But things change. The people who have been trapped in the ghetto of the pyramid eventually emerge to contaminate the world with their power and mirror back to this miserly universe its own terrible distortions. I am one of those people. An emergent. Combative. A literary terrorist. This dishonest globe, I thought, as I dragged all of my parts and their corresponding objects up the steep street, is inhospitable to writers and thinkers, not to mention members of the AAA. It has acted upon me with cold cruelty. I have been made an enemy. But I have endured the world with grace for long enough. I have been conditioned to become warlike by the perpetual war imposed upon my corner of the world, by the cultural assassination politely referred to as exile. Imposing myself on others in order to educate them is one of my duties. And Ludo Bembo, a literary amateur and underresolved member of the Pyramid of Exile, was in need of an education. He was a betrayer of exiles, an embarrassment to the legacy of the Bembos.

By the time I arrived at Ludo's doorstep, my ears were hot with fear and rage. As I knocked on his door, I thought to myself: What if he refuses my company? What if he invites me in? My thoughts spun and stretched. I knocked again, but no one came to the door. I was temporarily thwarted.

I was forced to spend the night on a bench in the mud outside Ludo Bembo's apartment. The bench was affixed to a dirt-covered overlook planted with a few young plane trees. It offered an astounding view of the foothills. The Pyrenees possessed an unnatural gleam. The range's dense black form, composed of deep grooves and ridges and moss-encrusted rocks, was shrouded in a fine layer of mist — vapor that appeared to have been backlit. I sat there with Taüt and stared into the distance until the curtains of night were drawn. The sky turned purple before it turned black.

"What is the nature of my predicament?" I asked Taüt. "I am from nowhere. Homeless, adrift, bewildered, crippled with endless estrangement."

Taüt nodded along in agreement with the calm patience of a man who has been locked up his whole life. He was weary from traveling, and his exhaustion had transformed him into a polite and cooperative being.

"What does that make me?" I asked.

He shrugged his wings as if to say, *How should I know?*

Just then, I heard a breathless voice yell: *Like the clear-eyed Edward Said, you are a specular border intellectual!* It was my father's muffled voice coming from deep inside my void. I barely recognized him.

I swooned over Said's name; it warmed my inky blood. It was true. As usual, my father's assessments were spot-on. Though mutilated by my perpetual exile, I, Zebra, was at home in my homelessness. I refused to blend the unreconciled veins of nationhood running through my body. I refused to produce a singular whole self, free of gaps and fissures, a being that poses less of a problem to the rest of the world. Instead, I, Dame of the Void, will continue to inhabit a liminal space between worlds, a position that affords me a vantage point from which to envision new formations of thoughts, to live beyond the frontiers of ordinary experience.

I was soon on my legs, standing before Ludo Bembo's home. The door had a hand-shaped metal knocker. I stared at that sick hand. It had a prophetic aura about it. It was moss green and freckled with rust, as if blood had been sprayed across it. I looked down at my hands. My fingers were hurting again, the way they'd hurt when Ludo and I had had sex and the way they had hurt when I'd nudged my father out of his stupor upon my mother's death. I felt noxious. I retreated to the bench and watched the violet fog roll softly over the mountainous frontier.

The day's rain had kicked up the faint smell of my father's death. I leaned back into the bench and put my legs over the miniature museum. I comforted myself with the thought that Ludo Bembo would have to return home eventually. Soon, I thought, I will have to introduce myself to his friends. I found a muddied piece of old string in the dirt and tied Taüt to the bench. He had begun to strain my shoulder. I walked over to the young plane trees, which had barely taken root in their terra-cotta planters, and introduced myself to them as if they were Agatha, Fernando, and Bernadette.

"Hello," I said to the first tree, shaking a handful of its thin and supple branches. "I am a non-Western encroaching on the territories of the West."

I stepped back to reflect. *A non-Western encroaching on the territories of the West.* The phrase fell short of what I'd wanted to say. It was an approximate unit of thought, incomplete, reductive, uncomplicated. It didn't account for the fact that the West had aggressed upon me while I was still in the East and that this invasion, the cultural assassination imposed upon me by the West, had forced an agonizing and psychologically maimed version of me to cross over into the West and contaminate its territories with the very distortions it had caused but now refused to acknowledge — that, on top of everything else, the West was gaslighting me. That's right. I had been gaslighted by the imperial powers of the world. But, much like the New World, this tree was too young to understand. It said nothing in return. I gave it a little kick and moved on.

Taüt, whose fate was no better than a hostage's, expressed his delight by hopping up and down on the rim of the bench as far as the string permitted.

"Hello," I said, petting the soft foliage of the second tree. "I, Zebra, am recrossing borders I have already crossed in order to map the literature of the void and prove once and for all that any thought worth preserving in our pitiable human record was manifested in the mind of an exile, an immigrant, a refugee" — my mind and my mouth had aligned themselves to perfection — "persons fleeing from persecution, and/or otherwise homeless beings."

The tree bowed.

"At the center of the archive of Western thought," I continued, encouraged by the tree's grace, "is the pain of those who have suffered at the hands of the xenophobic and militant fascists of the West and their puppets in the East."

I looked at the tree. It was sulking empathically. The tips of its branches were pointing despairingly at the ground.

"Spain, of course, is no different," I informed the doting tree. "Spain is the original culprit. It is singularly responsible for the establishment of the so-called New World, for the invention of the West. The Spanish of yore were expert annihilators and inquisitors, all of them."

Just then, the moon emerged and with it a soft Sephardic tune of loss and longing rose from the Museum of Jewish History, which was directly downhill from us. The church bells at the Cathedral of Saint Mary of Girona chimed in.

"Why would the Catalans, who so wish to distance themselves from Spain, want to claim Christopher Columbus as one of their own? Why would they have erected a statue in his honor at the Port of Barcelona? The ego!" I said, resuming my lecture. "The ego! It renders all of us incoherent!"

The tree bowed again. I had never encountered a more deferential tree, a tree with more moral integrity; it was dignified, wise beyond its age, destined to take its place in the highest ranks of the intelligentsia. I decided not to bother with the third tree. For once, I thought, why not end the night on a good note?

I spotted a rock in the moonlight. I picked it up. It made for a great pillow. I lay down on the bench. Taüt settled between my legs. We slept badly, but we slept.

Hours later, through my slumber, I heard Ludo's sighs of despair. He had arrived to greet me with his petulance.

"Mamma mia, mamma mia," he mewled.

I opened my eyes. There he was, walking in circles around the bench. His hands kept flying up to his head, his fingers anxiously working his curls or pulling at his earlobes before dropping down to rest at his sides, as stiff as sticks. I let him exhaust himself. Eventually, he gave in, sank into the bench, and stared into the distance with his dilated pupils.

"What's this?" he finally groaned, pointing at Taüt.

It was a dreary day. It had rained on and off through the night, and the ground looked like it had been punctured. My temperature had been dropping and spiking in cycles. I gazed at Taüt, half-asleep. He looked more haggard and unwilling than ever.

"This?" I rejoined groggily. "This is Taüt!"

"Why does it look like a rat caught in a drain?"

"He," I corrected.

Ludo rolled his eyes. In the morning light, the stone buildings of the Old Quarter looked chalky, straw colored.

"Besides, your supposition is preposterous. Have you ever seen a rat with a sulfur crest?" I turned to Taüt. "Show him," I emitted laterally to the bird.

The creature fanned open his crest with moderate difficulty. His feathers were sticky from the dampness in the air.

"Look," I said to Ludo. "You could take that crest to a flamingo show and fan yourself with it if you wanted. A rat!" I huffed dismissively, rubbing my temples to soothe my headache. I'd had a mild fever through the night.

A group of drunk men ambled into the parking lot adjacent to the overlook, directly in front of Ludo's door.

"Here we go," Ludo mumbled under his breath. He was at his wit's end. Nothing unusual there. In the short time I had known him, one startling fact had become clear: His cup was always full, about to spill over.

"Returning from the house of the Tentacle of Ice?" I posed. His hair was uncharacteristically tousled, a clear sign he'd engaged in frigid and mechanical sex acts with her.

His mind grasped the notion with a delay. When it did, his tongue mischievously pushed up against the gap in his teeth. I had forgotten about that crack, that window into the void at the center of his wide, handsome face.

"No," he lied, averting his gaze. He pushed his glasses up the bridge of his nose. When he looked at me again, his tongue had settled neatly on the floor of his mouth once more.

"A corpse in a coffin," I murmured.

"What?"

"I'm referring to your tongue," I said. "We should get it moving again."

One of the drunks, a man with a round red face and eyes so small and shiny that they looked like they had been lacquered and squeezed, bellowed something incomprehensible into the air.

"Mannaggia a te!" Ludo said. "Bunch of loiterers!"

The drunk's friend, a skinny man with a wrinkled face, pulled his pants down and spread his butt cheeks open. "Say it to my anus!" he yelled in Catalan.

I was pleased to see that there were holes and crevices everywhere I went. A good sign. I turned to Ludo, and asked: "Aren't you going to invite me upstairs?"

"Upstairs?"

"I'm not your whore," I said.

"My whore?"

"Produce your own language," I commanded. "It's the only way forward."

I felt his body go rigid. His muscles clenched to his bones; his jaw clasped down. The usual.

"Listen," I said. "You spent a great deal of time sliding in and out of my vagina in Quim Monzó's apartment. Surely you remember?"

He nodded reluctantly. The drunk's skinny friend, unable to get a rise out of us, pulled his pants back up.

"The decent thing to do would be to invite me upstairs, offer me a cup of tea, introduce me to your friends. I traveled through the rain all day and night to get here."

"It takes an hour to get here from Barcelona," he said sternly.

"Ah," I said. "Always the corrective."

The swollen, shiny, red-faced man bellowed again, like a wolf at midnight. But it was morning. The day's show had only just begun, and here we all were, taking a jab at it before it dragged us down with its dead weight.

"The early bird gets the worm," I said.

A terrible pause ensued.

Then Ludo muttered, "You refused my love." The words slipped out of his mouth despite himself. He seemed embarrassed by the admission, by this uncharacteristic loss of control. He sat there solemnly searching the ground, the corners of his mouth quivering. I was startled. I couldn't bear to see him that way, as if he were about to weep.

"I've changed my ways," I lied, though I knew there was a kernel of truth to it. After all, in addition to wanting to reeducate the man, I had also missed him; I had spent weeks aching bitterly because he had not grabbed my hand when I'd reached for him from the tub. And even though I couldn't trust him due to his interference with my notebook, my life, I knew at least one of my many fractured selves wanted to.

Ludo said nothing. He sat there sulking, puckering his lips. I untied Taüt. The bird stretched his talons, first one then the other. He groomed himself with his beak. But Ludo didn't move. He needed further persuading.

I got up and stood before him. I tried to lift his spirits the way my father had lifted mine through the interminable war. It was the only recourse I had.

"*Put away your sword in its sheath,*" I recited dramatically. I couldn't believe the words that were coming out of my mouth. *"Let us two go up into your bed so that, lying together in the bed of love"* — I looked at the wise tree and bowed respectfully —*"we may then have faith and trust in each other."*

"Why are you talking like that?" Ludo said, eyelids partially drawn.

I stood there and took in his face. Once the shock of seeing me sitting on the bench outside his door had passed, his expression had betrayed a terrible anguish. In response, I'd felt my face slacken and turn blank. My emotions went into overdrive and became indecipherable to me. I recognized the shifts — the pulleys of my mind hoisting my feelings and storing them in the recondite corners of my labyrinthine consciousness only to be extracted once I was well enough to cope with them, once they had turned as sour as spoiled milk. Ludo's eyes grew damp, his face despairing. I heard my father's guttural wails echo through my void. I thought of his anguish at my mother's death. I remembered that in order to get my father to move, to do something, to lift those rocks off my mother, I had pushed everything inside me away. What choice had I had? What choice does anyone ever have? I wondered. We cannot all lose our strength at once. I watched Ludo remove his glasses and rub his eyes. I realized he was still there, awaiting a response.

"The Odyssey," I heard myself say. "Read it and heal!"

Ludo let out a cautious laugh. He reached for my hand. Our tacit peace had been restored. Before I knew it, we were pushing open the door, leaving the drunks whistling in the background. We entered the dark vault of his building. He helped me carry the Mobile Art Gallery up the stairs.

His roommates were all standing there when he opened the door: Agatha, Fernando, and Bernadette. The first two had knowing grimaces on their faces. It was clear Ludo had filled them in on our encounters. Bernadette stood facing away from us. All I could see was the back of her head.

Ludo put down the miniature museum, looked at Bernadette, and leaned into my ear.

"An aberration," he proclaimed impatiently before turning back to the group, and saying, "Everyone, this is Zebra and her bird, Taüt."

"Zebra?" they asked in unison, emitting a pleasant hum.

"Yes. Zebra."

He sounded like himself again: strong, unfazed, those dreamy eyes limpid and alert. I, too, had recovered, content to have a roof over my head.

"Thank you, Ludo," I said. "It pleases me to hear my name echoed so many times because, as you know, I stand in possession of multiple selves."

He rolled his eyes.

Bernadette turned around. She was as pale as chalk, and her eyes were wide and black. She seemed startled and quickly began moving along the walls sideways, with her back against the surface, like a crab. She disappeared into her room and quietly shut the door behind her.

"She has such polished cheeks," I said.

"Yes," Agatha answered softly. "She is very pure, very Catholic. She is probably on her knees now, conversing with the pope."

I liked Agatha already. I looked down the hallway toward Bernadette's door. Clay busts of Agatha's face had been set out to dry on stone columns on either side of the corridor. I assumed they were by Fernando, who I knew to be a sculptor. Some were reproductions of her face in its current manifestation — the present Agatha, circa thirty-two years — while others were imagined versions of her face in old age, variations on a future Agatha, slightly wrinkled, cheeks sagging, eyes less willingly open. I apprehended her gentle and voluptuous figure. Agatha, I concluded, allowing my nose to guide me, is a well-turned-out person; she is delicate, obstinate, and she smells good. There were hints of vanilla and lavender wafting off her skin. No wonder Fernando was possessed by the impulse to reproduce her countenance.

"Fernando doesn't speak English," Agatha said kindly, perhaps in an effort to explain why he stood next to her with his brows knitted, as if he understood nothing. Then she asked: "Where are you from?"

"That is a very complicated question," I replied, undeterred.

"I have all the time in the world," she said, smiling.

Fernando's gaze intensified. He had dark black eyes that shone with a disquieting force. It seemed his face was set in a permanent expression of confusion and disgust with the state of the world. A man of strict conscience, taciturn, noble, and principled to the extreme.

Agatha took me by the arm and led me down the hallway. She escorted me into a living room. The floor was covered in pink, white, and black tiles meticulously arranged in geometric patterns. The room had cracked walls that had been painted a soft yellow, a high ceiling, and a narrow stone terrace dressed with green shutters, which Agatha immediately opened, letting in a chilly breeze and the boisterous clamor of the drunks. The room had a view of Girona and the mountains that outdid the overlook. Ludo and Fernando hung behind. I could hear them whispering at the end of the corridor. I heard them open the lid to the Mobile Art Gallery. They gasped in horror. The combination of *The Hung Mallard* and the gas mask offered a ghastly blow.

I turned my attention back to Agatha. Why beat around the bush when the sensitive beings of the world are so scarce? Agatha was clearly one such being, and she was very pretty, too. She had lilac-colored eyes and high cheekbones and a wide mouth, inside which were two rows of perfectly aligned pearly white teeth that seemed to smile at the world.

"I'll tell you where I'm from," I said.

Her eyes widened with delight.

"Please do," she exclaimed with an old-fashioned charm. She reached out and petted Taüt on the head. The bird fanned his crest.

"I hail from the land of not belonging, directly beyond the frontier of any nation." I unabashedly delivered my truth. "Your home is my periphery," I said.

Ludo intervened stiffly. "None of us are at home here. Can't you see we're all Italian?"

After that brief moment of tenderness, he had gone rigid again. I didn't want to compromise my positive outlook, which seemed to have presented itself in conjunction with Agatha's curious and welcoming nature, so I comforted myself by thinking that the two Ludo Bembos I'd been searching for, one austere and the other a hopeless romantic, had returned to my life.

Agatha sat down on the couch. She leaned into its flower-patterned surface, closed her eyes, and thought deeply about what I had just said. Ludo marched across the living room and walked out onto the terrace. I looked around. The room was sparsely decorated. There was a dying plant hanging from the rafters, a makeshift table, and a bookshelf bursting with books and papers, many of which appeared soiled. The walls were bare, and the cracks were full of gravel and dust. I noticed a filthy aquarium on the coffee table next to the sofa. The glass was covered in algae and slime;

something orange was swimming through the murky water. I decided to join Ludo on the terrace. I found him clutching the banister, his knuckles white. Taüt, still perched on my shoulder, opened his beak to inhale the morning air.

"What are you doing here?" he asked. "I haven't heard from you in weeks."

"I'm moving in with you," I said.

He said nothing, but I noticed his grip relax.

In the distance, the sky was beginning to open up. The fog, which had thickened through the night, was dispersing. It was rolling over the mountain range; the wind was pushing it out to sea.

"Strange way to go about it, don't you think?" he inquired, squinting as he looked at me through and through.

"I suppose," I said. "But I'm no stranger than you are. My strangeness is on the surface while you keep yours out of view. I applaud your methods. They are diligent, meticulous. But I have tried to warn you of the dangers associated with being cut off from your many selves, showing one face to the world while others lie hidden within you."

"You're one to talk."

A yellow sky emerged, smoky at the edges where a trace of the morning mist lingered.

"We can go on like this forever, passing around the ball of blame. But it's a terrible bore," I declared.

"Fine, let's change the subject. How have you been?" Ludo asked with the somber precision of a psychiatrist.

His question echoed in my ear. How had I been? As I scanned the sky, I felt myself grow wary. No one had ever asked me that. I wondered if he was feigning interest in order to gain information about the aftereffects of his unethical interference with my notebook. I decided to quote Nietzsche, the best armor in the world.

"*As summa summarum*," I said, "*I was healthy; as an angle, as a specialty, I was a decadent!*"

"Can't you ever produce an answer that's yours?" Ludo scowled, letting go of the banister and crossing his arms. He looked me straight in the eyes.

"Produce?"

"Yes," he said. "Produce."

There was something going on with the drunk men downstairs. Some disturbance that caused them to let out intermittent cries of anguish.

"I don't produce answers," I said. "Unlike you, I consider my speech acts very carefully. Besides, most of them come from beyond the frontiers of life. They are" — I swallowed — "sepulcher messages."

"Madonna santa," Ludo cried, looking away.

"Are you religious?" I asked.

"No," he said. "No, look."

He pointed his finger at the group of drunks. They were circled around a body. There was a great commotion outside, but I couldn't see or hear anything clearly. Just then, Bernadette reappeared wearing a furry pink onesie and proceeded to close all the windows and shutters, to draw the curtains. Her arms, covered in the pink, furry pajama suit, flailed about as she stomped around trying to seal us in.

Down below, the drunks emitted a long, steady howl. That howl was echoed by a weaker, whinier voice that seemed to emanate from whomever was lying at the center, supine on the ground, beneath their greasy heads.

I took advantage of the chaos to spy inside Bernadette's room. It was narrow, windowless, gray; it resembled the room portrayed by my great-great-grandfather, Shams Abbas Hosseini, in *The Hung Mallard*. All I needed to restage the painting in three dimensions was some rope and a dead duck. I took this as evidence that Bernadette's room was *my* room. Nothing could have been clearer. I inspected the space carefully. The closet was empty, the desk bare. Bernadette had packed her things in neatly stacked boxes. She was moving out. The only personal object left in view was a magazine cutout of Ratzinger, which she had pinned to the wall above a narrow bed with white sheets neatly tucked around a thin mattress. The bed looked like a gurney.

I returned to the living room, and announced, "Ludo, I can take Bernadette's room. You won't even know I'm here."

Fernando suddenly appeared, screaming at Bernadette.

"Ma che fai? Ma che fai?" He approached from the opposite side of the room and tackled Bernadette, who was drawing the shutters closed.

"Lasciala stare!" Agatha announced from the sofa.

"What's happening?" I asked Ludo.

"Fernando is telling Bernadette to stop closing the shutters, and Agatha is telling Fernando to let her be," he said resentfully. I was about to remind him that I didn't need a translator because both my father and Morales had dutifully taught me Italian, that what I needed was context, when he added: "Fernando needs all the light he can get to work on his sculptures and Bernadette likes to nap in total darkness."

"It's morning," I said.

He frowned. "It's all beyond the scope of my comprehension."

I could tell he was softening up again. The surrounding chaos had made of us a pair of adoring insects on a floating leaf. Even Taüt seemed more tender. Bernadette freed herself from Fernando's grip. She was going for it. She was closing the house down.

"Would you say she is perennially hopeless?" I asked Ludo.

"I would say she is."

It was a rare moment of agreement.

"What were you pointing at?" I asked.

"Didn't you see? One of the drunks slid off the wall," he said. "I think he's dead."

At that, his roommates all froze in place.

"Un morto? Ma che dici?" the three of them asked in unison, a traveling Italian chorus. It seemed Fernando understood the word *dead* regardless of any language barrier. I was beginning to like him as much as I liked Agatha. I was surprised to feel this way. I was surprised to like anyone at all. Perhaps I had found my tribe of exiles. I imagined stitching my life — which is, of course, a living death — to theirs.

Agatha rushed to the terrace. She pushed the shutters open. We all leaned out to see. It was true. One of the drunks had slid off the wall and fallen face-first onto the concrete of the parking lot. His carton of Don Simon had exploded from the impact. There was red wine running in serpentine paths down the cracks in the parking lot. His friends had vanished.

"Is he *really* dead?" I asked, remembering the way my father's skin had turned pale and his muscles had gone stiff after his death. I felt my face slacken again, become blank and expressionless once more.

"I think so," Agatha said somewhat desperately.

I had a vague feeling that the man, like my father, would find another way to go on. Even while lying there dead, he seemed as stubborn as wood.

"We shouldn't all be standing here," Agatha said. "This terrace isn't trustworthy. A view like this comes at a price," she said, looking in my direction and then past me at the man lying face down on the ground and then farther out at the Pyrenees, bald and exposed without the dense morning fog.

"Which drunk is it?" I asked.

"The one who showed us his asshole," Ludo said with some hesitation.

A dog scuttled onto the terrace.

"Petita!" Agatha said, and leaned down to kiss the dog on the forehead. It was a miserable little thing. Taüt guffawed at the sight of her. Next to that mangy dog, he looked like a finely groomed prince.

Just then, the neighbors burst out onto their respective patios and terraces, each of them holding their phones to their ears with one hand and gesticulating at us, the only ones with an aerial view, with the other.

"What's going on?" The question resounded in Catalan from every corner of the quarter. It lingered in the air. "Is he dead?"

Ludo hurried down the hallway. He returned a moment later, cell phone in hand.

"No, officer," he shouted into the phone. "He is not asleep. He is D-E-A-D!"

His face was red. His ears were crimson. I had never seen him annunciate a word with so much fierce passion. He removed his glasses and threw them on the sofa.

"You tell him!" I said.

There was a helpless look in Ludo's eyes. Without his glasses, his vision was strained. He searched the room indecisively, bleary eyed, as if he couldn't tell which figure was mine.

"I'm right here," I said, once he had located me.

He almost smiled. He hung up the phone and dragged his hands over the sofa to recover his glasses.

"Madonna santa!" Fernando said impulsively. The neighbors across the parking lot leaned over their terraces, and the family who lived adjacent to the lot dragged their chairs to the edge of their patio and stood on them so they could see over the wall.

The situation had gone from bad to worse. One of the dead man's friends had returned. He was pacing violently in front of our door.

"Dear god," Agatha said with that melodious voice of hers. "The cocaine addict is back."

The dog circled at my heels, looking up at the bird. "Don't touch that dog. It's a sack of fleas," Ludo said menacingly. His eyesight was twenty-twenty again. "You see all these locks on my door? I put them in so this sack of fleas wouldn't enter my room. But still I come home to find dog shit on my carpet, or a torn-up bag of rice on my bed."

"And you still haven't learned your lesson?" I said, opening the door. "How about an apartment without frontiers? A home without borders? That is what this dog is here to teach you. Why put up such harrowing barriers when the world is grossly impermanent? Think about it: Is there any guarantee that you or I are not going to die today? The same thing goes for animals. Petita, Taüt — even that miserable goldfish!"

Ludo stood there measuring his thoughts, head down, lips pinched. Bernadette was standing behind Fernando, as mute and pink as a flamingo, as if he were her guardian and friend.

"So you're sure?" Ludo asked. "You want to move in?"

"Yes," I said. "I'm here to stay."

"Fine," he said curtly, and walked back into the living room. I saw a small smile wrinkle the edges of his lips. He had missed me, too.

I decided to stake my claim. I dragged my Mobile Art Gallery into Bernadette's bedroom. I had to move her boxes aside to make space for the miniature museum. Once I was done with that, I looked at Ratzinger's face — stern, secretive, resolved — until I felt Bernadette approach me from behind. I turned around and in my best Italian told her that I could take her down a lot faster than Fernando if I wanted to. I said, "Why should I be the only one without food and warmth?" She scurried away like a crab alongside the wall. Everything Ludo had said about her was true. I was astonished.

I went back to the terrace. The cops finally arrived. The cocaine addict slammed his hands down on the car hood. His hair, which already looked like the greasy end of a mop, stood up; he appeared to have been electrified.

"Everyone, please remain inside your homes," the cops announced uselessly through their megaphone.

Across the parking lot, on the roof of a narrow stone building, a middle-aged woman was hanging white sheets on a line. They were as starched as the white sheet my father had been wrapped in before being slipped into the mud of the earth.

"Is she running a hotel?" I asked Ludo in Italian.

"No," he replied. "The sheets are her alibi. She uses them to spy on the neighbors." I wanted to swallow those elongated vowels of his.

Agatha came up to me, and said, "She has a bit of a crush on Ludo!"

Fernando cast her a punitive look.

"Well, it's true!" she said.

The paramedics wrapped the dead man in foil, lifted him onto a gurney, strapped him down, then carried off the body. Soon, he too would be swallowed by the ground and, depending on the frequency of his brain waves, absorbed by the mind of the universe. The drunk's friends, who had returned to the scene, lingered in the parking lot. One of them said something restless. Another let something slide out of his mouth that was of great offense to the third, a man with a head the size of a volleyball. He turned red with fury. The last man walked up to the wall where their dead friend had sat and delivered a long, eloquent aside. This show unfolded to the great indifference of the police officers who were busy pushing the cocaine addict into the back of their car. Once they drove off with him, all that was left was the puttering of feet, the chiming of the church bells, the ruffling of leaves in the cold wind of winter.

It was a stunning performance on the part of all involved. There it was, the theater of life rudely reminding us that we were still alive. The backdrop to all that death was tremendously beautiful. A raw light emerged over the mountains and came rushing through the windows. It was so bright that we all felt naked in it. No one said anything for the rest of the day.

By the next day, I had settled in, and Bernadette had moved out. No one knew where she went. No one cared. Ludo Bembo was in a good mood —a rarity—and he gave us all a laugh by imitating her by sliding down the corridor like a crab while pushing his glasses up the bridge of his nose with his index finger. Agatha joked about how Bernadette was probably drinking her pale tea and eating a bland lunch — bread with mayonnaise or Nutella with a bread stick — under a tree at the Vatican, pulling her skirt down over her knees if it hiked up in the wind.

Over the course of the next few weeks, I began to get a sense of everyone's lives. I learned the neighbors' names, watched them all come and go, amble about, loiter, walk to the green hills of Sant Daniel to fill their empty jugs with stream water; they bought groceries; they laughed, cried, soothed, or shouted at one another depending on the day. I felt safe among them — safer than I had when I'd been alone in Quim Monzó's apartment. There was Ester downstairs, a baker, whom we ordered our bread from every week. There was Mercè, who could almost always be found on her rooftop balcony spying on the neighborhood while removing dried sheets from the clothesline and pinning freshly washed items up in their place. Another, Agnès, appeared at dusk holding a fishnet with an extending pole handle, which she used to capture the neighborhood's stray cats. She would then release them back into the parking lot a few days later, and they would disappear faster than comets in the night sky. Agatha informed me that Agnès believed this form of catch and release would warp the cats' minds, effectively dampening their savage DNA, allowing them to lead happier lives; confused by the bewildering comings and goings of the other cats, they would be unable to engage in sustained fights or form enemy camps.

Inside the apartment, Fernando spent his mornings sitting quietly at the dining-room table, drinking tea and staring intently into the distance. He never said a word to anyone about what he was thinking. At noon, he would abruptly get up, march into the living room, and chisel away at a block of clay until another one of Agatha's faces emerged. Petita slept on the sofa as Fernando worked. The fish came in and out of view with a regularity that depended on how long it had been since someone had last cleaned its tank. It was a fat goldfish with bulging eyes and tiny transparent fins; it was unclear how such disproportionate fins could propel its bulbous body through the water, which was usually thick with grime.

Fernando refused to speak while he was working, and often he refused to speak even after he was done, especially if the expression on Agatha's bust didn't correspond to the expression he had intended. The only time he spoke was when he had a grave vision; that's how he referred to his dreams, as *grave visions.* One night, he dreamt that a balding, acned child with torn overalls and an ancient expression lived in their bedroom, a dark room at the back of the apartment with a small window that overlooked the courtyard next door.

"What's the child's name?" I asked, standing in the kitchen with Taüt on my shoulder. I had begun to feed him directly from my mouth. It was the only way the bird would eat. I chewed a piece of bread and then extended my tongue to the bird, who quickly retrieved the masticated clump.

"His name is Fernando," Fernando said.

"Fernando?" I swabbed my mouth with my finger to get rid of the remaining bread. I hated it when it got stuck to my gums.

"Fernando," he insisted.

That was it. From that day on, there were two Fernandos living in the house: the flesh-and-bone Fernando, the adult sculptor, and the child-ghost Fernando who, according to the first Fernando, had suffered a terrible and frightening death. To help the child heal, Agatha placed bowls of salt around their bedroom.

"Salt absorbs negative energy," she said. "The bigger the crystals, the more they absorb."

I told her there was no need to explain the obvious. Agatha worked in a health-food store selling macrobiotic products, incense, herbal infusions, salt lamps, teas. Later that day, she returned from work with a gift for me: a bag of Himalayan salts, which she insisted I put under my pillow in order to eliminate the residue of Bernadette. I told her I live for residue, though perhaps not Bernadette's, a comment that caused Ludo to roll his eyes from across the living room, where he was seated, legs elegantly crossed, on the sofa.

Ludo's mood, which had initially been generous, perhaps even exuberant, had soured over the last few weeks. He had become consistently petulant and unforgiving, stern and hard to read. I didn't know how to approach him. I didn't know what to think. I had no idea what he did with his days. Sure, he taught a few classes at the university, but he would often leave in the morning and come back at night, exhausted, shut down, gassy, and disgruntled, unwilling to have sex.

I had to work on him every evening, tune him up. This was his home, his hearth. Instead of him coming and going in Quim Monzó's apartment, being pushed out by the putrid fumes of my past that would rise at random to pay me a visit, demanding my attention, here it was I who was subjected to Ludo's whims. Here, his manners seemed strange, mysterious, ethereal. If I approached him with questions, he would answer some but not others. Certain topics, I had come to observe, he avoided altogether: anything having to do with death, illness, the injustices the powerful minority assailed against the abject majority. There were days when his dismal temperament caused me to feel visible and invisible in rapid succession, as if I were constantly appearing and disappearing from the stage of life. This experience hooked a familiar sensation out of my past and replayed it until I felt obliterated: the awareness of finding myself *in a dark wood, lost*. I felt yanked around by his ups and downs. I felt dizzy. I couldn't tell if I was ascending or descending humanity's abysmal pits.

At times, I would think: What is my part in this? Whose hand had failed to remove the thorn from the other's foot? But then I would remember that it was his job, as a privileged member of the Pyramid of Exile, to help *me*. After all, he was gulping down all the oxygen available from whatever small opening existed at the top. He could even squeeze his way out to interact with others or, I was sure, to have sex with the Tentacle of Ice. This was a pernicious thought that had wormed its way into my brain, and I couldn't figure out how to exterminate it. After all, in addition to spending most of his time outside of the apartment, he seemed to have lost interest in having sex with me. What else was I to conclude? The Tentacle, a nonexile par excellence, likely offered him a much simpler exchange. I imagined her letting him off the hook, encouraging him to deny his pain, rewarding him for leading an unexamined life.

One night I left Taüt in my room, which resembled a prisoner's cell, shut the door behind me, and walked over to Ludo's. I was naked. I let myself in without knocking. He was reading a book in Occitan. I couldn't make out the title. I saw my figure reflected in a mirror on his wall. I looked thin and brittle, but I was more resolved than ever. My eyes were shining with the fixed purpose of a rebel; I was preparing to express my whole fragmentary self in a wild deluge. Ludo lay his book down to rest on his chest.

"You shouldn't walk around naked. There are other people living in this apartment, you know."

I could see his penis rising in his pants.

"Don't be so resentful," I said, kneeling on his bed. I examined his head of precise curls. I reached over and removed his glasses. His pupils dilated as his eyes adjusted to seeing without them. He looked lost and helpless.

"Is it easier if you can't see me clearly?" I teased, gently placing my hand on his bulging organ.

"You've worn me down," he said. "I can't make sense of your moods; they exhaust me." He removed my hand as he said it.

My moods? I thought. I was appalled, but I didn't want to get into it. Instead, I said, "According to Scheler, resentment is an *autointoxication — the evil secretion, in a sealed vessel, of prolonged impotence.*"

"Who is Scheler?" he said with an air of desperation.

"Who is Roquentin! Who is Scheler!" I said mockingly.

"Do you think this is seductive?" he said, reaching for his glasses and putting them back on his face. He looked at me through the lenses. His bulge had, in fact, deflated.

"Who cares!" I said. "How can you talk to me about moods when your own are abysmal and likely designed to distract me from the fact that you have a dirty conscience?"

"A dirty conscience?" he inquired, offended, as if he had never interfered with my notebook.

"Yes, a dirty conscience," I repeated. Then I got up and I left. Hours later, I slipped a note with the word *inquietare* under his bedroom door. That was as much of a clue as I was willing to give him.

We didn't speak for days. During that time, I swung between feeling sullen, dispossessed and angry, betrayed. But then, somehow, we got back to business as usual. He came home one night, pushed me up against the wall, and stuck his tongue in my mouth. He grabbed my arm and pulled me into his bedroom. "Leave Taüt with the ghost of Bernadette," he said breathlessly, when I tried to retrieve the bird. It didn't occur to me then that he sounded like me. I left the door to my room open. Taüt was perched on the edge of the wooden desk chair. He will likely stay put, I thought, following Ludo. We fucked like animals.

"Why does your pussy feel so good to me?" he cried out.

His mouth smelled like another woman. The Tentacle of Ice, I thought, as I finished. My suspicions were finally confirmed: During the weeks we hadn't seen each other, she, a member of the unthinking masses, had returned to his life to provide him with uncomplicated pleasure. He had sought solace in a woman — the Tentacle of Ice — who was, relative to me, in less pain and whose desires had nothing to do with art or literature or the *total problem of life*. As I went over these thoughts, I often felt a cold draft blow through my void. It stung the flattened sheet of my heart that had begun to thicken, to gather dimensions, to warm up — an entirely disorienting sensation.

The next morning, confused and hurt, I went back to my room looking for Taüt. I needed to take solace in his company, but he was nowhere to be found. The bird had disappeared. It was one thing when the bird had vanished in Quim Monzó's apartment, but another thing entirely in Ludo Bembo's. I organized a search. I put Agatha in charge of looking through all the nooks and crannies of our respective bedrooms.

"Don't hesitate to search inside pillowcases," I ordered, "even if they are stuffed with pillows; that bird knows how to shape-shift. And make sure you look under mattresses, behind wool sweaters piled in our closets, and inside drawers with handles he could have hooked his beak onto and drawn open." She proceeded with her usual convivial manner, spreading her soothing scent through the apartment as she conducted her search.

I put Ludo, who was grumpier than ever, in charge of the kitchen. "Open all the cabinets and look under the kitchen sink, inspect the pots and pans, especially the large ones you reserve for boiling your noodles."

"You mean pasta," he rudely interrupted.

"And make sure you don't forget to look inside the fridge and the washing machine; Taüt may have needed to tumble around a bit or sit privately for a moment in the chilly air of the refrigerator."

Ludo stood there, staring at the dining-room wall, which was blue and bare. He would make a terrible soldier, Ludo Bembo, with the protracted firing of his neurons.

"Can you go about your business in a more committed fashion?" I asked, pushing him through the kitchen door.

But to my dismay, he began brewing coffee. He was determined to be idle. I watched his nimble fingers unscrew the moka. Outside, the tramontana was thundering down the streets, rattling doors and windows, banging shutters. All the noise of a firing squad, I thought, looking at the composition of colors beyond the window, the mustard lichen covering the neighbor's terra-cotta roof. The colors reminded me of the Catalan flag, that blazing gold overlaid with four stripes of blood.

"Well?" I said, pressing Ludo with a businesslike dryness.

He cast me a defiant gaze, lit the stove, put the moka on the grills. Then he removed his glasses and calmly wiped the lenses with the edges of his pajama shirt.

"This is the best I can do given the absurdity of the task," he stoically answered, putting his spectacles back on.

I looked out the window at a misty-eyed pigeon, hoping it would turn into Taüt. Its pink feathers gleamed in the cold winter sun. It was February. I listened to that reckless wind howl furiously as it swept through Girona. What am I doing here? I silently wondered. What am I ever doing anywhere? The coffee brewed, filling the kitchen with a light steam that carried the scent of chocolate and lemon peel, with a hint of cow dung. Love. What is love? Was it the bird-shaped hole in my heart? I looked at Ludo.

"I don't want to hear the word *love* come out of your mouth ever again," I said bitterly. "It is as clear as the sky, crystal clear, that you have understood nothing."

"Nothing?" he posed with an implacable inquisitorial expression.

"Nothing."

I walked away, nearly in tears. I felt myself to be the unhappiest person in the world. I could feel my hands and lips trembling. Where was Taüt? Had someone left the door ajar? Thrown the windows open? He couldn't fly. He was a bird whose wings had been clipped so often, they had refused to grow back. But he could have scaled the walls. Did he suffer from phantom-feather syndrome? I shut myself inside the bathroom and silently cried. I cursed the disastrous calamity of my life. I looked in the mirror. "Is this me?" I asked. I watched my lips form the words in the mirror. The coarse hairs of my father's mustache floated across the black sea of my void. There was hardly anything left of him. "Does everything I touch have to disappear?" I mumbled. I looked down at my sick hand. Then I cupped it over my mouth and shoved the screams of pain that were on the cusp of emerging back inside.

Hours later, I'd finally calmed myself down. And who did I think of? Fernando. Where was Fernando? I burst out of the bathroom looking for him. He was hovering over another one of Agatha's false faces in the living room. Time had swept past; it was midafternoon. The glass doors leading out to the terrace were open. I closed them immediately, then I stood there and looked at the prune-colored sky through the window. It was radiant, breathtaking. The crystalline blue of the morning had bloomed into a metallic violet that shone with the cool light of the winter sun. In the distance, the Pyrenees looked like silver needles lined up to sew the regal fabric of that purple sky. I turned to Fernando.

"Fernando," I said with rehearsed calm. "Taüt has disappeared."

"Sparito?" he asked rhetorically.

Where had he been this whole time? Where were Ludo and Agatha? No one had come knocking on the bathroom door; they hadn't even told me they were leaving.

"Sparito," I answered with a funereal gravity.

He put his chisel down. I told him I needed him to sit at the dining table, close his eyes, and retrace Taüt's footsteps in one of his grave visions. I told him, "That bird walks everywhere like a dog." Then I looked at Petita, who was curled on the couch; her ears perked up immediately. Had she eaten the bird? I walked over to her and lifted her flews. I smelled her mouth. Her saliva smelled like metal. I forced her mouth open. She was innocent: no feathers, no blood. I let her go back to sleep again.

Fernando did as he was told. He sat at the table with his eyes closed. When he opened them, he said, "Taüt will be back in his own time."

"Where is he now?" I asked, leaning across the dining-room table. The wood felt cold against my palms.

"I have no idea," he said. "All I see is darkness. Everything is black."

I wanted to bang my head against the wall. I wanted to slap him in the face.

"Taüt?" I called out in a shrill voice, hoping the bird would appear at my heels. He did not.

Afternoon turned to evening. It was unclear when Ludo and Agatha would be back. Perhaps, I wistfully thought, they were searching the streets. I hadn't wanted to leave the apartment. I wanted to be there in case

Taüt returned. The sky turned a velvet black. I felt despondent, foolish. I thought to myself: Being with others only leads to more loss, more pain. I was humiliated. I reached for my notebook. I looked around, searching for a hole or a crevasse to sink into, to be alone with my endless wretched thoughts.

ALBANYÀ

The Story of How I Oxygenated
My Multiple Minds in the Verdant Valley
of the Pyrenees and Engaged in a
Socratic Dialogue with Nature

B Y THE NEXT MORNING, I WAS HARBORING A TERrible resentment toward Ludo. I considered pelting hot coals of anger at him, but if I did, my sick hand would burn. I wasn't sure how much more pain it could hold. I decided that the best course of action was to take a temporary leave of absence. Besides, Bernadette's room, despite being a dark and damp hole, was too close to Ludo; it was no place to think. I needed to bathe in forests, to breathe oxygenated air.

That afternoon, while nursing a violent headache, I boarded a bus to Figueres, the stomping grounds of Dalí, that mustached genius. There, I changed buses. I headed northeast to Albanyà, a tiny village in the valley of the eastern Pyrenees situated along the Muga, a river that passes through Boadella i les Escaules and Castelló d'Empúries, and that proceeds to deposit its chilled waters into the Sea of Sunken Hopes at the Gulf of Roses.

As the battered bus pitifully made its way north, I realized that my very ability to think had been corrupted by Ludo's destructive pattern of advances and retreats, the constant making and unmaking of our relationship, not to mention his remorseless indifference toward Taüt's tragic fate. Ludo's moods, I hypothesized, had several origins. Primary among them was the fact that, due to his unresolved issues with literature and death, and therefore with his ancestors, the Bembos, he was simultaneously attracted to and repulsed by me, final descendent of the Hosseinis. By keeping me in close proximity, he was both working out his issues, which he longed to do — hence his confessions of love — and, concomitantly, was perplexed by the disturbance such processing required of him — hence his sudden withdrawals and subsequent numbness. So what lesson had I taught him regarding love's false and intrusive nature? None. I had been a fool. My defenses had been blown. I had walked straight into the trap of love. I felt as though someone had gutted my organs.

We reached the lofty peaks of Mare de Déu del Mont and Puig de Bassegoda. As the steep cliffs and deep ravines of Albanyà came into view, I was reminded of the mountainous terrain of that no-man's-land my father and I had traversed, our harrowing exodus. Neither love nor home, I thought despairingly, apprehending the high mountain crests that sliced away at the sky, are capable of keeping anyone alive.

I got off the bus. Albanyà was deserted. There wasn't a soul in sight. A stray dog was lying lazily at the end of a gravel path. A few pigs were sniffing at the muddied grounds behind him. There was a lonely horse standing by the edge of a corral, whipping her tail. I imagined Ludo's voice coming at me from afar.

"Where in the world are you going?" he asked, swiftly exposing his annoyance.

"I found a room for rent on the World Wide Web!" I told him.

"In Albanyà, on the Internet?" I heard him ask, bewildered.

"World Wide Web, World Wide War!" I declared, though I had no clue why.

He said nothing after that.

I walked to the end of the gravel path. The dog, a white mutt, raised his head and let out a halfhearted growl. I knocked on the door of the farmhouse, which was tucked behind a row of cedars out of view from the road. A clean-shaven man with a round pale face opened the door. He grunted something; it was barely audible. He was either very timid or very drunk, round at the waist, and his eyes looked bruised. *Widower rents room in quiet Albanyà farmhouse*, the ad had read. He let me into the living room. He kept his eyes on the rug that ran across the floor, as if he had lost a few coins and was searching the ground, hopeful but demure. There was a grandfather clock in the back of the room. It ticked and tocked. I watched the golden pendulum swing inside the glass case, then I looked at the walls, which were covered with a vivid floral wallpaper that featured peonies, chrysanthemums, roses, pinecones, and cinnamon ferns on a green background. It was a tasteless hodgepodge affair.

Without lifting his eyes from the floor, my chubby host, whose face turned crimson upon speaking, told me that coffee and a boiled egg would be served in the morning—breakfast was included in the price of lodging. If I insisted, he continued, turning as red as a plum, he could add a piece of toast and some peach jam he had preserved last year. But I insisted on no such thing.

He promptly showed me to my room, a small rectangular enclosure perched atop a spiraling flight of wooden stairs, furnished with a single bed and a child's desk and chair. I saw myself as a child, sitting at that desk, my father standing over me.

"What are the major and minor cities of our sorry nation?" my father inquired.

"Isfahan, Shiraz, Tehran, Qom, Tabriz, Ahvaz, Mashhad, Bandar Abbās, Kerman, Zāhedān, Yasuj, Hamadān, Izeh, Behbahan," I heard my-self answer.

I felt something sweet and tender in my mouth. The taste of dates from our palm trees in the Caspian.

"And who are we?" he inquired, his mustache still dark with youth.

"Autodidacts, Anarchists, and Atheists," I answered.

"Good child!" he declared. And with that, the chair was empty again.

The timid host had long retreated. We didn't bother each other again until the next day at breakfast.

That night, before going to bed, I said out loud to no one: "I have come to Albanyà to rake the floor of my void and think spontaneously far from the unforeseen interruptions of Ludo Bembo's testicles." I swallowed my saliva. I was hungry, but I refused to eat. Fasting clears the mind, I in-sisted, and persevered, retrieving my notebook whose inky pages were, by then, full of prophetic declarations made by the writers of exile; authors of death and discontinuity whose words implied a metaphysical rebellion, whose sentences communed together in the limitless expanse of the ma-trix. These writers' sentences deposited me at the edge of the unknown, far from the repulsive banality of reality others refer to as life.

I pushed my fingers into my notebook as if it were the oracle of Hāfez. My notebook, I considered, is currently bursting at the seams with tran-scriptions of my father's Catalan oeuvre, which was itself a series of tran-scriptions of Rodoreda, Dalí, Pla, Verdaguer, Roig, and Maragall. "Ah, Maragall, that failed anarchist," I muttered. After the bombings of the

Tragic Week and the defilement of the corpses of nuns, the man had turned soft. He had become a protector of the bourgeoisie. Yet my notebook was spilling over with retranscriptions of my father's transcriptions of Maragall's translations of Nietzsche's oeuvre from the French, since Maragall, known as the poet of "La Paraula Viva," hadn't learned a lick of German. *La paraula viva*, the live word, I thought, laughing hysterically and sitting bolt upright to bang my notebook against the mattress.

"As if there are any dead words!" I spoke into the smoky air of night. Somewhere in the house, a chimney had been lit, logs stoked, embers sent flying.

I looked out the window at the verdant valley; the tops of the trees, shimmering with the reflected light of the moon, appeared as white as craniums against the black sky. I had no idea what time it was. Time, that remorseless thief. But, in the depths of my mind, I knew that whatever time it was, I wasn't yet ready to open my notebook. I wasn't hungry or lucid enough. To pass the time, I stood up and exited the room. In the absence of a corridor, I began to pace the stairs, muttering various incendiary phrases into the atmosphere as I ascended and descended the creaky wood.

"I am going to use my sick hand to grab hold of the Matrix of Literature," I cried out on my first downward flight.

"I am going to leap headfirst into the senselessness of the world," I added on my upward climb.

Once I was at the top of the staircase again, I yelled: "I am going to hurl my void, which hosts literature's spears and daggers and the pain of my multiple selves, at life. I, a literary terrorist, am going to force life to dissolve its resistance toward me."

I started back down again.

"I, Zebra, Dame of the Void, am going to express my *desires, enigmas, obsessions, and passions* for everyone to see."

I paused and sniffed the fiery air.

"Long live Zebra!" I projected, just as my host's round face, red from the heat of the fire, appeared before my own.

He had a disconcerted look in his eyes. *You, whose wife is dead — what is a being?* I wanted to ask him but held myself back. Instead, I bowed before him. He had been eating. He finished chomping the remains of his dinner and then asked me, rather irresolutely, if I could contain my activities to my bedroom. The man has suffered, I thought, and complied.

Back in my little rented room of writing, my *room of ghosts*, I surveyed the countryside through the window. I heard dogs howl, horses neigh, pigs snort hefty doses of muddied earth. I caressed the soiled pages of my notebook. The trees looked like wrinkled silk amid the folds of the night sky. The moon, pocked and slung low, looked like a wheel of cheese. A chilly draft came through the seams in the door and the window. It was time. Suddenly, impulsively, I opened my notebook. The following oracle emerged: *Even the most perfect reproduction of a work of art is lacking in one element: its presence in time and place, its unique existence at the place where it happens to be.*

"Ah, Benjamin, martyr of thought, sublime member of the Matrix of Literature!" I said to no one. A man much like Barthes, Borges, Blanchot, and Beckett — the writers of the *B* who had emerged in Quim Monzó's corridor on the eve of one of Ludo's first departures. Taüt, fellow steward of death, had spent that evening walking at my heels. "Where is he now?" I cried. I could feel the tightly woven tissue of my heart being pulled and stretched to make room for yet another absence. It was excruciatingly painful. I let myself weep. Then I redirected my attention to Benjamin, who, unlike Ludo Bembo, was a man unafraid of holding a candle to the night in order to measure the immensity of the darkness that surrounds us.

I reflected on Benjamin's words. What message lay hidden in their nimble sound? I experienced a torrential sequence of digressive thoughts: like me, Benjamin was hyperconscious of his poorly designed fate. Stuck in Portbou, he had killed himself at the edge of the Catalan territories a day before Spain opened up its borders to those who were fleeing from Hitler, that evil despot, man of grotesque afflictions whose presence on this soggy earth we might never recover from. This, in turn, led me to think of Mohammad Reza Shah Pahlavi, self-proclaimed King of Kings, walking around the ruins of Persepolis in his bejeweled clothes looking like a torero. The smell of putrefaction arose from the ashen corpse-strewn landscapes of my childhood and tickled my nose. Before I knew it, my father's ghostly voice was trumpeting through my void, that echo chamber of literature that I carried within me and that I had funneled an infinite number of words into.

"The Catalans are against bullfighting," my father solemnly relayed. "A sign of their dignity, which was arrived at through excessive suffering at the hands of Franco." He sighed deeply, then continued: "That fraudulent man with his Hitlerian mustache, against whom I rebel by growing a mustache of Nietzschean proportions . . ."

His voice faded as suddenly as it had appeared.

"Father?" I called, projecting my voice like a searchlight into the depths of my void.

But my father did not answer. He had been reduced to dust. He had been absorbed back into the mind of the universe, where he ultimately belonged. He was gone. Had the trace of my mother left along with him? I wondered. I felt my throat clog with tears.

I lay down on the bed, unsure of what to do. I closed my eyes. I pictured Walter Benjamin sitting with his head in his hands in Portbou, then I, too, sat that way. Hours later, I got myself together and read his mystical sentence several times in the bleak light of the lamp. *Even the most perfect reproduction of a work of art is lacking in one element: its presence in time and place, its unique existence at the place where it happens to be.* The more I lingered on the phrase and its community of ideas, the more I felt as though I had encountered a loose thread from my own multiple minds, smeared and flattened onto the page.

In my father's absence, my thoughts began to congeal like the night air. They became focused and took on gargantuan proportions. I, too, am a reproduction. My consciousness, battered by multiple exiles, is a constellation of distorted reproductions of my childhood self; in other words, just like a reproduced work of art, I had been detached from the domain of tradition, expelled from my home, banished from my origins; like an uprooted tree, I had been cut off from fertile soils and light, drained of my verdant aura, tossed into the shadowy pile of ruins. I wished Morales was around so I could share my revelation with him. But how was I going to push Benjamin's thought further? How was I going to borrow his thinking to do what I intended: to hurl my void — that palimpsest of literature and my multiple stratified selves — at life in order to simultaneously expose its infinite multiplicity and its fundamental nothingness? Surely, Benjamin had gone far enough for his time. But years had passed since his life and death, decades. It was a whole new century, the twenty-first, a century with fangs, habituated by its predecessor, the twentieth, to drawing huge amounts of blood from us sorry little rodents.

I sat on the edge of the bed, clueless and yet certain I was on the cusp of an earth-shattering idea. I reveled in the euphoria of that liminal zone, the blissful space of potential between the germination and the harvesting of an idea. The sheets were rough against my feet. The room was growing draftier by the minute. I was shivering. I looked out the window. I saw my reflection in the glass. I looked through it at the moon, which was wheeling its way across the sky. I fell asleep, thinking only of the capricious cascade of thoughts that awaited me the next day in the remote village of Albanyà, with its glacial river and backdrop of granite and slate.

The morning unfolded like a reel of paper. I took my coffee and boiled egg at the dining-room table while my host stood motionless, staring out the east window in silence. We had our backs to each other.

"Is this yesterday's coffee?" I asked.

He turned around and nodded. His face looked marbled in the filmy light of morning. He looked even sadder than the night before.

"Did your wife die in the morning?" I asked.

He retreated into the kitchen rather unhurriedly, then returned with the pot of coffee and refilled my mug with the liquid tar.

"She died at dawn," he confirmed. His face shrank as he said the words.

I offered him my condolences. Useless to ask if he had absorbed her through metempsychosis, I contemplated, as I observed his deflated demeanor. It was unlikely that his body or mind could accommodate two people.

"No wind or clouds today," he said with a sinking voice, as he returned to the window and looked through the polished glass at the boulders and rocks hemming in the valley.

"Nothing like a clear sky," I replied. "A personification of the void," I murmured.

Then, thinking of Benjamin, I told him that I had to get going because I had my work cut out for me, that my life was composed of a series of appearances and disappearances (I said nothing of Taüt), that as a result of this profound disorientation, I had been retracing the crooked path of my exile in order to map on the page the uselessness of my suffering, and that I have been waiting for myself — my multiple selves, I corrected — to appear in my notebook legibly, which so far had been an inconclusive affair, derailed by an unforeseen enmeshment with a man so profoundly attached to rationality, a man with an inflexible mind, a mind as linear as the stick of a broom! A man *ready to deny the evidence of his senses*, I told the man angrily, echoing Dostoyevsky's words. A literary amateur, who only has thoughts about the thoughts of others and not a single one of his own, like most scholars, who, on the whole, are thoughtless and witless heretics who approach literature with their rational mind as if it were a technical tool, purely mechanic. My timid host looked shocked and bored — perhaps slightly more bored than shocked. The good news, I barreled on, gurgling my saliva, is that I have come to Albanyà in order to get back on track; it is my conviction that I will be able to get to the bottom of things in this remote and verdant valley, and finally enter the red-hot center of this sinister journey I have come to refer to as the Grand Tour of Exile.

He looked at me with those wet eyes of his but said nothing. He peeked inside my cup to see if I had finished. I had. He removed the cup and the empty plate where the egg had been. Indifference, I concluded, is the driving force of his character; his wife may have killed herself out of boredom. I wiped my mouth and flew out the door with that shiny boiled egg bouncing around in my intestines.

I walked over a bridge into the town cemetery. I stared at the remains of the dead. Small vases were affixed next to each headstone, and a variety of pink and white plastic flowers, their leaves weathered and paper thin, sat in sooty containers. I could smell the stench of the decomposing corpses through the wall, an overpowering bacterial smell that brought to mind fungi, rotten meat, bile, shit. When I'd had enough, I walked back and stood on the bridge that was suspended over a glacial sapphire brook that widened into a small crystalline pool. I spotted an opening in the hilly surroundings and made my way through a cluster of trees. Once there, I sat on the rocky shore and cast smooth stones into the emerald green waters, prepared to unleash my most fanciful and mercurial thoughts.

With each stone I sank into the water, I verbally reproduced Benjamin's sentence. I duplicated and quadrupled the phrase until I'd worked myself into a frenzy. The seeds of my thoughts were sprouting. I arrived at a more nuanced edition of the revelation that had presented itself to me the night before: By hurling my void at life, I, Zebra, was putting all my many disparate selves, the seemingly distant "realities" they pertained to — modernity and tradition, the New and Old Worlds, life and literature — on a collision course.

I disclosed my thoughts to the trees and the sky and the birds in the bush.

A response emerged from the rugged surroundings, and I repeated it for the world to hear: "You are going to continue to reproduce yourself, thereby preserving the discontinuity of exile and confronting the self-satisfied ignorance of the unexiled, but you are also going to embed yourself again in the fabric of tradition, the depths of your childhood self.

"How?" I asked.

"By stitching your multiple brains to the landscapes that have produced them.

"And what will I use to thread the needle?

"The spooling lines of the literature of exile produced in the very places you will traverse!"

I was having a Socratic dialogue with the environment. I was speaking to the poetic consciousness of nature and nature was responding. The wind blew, the trees bowed, the birds chirped, the water rippled along its stony path. And as each thing moved, my conviction that I was on the right track was reinforced. I pressed on.

Finally, the hidden message in Benjamin's prophetic line arrived. It sounded out from the smooth granite of the Eastern Pyrenees and inserted itself into the labyrinthine corridors of my mind. Once there, it scurried about like a rat in a maze: "Replace the word *reproductions* with the word *retranscriptions*," the mountains seemed to say. I opened my notebook. I wrote: *Retranscriptions lack one element: their presence in time and place.*

Suddenly, all was clear. Displaced transcriptions would no longer do. I had to retranscribe Josep Pla's literature in the places and spaces represented within its pages — namely Girona and Palafrugell — Joan Maragall's in Barcelona, Walter Benjamin's in Portbou, Jacint Verdaguer's on a hike to the peak of the Canigó. I had to retrace the long walks my father and I had embarked on in the Corridor of Exile in order to transcribe literature in situ. And what did this exactness, this topographic precision, provide? The opportunity to impose the truth of my complex and many layered void on any nonexiles who would be walking along those same routes engaging in some banal form of literary tourism out of the delusion that there is such a thing as an original or a singular self, a coherent "I" conducting an apprehensible life — the delusion par excellence of the imperialists of the so-called New World, of the supposed march of progress. After all, where was Walter Benjamin or Unamuno or Mercè Rodoreda? These writers were everywhere and nowhere at once; their consciousnesses — the network of sentences into which they had breathed life — were being reproduced, plagiarized, lifted from this or that text to be infused back into the world. By transcribing those sentences in situ, I would be producing a thread, however meager, of hope that the willfully blind, the nonexiles who would be slogging along the same literary routes as I, would finally acquire the courage not just to see but look.

I smiled at the thought of it all. I had struck gold. The harvest was approaching. It was clear to me now, crystal clear, that it wouldn't have been enough to drag the Mobile Art Gallery hither and thither at random. What a premature idea that had been! What an oversight! I remembered standing alongside my father staring at the landscapes Josep Pla had written about: the cork trees of Palafrugell, the cauliflower heads that burst out of the village's moist red earth, the rusty masts of the fishing boats that rock hypnotically in the wind and the waves. I saw my future self returning to Palafrugell at a time when *half of Europe* was again *collapsing like a battered building that's subsided and falling apart,* as it had been during Pla's youth, when he'd written those words. I felt emboldened, powerful, buoyed by my many former selves. I thought, I am a person capable of simultaneously existing in multiple planes of time. What an exhilarating thought that was! I repeated it inwardly, and then I said it out loud to be absorbed by the trees and the sky and the birds moving through it like missiles.

The entire province of Girona was Pla's territory. This was an undeniable fact. Just like Cadaqués, Port Lligat, and the Cap de Creus had been Dalí's. And Portbou, at the end of the great calamity that was his life, had been Walter Benjamin's.

I wrapped up my thoughts: It was clear I needed to resume my pilgrimages. I had to design literary routes for each of these writers — the primary authors of my father's Catalan oeuvre — in order to merge the metaphysical experience of the Matrix of Literature and its network of archives with a physical experience in situ. I opened my notebook at random again to make sure I had pushed my thinking as far as it could go.

"*Dante, vindictive and severe as any artist in exile,*" I read, "*used eternity as a place to settle old scores!*"

Who had said that? I could not recall. I took my thoughts one step further. I was reaching the bottommost plateaus of my void, the icy, burning center at the core of my existence. What did I find there? A raw and savage pain: rejection, humiliation, despair. The world had planted within me the seeds of its own ruthlessness. Just like Dante, I was going to settle my old scores; only I was going to do so in Catalonia. I was going to stage a metaphysical insurrection and reclaim my place among the other beings of this trifling universe. Because how, I wondered, was I going to sound out the Hosseini alarm while living apart from others, barred from the good life, invisible? I couldn't stand the way people looked through me as if I were transparent. Who would be able to ignore me, or literature, which is my life, if I, Dame of the Void, walked along literary routes dragging the Mobile Art Gallery behind me and transcribing literature as I went? The nonexiles and imperialists of the world, all those who had made of me a monster, a sublime and ghastly being, would have to stand in awe and fear of me. They would have to stop and look at my pain.

I understood, finally, that this was why I had invented the Mobile Art Gallery. I was going to use that miniature museum on every single pilgrimage; I would use all the decrepit writing machines I had embedded within it to contaminate life with literature, modernity with tradition, the New World with the Old. I walked through the herd of trees. I went back over the bridge, shoes in hand. Words, suggested by the scenery, started flowing freely from my mouth. "I am a wandering *speculative border intellectual*, surviving by my wits, roaming the land. Not unlike Ibn al-Arabi, Bashō, Omar Khayyám, and Badi' al-Zaman, those solitary walkers, extemporaneous philosophers, literary tricksters, the wise and wicked ancestors of Cervantes, Rousseau, Rimbaud, Baudelaire, Acker." My void caught fire. I thought I was going to lift off like a balloon and fly into outer space. I pressed my feet into the ground. The asphalt was cold and pebbly. Like any good guru, I thought, all I need are pilgrims, a roving pack of the world's marginalized and exiled, other .1 percenters, who, unlike Ludo, would understand my poverty, the sting of my uninterrupted loneliness.

"Why?" I heard the trees ask.

"Because rebellion means nothing when done alone," I answered, thinking of Camus. "But rebellion means everything when the wronged rise together against the toxic secretions of the world's evildoers and despots."

I skipped down the glum road, energized by this superabundance of thoughts. Halfway to the farmhouse, I sat on a chopped log on the side of the road and listened to nature. It was breathing all around me, and I was breathing alongside it. The sky was nourishing my mind. I sucked in little puffs of air. I held my breath. I absorbed the atmosphere into my cells. Instantly, my brain amped up its revolutions. I opened my notebook. I closed my eyes. I let my sick hand move across the page without thinking. I wrote: "I, Zebra, Dame of the Void, am convinced that the world will yield its mysteries to me so long as I embark on a series of pilgrimages, pilgrimages that would require me to travel physically through the Old World while simultaneously traversing through its mirage in literature, submerging myself in literature's radical genealogy, yes, but also reproducing its pages, exhuming the corpse of the past." My hand hurt, as if by writing I was spilling my own inky blood. "The landscape, as far as I am concerned," I persevered, "has become my library, an archive that lays bare the subtexts of time, the tangled meanings I need to excavate in order to sound out the Hosseini alarm loud and clear."

I sealed my notebook and opened my eyes. The air was full of mist. I could barely see the end of the road. How quickly the weather changes in these mountainous parts, I thought, as quickly as history itself. I got up and walked back to the farmhouse. "My next move," I declared, as I walked past the horse, "has been decided." The animal clapped its tail against the mist. The pigs made way. The dog bowed. Already I was more visible. I had thought my thoughts alongside the mind of the universe. The next day, whistling into the wind, I returned to Girona. There, I would forge my plan: I would map out my literary routes; I would find my fellow Pilgrims of the Void.

GIRONA

The Story of How I Traveled Across
the Corridors of Exile in the Company
of the Pilgrims of the Void

M Y PLANS WERE YET AGAIN STYMIED BY A STRANGE unfolding of events. The following morning, I returned to Ludo Bembo's apartment, and immediately upon opening the door, I heard whispers in Farsi float up through the corridor. It had been so long since I had heard those melodic sounds that my ears grew hot, my knees buckled, my mind spun dizzily. I exited the building and stood dumbfounded on the cobblestone pathway. I observed the recessed door with its hand-shaped knocker. I was at the right door. I climbed back up the dusty steps.

I walked across the threshold cautiously and proceeded down the hallway. There they were: Ludo and Agatha, sitting cross-legged on the tile floor, reproducing the sounds of my mother tongue. They were passing a book between them: *Persian for Italian-Speaking People: A Guide for a Journey into the Unknown.*

They were so entrenched in the book, they'd taken no notice when I walked in. I stood there like a ghost and watched the spectacle unfold. Ludo was wearing a striped silk robe over his pajamas and his hair was uncombed. His curls, usually so precise, had an electric frizz that made it look like he had a halo. He was holding the book.

"Is there a dining car?" he asked in Farsi, returning the book to Agatha.

"What time does the train leave to Isfahan?" Agatha posed. She, too, was in her house clothes: thick sweats and a purple cotton shirt with a green wool sweater over it. She gently passed the book back to Ludo.

"Does this train make a stop in Herat?" Ludo asked.

Their accents were terrible. They might as well have stuffed their mouths with stones. I wanted to stop them from butchering my mother tongue. My mother tongue, I thought, and imagined my mother turning in her makeshift grave. My eyes welled up.

"Can you direct me to the bridge, please?" Agatha asked.

What if a strong wind had blown? What if her body lay there exposed next to the ruins of that demolished house? I stood there unable to speak or move. I had calcified. I had turned to stone.

Ludo took the book from Agatha and then brought it down to his knees.

"What's the matter?" he asked in Italian.

"She's here!" Agatha cried out, nodding in my direction.

"Who?" Ludo shuddered.

"Zebra! She is standing there like a statue."

Those words delivered me from my sorry childhood. Me? A statue? What about her and her many busts? Ludo turned around, wide-eyed and bushy-tailed.

"You're back," he said cheerily, as though we had parted on a good note. Then he spoke to me in Farsi. He opened the book at random and asked the first question that stood out to him on the page. "Do you have a light?" he asked, retrieving his pipe from his robe and placing it rather seductively between his lips.

"I understand nothing!"

"Isn't Farsi your mother tongue?" he asked, perplexed.

His eyes had drifted apart. His face always looked so distended when he was confused. I enumerated Ludo's missed opportunities for demonstrating compassion: He had grown silent at the mention of my dead mother during our first meal; he had abandoned me in a lukewarm tub; he had neglected to search for Taüt. What right did he have to ask me about my mother tongue, to utter those words — *mother tongue* — before I was prepared to speak them, let alone hear them spoken by a pair of expatriated Italians? That pair of words was reserved for me to contemplate on my own time, in solitude.

"That language — Persian, Farsi, Pars — whatever you want to call it," I lectured him (my voice was unleashed), "is reserved for my mustached father. To what end are you, Ludo Bembo, an Italian subject expatriated to Spain — to Catalonia, to be precise — employing it?"

He looked as though I had slapped him across the face. I went on to tell him that where I come from there is an inner and an outer form, and that the rules governing my internal state don't have to correspond with those dictating the terms of my behavior in the world. "Do you understand?" I screamed. "Farsi is relegated to the latter so as far as you are concerned," I warned, "I have no idea what you are saying!"

Agatha retreated from the living room. She gently squeezed my arm on the way out and cast me a pleading look, as if to say *I swear he made me; it was all him.*

"Give me that book," I demanded, once we were alone. I looked at the title, and yelled: "What does the unknown have to do with Iran? The unknown is not a nation no matter how like a chameleon that nation is, no matter how many times it shifts its shape!"

Ludo got off the floor. He was disenchanted. His mouth was down-turned; his eyes and eyebrows drooped.

"Any updates on Taüt?" I asked, forcing my mouth to form the words.

"No," he said. "We've been home all weekend, but he didn't show up." He sounded remorseful. "You know," he said, shaking his golden halo. "You make no room. No room for being understood."

A terrible silence spread its wings between us.

I watched him trail out of the room. I sniffed him on the way out. He smelled like blood oranges, mint, eucalyptus, sand, rotten watermelon rinds, salt, and mist. He smelled like the Caspian Sea, like the Oasis of Books. I stood there simultaneously defiant and disoriented, aware and repulsed by the fact that the codes those who are less burdened with history live by would forever be illegible to me.

I looked out the window. The clouds were swollen. They were loaded with rain. I stood there for a long time, alone, holding the book of Persian phrases and idioms. I could hear Ludo and Agatha putting the dishes away in the kitchen. I heard Fernando come home. To sink, I thought to myself, to slide down the craggy walls of despair would be the easiest thing to do, to indulge in my misfortune, to stop kicking against the current of injustice and the rising tides of evil. Just then, the clouds burst open and released massive globular drops. The windows fogged. I heard Agatha say sweetly, "It's a monsoon!" I sniffed the air. It, too, smelled like the Caspian of my lost childhood.

Shards of memories floated through the misty room. I saw my mother standing in the corner burying her face in her hands. Then I saw her standing in our kitchen on the Caspian. The village fisherman was on his knees on the terra-cotta floor. He was cleaning a sturgeon he had caught, and she was sweeping the blood into the drain. She looked spent, famished, sapped. I saw myself running through the topiaries looking for our three dogs only to find them lying dead under a date palm. They had been poisoned. I touched each one. Their bodies were still warm. I ran back to my mother, knees soiled from crouching next to our dogs, hands bloody from wiping their nostrils.

"Who would do such a terrible thing?" I asked.

"Ask your father," she said sorrowfully, and his figure appeared in the room.

"Life is full of loss," he said. "It's the war. It's always the war. The war has become a state of mind. Our brethren have turned on us. We should consider this a warning for what awaits us if we do not leave."

After that, he walked me to the oval library and resumed my lessons. He asked, "Child, what does an Autodidact, Anarchist, and Atheist always have to do?"

"Compartmentalize," I recited. "And carry on. It's the valiant thing to do!"

There was a burst of thunder. I looked through the window. The image resolved itself. The memories diffused like smoke in the air. I heard a crowd run through the streets laughing hysterically as they went. I stood there in the living room in Girona staring into the distance for a long time. Petita came scurrying in. She sniffed the air. I reached down and patted her on the head; her eyes grew sleepy and full of mist. What now? I thought, looking at her with a troubled mind. I thought of the insurmountable loss, the irreparable wounds that had led me to retrace my footsteps halfway across the globe. And to what end?

I retreated to my room and reached for my notebook in the dark. My sick hand always knew how to find it. I turned on the table lamp. I cracked open the book in the exact same way I had been for decades, years, to soothe myself. Goethe's lines swam up from the page: *There are two souls within my breast, one clings to the earth in search of rough passion, while the other violently shakes off the dust and flies toward the kingdom of its sublime ancestors.*

There was a knock on the door.

"Come in," I said.

It was Agatha. She was standing there with our downstairs neighbor, the baker, and her daughter.

"We're putting in our weekly order for bread," she gently said.

I put in my order. I looked at the child. She floated down the hallway, moping, crestfallen. "*Through love, life is reborn,*" I heard. Who had said that? Life, I thought, as the child returned, horrifying to begin with and now it's duplicating itself. The girl buried her face in her mother's skirt.

An hour later, I knocked on Ludo's door. I was prepared to extend an olive branch. What else was there left to do?

"Come in," he said.

I released the Petita-proof locks and let myself in. But as soon as I saw him, I thought better of it. He was distant, cold, removed. He was lying on his bed with his head propped up on a stack of velvet pillows, his body still wrapped in that silk robe, a sight to behold. He was drawing contentedly on his pipe. I could no longer see his halo. A vaporous cloud filled the room; a soft dawn mist lightly veiled his features. An amateur dressed to approach literature, I thought, as I apprehended his figure. A dandy. Papers and a few dictionaries were scattered across his mattress.

"The only thing you are missing is a lighter on a pulley," I informed him.

"That's what you've come to say?" he asked reproachfully, not even bothering to lift his head. He sucked on the end of his pipe and held the smoke down in his chest.

"No," I said, attempting to break our cycle of misunderstandings. How many senseless blows could we withstand to receive from each other? "I have come to make myself understood."

He exhaled from his nose and the emerging smoke made me think of a bull breathing in the middle of a frost.

I spoke my truth. I shared the words I'd gathered from Goethe.

He reflected quietly for a moment. The dim light coming from his lamp illuminated the wall behind his bed and cast the others in shadow. I felt as though I were standing in the chiaroscuro of a Renaissance painting — an annunciation of sorts. He sat up and set his pipe on the wooden side table. It, too, lay supine in the light of the lamp. I looked at all the wood in his room, at the walls, which were painted a soft yellow. His face recomposed itself. He looked grave, a man on the cusp of delivering a verdict he has been patiently waiting for. He licked his lips.

"*To do two things at once,*" he said somberly, "*is to do neither.*"

Ah, Publilius Syrus: the Iraqi thinker who had been enslaved by the Romans, my estranged brethren. I pushed my way deeper into his room and sat on the edge of his bed. I crossed my legs.

He leaned back and slipped his pipe between his lips again. In the back of my mind, I saw soldiers in camouflage marching single file behind a wall of sandbags on the shore of the Caspian. A leftover memory shard emerging from the ruins of the first, I reasoned, and suppressed the image.

"You look tired," Ludo said, exposing the thread of tenderness that ran beneath his stoicism like a subterranean river. "You should get some sleep."

I turned to look at him. He was holding his pipe away from that seductive mouth of his. The vaporous cloud had diffused, or else my eyes had adjusted to the smoky veneer of the room.

"*Everyone has the face they deserve* by the time they approach thirty," I said, looking at myself in his eyes. Orwell. He, too, had gone to Catalonia. He had fought alongside the Republicans. And what for? Injustice always reconstitutes itself. My reflection shrank from Ludo's eyes. A second later, he blinked and I was gone. I sat there somber, silent, servile, until Ludo Bembo, unaccustomed to my sorrow even though it seemed to have been what he had wanted all along, finally spoke.

"You want platitudes, I'll give you platitudes: *Anyone who doesn't take love as a starting point will never understand the nature of philosophy.*"

There was Plato again. There was Ludo's false rhetoric of love.

"Put your money where your mouth is," I said, and left his room.

The corridor, as usual, was like a Greek temple. I paused for a moment and examined the clay busts. In that strange caesura, Nietzsche's voice came rushing at me. *The whole of European psychology is sick with Greek superficiality!* Due to their excessive number, Agatha's busts were both a reproduction and a dissolution of life. I stood there staring at them, lost in that dim corridor. My thoughts looped and spun. Love. What is love? Had I ever received it? I couldn't be sure.

////////////

After that, I treated the apartment as a hospital where I was convalescing. I sought refuge in my books. I needed to regain my strength. I needed to sharpen my wits, bolster my willpower. How else was I going to execute the plan that the poetic consciousness of nature had unveiled to my many minds in Albanyà?

One morning, as I continued honing my plan, I walked in circles around the dining-room table while the others ate their breakfast just as I had in the oval library of my childhood. I whispered Dante's verses in ghostly tones while I went.

The three of them — Agatha, Ludo, and Fernando — whispered to one another. "She has turned into a goat," Fernando dryly said.

"She is like a clove of garlic!" Agatha humorously agreed.

They were speaking in Italian but using Spanish idioms to agree with one another that I had lost my wits.

"Me? I've turned to stone," Ludo uttered resentfully. "This is beyond words." He poured sugar into his espresso cup and stirred the granules until there were no uneven surfaces left. Is that what he had wanted to do to me? Grind me down, sculpt me until all my rough edges were gone?

"I can hear you loud and clear!" I said to them. "And if you want a Spanish idiom, I can give you a Spanish idiom: I am healthier than a pear!"

Immediately, I thought of Ortega y Gasset's words: *the gem like Spain that could have been* were it not a country obsessed with foreign imitations. This, I thought, is where the Catalans distinguish themselves. "They are no imitators," my father would have said. Just then, the words of one Ehsān Narāghi, a man whose work I had once encountered in my father's library of unatheist books, cascaded down the walls of my void: *What should be done to allow the Oriental countries, and Iran especially, to become conscious of their national and cultural existence and be "for-themselves," without falling either into blind imitation of Western patterns or into extremist reactions to such patterns?*

A torrential outpour followed. The floodgates had opened. I waited for everyone to leave the apartment, and then I walked up and down the corridor, sobbing for hours. In the wake of the Islamic Republic of Iran, these questions had been extinguished. There had been a near total physical and psychic massacre of the country's leading thinkers, writers, intellectuals.

Contemplation, musing, and doubt were no longer allowed; an extreme line of zero tolerance had taken root. I wept at the thought of the damages we had endured. When would Iran show its true colors? I wondered, sipping on my salty tears. Its radiant and stratified pluralism?

I felt as if I had either arrived too late or too early to my own life. I thought of my truncated voyage. It dawned on me: My plan to retrace the path of my exile was impossible. I could make it all the way to Van and salute the Iranian craggy border, but I could go no farther. I would be killed instantly for being a woman traveling alone or for being a Western spy. Me, a *speculative border intellectual*, a Western spy! My future self took offense at the potential insult. What good would it do for me to be buried in that no-man's-land alongside my mother? What use would I be to the world?

I was caught off guard by my sudden impulse to remain alive, by the savage energy of survival. I realized that the Pilgrims of the Void would need me, their dame, to be in tip-top shape. I needed to train my mind in the lucidity of death through the limpid territories of sleep. I returned to convalescing in that borrowed room of mine, which still smelled of Bernadette, of the unlikely pairing of frankincense and toilet-bowl cleaner. Sequestered in my bed, I slept for days.

Whenever I woke, I found I was totally lucid, consumed by hunger, and began furiously making plans. I mapped out various routes. I designed the Pilgrimages of the Corridor of Exile: Pilgrimage of the Memory Man (Josep Pla), Pilgrimage of the Wide-Eyed Genius (Salvador Dalí), Pilgrimage of the Catalan Resuscitator (Jacint Verdaguer), Pilgrimage of the Martyr of Thought (Walter Benjamin), Pilgrimage of the Perseverant (Mercè Rodoreda), Pilgrimage of the Tireless Excavator (Montserrat Roig). The list went on and on.

Afterward, I dusted off the Mobile Art Gallery. I tended to it. I made flyers calling on interested parties to attend the first meeting of the Pilgrims of the Void, scheduled to take place in March, at the site of the ruins of Josep Pla's childhood school directly adjacent to the parking lot beneath Ludo Bembo's apartment. I couldn't believe I hadn't noticed the plaque on the side of the wall until the day before: *Here Josep Pla went to school.* A formidable sign!

On a crisp morning, I left the apartment to distribute the flyers among the regulars at the soup kitchen, among students in the hallways of the university, among those going up and down the steps of the cathedral. I was looking for people who, despite searching, had been unable to fill their void and who were willing to dive into the depths of their doubt. In addition to other bits of useful information, I had included the following points of reflection on the flyers: "Are you willing to drown in inquiry? There is no point in rebelling alone!"

I was hopeful I'd get a good crop.

After several days of this, Ludo finally knocked on my door. He let himself in, holding a plate of rice stained black with squid ink and a salad of arugula and radishes. He put the food down on my desk.

"You have to eat something," he said. He had a look of concern on his face. "I can bring you some wine. Do you want some wine?" he asked.

"Yes, bring me some wine."

I wanted to send him off again because I was in the midst of my thoughts. Literature, I had been thinking, happens in advance of history; it is a form of precognition. Why else would my notebook operate as an oracle with such finesse?

Ludo returned and stood over me, silently observing. Then, finally, he asked: "Why do you spend so much time alone?"

He was looming over the bed, peering down at me. He looked huge to me then and rooted into the ground, as if there were a whole other Ludo branching from his feet into the earth, pinning him to this trifling circumference. I, in contradistinction, had been blown hither and thither by the whims of time. I had been gored to death by the bull of history. I would have needed so much more tenderness than what could be offered in a plate of food and a ten-minute display of affection. I needed to be held. I needed fresh layers of skin to wrap around my raw wounds. I needed someone who didn't retreat so easily to show me how to love them in return.

I dug deep and grabbed hold of my voice.

"Because I can smell character. I can smell bad blood," I said, without looking at him. "I can smell the shit that's gathered at the center of any given person."

He turned stoic again and stared at me with the cold remove of a stately marble statue. Who did he think he was? The embodiment of God? The questions rose like steam from the frozen lake of my heart.

Finally, I mumbled: *"God is an indelicacy against us thinkers."*

"What does that even mean?" he cried out, before disappearing into the corridor.

I threw the plate of food at the door to close it shut behind him.

But just a few days later, in early March, my luck finally turned: Taüt reappeared. I took his spontaneous reappearance as a validation from the mind of the universe and, therefore, from the fumes of my father for the direction in which I had chosen to take the Grand Tour of Exile. I had spent the morning in my room hunched over Bernadette's old desk, transcribing Maragall's translation of Nietzsche in reverse, from right to left, a departure from my previous methodology, which had followed the Western order of reading and writing. What was my purpose? To recover the fumes of my mother, which I had likely absorbed upon her death. In other words, now that my mother tongue had been uncovered perhaps I could also uncover my mother. I contemplated the matter: Who's to say my father had been the only one to absorb her? Or that I should consider sufficient the impoverished traces of her that I had absorbed through the absorption of my father? After all, I had been at the site of her death. My fingers were still sore from digging her grave. Furthermore, I reasoned, there was no chance I could have expelled her. Because before expelling my father, I had conversed with him, his voice had echoed through my void; no such phenomenon had occurred with my dead mother. Her fumes, I concluded, remained lodged in my consciousness, waiting to be discovered. And, if I was going to go on various Pilgrimages of Exile, I wanted her to be present to inhale the brackish Mediterranean air!

I thought about her life. Bibi Khanoum's fate had been one of total extinction: metaphysically assassinated by the confused politics of our nation — Free women! Let them live in bondage! Cover them up but allow them to be educated! Women are our warriors! They must be hanged if they are immodest! They must be jailed if they do not expose their bodies and acquiesce to Western standards of progress! — physically pounded by the house of ruins that collapsed on her head while she was searching for food in that corpse-strewn no-man's-land, and psychologically outmaneuvered even in death by my father's absolutist positions, beloved Autodidact, Anarchist, and Atheist, head of our family.

As I continued with my reverse transcriptions, not only did I recover the parts of my childhood self that contained my mother but also the fumes of my father, his final residues. Flakes of skin. Balls of hair. Nails. All these, I recalled, my mother kept and trimmed for him. At one point, my father's right ear floated up to the surface of my void. It bobbed around the dark folds of my personal abyss like an abandoned boat in a vast open sea. Who was my mother? I asked, but his ear, eroded and soft, capsized and disappeared. I placed a period at the beginning of a sentence and went into the kitchen to make myself some tea. There was no one home. I spoke aloud, addressing the many busts of Agatha's face.

"My mother was Bibi Khanoum," I said. "A woman with infinite patience and an uneven gait. That is all I know about her."

Agatha's busts nodded and smiled empathetically.

"Long live Zebra," they whispered.

I opened the cupboard to grab a glass, a spoon, some sugar; and there, much to my surprise, in the midst of the tableware, was Taüt. He was roosting in a silver dish as if he were an exotic bird prepared by a Roman chef to be served to Julius Caesar. I couldn't believe my eyes.

"Taüt!" I screamed.

He lifted his head and, drawing a deep breath, looked hard at me. His head was glowing. I removed the dish and set it down on the kitchen counter. His whole body was glowing!

"What have you done?" I marveled.

The bird looked at me smugly. He was in the pink of health. Had he been oiling his feathers? I remembered that some days earlier I had overheard Ludo militantly drill into Agatha and Fernando the proper use of olive oil, which he, I discovered while eavesdropping, bought from rare artisanal producers who cultivated the flanks of Mount Etna. "Cold-pressed virgin oil stored in dark chambers," he said, "so as to avoid being ruined by the light of the sun." He paused before stating firmly, "Hence it's bright, almost neon green, glow! Do you know the value of that oil? At any moment those trees could be turned to ash in an outpouring of lava." Neither Agatha nor Fernando could defend themselves, Fernando because of his habit of carefully weighing his words and Agatha because of her sweet disposition, which could tame a wild boar. "We've barely cooked, Ludo," she said in honeyed tones. "It's you who does most of the cooking." I remembered Ludo's final words: "I always use the oil with great discretion."

My fate really did seem to have taken a turn for the better. Taüt had been on a spa vacation, dipping freely, presumably in the night, into Ludo Bembo's precious oil, and Ludo was not home to make the discovery. I stood there observing Taüt. How had he gotten into the cupboards? Where had he been all along? How many deaths had he survived during his disappearance? How many lives had he led? Clearly, he had been spoiling himself. But what had he endured before giving himself such a lavish full-body oil bath? I would never know.

I stood there until, rather suddenly, it occurred to me that Taüt must be my mother. A thought of dizzying proportions. Why else would he have reappeared right now just as I was recovering all that was left of her? She must have reincarnated into this bird, and Quim Monzó had been keeping her for me without even realizing. Or, I thought, maybe while I'd been releasing the fumes of my father in Quim Monzó's house, I had also released some of the fumes of my mother, and the bird — through the power of metempsychosis — had absorbed them. I hadn't stolen him for nothing!

I scooped Taüt out of the dish. He protested and whined, but I didn't care. I had to wash him off before Ludo returned. I had to protect whatever of my mother remained inside him. I shoved him under my shirt. I pressed him against my chest. I only let him out once I was in my bedroom with the door closed. There, I gave him a lecture. I told him that as my only remaining frame of reference he was no longer allowed to disappear. He took offense. He squatted down on the desk and fluffed his sticky feathers, which stuck out like needles.

"You look like a porcupine," I said, and he turned and looked the other way.

I bathed him several times in a bowl of tepid water, scrubbing him with mild oatmeal shampoo. He seemed to enjoy his bath, to perceive it as a welcome extension of his retreat at the spa. He cooed and rubbed his head against my hand. I took this as a sign that he had missed me as much as I had yearned for his haggard and unwilling company, for that bass voice of his. I went into Agatha's bedroom, grabbed a fresh towel, and rummaged through her jewelry until I found an amber bracelet that was too small to fit her wrist.

I dried Taüt off and put the bracelet around his neck, an amulet that would serve to protect him and, in doing so, also protect the fumes of my mother.

"You look so handsome," I said to him.

"You look so beautiful," I said to the part of him that contained my mother.

Taüt cocked his head. His jaw dropped open. I scratched his neck.

A moment later, everyone came home. I announced the good news. Immediately, Ludo and Agatha rolled out a birdcage — huge, ornate, rusted — that they had purchased at the antiques market as a gift for me in case Taüt ever reappeared. It was clear that Agatha had talked Ludo into making the purchase. She strode forward and pushed the cage over the uneven floor with a radiant smile on her face. He, on the other hand, proceeded sternly, a severe-looking silent man whose arm had been twisted into expressing a form of kindness he found difficult to bear. He had made it abundantly clear that he felt the bird infringed upon his rights as a human. He had entered into direct competition with that bird, and this loving exercise, pursued by Agatha, had forced him into an uncomfortable position: that of preserving the bird within our company and therefore securing the possibility of an ongoing battle between the two of them for my attention. A childish man!

They made their way around the clay busts with great care while Fernando watched from a distance. "It is all upward from here," I said, presenting them to the new and improved Taüt.

"Oh, my childhood bracelet," Agatha said. "It looks gorgeous on him!"

I considered telling her about my mother, but I didn't. My mother had never met the Catalans or the Spanish, let alone Italians living in Spain. I wanted to protect her. To keep her safe from the pitying gaze of strangers.

They set the cage in my room, and together said (Ludo surely having been primed by Agatha): "Voilà!"

I knew it had all been rehearsed, but I still gave Ludo a kiss for making an effort. I squeezed his hand the way he had squeezed mine on our first night out together. I felt his muscles relax under my touch.

The pair of them, seeing me deep in thought, retreated from my room. I was alone with Taüt again. Had I ever been alone with my mother? My father had been omnipresent even in death. I looked at the cage. I cringed at the thought of putting Taüt in there. What would my mother do, trapped in that opulent prison?

I searched the house for a ball of yarn and ornamental bells. I tied one end of the yarn to the frame of the bed and the other to Taüt's right talon, to which I also secured the bells. I let him walk freely through the apartment. He spent the evening trotting from room to room. Petita followed close behind, sniffing at the oatmeal fragrance he released along the way. She was a peaceful dog; there wasn't a mean bone in her body.

I followed their hypnotic movements, watching as Taüt crisscrossed through the apartment, folding back over his steps, leaving behind a trail of yarn like the lines one draws between stars, like the Matrix of Literature itself. I was entranced.

Finally, with Taüt restored, the fated day, the day of the gathering of the pilgrims, arrived. I had counted my money — I was two-thirds of the way through it — and asked the baker downstairs to bake me a few loaves with three As cut into them. I bought wine as well, many cartons of Don Simon.

It was an unusually blustery spring day. I was waiting for my disciples to show up in the parking lot in the very spot where the corpse had fallen. In addition to food for thought, the signs I had distributed contained the following information: The Bureau of Spatial-Literary Investigations is searching for participants interested in embarking on the literary expedition of a lifetime. Meeting to be convened on March 17 at four p.m. in the parking lot adjacent to Calle Claveria. Participants must concede to being referred to as Pilgrims of the Void. Prerequisites include: experiences of disenfranchisement, alienation, abandonment, banishment, rejection, voluntary or involuntary exile, financial or psychic poverty (defined, in the case of the latter, as the involuntary drainage of energy through the fissures in one's fractured consciousness, a direct consequence of the aforementioned experiences), and, last but not least, physical exile (defined as a lack of correspondence between one's mind and body). I included the Hosseini family logo on the bottom, three As followed by our timeless motto: *In this false world, we guard our lives with our deaths.*

I had arrived an hour early in order to forestall eager candidates from gathering in my absence to gossip about our collective objectives. I wanted them to apprehend my ruminating figure as they advanced from a distance, which would predispose them to identify me as their leader. To keep warm, I paced around in the spot marked by the famous corpse of that butt-exposing drunkard. I could still smell the fumes of his death. Even so, I managed to admire the view: the lichen-stained roofs of the houses; the trees of Devesa Park, their branches gently swaying in the midday air; the mustard dome of the post office; the three young trees of the overlook that I had aired my feelings to months earlier; and, on the corner adjacent to Josep Pla's childhood school, a convent with an austere facade that permanently hemmed in a group of self-loathing nuns. The school was missing a roof, and there were trees growing inside it.

Just then, a few disciples arrived. They streamed into the parking lot one at a time. First, a girl with sunken cheeks and hair parted at the center, who claimed to be devout and kissed the small silver cross hanging from her neck as she introduced herself. Her name was Remedios. She had a droopy nose and her eyes were leaking; the skin beneath them was red and worn. It was clear she was going to be a bore.

After her, a drunk by the name of Gheorghe arrived. I had seen him before. He was a friend of the dead man's and a nemesis of Ludo's. Ludo had a bone to pick with him because, during one of his drunken spells, Gheorghe had stood on the parking lot wall and peed on the hood of Ludo's car. Gheorghe was chubby and bald, and his ears looked as though they had been pressed against the sides of his head. He stuttered as he spoke. He had a black mole on his chin, which was the double kind, round and fleshy; naturally, the second layer wobbled as he struggled to dispense his words.

Then came Mercè, the middle-aged woman with a blond bob who hung sheets on her roof while spying on her neighbors and who, according to Agatha, had a crush on Ludo. She also had about thirty years on him. In the absence of sheets, she hid behind her hands, which is to say she spoke through her fingers, and every once in a while, during a pause in conversation, she spread them open and peeked out at her interlocutors. Nevertheless, her face lit up when Ludo arrived. I had given him an ultimatum: *Become a pilgrim or forget we ever knew each other.* He had acquiesced with reservations. He was learning to come along.

Ludo looked equal parts captivated and peeved. His lips were pouty, but his eyes were alert and expressive. He saluted Mercè with the warm grace of a dandy and a gentleman (she blushed, lowered her hands, and held them over her mouth like a fan so he could see her eyes), then he cast a defiant gaze at Gheorghe, who, having no memory of his drunken adventures, responded to this passive assault by nervously shaking the double flap hanging from his moley chin. He moved on to Remedios; he acknowledged her with a wry smile.

Agatha and Fernando arrived next. I waited five minutes for possible latecomers, but there were none. This was our lot. A crew of misfits. I counted their oily heads: There were six of them, seven if I included myself.

"All present?" I asked.

No one answered.

"Is this a pyramid scheme?" Mercè mumbled into the palms of her hands. She had recently gotten caught up in one and had lost all of what little money she'd had.

I assured her that it wasn't, then looked over that sea of heads, fixed my gaze on the horizon, and, employing an oratorical manner, said: "This is a remedy for the ill-fated, the oppressed, and the disenfranchised, like yourselves, who knowingly or not live within the metaphysical ghetto known the world over as the Pyramid of Exile, which is shaped similarly to Dante's triangular purgatory."

At the word *purgatory*, I heard gasps of recognition. The cathedral bells tolled.

I informed them that in the Pyramid of Exile we are all desperately alone; no one is in the position to extend a hand to another.

"This world has a way of abandoning the weak to their weakness and of encouraging the powerful to further attach themselves to the objects of their greed and avarice," I declared. "But we, the ill-fated, must resist becoming pawns in their hands. We must rebel together against the injustices assailed on us! Now, who here can define exile?" I asked, pacing the narrow spot where that hairy-assed man had died. I hung my head humbly and looked down at the ground.

Agatha, with that frank and straightforward presence of hers, said, "A depressed state of mind!"

"Excellent," I said. "Who else?"

Mercè, looking pleadingly at Ludo, said, "A loveless life."

Gheorghe stepped forward, encouraged. He stuttered, "A p-i-t-i-f-u-l m-a-n."

The leaky-eyed girl said: "Earthly life. We have been locked out of the gates of paradise. All of life is exile from the sanctity of the almighty creator."

I paused and looked at her. I could see now that she had a rash on her neck. She had a tissue in her hand, and she kept dabbing the red protrusions. How had she landed in our midst? I refrained from giving her a lecture on Nietzsche. She had no idea what the last A in AAA stood for, and I wasn't going to be the one to tell her.

"Ludo," I proceeded with an inquisitorial tone. "Any thoughts?"

He took on that stoic, arrogant look of his. He seemed ready to bolt. Then, clearly reciting from the dictionary, he delivered a pedantic outline of the etymology of the word: "Exile (v.) c. 1300, from Old French *essillier* 'exile, banish, expel, drive off' (12c.), from Late Latin *exilare/exsilare*" — his tone was getting progressively haughtier — "from Latin *exilium/exsilium* 'banishment, exile, place of exile,' from *exul* 'banished person, from *ex-* "away" (see *ex-*)'; according to Walters, the second element is from PIE root **al-* (2) 'to wander'" — he was articulating each comma, open parenthesis, closed parenthesis, asterisk — "(source also of Greek *alaomai* 'to wander, stray, or roam about')."

Fernando, eternal lover of knowledge, considered Ludo's etymological breakdown sacred information and listened with his head hung over his muscular body, eyes closed, ears finely tuned. Remedios, Gheorghe, and Mercè seemed disenchanted; none of them had understood Ludo's soliloquy. He took note and assumed a more casual approach: "He who walks out," he intoned. "In other words, he who is driven out." At this, he gazed defiantly in my direction.

"He, she, they who walk out," I corrected Ludo. "This," I said, waving my hands over the area of death, "is a safe space where all the marginalized are welcome."

Ludo scoffed and looked away. He was in a terrible mood. He stood there looking snubbed, as stiff as a mummy. A specialty of his.

With Agatha's help, I had brought down the Mobile Art Gallery and left it in one of the parking spaces. It looked like a casket on wheels. There was some wine inside and the bread and, of course, Taüt. I had drilled a few breathing holes for him. I rolled the miniature museum to the center of our circle. I opened the lid and let Taüt out. He promptly climbed my arm, settled on my shoulder, and stared with such a villainous glare at the pilgrims that an icy silence ensued. To compensate for his charged presence, I distributed the bread and wine.

"A gift," I said, giving each person a piece of bread and a carton of Don Simon.

Again, the cathedral bells tolled; their peal cut through time, through stone, through the entire atmosphere. We had been there a good while. The sky was beginning to take on a purplish hue, and there was a terrible chill in the air. I lifted *The Hung Mallard* and pulled out the four retractable glass panels I had added to the suitcase, each adorned with a map of the coordinates of my life — Iran, Turkey, Catalonia, America — and then unfolded the side tables. On these, I placed the typewriter and the telephone. I showed everyone the gas mask. It was a huge success. I handed it to Mercè, forcing her to expose her face momentarily — pale cheeked, red nosed — and told her to pass it around. Ludo, despite his stoic demeanor, no longer looked like he was going to bolt. Agatha clapped with childish ebullience when it was her turn to hold the gas mask. She slipped it over her head and looked each of us in the eye through those rounded glass panels. Then she removed it, and sweetly declared, "It smells terrible in there!"

"That's the whole point!" I said. "We have to rub our noses in the accumulated shit of history, in the pile of ruins. It's our job and burden as Pilgrims of the Void to blast open the gates of life and let the nonsense of death through. In order to apprehend totality," I declared with sagacity and resolve, "we have to annihilate the notion that life and death are two antagonistic blocks. That divide," I persevered, taking a more populist approach, "is the source of our pain. We must go deep into our pain," I insisted passionately. "Deep into it and come out the other side."

"How?" Mercè asked, almost choking on her spit, fingers trembling over her face.

"Believe it or not," I said, "it all comes down to the relationship between exile and ambling about, which Ludo so dutifully outlined for us." I looked straight at him.

To my surprise, he winked at me. It may have been the wine — Ludo was halfway through his carton — but he was finally looking at me, smitten. I could tell he felt a part of something. His shoulders had relaxed. His curls had recovered their bounce. I winked back at him, and he let out a hot groan.

After that, I picked up a loose branch. It made for an excellent walking stick. I used it to point at the various maps in the retractable vitrines. It was time to introduce myself. "I am Zebra, Dame of the Void," I said, tracing the path of my exile from Iran to the New World. "And my father, Abbas Abbas Hosseini, was my companion as I wandered in exile after my mother's death. It is his life's labor I honor by oiling the archival machine of my mind through a devotion to rigorous reading, dictation, memorization, and dramatizations of read materials." I moved across the maps in reverse order, folding the path of my exile over itself, and concluded somewhat wistfully: "Let it be known that landscape and literature are entwined like the helix of DNA. And we," I said, rehabilitating my tone, adopting a more convincing timbre, "are going to embark on collective Pilgrimages of the Corridor of Exile across these territories!" I pointed my stick at the Alt Empordà and then raised it to point beyond those flat fertile fields to the craggy range of the Pre-Pyrenees. "Why?" I asked rhetorically. "In order to retrace the path of the writers of exile who lived in or passed through these regions, stretching from Barcelona to Portbou, and transcribe their literature in situ on this typewriter."

I pointed at the writing machine with my walking stick. I scanned the pilgrims' faces, some of which were aglow, others swirling with confusion, their eyebrows stitched and foreheads pleated. Ludo, as usual, felt the need to set himself apart. He was mesmerized, perplexed, turned on.

"And why, you might ask, should we, the Pilgrims of the Void, focus on the literature produced by exiles? Because *exiled poets objectify and lend dignity to a condition designed to deny dignity*," I said, citing Said. "By transcribing the literature of such writers, we will be restoring dignity not only to literature but also to ourselves; not to mention the fact that we will be retroactively restoring dignity to those great writers of the past. An act of posthumous salvation," I said somberly, looking at Remedios, who was so entranced she had stopped fiddling with the oozing rash on her neck.

"Enough," I finally said. "Enough. None of this means anything if we don't put it into practice." The collection of eyes staring at me all widened in unison. I told them I'd prepared an icebreaker, a bonding activity for the future Pilgrims of the Void. "I am going to read two quotes to you and you are going to provide your personal interpretation within seconds of hearing the quote. I want gut-level responses!" I declared fiercely.

A few of them shuffled around to get their blood moving. It was getting colder by the minute. The night air was being drawn over our heads like a dome. I persevered, rubbing my hands against each other and then holding them one at a time against Taüt's feathery body. We had to remain close to the ruins of Josep Pla's childhood school. We had to breathe in his fumes, allow them to alter our consciousness.

QUOTE #1

TITLE: *Bleak House*

CHAPTER: "In Fashion"

AUTHOR: Charles Dickens

ORIGINAL TRANSCRIBER: Charles Dickens

TEXT: It is not a large world. Relatively even to this world of ours, which has its limits too (as your Highness shall find when you have made the tour of it, and are come to the brink of the void beyond), it is a very little speck. There is much good in it; there are many good and true people in it; it has its appointed place. But the evil of it is, that it is a world wrapped up in too much jeweller's cotton and fine wool, and cannot hear the rushing of the larger worlds, and cannot see them as they circle round the sun. It is a deadened world, and its growth is sometimes unhealthy for want of air.

QUOTE #2

TITLE: "On Exactitude in Science"

AUTHOR: Suárez Miranda, *Viajes de varones prudentes* (Travels of Prudent Men), Libro IV, Cap. XLV, Lérida, 1658

ORIGINAL TRANSCRIBER: Jorge Luis Borges

TEXT: . . . In that Empire, the Art of Cartography attained such Perfection that the map of a single Province occupied the entirety
of a City, and the map of the Empire, the entirety of a Province.
In time, those Unconscionable Maps no longer satisfied, and the
Cartographers Guilds struck a Map of the Empire whose size was
that of the Empire, and which coincided point for point with it.
The following Generations, who were not so fond of the Study of
Cartography as their Forebears had been, saw that that vast Map
was Useless, and not without some Pitilessness was it, that they
delivered it up to the Inclemencies of Sun and Winters. In the
Deserts of the West, still today, there are Tattered Ruins of that
Map, inhabited by Animals and Beggars; in all the Land there is
no other Relic of the Disciples of Geography.

"Reactions?" I asked, leaning into my cane. "Thoughts?"

Through her hand, Mercè said, "I don't feel a connection to the second
quote. For example, what is an unconscionable map?"

Fernando leaned in. "A false map," he said with acuity, "is an incomplete
map."

I should have known that he, a man with the strictest of consciences
who had predicted Taüt's return, would have caught on immediately.

"But all maps are incomplete," Gheorghe protested ineffectually. "I had
to buy so many on my way from Romania, and not even putting them all
together —"

"Bricolage!" Agatha interrupted whimsically.

"Indeed," I said. "Gheorghe, your thoughts on the Dickens?"

"Ah," he said with unexpected clarity and confidence. "That went
straight to my heart. I felt the void in the depths of my heart, and when I
feel that void, I don't want to drink." He looked at his carton and suddenly
disposed of it.

Agatha looked at him. She was beaming with delight.

"A genius," she said to Ludo. "A genius!" She was referring to me.

Ludo rocked back on his heels and let out a charming little laugh. Who
knew what was going on with him!

Remedios came forward. She said, "I prefer to live with a view to the afterlife. Why focus on the darkness of the present when one can pray —"

"All the way to the grave?" I interrupted. Then, more sternly, I said, "Someday you will understand that darkness is your greatest asset, the void your most powerful strength."

She didn't look convinced, but she said nothing more after that.

I turned back to Ludo. He was drunk. He had squeezed every drop out of his carton. His cheeks were flushed and his lips stained purple. He looked delightfully effeminate. Then he opened his mouth, and recited: "*I hardly feel constrained to try to make head or tail of this condition of the world.*"

A quote from Benjamin via Arendt. Ludo had been reading my notebook again! Or had he secretly been reading what I had been reading in order to gain access to the inner workings of my consciousness? I had no idea. Soon enough, I thought, I will get to the bottom of things with this mysterious Bembo.

By then, it was time to go. We arranged to meet again at the parking lot in exactly one week's time. "The first literary pilgrimage," I said, "involves a trip to the terroirs of Josep Pla's birth and eventual death, Catalonia's infamous Memory Man. But before we depart, dear pilgrims, I'd like you to repeat the following sentences after me: We are aware," I said.

"We are aware," they repeated.

"That each literary pilgrimage we undertake will unleash a chain of events that, like any event . . ."

"Will unleash a chain of events that, like any event," they chimed in.

"Once set into motion, will enter in contact with other events and give rise to sublime and banal phenomena." I let them catch up, then said: "We understand that while every event occurs in the present it also casts a shadow forward and backward in time and space and that there is no way of knowing if that shadow will serve to protect us or if it will keep us in darkness, submerged in a sea of opacity. But we, Pilgrims of the Void, are willing to sacrifice ourselves." They followed along swimmingly. I didn't give them a chance to pause and reflect on what was being said. "Our findings will be as inconclusive as life and we will defend them for that very reason, for their total disordering of so-called reality. Now let's bring our hands together."

We came together.

"In the words of beloved Shakespeare . . . ," I said.

"In the words of beloved Shakespeare . . . ," they repeated.

"What's past is prologue!"

"What's past is prologue!" they echoed into the air.

A week later, I gathered the Pilgrims of the Void at the Centre Fraternal in Palafrugell, a modernist-style casino and bar with a yellow facade and several Catalan flags that hung over its windows and awnings. This was the cultural center where Josep Pla used to spend his evenings drinking with his friends, practicing objectivism, discussing literature into the wee hours of the morning.

The waiter, seated at a stool behind the bar, refused to rise when we entered. He simply waved us in the direction of a round table at the far corner of the large rectangular room. We walked single file across that tiled floor, navigating the tables and chairs, the scrutinizing gaze of the other customers — four wrinkled men, all dressed in brown slacks and green wool sweaters, whose eyes momentarily drifted away from their plates and their newspapers to apprehend our collective figure.

We sat at a table sandwiched between a floor-to-ceiling window and the bathrooms. A good omen. Ludo whispered something to Agatha. He, the King of Food, was in charge of ordering for us. We had each chipped in four euros. That was all we had. I looked at the waiter. He had a phallic nose and bloodshot eyes and gnarly little fingers, which he had likely plunged into the earth, digging up roots and planting seeds his whole life.

"The man looks so powerful fixed to that stool!" I declared under my breath.

Gheorghe, who had taken to me, leaned in, and whispered, "Too true." His belly awkwardly grazed my arm.

"Gheorghe," I said, seeing that Ludo was about to order a round of tap beers. "You are not to drink. You are a pilgrim now, and you need to keep your wits about you, protect your faculties."

He looked crestfallen. The flap of skin that ran from his chin to his ears, a fleshy bib, shook each time he felt despair. I could hardly stand to see him that way. I wanted to cheer him up.

"I've assigned you a central role in today's pilgrimage," I said. "You are going to be the corpse of Josep Pla."

Remedios gasped in horror and reached immediately for a napkin from the dispenser at the center of the table. She dabbed her rash, which had taken on a glossy finish in that steely light.

"Do you want to volunteer as a corpse?" I asked her.

She said nothing. Mercè sat there with her face in her hands, her yellow bob spilling over her fingers. She looked like a mop that had been used to sweep up urine.

"It's a time-honored tradition, Remedios," I said, turning back to Gheorghe, who was nervously weaving his fingers because the waiter had finally detached himself from his stool and was carelessly setting down the cold steins of beer on the table. The foam ran over the lip of the glasses. Ludo cleaned each one.

"Gheorghe!" I called out, trying to claim his attention. "Josep Pla, too, had a mole that looked out at the world like a third eye" — I stared at his mole as I delivered my lines — "so astute was his gaze among the world's commoners, the willfully blind."

He regained his resolve. The rest of us chugged our beers. We each ate a plate of sausages and rice. Ludo, who had more money than all of us combined, ordered coffee and *crema catalana*. He used his spoon to crack the crystallized surface and then proceeded to consume the entire concoction without offering any to the rest of us. Self-centered beast, I thought. But there was no time to pick a fight with him. We had a long day ahead of us.

I'd left Taüt inside the miniature museum. As I had walked away, I'd heard him hissing and pacing, sucking in air through the drilled holes. He released macabre screams at fixed intervals throughout our meal.

"He's calling out in panic to see if I'm around," I announced to the pilgrims. Everyone except Ludo nodded in agreement. To distinguish himself, he rolled his eyes.

"Taüt!" I yelled. "Taüt!"

Remedios nearly jumped out of her seat.

"So he knows I'm here," I assured the pilgrims, turning to look at Ludo's face, which was flushed. The other men in the casino were staring at me wide-eyed, jaws dropped, newspapers in their laps, cigars hanging from the rafters of their mouths. Ludo took it upon himself to cast a regretful gaze in their direction.

"Offering apologies on my behalf?" I asked, pointing at his empty dish of dessert.

He got up and went to the bathroom. His chair almost flew out from under him. A few minutes later, he returned with an artificial calm. He leaned back, removed his pipe from the pocket of his tweed jacket — all his actions rehearsed — and placed it between his lips with those nimble fingers. He smoked with a superior air.

The Pilgrimage of the Memory Man was not without obstacle. It took us three hours to walk the old road from Palafrugell to El Far de San Sebastià, where the young Josep Pla would sit, crack open his notebook, and record triumphant descriptions of the glorious landscapes of his birth. We got lost on the way. We didn't have maps. We ended up on a rugged downward pass that led to a cluster of trees. Taüt, thrilled to be out of the casket, was miming the noises of the wild: the ping of a walnut falling from a tree, the sound of rocks detaching from the hills and knocking against one another in those vast tracts of forest densely packed with cork oaks, pines, eucalyptus.

"No sense of direction!" Ludo said breathily.

I was the one leading the way through that abysmal network of unpaved roads.

"No sense of direction!" Taüt mimed. Then he chirped like a canary because he heard a canary chirp in the dense fabric of shrubs.

"That wretched bird!" Ludo said.

"That wretched bird!" Taüt echoed.

"Agatha," I said. "Can you tell Ludo that I can hear everything he's saying?"

Agatha threw her hands up in the air.

"So now you won't speak to me?" Ludo huffed from the dusty cul-de-sac. He reached up and yanked a tree branch. He had a wool scarf tied around his neck and a red cardigan under his tweed jacket. He looked like a fussy Englishman.

"Are you going to fan yourself?" I posed.

It wasn't as cold as his stuffy outfit suggested. Winter was finally giving way to spring.

"Fan!" Taüt squawked, raising his sulfur crest. Ludo released the branch. I had never seen the bird so animated. I secretly rejoiced that my mother was getting to see other parts of this woolly world.

We were lost in the hilly folds separating Palafrugell from the sea. I could hear the noise of those waters batting against the earth from across a vast distance. A roar at the margins of the universe that reminded me of the deep roar of the Caspian. I looked at Gheorghe. What a vulnerable being! He looked exhausted. He and Remedios — the corpse and the devotee — had been in charge of either dragging or lifting the Mobile Art Gallery over their heads as if it were a casket. Fernando, who had been groggy that morning, even more introverted than usual, had refused to join the pilgrimage. His loss! I thought, and ordered Gheorghe and Remedios to put the miniature museum down because I had decided that this dead end offered the perfect conditions for delivering my lecture on the dim forests of Josep Pla's interior exile.

I told the pilgrims to gather around, that it was time to edify them on the nuances of our collective mission. Ludo, in a petulant mood, lingered at the edges. I refused to care.

"Soon we will find our way," I said to them, as they gathered before me. "But even if we don't, nothing is lost."

Gheorghe nodded along. He had caught on rather quickly; a sharpness lay hidden beneath all that flesh. Remedios, on the other hand, looked more leaky eyed than ever.

"My rash is burning," she interrupted shyly. "From all the sweat."

"My dear Remedios, discomfort is a literary experience you have to learn to bear. Imagine how you will feel once you are standing in the center of the void. Terrible! That's how! You have to build your endurance."

She was quick to retreat, her saving grace.

Mercè, having caught her breath, brought her hands over her face and, with a stutter more appropriate to Gheorghe, asked, "Ex-cuse me, b-but who is Josep Pla?"

Who is Josep Pla? What kind of Catalan was she?

I heard Agatha let out a gasp. "Everyone knows who Josep Pla is," she said sweetly.

Mercè shook her head of hair, a sign of distress.

"Mercè," I said, with rehearsed patience. "Josep Pla, alias the Memory Man, is" — "was," I corrected — "the most prolific and controversial Catalan writer of the long and cruel twentieth century, which concluded just a few years ago, though the brutality it unleashed is still showering down on our heads. And the life of Josep Pla," I said, suddenly — decisively — connecting the dots, "registers the trauma of that century; one just has to look at his comings and goings to see the irrevocable damage of the times on his person. The man, a provincial boy turned cosmopolitan dandy, was forced into interior exile in Palafrugell several times throughout his life. That is why we are gathered here today."

Mercè's blood pressure leveled. She was peeking at me through her hands, listening intently.

"We should keep moving. It's getting cold," Ludo rudely piped from the end of the path, an army of trees behind him.

"The voice of reason!" I yelled back. "The march of progress!"

He kicked the pebbled ground.

"Care to join our lecture?" I asked.

"Care to join our lecture?" he mocked. He had lost his mind.

Taüt, dignified creature and charitable host to my mother, didn't perpetuate the thread.

"To each his own," I said, turning back to the crowd.

"Now, Pilgrims of the Void, memorize the facts of the life of Josep Pla." I saw their ears fan open like flowers in the sun.

"ONE," I declared, employing a pedantic tone. "Josep Pla, born in Palafrugell on March 8, 1897, a shy and suspicious soul and a terrible student, studied law in Barcelona until he was forced to retreat to his hometown in October of 1918 during the second and deadliest wave of the Spanish flu. This retreat led to his first literary adventures, adventures cultivated in an atmosphere of mass illness and death. He read and wrote under conditions of interior exile. It was in this cruel atmosphere that Josep Pla, the writer, was brought into existence, overtaking Josep Pla, the imminent lawyer."

I paused briefly to catch my breath.

"TWO," I spat. "In the aftermath of the Spanish Civil War, which lasted from 1936 until 1939, after traveling across Europe and North Africa conducting acts of reportage, the Memory Man, who was both Catholic and Catalanist — a contradiction during the inflexible trials of war, which reduce the world and all its citizens to good versus evil — was banished by both factions. The Catalans accused him of being a fascist and a betrayer, and the Francoists dismissed him for being a Catalanist and therefore also thought of him as a betrayer. So he again retreated to Palafrugell."

At this, I lunged forward and took in a deep breath, and said, "THREE. Last but not least, at the end of his life, Josep Pla, suspicious of his fellow man and aware that monotony is the only counterweight to our perpetual fear of death — a little factoid that I, one of the unlucky, learned early on — returned again to the nauseating boredom of Palafrugell and there he rewrote — no, he falsified — his diary, which he had originally composed during his first exile when he was just a failed young law student. He thereby plagiarized and regurgitated his younger self, and then published his fabricated 'diary' as the work we now know of as *The Gray Notebook*, thereby also," I said, faint with vertigo, "proving Nietzsche's theory of the cyclical nature of time as well as Borges's philosophy of the eternal return, notions likely borrowed from other sources, Eastern sources," I said, nearly out of breath, "which I shall later consult!"

I almost fainted. Who was I lecturing? I suddenly wondered. Everything was a blur: the trees, the pebbled road, my hands. But I couldn't stop; a final message was pushing its way up.

"In 1918," I mumbled into the misty air, "while the Memory Man walked the streets of Palafrugell under the gauzy light of a gunmetal sky not unlike the sky we have above us today and thought of Montaigne, Proust, Stendhal, Mallarmé, and Nietzsche, death was making its rounds in the form of the plague. In other words, Pla's literature dawned in the dark and drafty abysmal void of death."

My thoughts were doubling over themselves. I thought of the pile of ill-fated corpses. That image, I realized, had a prophetic quality to it: It was a kind of afterimage, reoccurring both as memory and premonition. I remembered my father and me, paper-thin as we had traveled across that ashen no-man's-land, repeating: *The world is a savage place; we are crossing not death itself but the death of life; we are becoming literature.* He would have been proud that I had found others — the marginalized of the world — to join me. I saw the pilgrims sitting before me, listening with their inner ears. I felt my heart turn to flesh, blood pumping through its corridors. I was overcome with gratitude. This cluster of humans, I thought, who had appeared in the most ordinary way, were helping me move along my path toward nothingness. We were going to cross the event horizon of the black hole we each harbored at the center of our lives and kick up the dust, rove the depths, until the information the void had swallowed — our multiple selves from which we had been severed — would rise out of it as residue, transformed, ready to sound out the alarm of truth: that death will send the Four Corners of the World collapsing and that no one, no matter how astute, wealthy, or robust, will be spared. Our bodies will be reduced to ash. But, I comforted myself, our minds will barrel through this cosmos again and again, a continuum that would exist everywhere and nowhere at once. And how long would this cycle perpetuate itself, this mirage? There was no way of knowing. This, too, was a certainty, a terrifying, malodorous truth.

By the time we reached the summit of San Sebastià, the lighthouse situated at the top of the cape had taken on a mythical quality. Its beaming light, enclosed in a crowned glass dome, roved the sparkling silver waters of the Mediterranean. The shrubs and trees — the bushes of lavender and thyme, the juniper and olive trees, the maritime pine, the broom plants and palmetto scrubs — all woven into the rocky shelves, formed an avalanche of granite and foliage that led to the Calella de Palafrugell, where wooden fishing boats had been pulled out of the water and left strewn across the sandy coast. Behind the lighthouse and El Far Hotel, abandoned in winter, was an archaeological site with ruins of an Iberian settlement.

"Look around," I said to the breathless pilgrims. "This stunning view is what Josep Pla observed daily during the plague. He hiked up here and sat for hours with his notebook, searching for well-endowed adjectives to describe the landscape."

I could tell they were impressed, but they also seemed exhausted from the laborious journey of digressions it had taken to get there.

I observed Ludo from a distance. He stood on the hotel terrace taking in the view. Then he lit his pipe and sucked on it with his eyes closed, head tilted back, face pressed into the radiant metallic sky. He seemed at peace. I wondered if he had come to terms with our collective endeavor, if his wall of defenses had come crumbling down. But I couldn't be sure, and I knew that even if he had opened up his heart to our objectives it wouldn't last long. He had become shifty, a woeful, unpredictable man.

I busied myself with setting up the Mobile Art Gallery near the light-house. Against the mercurial waters of the sea, *The Hung Mallard* truly looked like a pirate's flag. I set up the telephone and the typewriter. I un-wrapped the gas mask. Then I went in search of the pilgrims who were prowling around, breathing through their mouths. It was time to tran-scribe.

"Pilgrims," I announced. "Report to the miniature museum immedi-ately!"

Everyone showed up. Mercè looked on anxiously, hands over her mouth, eyes peeking out. I offered her the gas mask.

"For your personal relief," I said.

She turned her back to us and slipped it over her head, then turned around again and looked at us with her rubber face. I picked up the tele-phone and listened to the devastation coming through it, to the residue of silence left over from the worldwide wreckage, a portion of which had annihilated the Hosseinis. The world had slit its own throat with such reckless abandon! I ordered Gheorghe to stand at the typewriter. Agatha broke into a premature applause. She looked up at Ludo's face, and boldly said, "What a show she is about to put on!" I thought Ludo might bolt, but he stayed put, firm in his spot. Mercè stood next to him. With the gas mask covering her face, she had no trouble gazing at him lovingly. He looked down at her a few times and forced a polite smile. The architecture of Ludo Bembo's interior life is as knotty as an irregular home full of in-terlacing staircases, hallways, rooms. Who could read the tides of his emo-tions? He's a man with a Byzantine character and a Roman nose!

"Gheorghe," I said. "Lay your hands on the polished keys of the type-writer."

He did.

"Your life has been evacuated of meaning; it is, therefore, a welcome campground where Josep Pla can pitch his tent. It is as if you were an empty house beckoning for a squatter. See Josep Pla walking around the labyrinthine corridors of your mind. He lifts his head to stare at the ghastly void of your existence. He presses his face against your void, and for a moment, you feel a reprieve from your loneliness. This is a sign that his words are being transmitted to you. See his beady eyes, his crooked nose, his square and narrow smile, his slick pink tongue sticking out between his teeth — the mouth of a misanthrope, of a person repulsed with life. It feels as though you were looking in the mirror, doesn't it? Now transcribe in situ!"

Gheorghe began to type before I had a chance to dictate the transcription to him. I stood there staring at him in awe. Had he usurped the spirit of Josep Pla? He removed the paper from the platen and read what he had written to us. His beady little eyes glowed with the reflected light of the paper.

> *I was born in Palafrugell (Lower Ampurdan) on March 8, 1897. My family is entirely from the Ampurdan. The landscape of my life encompasses Puig Son Ric, in Begur, in the east; the Fitor mountains, in the west; the Formigues Islands, in the south; and the Montgrí in the north. I have always felt this a very old country. All sorts of wandering peoples have passed this way.*

"Wonderful factoids," I said. Gheorghe nodded, his eyes closed. I scanned the crowd of pilgrims. Remedios's eyes were wide and dry. Her rash had calmed. It was no longer oozing. It was pink instead of a glistening red. And Mercè was wheezing happily next to the object of her longing, Ludo Bembo, who looked on with a gravity usually reserved for those men who diligently attend church but understand nothing. Agatha was standing with her arm wrapped around his, a saccharine smile spread across her lips.

"There's more," Gheorghe stammered. "*Hardening of the heart isn't congenital,*" he said forcefully, between fits of coughing while everyone looked on, entranced. I recognized the words. He was reciting quotes from my notebook. "*It's an acquired condition. It depends on experience of life. What poets and novelists call narcissism is generally congenital and is symptomatic of genuine abnormality.*"

Gheorghe snorted several times. I felt Ludo's gaze on me. When I turned to look at him, he was mouthing the words *genuine abnormality* at me. I felt as though I had been punched in the gut. Gheorghe looked over at him nervously before carrying on. He coughed distinctly before speaking.

Taüt paced nervously between my shoulders. Then he paused and hissed in Ludo's direction. Remedios began to scratch her rash again. It started to peel and form little patches of blood that caught the silver light of the sky here and there.

"*The level of loathing reality brings,*" Gheorghe stuttered, "*clearly can increase in relation to one's experience of life. But it would be pretentious*" — at this, Ludo mouthed *pretentious,* confirming my suspicion that he had paid Gheorghe off — "*however painful the experience has been, to act like someone who has overcome everything and is completely coldhearted.*"

Gheorghe cast a pleading look in my direction. "*I look on in horror,*" he said, "*as everything drives me into a state of callow indifference, but I'd be a clown to act as if I've touched rock bottom.*"

The whole lot broke into nervous applause. Gheorghe bowed, pleased with himself. I felt humiliated, devastated, as if the very Matrix of Literature had turned against me, along with the Memory Man, for whom I had organized such a lavish homage. I walked off with Taüt and settled on one of the chairs on the terrace. That fleshy mole-covered face came running after me.

"Did he pay you?" I asked, pointing at Ludo Bembo.

"Pay me?" he repeated stupidly. "I spent everything I had on lunch. I don't have a euro to my name!"

"I'll forgive this trespass," I said, breathing deeply in order to gather my wits again. "But you are not to trust him. I'm beginning to suspect he is not a Bembo at all. He may very likely be the reincarnated spirit of the murderer and philologist Eugene Aram, whose terrible actions and personality are referenced in the literary works of Hood, Wills, Orwell, and P. G. Wodehouse. Do you understand?"

He shook his fleshy chin and walked away with his head hanging over his body in shame. I sat there staring out at the vast sea below. I was dumbfounded. I understood nothing. I had tried to hurl my pain at the world, but it had been intercepted by Ludo's scheming. And where were my witnesses, I thought, the pitiless and inhuman members of society, those who don't hesitate to make the less fortunate pawns in their provisional game of chess? I thought again of Ludo.

We had come to Calella before, Ludo and I, in the autumn. At the end of a long day spent foraging the forests for mushrooms — bloody milk caps with their red and orange hues and green flecks; king's testicles; yellow-footed chanterelles; and my favorite, black trumpets, the trumpet of death. We had eaten a feast of pig: foot cartilage, cheeks infused with beer, *jamón* cut from the flanks of hogs fed on acorns. At the end of the day, we lay on the sandy shore locked in an embrace to keep warm. We had fallen asleep like that on the beach.

What had happened now? Who is the victor? I thought, looking over at him. He was watching me in pain. Who is the victim? There was no way of knowing, I thought, *no way of making head or tail of this condition of the world.* The moon rose. Its round face shone in the sky. I felt low, down, lackluster. Another day had been ineffectually swept into the ruins of time.

Ludo and I didn't speak for three days after the pilgrimage. If our eyes accidentally locked while passing each other in the hallway, he looked down at his feet. I counted the busts of Agatha's face, which seemed to multiply like the miracle of the fish.

On the fourth day, I considered giving him a piece of my mind.

In the feeble light of evening, Ludo looked like a ghost of himself. I looked at Agatha's busts planted in rows along the walls on either side of him. They resembled garden topiaries in the obscure light. I could hear Petita in another room scratching herself. Taüt was at my heels, his countenance majestic, resolute. He had the loving aura of Bibi Khanoum. Ludo pursed his lips. He looked down. A shadow fell over his face. Then, as if from the subterranean channels of the world, his voice emerged before mine. His words — each one a sword, a dagger — dangled in the air.

"According to Montaigne," he said, "*Plutarch says of those who dote over pet monkeys or little dogs that the faculty for loving which is in all of us, rather than remaining useless, forges a false and frivolous object for want of a legitimate one.*"

I scooped Taüt up. The bird protested and bit my finger. He tore the skin. I remembered lying in Quim Monzó's bed under that sagging ceiling, sucking on the blood Taüt had spilled. I put my finger in my mouth to stop the bleeding.

"Plutarch?" I said to Ludo, removing my finger from my mouth. "I'll give you some Plutarch: *There is no point in getting angry against events: They are indifferent to our wrath!*"

"You should tell that to yourself," he said, and rushed past me.

I managed to grab hold of his arm before he could storm out the door. He turned to look at me. His face had collapsed.

"Do you ever consider taking off your mask?" he pressed.

"What mask?" I asked reproachfully.

"The mask of literature!"

"You're the one speaking in platitudes," I insisted.

"Me? Me? Me? No, no, no," he said. He was shaking his head with a violent passion. I thought he was going to get stuck reproducing those two words forever. But then he steadied himself. "This is our problem: We have become entangled with each other!"

"With each other and the whole world," I said. "The self is a porous thing."

"Not *my* self."

He was facing the door again.

"You're an exception to the rule?"

He opened the door.

"You should get ahold of *your* self," he murmured into the threshold of the apartment. "You're the one dragging a bunch of lost souls up and down hills as if they were your indentured servants. You should try examining your thoughts before you decide to act on them!"

"Are you suggesting that I don't deserve to make friends? That I should suffer indefinitely from this ancient loneliness I carry within me?"

"By dragging those miserable wretches into our lives?"

"I am a miserable wretch!" I said, my eyes damp with tears.

His eyes welled up, but he just stood there in silence, as stubborn and impassive as a bull.

Beyond the door, the staircase was darker and dirtier than ever. I watched him walk down the stairs, turn the corner, and disappear. I was alone again. Alone with Taüt, Petita, with that slimy, stubborn fish. I stared into the darkness of the staircase and remembered looking down at the ruins of Van, my eyes sore from having been wrapped in the rough cloth of that black band. Do we ever see anything at all? I wondered. Everything in my life had turned into an afterimage; the past had transcribed itself onto the future, annihilating the present. I closed the door behind him. I put Taüt down. I let him roam at his will.

After that, I went to the bathroom and stood in front of the mirror. I saw my eyes, my nose, my lips, but I couldn't see my face. My features refused to come together; they seemed to either be drifting away from one another, an exploded view, or were stacked together, an overlapping mess of organs.

I retreated to my room to plan the next pilgrimage: a pilgrimage of Dalínian proportions: the Pilgrimage of the Wide-Eyed Genius. It wasn't easy. I felt both drained and panicked. But there was no turning back. I had gone too far. I had to carry on. Faced with the failure of the Pilgrimage of the Memory Man, I had decided that I would try again, persist until my nerves were raw — a wisdom born of all my mutilated parts blended together. That failure had made my desire to hurl my pain at the world even more assiduous. I experienced a rapid cycling of moods: a sense of exhilaration followed by sudden defeat during which my mind felt consumed, charred, burned to a crisp. I churned my mind. I forced it to produce more routes, to recall the quotes and maxims that my father had stuffed into it, that I had been feeding on through his old age, his macular degeneration, his death, his resurrection within my void, his return to the mind of the universe. But something was off. A tangible sense of estrangement.

I stared for hours at the surfaces of my life, my death: the high cracked walls of the living room, the shuttered panes of the terrace window overlooking the city — elegant, resolved, draped in gray stone. Hours later, deep into the night, I went on a long walk along the Onyar River. It was slipping silently past the houses lined up along its banks. I stared at their reflection in the water, at the bridges that arched across the divide, the seagulls that plunged into the water from the roofs and railings, remorselessly attacking the fish in the night — ugly, whiskered, lazy, sucking on the mud and waste of the riverbed — and then, finally, at myself. My own dumb, round face in the water, and next to it, Taüt's beaked countenance. I looked swollen. My eyes were puffy, my hair uncombed. Who am I? I wondered. How is it that I have ended up here, adrift and alone in the world with no money? For one brief, fugitive moment, I longed for Ludo's embrace, but were he to offer it to me, I couldn't be sure that I wouldn't refuse it. No one had ever been in a position to protect me. How could I trust someone who was offering to protect me now? I was bereft. My life was small and narrow. I didn't know what to do, how to generate love.

For days, I fell asleep and woke up at odd hours. At one point, I don't know if it was in the middle of the day or night, I sat bolt upright in bed. I had woken up from a dream in which I had seen my parents. Or not my parents. Not exactly. I dreamt I was standing in front of a tableau vivant of Goya's *Two Old Men Eating Soup*, but the two shriveled-up men in the painting, with their toothless jaws and hooded heads, had been replaced by my parents. My mother's bruised hand reached out from the dark shadows of the painting. She held the spoon out to my mouth, inviting me to take the soup of death. Her skin was freckled and spotted with purplish hues; it was paper-thin, a trembling hand. I drank the soup. Then my father reached out and wiped my mouth with the edge of his sleeve. He was still wearing that outmoded suit, but he was bald: no mustache, no hair on his head. Had I ever seen his mouth? I barely recognized them. "Where are you? What realm do you live in?" I stepped forward to ask, but they immediately retreated into the canvas, and the painting was static again. I ran my hand across the surface of the portrait. I was hoping my hand would go through so I could join them on the other side. But there was nothing there. Nothing except air. Air full of the residue of the living and the dead.

Finally, Ludo slipped into my room one night. He got into bed next to me and drew me onto his chest. "I have no other way of getting through to you," he confessed. "Your notebook is the only inroad, the only way in."

I didn't know what to say. I lay there and listened to the beating of his heart. It sounded like the deep roar of the sea, the white noise of the universe. Again, I thought, the parts don't add up to a whole; there is always a residue. At least I, I reassured myself, am trying to account for that residue.

"I have good news for you," Ludo said.

"Is that so?"

"National borders are an artificial construct," he said.

A protracted silence ensued. I am an orphan, I thought, as he ran his hands through my hair. He was trying to untangle the knots, but he gave up halfway through.

"Madonna!" he said.

"An artificial construct that has controlled the terms of my life," I finally answered. "There is nothing abstract there."

He didn't speak after that. I could tell he was sulking again.

"You know," I said to him, "according to Nietzsche, wisest Autodidact, Anarchist, and Atheist of all time, *those who remain silent are almost always lacking in delicacy and courtesy of the heart. Silence is an objection; swallowing things leads of necessity to a bad character — it even upsets the stomach. All who remain silent are dyspeptic.*"

I thought he was going to push me off his body and leave. But he didn't.

"Okay," he said. "Okay."

We drifted off to sleep.

Halfway through the night, I woke him up, and said, "You know, Ludo, there is nothing noble about my suffering. It is the result of an exhaustive investigation into the deepest recesses of human nature — its senseless-ness and propensity toward fakeness, its lack of honesty. We have made very little progress, Ludo Bembo. The march of progress is the biggest lie of the twentieth century."

I could tell that he was out of his depth. It was as if a tide had dragged him out of the shallows. He was half-asleep. He was struggling to keep his head above water.

He said: "I wish you would say you love me."

I wanted to speak, but I felt as though my mouth had been taped shut. The pilgrimages were the only way I knew to dissolve life's resistance to-ward me, my resistance toward it — but I had only just begun. I rolled away. I didn't want him to see me weeping. Ludo moaned. He reached out and tried to pull me back into his embrace. I swatted his arm. He faced away from me and went to sleep. The tides of his mood had again turned. Tomorrow he would withdraw from me. He would be obstinate, cheer-less, as ornery as a child. I got up and paced the hallway. How comfortable for him to escape into sleep, I thought, after returning to that word *love*. A love I was in no position to receive despite desperately needing it. No. Not I with my castaway, homeless body. Where would I store it? It would fall right through me, sink into the depths of my void. I would have needed so much love, more than any one person is capable of giving, to fill that gaping hole at the center of my life. And, besides, his love had been capricious, inconsistent, flighty.

When I walked back into my bedroom, I heard him murmur the word *unhappiness*. His eyes momentarily flooded open. He looked unplugged. An old wound seemed to have come loose and extinguished the light from his eyes. Later, much later, I would look back on this moment and realize that my hypothesis had been correct, that Ludo Bembo had come searching for me not only because our fates had been, as I had always known them to be, united in the poetic dimension but also because in my company, alongside the Dame of the Void, something Ludo had long suppressed could finally burst forth and arrange itself among his other memories — a certain darkness he secretly carried within that he, a utilitarian, an optimist, a linear-minded, rational man, would rebel against and use as an excuse to refuse me. Psychological morbidity is not for the weak.

Days turned to weeks. Time passed. Though the distance between Ludo and me began to calcify, we each held on to our relationship the only way we knew how: by yanking each other around. As a result, we both grew increasingly doleful, despondent, aggrieved.

Soon, March ended and April began. It was the anniversary of my father's death. The sky was glowing with a bright spring sun that cast a straw-colored hue on the gray stones of Girona. There was an uncharacteristic chill to the air. I again stood with my fellow Pilgrims of the Void in the parking lot.

I was wearing a Wagnerian mustache — an ode to my father. I had fashioned it from hair deposited in garbage bags outside of one of the city's hair salons. The pilgrims, with their sea of greasy heads, were looking at me with knitted eyebrows. They had multiplied.

Fernando had joined us. He was perched elegantly on the hood of Ludo's car. A finely sculpted man. Gheorghe, having repossessed himself of his person, had found a companion: a short blond woman named Paola, who was graced with leathery skin and sagging breasts and a protruding belly that hung over her skinny legs. Based on her appearance, it was clear that the pair of them had shared an alcoholic past and that now they planned to leap hand in hand into sobriety; from the pits of the abysses they had been avoiding within themselves, they would pump temperance and restraint.

Aside from them, there was the usual crowd: Remedios, whose rash had spread, covering her right cheek — she looked as though she had been freshly slapped; Mercè, who arrived wearing the gas mask, looking the part of a shiny beetle; Agatha, who had ornamented her face with Venetian earrings for the occasion; and Ludo, who had tied a silk scarf around his neck and was lying obscenely on the hood of his car next to Fernando, as if to say: *Here I am, Cleopatra's male counterpart.* He was up to something. What, I did not know. Only time would tell.

Taüt was nibbling on my mustache, smoothing the hairs the wind had ruffled.

"Why are you wearing a mustache?" Mercè's muffled voice emerged from the mask, a childish whine. I pushed the bird's head aside.

"Before disappearing altogether," I said, adopting a grave tone, "the growth of my father's Nietzschean mustache had miraculously increased. As you all know, we are about to embark on a Dalínian pilgrimage, and while Dalí commands all of my respect, his lifelong rebellion against Nietzsche's Wagnerian mustache also drains my deference. Dalí's fixation with Nietzsche's mustache paradoxically represents Dalí's lack of differentiation from him, making Dalí Nietzschean to the core" — I made a fist with my sick hand and vehemently punched the palm of my opposite hand — "Nietzschean in the depths of the depths of his heart."

I paused thoughtfully and scanned the faces of the pilgrims. They looked pained. I took a softer approach.

"We are all the very thing we rebel against. Take this man as an example," I said, pointing at Ludo Bembo. "In the depths of this man's soul lies a labyrinthine network of abysses not unlike mine, which explains why, despite his conscious efforts to go toward the darkness of life, he is continually attracted to me, whose life is a prolonged meditation on the *clear light of death.*"

In the presence of that word, *attracted*, Gheorghe and Paola exchanged a magnetic glance. Mercè hung her rubber-wrapped head in defeat. Ludo drew his legs together and sat up. I fixed my gaze on him and continued with uncompromising conviction. "In the depths of this Bembo's soul lies, like a madam cast in marble, the fear of his own mortality."

Ludo opened his mouth to speak, but a group of giggling American tourists flocked past us just then. I could smell the swamplands of their psychology, their disturbed intestines. They smelled like mildew and mud. I watched those abusers of history disappear under the archway and down the stairs that hug the convent walls. I felt the residual toxins of my childhood clog my airways. It was extremely painful and difficult to breathe. I closed my eyes. When I opened them again, a different figure was advancing toward us unflaggingly. It was the Tentacle of Ice.

"What's she doing here?" I asked Ludo.

"She is an interested party," he said tonelessly.

She took her place next to him, tossed her long curly hair to one side.

"What is the object of her interest?" I posed.

"L-I-T-E-R-A-T-U-R-E." He annunciated every letter. I could see each one float out from the gap between his teeth.

"Don't fool yourself. The only thing that woman is interested in is your sex organ."

Ludo smiled at me with false teeth. Who could trust a man with such incongruities? She leaned over and gave him a kiss on the cheek. She was twice my size: voluptuous, large breasted, with hips designed to procreate. Her hands were manicured. She had plucked her eyebrows, applied makeup to her face. Mercè, realizing she was third in line, had begun to cry. The glass panels over her eyes had fogged.

"Look what you've done," I said to Ludo. "Mercè is sobbing. She is falling apart. She looks like a heap of moist flesh."

"Is that not so?" I asked Mercè.

"I'm crying," Mercè lied squeakily, "because I spent the morning chopping onions."

"Onions?"

"Onions!" she insisted.

"A great symbol of putrefaction and decay," I said to Ludo Bembo, "of which you understand next to nothing!"

The Tentacle of Ice wrapped her frigid arms around him. She was reclaiming him. I stared at her smooth upper lip.

"Let's go," she said evenly. She whispered something hotly into his ear.

Ludo agonized for a moment, then swiftly assembled his thoughts and followed her. I felt my sick hand cramp in response to his absence. I felt as if the air were being squeezed out of my lungs. How could I have let a non-Hosseini into the craggy pits of my void? Ah, the redundant sting of betrayal, I thought, and forced myself to carry on without him.

I led the remaining pilgrims back to Calella de Palafrugell. We flipped one of the wooden fishing boats that had been abandoned on the shore and pushed it into the water. The sea was rough. We had to hug the coast. We sat around the Mobile Art Gallery, plunging our oars in the water.

Hours later, we rowed past the Medes Islands. They looked like the white teeth of a giant. The rocky plateaus of the coast changed textures along the way: the rock looked shaved one moment and as if it were peeling the next. The leathery water of the sea changed colors, too. It was black and laced with diamonds in the distance; aquamarine along the shore, revealing huge white rocks at the bottom of the sea; then icy fluorescent blue interrupted by shades of green farther out.

The tide almost pulled us out to sea a few times. We had to row fiercely to stay in line with the coast. No one spoke. When we were near land, we could hear the caves along the coast sucking in the sea then spitting it back out. Hours later, famished, exhausted, we arrived at the Cap de Creus, Dalí's *delirium of rocks*. I took in that mass of savage stone: It was pleated, wrinkled, dimpled, rounded, conical, stratified. It looked like the Matrix of Literature with its coiled and complex pathways of interconnected sentences. In other words, it looked like my life.

We arrived at dusk. We set up the writing machine in front of Dalí and his wife and muse Gala's house in Port Lligat. It was closed due to damages the building had sustained during a recent storm. Again, there were no witnesses. We, squalid misfits, were alone. What was I to deduce? I earmarked the thought and carried on. I had been inside that house before. Long ago. Or, perhaps, I thought, not so long ago. I couldn't remember if I had been there with Ludo Bembo or with my father. Or with both. Dalí's home was one of those houses with a complex network of interlocking rooms, each door leading to a window, each window showing a staircase beyond or an egg, white and smooth, sculpted in the terraced yard. It was opulent, magnificently irrational. I looked over at the pilgrims. They were sitting on the sandy coast, looking pale, overexerted from rowing, from the lack of food and water. They were at the brink of the void. Taüt, too, looked weaker than ever. The wind had sliced at his face, ruffling his feathers, as we had rowed. He was keeping to himself now, the way, it occurred to me, my mother had always kept to herself. He was on lockdown, wings tucked into his sides, neck turned, beak plunging like a dagger into his spine.

"How does one become what one is?" I suddenly asked, trying to lift the pilgrims' spirits. I stood behind the miniature museum, which we had prepared for transcribing, and preached at them in an oratorical tone as if I were standing on a pulpit.

Gheorghe put his arms around his lady to keep her warm. Remedios's face was so red from the chill that her rash blended in seamlessly with the rest of her wounded flesh. In Ludo's absence, Mercè had removed her mask. Agatha sat in Fernando's lap, smiling at her encouragingly. Fernando was examining Agatha's face, memorizing her expression, I assumed, for the next bust.

"After reading Nietzsche," I continued, "Dalí decided he would be the one to outdo the inventor of the overman, otherwise known as Zarathustra, Nietzsche's most transcendent, mystical, and lofty creation, by developing a Dalínian cosmogony, a cosmogony littered with anuses. In other words, Dalí flipped Zarathustra on his head by ascending to sublime heights through the grotesque."

Mercè turned as red as Remedios. Paola smiled coquettishly at Gheorghe. Aha, I thought, she has enjoyed it in the rear.

"Paola," I said, "would you care to transcribe?"

She leapt at the opportunity.

"We will be weaving together the voices of Nietzsche and Dalí, and sprinkling in some Lorca, who made several amorous advances at Dalí, all of which he solemnly refused — an incomprehensible decision, but let us not digress from the task at hand. Now, Paola, transcribe the following twice."

Gheorghe clapped to cheer her along. At the word *twice*, Fernando smiled wryly. He had understood. This exercise was not unlike his obsession with forging Agatha's face.

"I am a doppelgänger," I declared, reading from my notebook.

"I am a doppelgänger," Paola repeated into the typewriter.

I picked up the phone and listened to the devastating silence, to the signal of literature, the residue and ruins of the universe. I heard: *Much have I suffered, labored long and hard by now in the waves and wars.* I kept Ulysses's words to myself.

"*I have a 'second' face in addition to the first,*" I said to Paola, my voice breaking, my heart heavy with grief, "*and perhaps also a third.*" I was citing Nietzsche.

I have a "second" face in addition to the first, she wrote, *and perhaps also a third.*

"Now, on the same page, transcribe what Dalí said about his obsession with Nietzsche."

She paused and looked at me, an intelligent creature.

"*Nietzsche is a weakling who had been feckless enough to go mad, when it is essential, in this world, not to go mad.*"

When it is essential in this world not to go mad, Paola typed.

"*These reflections furnished the elements of my motto, which was to become the theme of my life: The only difference between a madman and myself is that I am not mad! It took me three days to assimilate and digest Nietzsche. After this lion's banquet, only one detail of the philosopher's personality was left for me, only one bone to gnaw: his mustache!*"

I scratched at my false mustache as I recited the lines to her.

"Don't write this down. Did you know that Federico García Lorca, fascinated by Hitler's mustache, said — be sure to write *this* down — *The mustache is the tragic constant in the face of man?*"

Paola typed the sentence twice.

I continued to read Dalí's words from my notebook: "*Even in the matter of mustaches, I was going to surpass Nietzsche! Mine would not be depressing, catastrophic, burdened by Wagnerian music and mist. No! It would be line-thin, imperialistic, ultra-rationalistic, and pointing towards heaven, like the vertical mysticism, like the vertical Spanish syndicates.*"

I surveyed the pilgrims. In their faces, I saw the cowardice of the world. We are all victims of its fecklessness and lies, I thought, thinking of the variations of Dalí's mustache: limp, two pronged, figure eight (infinity), lopsided (one side hanging over his mouth, the other reaching for his cheeks).

"A *counsel of prudence and self-defense,*" I said, quoting Nietzsche and ordering Paola to continue transcribing, "*is to react as rarely as possible, and to avoid situations and relationships that would condemn one to suspend, as it were, one's 'freedom' and initiative and to become a mere reagent.*"

The pilgrims all nodded their heads. Their faces were flushed again. An inky life had drifted back into their veins.

"As a parable," I recited, holding my notebook in one hand and the phone against my ear with the other so I could hear the sour winds of my childhood blowing through it, "I choose association with books. Scholars do little nowadays but thumb books. Philologists" — I thought of Ludo Bembo and the murderer Eugene Aram — "at a moderate estimate man-handle about two hundred books a day and ultimately lose their capacity to think for themselves entirely. When they thumb, they don't think!

"Transcribe my words," I said to Paola.

She nodded.

We are approaching the event horizon, I thought to myself smugly; a ring of light had been generated around our swirling void and it was warming up our hearts, illuminating our faces.

"The scholar is a decadent and an amateur," I said with a feverish en-ergy, riffing off of Nietzsche's words, stitching my lines to his. "How is it possible for one to be a decadent and an amateur at the same time? Let me tell you: I am a dangerous thinker, a literary terrorist.

"Scholars," I declared, thinking of Ludo, my sick hand hurting from the sting of betrayal, "would make better use of themselves raking fields. They are people who cannot think for themselves, who spend their lives think-ing about other people's thoughts. They are uninventive, square, insecure. They don't possess a single authorial thought; all they have is the ability to say yes and no. In a world that is predominantly gray, they raise their finger and say yes and no."

After a brief silence, I released a razor-sharp "Ha!" into the air.

"Did you get that?" I asked Paola.

"Ha!" she said.

"Ha, ha, ha," I said.

"Ha, ha, ha," she repeated, and we all fell back into the abyss with our false laughter; it resounded against the walls of our void. Our laughter was as loud and dark as that roaring sea, that Sea of Sunken Hopes at the bottom of which so many bodies lay dead.

We signed the paper: *Manifesto of the Pilgrims of the Void*.

Then we each transcribed that sheet. We took our transcriptions and taped them to Dalí's front door. We abandoned the boat. We hiked down to Roses through the dark folds of night. At dawn, we caught the first bus back to Girona.

The following night, I dreamt I was standing on the Cap de Creus. *Cap de Creus*, I kept saying to myself in my dream. The words echoed back. I heard *Head of Christ*. I was standing on Christ's head. It was charred, black, burned to a crisp, full of craters and holes. From that humble bowed head of his, I could see the savage coast below. The chilled water of the Mediterranean was scrubbing his cheeks with salt and foam. The sea to the east was deep, blue, brilliant; to the west, silver like aluminum foil.

Blades of rock jutted out of the water. They looked like razors. *If you lean over the edge*, I heard, *you might be able to get a glimpse of the Cova de s'Infern*. It was Ludo's voice. I leaned over and looked at the Cave of Hell. I was so terrified of being attached to him, of losing him, that I almost slipped off the edge of the cliff.

Moments later, I woke up confused, thirsty, my mind a tangled mess. Why hadn't I been able to say that word — *love* — the only word Ludo had wanted to hear? Because, I reasoned, in order to love properly, one must also be predisposed to feelings of hope; one must believe that the object of one's love is capable of remaining alive long enough to feel loved. But could you expect that of anyone given the conditions of our sorry world? In the feeble light of morning, I reminded myself that I am an atheist relegated to a lifetime of sublime doubt, not easily inclined toward the winged pair, *love* and *hope*.

My thoughts spun dizzily. For a moment, I saw freedom close at hand. No witness, however wise, however ancient, however many times their mind had circulated this trifling earth, would dissolve my pain. Even if their eyes were as sharp as my nose. I had to gnaw on my pain alone, breaking it apart and digesting it as if it were a bone. I had to know its taste intimately. And as if that were not enough, it was my good fortune that I would have to live with its aftertaste lingering in my mouth: bitter, acerbic, sharp.

I sat up in bed. I looked around. Taüt was sleeping on a pile of clothes. Petita was curled up next to him. Had they figured out how to love each other? I pushed that word — *love* — down into the deepest recesses of myself. I lit it on fire. I watched it burn to ash. I extinguished it from my repertoire of emotions so that it, too, could be reborn like a phoenix in all the scattered ash of this sooty globe.

A few weeks later, Ludo came to me asking for forgiveness. He kneeled on the floor, put his head in my lap, and wept. He was sobbing over the twists and turns of our mangled fate. He kept saying, "No matter how hard I try, you keep pushing me away. What's the point of living as if you were already dead?" I didn't know what to say. I cupped his head in my hands. I brushed his hair out of his face.

A week later, having barely recovered from our bitter wars, we went on a solo pilgrimage to Portbou, the burial ground of Walter Benjamin. We ate macarons, walked along the oxidized rocks lacerated by the sea, and took turns listing the names the Mediterranean has been called throughout history: *liquid continent, bitter sea, the great green, sea of refugees, Sea of Sunken Hopes.* At the end of the day, holding hands, we walked to the Walter Benjamin memorial. We entered the steep narrow passageway carved into the seawall as if we were entering a tunnel to the afterlife. We descended the stairs toward the aquamarine waters, stood on the last step, and watched through the protective glass panel that seals the memorial from the sea as the Mediterranean knocked its head against the limits of the land.

We stood there in quiet contemplation for a long time. It was I who broke the silence. I couldn't help myself. I had toned down the literary activities of the pilgrimage as much as possible. I had left behind Taüt and the Mobile Art Gallery. I couldn't restrain myself any further. I pointed at the engraved panel of glass, and said, "This is symbolic of the potential escape the philosopher hoped for but never achieved. Walter Benjamin was forced to take his own life. Where does that leave the rest of us? Our destiny is no brighter."

Ludo let out a generic grunt. I moved on. I took a picture of the glass panel, which is to say I took a picture of the future that had been forbidden to the philosopher by way of that dark and stormy event at the center of modern history, that old persistent wreckage of the world wars, the human carnage, the unutterable scale of that mass genocide from which I doubt we will ever recover. In the picture, my shadow was superimposed both on the glass surface, which is inscribed with a German verse I couldn't read, and on the sapphire waves churning in the background: my death, my ghostly pewter-colored double, my shadow, superimposed on that impossible future.

"Let me see," Ludo demanded. The camera fell out of my hands. Ludo swatted at it like an impetuous child. Now he was holding the camera, looking at the photograph. "Try again," he said, with a dismissive wave of his hand. "This time without the shadow." He acted as if my shadow, my negative — and I, by extension — were a problem, an interference that needed to be eradicated. I didn't say a word after that. I emerged from the Benjamin memorial and stood under a struggling olive tree near the cemetery. Ludo sat on a rock like Rodin's *The Thinker*, head in hand. I ignored him. At some point, he lit his pipe. He leaned back on a rock to stargaze. I watched that same sky in silence. The dark silky folds of evening descended through the retreating light. Ludo's trail of smoke rose against it, a ghostly thread eclipsing, like a secondary ethereal world, the falling darkness.

We started to drift even further apart after that. Ludo started coming home late. A few times, unbeknownst to him, I followed him to work and saw him leaning in the door frame of this or that colleague's office, casually drawing smoke through his pipe. Once I saw him sitting at his desk, leaning back, enlarging his chest. The Tentacle of Ice was standing over him. I stayed away. I kept to my bed. I convalesced from the fresh punches of life. The apartment took on a morose atmosphere. Ludo and I started to take bigger stabs at each other, to punish each other with silence. Even Agatha seemed disconsolate. I could hardly stand to see her that way. One night I walked in on Ludo while he was working at his desk. He was leaning over a stack of books. He turned to look at me. He had a weary expression on his face. I proposed we go on another pilgrimage.

"Pilgrimages heal the heart," I suggested, picking up his umbrella and pointing it at his chest. He pulled on the end of the umbrella and reeled me in.

"Straddle me," he said.

We undressed. I got on top of him. When we were done, he leaned his sweaty head against my chest. He panted like a traveler spent from a long journey around the world. Our boundless magnetic lust helped us to recover. Sex had become the only thread holding us together. I felt limited, empty in a different way than I usually did, sick of my own story.

A week later, on the first day of spring, we set off to hike the Canigó with the other pilgrims. We embarked on the Pilgrimage of the Catalan Resuscitator.

It was June when we crossed the Spanish-French border in Ludo's car. We were headed to Saint Michel de Cuxa, in the Conflent region of France. Agatha, Mercè, and Remedios slept in the back seat. Gheorghe and Paola followed close behind on her scooter. I watched the stars shine through the black sky with their dead light. I watched spongy patches of fog drift over the plump moon. When the sun finally rose, it released a peach-colored light. The moon looked thin, transparent. I looked in the rearview mirror. Gheorghe had his arms wrapped tightly around Paola's slim figure; he had a highly unpleasant expression, likely the result of hardly being able to breathe against the wind. He had forgotten to bring a helmet.

Ahead of us, the Canigó was in full view. A gorgeous beast.

I turned to look at the pilgrims in the back seat. Agatha's face looked pudgy in the morning light. Remedios's cheeks had acquired a purple hue; she looked as wounded as ever. Mercè had hung a black cloth over her head. She looked like a corpse mourning her own death.

"Get that bird away from me," Ludo briskly ordered. Taüt, who was perched on my shoulder, had extended his neck across the divide to nibble on Ludo's ear. The bird had a knack for provoking him. Ludo turned to look at me with a troubled visage. I didn't appreciate his rejection of the fumes of my mother. "Stay in your own zone," he reproached. His breath smelled like garlic.

"In case you'd forgotten," I observed, "as exiles, Taüt and I lead a zoneless existence."

"Jesus Christ!" Ludo exclaimed. He was extremely agitated.

///////////

A few hours later, we were standing in the verdant valley surrounding Saint Michel de Cuxa, looking at the Benedictine abbey's cloister and crypt, parts of which had been dismantled and transferred to New York City. I remembered standing with my back to the Cloisters in Fort Tryon Park. Time folded over itself, an unconscionable map. Behind me were the Cuxa, the Bonnefont, the Saint-Guilhem, the Trie. Below me, the Hudson, green, serpentine, slithered lazily by. More than a year had passed since my father had been swallowed by this soggy earth.

I stepped back and searched the steely summits of that wide mountain. There was something violent about the Canigó: the mass of elongated rocks, the snowcapped summit, the alpine forests that grew out of its flanks and passes. I looked at the pilgrims. There was nothing lithe or nimble about any of us. The only athletic being among us was Petita, whom Agatha had brought along for the day. She was sniffing at my heels.

We began our climb. Two hours later, we were barely one-third of the way up the mountain. Already, we needed rest. The pilgrims sat on a pile of rocks near a brook. They ate their sandwiches, caught their breath.

"Sensitive being of the world," I said to the dog. "What can I do for you?"

"You're enabling that dog's anxiety," Ludo interfered righteously, fixed to his station under a row of trees.

"How do you know that her anxiety isn't a direct consequence of her awareness of the deep and irresolvable contradictions of the world?"

A crow landed near Ludo's feet and busied itself pecking at the gravel. I approached him. Petita followed at my heels.

"How is she supposed to reconcile being beaten and abandoned with the grace bestowed upon her by Agatha and, except you, the rest of the household?"

I had never had a home in my life, and yet that word — household — rolled right off my tongue, leaving behind a saccharine taste in my mouth. Ludo broke off a piece of his sandwich and threw it at the crow.

"And what you are doing to Taüt?" he said. "You think that's normal?"

Doing? I wasn't doing anything to the bird that hadn't already been done. I told Ludo that the abusive machinations driving Taüt's domestication had been set into motion long before I came into the picture. I had stolen the bird, but only because I had detected that the bird carried the fumes of my mother. Still, I somberly wondered, what was the effect of this transition on Taüt? I reflected quietly. Had I further distorted the bird through my actions? Had I intoxicated him with and then squeezed the fumes of my mother out of him? I felt a gnawing ache in my gut.

"We are all in the mud," I finally said to Ludo. "Thinking beings and feeling beings and trees and the wind and the objects we surround ourselves with. We are all in the mud together."

"But you," he said, "spend most of your time ignoring reality!"

"Reality? Whose reality am I ignoring? Because I'm sweating bullets trying to untangle the great knot of my past."

"At the expense of the present?" he retorted sarcastically.

"Yes," I said, with the cool detachment of an investigator. "I plan to salvage my integrity even if it causes me pain. And besides, time isn't linear. Minutes don't stack in an orderly fashion. They aren't soldiers."

"Even if it causes *others* pain. Try to wrap your mind around that," he said.

I looked up at the sky. A thick fog had begun to roll in. Suddenly, it was evident: I had caused Ludo Bembo pain. I felt as if someone were drilling holes in my heart. I imagined those holes, and an image of Dalínian proportions appeared to me. I tried to push the image away.

"We have to get going," I said. "A rational man would understand that."

The weather was shifting. We had a long way to the Pic del Canigó. I had been there with my father in June, on the night before Saint John's Day when a fire is lit near the cross at the summit, which is covered in the Catalan flag. We had kept vigil with strangers through the night and lit torches on the fire. Not in the spirit of Catholicism but in the spirit of Catalan identity. I remembered watching the torches light up, one after the other, down the flank of the mountain. I remembered seeing the chain of people, their silhouettes against the orange flames that licked the dark night air. Now, a gelid breeze was barreling down the mountain pass. It didn't matter what time of year it was. The weather turned quickly in the Pyrenees.

"Save your sandwiches for later," I said to the pilgrims. They all got up. One injured soul after another. A sour mood hung over them.

We hiked up the plateau for several hours in silence. I could hear the pilgrims panting behind me. Ludo, that shortsighted amateur, hung his head and stared at the ground. I gazed into the distance, into the future of my past, which we were fast approaching. What lay before us were abrupt cliffs, ravines, slender cascades rippling into small pools, twisted strata of crystalline rocks. Up ahead, there was an elongated terrace of creased and pleated rock marked by depressions where the mountain seemed to suddenly drop off. I took in that crisscrossing labyrinth of sierras, massifs separated by bright valleys and shallow glaciers. To lift the mood, I turned around and recited verses from "Canigó," Verdaguer's epic poem. My mustached father had recited those same verses to me.

"*The Canigó is an immense magnolia,*" I declared, "*that blooms in an offshoot of the Pyrenees.*"

"The fog is thickening," Agatha gently observed.

"What does that have to do with anything?" I asked.

"There's no one else walking these trails. We don't even have a map," Mercè protested through the black cloth that continued to hang from her face. She was walking arm in arm with Remedios.

"The blind leading the blind," I said.

"No one is blind here," Ludo interjected. "This is a bad sign — a sign of dangerous weather."

"Dr. Bembo, fog is the state of the world, nothing more, nothing less," I retorted. "It is our job as pilgrims to stand at the brink of the void. You cannot be a pilgrim and be invertebrate!"

An argument ensued. Here and there, I heard sighs of despair. I heard Paola complain to Gheorghe about her hip. The pair of them were in a grave mood.

"We're lost," Mercè cried out through that cloth of death. "We're lost! We won't be able to find our way back again."

"And the light is already waning," Remedios added.

"Isn't that what God is for?" I asked her. "To fill your spirit with light when you most need it?"

She fell back silent. But it was true. The light was waning. It was also true that we had all overexerted ourselves. We had pushed our bodies up the wide pedestal of the mountain. We had hiked through forests and past streams, up steep green slopes, and crossed paths flanked by sharp sheets of silver rock.

"Mercè," I said. "I suggest you remove that cloth from your face. What is wrong with you?"

"There's nothing wrong with me. I'm just shy," she said.

I couldn't take it anymore. I grabbed a stick and whipped it at their ankles. "Onward!" I barked like a shepherd's dog. I herded them up the mountain. We pushed our way up the steep slopes in fits and bursts. I could see their arms and legs pumping through the thickening fog. Vertical walls of rock were closing in on us. Gusts of wind were barreling down. It sounded like a million knives were being sharpened at once. The wind was burning our skin. I scooped Taüt off my shoulder and held him in my arms. Agatha put Petita on a leash. I could hear the dog chattering in the cold wind. Finally, I admitted that we were lost. There were no signs anywhere. We had gone off the trail. I no longer had the faintest notion where we were in this maze of peaks and knolls.

"Let's take five," I said, and we sat down against a wall of rock. I opened my notebook to a random page.

"Not this again," Ludo said.

"How many times do I have to tell you that these sentences are our roadmap to the future?"

There was a strong gale, after which Remedios finally broke.

"What does the book say?" she asked, on the verge of tears.

"Thank you for asking, Remedios," I said, rather joylessly.

"According to the book, this book that is the book of books, its sentences highways that allow readers to travel in multiple temporalities simultaneously" — I took in a breath against the wind that was blowing everywhere — "according to this book, *terrorists are those who desire absolute freedom and who behave during their lifetimes not like people living among other living people*" — I paused to swallow the soot spreading through the atmosphere — "*but like beings deprived of being, like universal thoughts, pure abstractions beyond history, judging and deciding in the name of all of history.*"

Ah, the prophetic Blanchot.

"We are literary terrorists," I said to my companions. I heard that word — *terrorists* — echo back from the mess of rocks. I looked up. There was no one there. Everyone had dispersed. One minute they were sitting against the chiseled facade of the mountain, and the next they were nowhere to be seen. I was alone with Taüt, sitting in a dusty bowl. I felt abandoned, alone once again with the heavy burden of my ill-fated past.

Time folded over itself. The gates of memory opened. I leaned over the edge of the mountain and took in the dizzying expanse beneath me. Memories emerged like troops from the dark recesses of my consciousness. I tried to push them away from my face with my sick hand. I felt the present distend into the past, contract toward the future. I heard my father's muffled voice pour out through the gaps in his waning mustache. I was standing next to him at the top of Mount Sahand.

"I spit on you," he said, "you bunch of patriarchal nepotists!"

Our hands were sore from burying my mother.

Then, suddenly, without warning, the sky cleared. It was limpid again. I was standing on the bald summit of the mountain. I had, despite all the obstacles, ascended the Canigó. I could see Casteil, Taurinya, Valmanya, Vernet-les-Bains. I looked beyond France at Italy. I turned and looked in the direction of Spain. Then I looked beyond it at the New World.

"Pitiless persecutors!" I said, thinking of Franco, Mussolini, Hitler, the King of Kings, Bush. "This is not the end of them. The fascists will keep reconstituting themselves!" I declared, and tried to get up, but I couldn't. I felt as though I had been fused to that delirium of rocks. Had I made it back to Iran? I wondered. To that mercurial country of my youth? My mind was unreeling. My thoughts were spooling, spilling over. And what, according to my father, was so vile about Iran? How, I wondered, could he have considered it worse than Spain with its rampant colonialism, its inquisitions, a country with centuries' worth of blood on its hands? And what about the so-called New World? How had we ended up there, caught up in its lies and dissociations? The New World, I thought, a direct extension of the Spanish and the British imperialists? We, whose lives had been shaped by the interests of the British, had returned to live among their descendents in the New World, to be pulverized again and again by them.

"What is wrong with us?" I said. "What is wrong with us all?"

"Who are you speaking to?" It was Ludo. I turned around. He looked crestfallen, wind battered. He said, "We lost each other. I came looking for you." Petita was at his heels.

I wanted to go toward him, but I couldn't. The storm picked up again.

It sprayed the dirt of the world into our faces. We were both squinting in the wind. Ludo asked, "How can someone who hates love love literature?" His voice was shattered, spent, consumed.

"Literature is risk free," I lied. "Each book is a perfect boat you ride into the darkness, but you are guaranteed to emerge unscathed."

"Are you sure about that?"

Petita scurried over and sniffed Taüt's tail. The bird bowed in response. Sure? Sure about what? I wondered.

"So you are advocating a categorical absence of risk?"

There was a strong wind. My life, I thought quietly, has been subject to one putrid gale after another.

"Listen to me," Ludo said desperately. "Do I have to bear the risks of loving you alone?"

His voice was being carried across the mountains on the wind.

"Look at me!" he demanded pleadingly. "Look at me!"

I looked at him. His face looked ancient, familiar. His shirt was torn. His hands were scarred. I plodded through my mind. I came across roadblock after roadblock. *Love is the enemy. Love is a thought. Love needs reinventing. Hate I shall if I can; if I can't, I shall love, though not willingly.* There were no words. I had run out of lines of defense. I said nothing.

"Enough," he said. "Enough. I'm here, aren't I? Through all this absurdity?"

My voice released in weak bands. "Absurdity? There is nothing absurd about any of this. I am simply living by the laws that have governed my life."

"And these poor impressionable nitwits you've dragged into this mess with you?" he asked.

Nitwits, I thought. As if those people had no willpower, no agency of their own. How could I explain that to a man like Ludo? I would have to destroy him in order to reconstruct him from the ground up. And how could I know that I wouldn't get shattered in the process?

"Where is everyone anyway?" I asked.

"They headed back down the mountain," he said. "And I suggest you do the same. There is a terrible storm on the way," he warned. "This is the calm, the calm before the storm. I can't take care of you. You have to decide to do this on your own."

Is that the best you can do? I wanted to ask, but I didn't know who I was addressing the question to. Ludo? My dead parents? The wretched leaders of my lost nations?

I started walking. My legs were trembling beneath me. Petita led the way, sniffing the ground. An hour later, we had come to a valley that sliced the mountain in half. I felt as though we were walking up and down the craggy plateaus of hell. I thought of Dante the Pilgrim. I heard Virgil's voice: *Ruthless striving overcomes everything.* I heard the anxious neighing of horses. I heard the creaking sound of trees folding at the waist in the wind.

I stopped in my tracks. I turned around to face Ludo.

"I have been pushed by the world into a state of psychic feudalism. And you want me to make myself vulnerable to you. How much vulnerability do you think one person can take? Do you want me to rip my skin off and stand in the wind, bleeding and raw?"

"What do you want me to say to that?" he answered, pushing me along.

We walked another hour against the wind. I could barely breathe. I sat down on a chopped log that had mushrooms bursting out of its wet peeling bark. Then I got up again. Through the alpine forests, I had spotted a house in ruins. I thought of my mother searching for food. Before I knew it, I was standing in that ruined house and Ludo was standing on the other side of it, begging me to come out, to keep going.

"You're taking this too far," he cried. "You're putting our lives in danger."

It was true. I had taken things further than anyone had before.

"It's going to come down on your head," Ludo protested.

"Let it," I said.

The wind was howling and wheezing; it was dragging everything down. I crouched on the ground.

"I'll relive that, too," I said.

"Relive what?" he asked. His voice was breaking. Petita was pacing anxiously. Taüt let out a shrill scream.

"My mother's death!" I declared.

Ludo's eyes widened in horror.

Rain started pouring down. It was the hardest rain we had seen that year. I was standing at the epicenter of my life. I could see toxic fumes radiating outward. The drops were the size of my hands. We were drenched within seconds. Torrential cascades of water were pouring down the mountain. I started looking under the rocks for food. What was the first thing my mother would have laid her eyes on when she walked into that house of ruin? The last thing before she died? Did she swallow the dirt of the world? I grabbed a chunk of mud and ate it.

"You are a lunatic," Ludo said. "You are acting like a savage."

I wiped my mouth. I swallowed the clumps of wet dirt.

"I have been made an enemy," I said. "I have endured the world with grace for long enough."

Then I remembered my mother leaning over me, whispering into my ear: *Somewhere, deep inside you, hidden by all sorts of fears and worries and petty little thoughts, is a clean pure being made of radiant colors.*

So I had remembered her words all along. I recognized the quote. It was by Shirley Jackson. My mother, too, had embedded sentences into my body; the words of literature, like my mother and father, were everywhere and nowhere at once. She had appeared to me in the most ordinary way. This, I decided, implied that she had been there all along and that dead or alive the minds of the sensitive beings of the world were slogging through the cosmos even if I could not perceive them with my eyes.

Hours later, the storm subsided. Ludo, Taüt, Petita, and I made it down the mountain. We had no idea where the other pilgrims were. We stood in front of Saint Michel de Cuxa, dumbfounded, stunned by the strange unfolding of the day. The abbey's cloister and crypt were stained by the rain. I again remembered standing with my back to the Cloisters in Fort Tryon Park. Behind me were the Cuxa, the Bonnefont, the Saint-Guilhem, the Trie. Should I leap into my death? I wondered. My memories were recycling themselves. Then all my thoughts were interrupted by the sound of Ludo's scream.

"My car!" he exclaimed. "Where is my car?"

Rainwater was dripping off the trees, off the red-tile roofs of the abbey, off the stubborn granite of the mountain. We were standing knee-deep in the muddied waters of the earth. We trod through the waters until we found Ludo's car. It had slid off the road. It was sinking in the river. We watched the hood disappear.

"No!" Ludo cried. "No!" He kicked the ground, then he stood there with his hands on his head, speechless.

I watched that car sink. We had left the miniature museum — my father's casket — in the trunk. It was too awkward to carry up the steep mountain. It drowned with everything else. It disappeared. I felt a weight lift from my shoulders. I felt my life dissolve, as though the person who had set off on the Grand Tour of Exile no longer existed. I am from nowhere, I thought, as that car sank into the river; I was born in the nothingness that contains everything within it. I petted Taüt gently on the head. That, I said to my dead mother in the depths of my heart, is my only essence.

THE LIQUID CONTINENT

The Story of How I Traveled Across
the Sea of Sunken Hopes

LUDO WAS WEARING A TWEED JACKET OVER HIS RED wool cardigan even though it was summer, and he had a gray cashmere scarf tied around his neck. He was leaving but not before giving me one last admonishing look. He planted his umbrella into the floor of the landing and leaned into it, that umbrella he had begun to carry with him everywhere, using it to point at things as if it were an extension of his arm. His eyes betrayed no remorse. Anger, maybe. And pity. But remorse: none at all.

"At last," he said with labored breath. "Finally."

He stood in the shadowy landing, pipe tucked neatly into his breast pocket, copper curls perfectly conditioned. The landing was dark and dusty, full of residue from times past. The walls were perpetually damp; the Mediterranean humidity had gotten into the building's bones. In that wet, ashen bleakness, Ludo lay bare his reasons for leaving: He was departing because of my self-prescribed cure for the long dark history of my past: my literary pilgrimages into the void of exile.

When I pressed him for more information, Ludo set his leather suitcase, which matched his shoes, squarely by his feet. Kindly but with a certain formal distance, he said, "Look, the way you choose to cope with your past is unbearable to me. The fact is there are toxic side effects to your writing behavior, effects I can't stand."

I looked at him, astonished. He proceeded, blasted past my bewilderment, to deliver the bullets one by one.

"ONE," he let out, as stern as a drill sergeant. "Sudden disappearances." I told him I knew perfectly well where I was at all times.

"TWO," he declared. There was no stopping him. "Pathological indifference toward the living. THREE. The worst transgression of all —"

"I hardly agree," I said, somewhat helplessly.

"THREE," he continued, deaf to me. "Consecutive days during which you remain in bed, stinking up the bedroom as if you were a corpse!"

I told him this was no way to say good-bye. I told him he had a lot to learn from Agatha on the art of politeness. I looked around. Where were Agatha and Fernando? Petita came rushing to the door. The clay busts of Agatha followed the dog with their eyes, an army of Agathas. The dog sat at my heels. I sucked in little patches of air between gasps of disbelief. I could feel shock spreading through my veins. I gathered myself.

A shaft of light shone through the skylight, burnishing the tip of Ludo's umbrella, the silver buckles on his leather suitcase. He was returning home to Florence. He had stuffed his suitcase with English wool, tobacco, his collection of historical dictionaries, and left everything else. He told me his elderly father had fallen ill; his bones had grown brittle, his heart was weak, and as a natural consequence of that, his mind was engulfed in a fog through which he could no longer see clearly.

Does your father have a mustache? I was tempted to ask, but I kept my mouth sealed. I am no fool. I could see that Ludo was lying. My duty to my dead father, whom I had absorbed through metempsychosis and whose presence I had carried within my void, had eclipsed my relationship with Ludo, limiting the attention I was able to bestow upon him. Now this literary heretic, uninventive descendent of the Bembos, was using my narrative to justify his own. He was pelting his father at me. He was taking revenge.

I remembered, as lucidly as a déjà vu, when Ludo had asked me after a terrible fight, his voice exasperated, guttural: "What are you hoping to find? It's not a treasure box," he had said, referring to the void.

With great theatricality, I had responded: "My friend, my dear, dear friend, I am searching for a flame in my void that will shine so brightly, brighter than the brightest dawn, that it will roll back the shadow of death!"

But that wasn't true. It was just something I had said. What I had wanted to confess to him was this: *My wound is inside me. It is the wound of a lack of love.* But I couldn't bring myself to expose my weaknesses, my vulnerabilities. Too much had come to pass. All I could see was history's chain of frauds. The world had turned into a reckless mirror image of itself and cut off my oxygen. Who was I to trust? The world had no solidity.

Petita let out a cry of anxiety. I opened my mouth. I said: *"This is love, when death's involved."*

Ludo stared at me. I couldn't tell if he was bemused or disturbed. I stared back at him. I rolled his name on my tongue: Ludo, a living being among other living beings, who was standing at the threshold, suitcase in hand, about to depart forever; Ludo, who had turned a blind eye to all signs of turbulence when I needed him most, to the generalized disturbance being alive engenders, to the nothingness that is inherent in everything we do.

Ludo reached for his pipe and then swiftly slipped it back into his pocket and patted his chest. For a moment, I thought he might change his mind, that he would step over the threshold and cross the boundary he had drawn to protect himself from — as he had so crudely intoned in the past — the death-slapped and warped nature of my mind. I pictured him dropping his leather suitcase, detaching himself from his umbrella to embrace me. I imagined our bodies collapsing into each other. I imagined him pushing me backward into his room, furiously unbuttoning my shirt, caressing my breasts, lowering his head to lick my hardened nipples; Ludo, salivating, impish, ready to take on the task of mending the disrepair our relationship had fallen into. Sex has a way of doing that, of raising our courage.

But instead, he stood in the doorway scratching his beard. He had let it grow. Until now, Ludo had always been clean-shaven, tiresomely groomed. I interpreted the stubble on his face as a sign of his grief. I looked into Ludo's eyes and saw myself there, a shadow in the glassy pond of his irises looking back at me. I saw the love and the hate that had bonded and repelled us, the sexual appetite we had untethered in each other. The black surfaces of his pupils shrank; my image vanished. I was exiled. He was sweating. His nostrils flared again. I didn't know what to expect. Sexual attack? Sudden departure? The odds were even. Then, poof, the moment vanished. He was steady and severe.

I examined his face. I told him he had a lovely Roman nose.

"It gives you the look of a man capable of building things — aqueducts, roads," I said. Ludo lifted his upper lip and bared his teeth.

"You," he said, lifting his leather suitcase with one hand and whipping the shaft of his umbrella against the door frame with the other. "Have come into my life to torture me."

Ludo clutched his departure paraphernalia the way a man lost at sea clutches a raft. He left abruptly, vanished before I could respond, before I could remind him that he was the one who had pursued me, muttering the word *love* all along and confessing that my vagina was like a tunnel of light he could swim into the way a fish swims into a channel to protect itself while the world is being lacerated by a deathly wind.

I walked to the living room and — spent, shocked, bruised — pressed my face against the latticed panes of the terrace doors. I watched him march down the street. He was soldiering his way to the train station. I peeled the shutters open and stepped onto the terrace between our dying plants. I was as empty as the wind-beaten sky. I didn't know what to do. Against my will, against my better judgment, I yelled: "We all wake up to realize we are stuffing the wrong holes with the wrong things!"

The earth was finally beginning to warm up. A hot wind whistled through the crooked cobblestone streets of the medieval quarter; it moved in broad strokes, polishing the sky. A vermillion band of light was beginning to form over the mountains in the distance. I heard the wind pick up; it cartwheeled its way through the streets of Girona. The Catalan flags of independence, hung here and there on poles, the buildings, the terraces — they all clapped as if in response. In the midst of the narrow alleys, flanked by their dense stone walls, I spotted Ludo.

He emerged through the arch at the end of the stairs that hug the convent. The wind knocked over empty bottles of wine that had been left at the door of a wine bar the night before. They rolled, trailing behind Ludo, chiming against the cobblestone street. The wind cast aside anything that hadn't been bolted to the ground. I watched Ludo duck menus and plastic patio furniture. He was walking down La Rambla now, the city's main promenade. He crossed the bridge, the Pont de Pedra, rushed over the river, then disappeared into a flood of light. A white sheet Mercè had hung out to dry on her rooftop tore away and floated upward, softly at first, and then in a panic, the way a dove released at a funeral jets into the sky, eager to get away from all the grief-stricken people left on earth.

Once Ludo crossed the Pont de Pedra, I lost sight of him. I knew him well enough to know he would take the road we always took. I also knew that those streets operated as corridors for the wind, that the wind would have to narrow its scope in order to push through them, and that in doing so it would pick up pressure and speed. An unusually strong *xaloc* was blowing up from the Sahara. Ludo would have a hell of a time getting to the train station. He would have to throw all his weight into the wind to avoid falling backward. He would have to lift his legs one by one with tremendous focus, as if he were walking across the moon, and even then, he would still arrive at the station panting, out of breath.

The bells tolled again. I stepped back in and sealed the shutters. I looked around the apartment. Where were Agatha and Fernando? It seemed they had been gone forever. I had been deserted in an outdated apartment, left to rot among the broken telephones and VCRs, the old vacuum parts, those bits of technology the three of them — Ludo, Agatha, Fernando — had kept in the event that the ones in regular use ever broke. They had been taught to do so by their parents and grandparents who had survived the world wars. Those shattered bits of technology were proof that the ravenous events of the twentieth century were still hungry for fresh blood. They may deny that proof, but I saw it clearly: the rupture in communications, the feelings of uncertainty activated by the world wars, had barreled on from generation to generation with an increasingly greedy appetite. I felt the blood, which had only just begun to course through the fleshy corridors of my heart, halt and retreat.

I walked past Agatha's busts to Ludo's room and sat down on the edge of his bed, numb. I was as empty as the sky. I felt as though someone had wiped my chest clean. I felt a harrowing, ancient terror begin to rise. The yellow walls of Ludo's room closed in on me. I wondered if I was suffering from a nervous disorder. I thought, this must be what it's like to be born. This must be why infants scream when they first exit their mothers' wombs. Their scream is a scream of confusion. I calmed myself. I reminded myself that this is what I had asked for in retracing the path of my exile: to die in order to begin again. Only I hadn't expected to feel so increasingly disoriented. I felt like I was trapped in a maddening replicative mirror that kept projecting the dark and stormy event at the center of my life: the void of exile. Was this life? I wondered. A web with no center? An eternally repetitive sequence of events without origin?

Hours swept by. I walked onto the terrace a few times, as though it were a landing with a vantage point from which I could see Ludo regardless of where he might be. What else did I have now that Ludo was gone? The goldfish was circling its tank, pumping the slimy green waters with its extraordinary gills. Taüt was walking the corridor. Petita was trailing behind him. I had only the company of these animals.

I returned to Ludo's room and threw myself on his bed. I stared at the ceiling. I listened to the calm susurrus of Girona through the walls. I sank into the swampy Matrix of Literature. In my mind's eye, I navigated its dark waters until I felt time collapse into a single surface, indicating that everything had both already happened and was about to happen. So, I said to myself as I drifted off, neither here nor there: Ludo has left me before; Ludo will leave me again.

Sometime later I awoke. Was it yesterday, today, tomorrow? I couldn't tell. The first thing I saw when I opened my eyes was Taüt. A cyclone of thoughts unreeled in my mind. How am I supposed to reconcile being an exile with loving someone? Where is my mother? My father? Where is the archive of my nation? What nation? Which one? Which one could I claim to call my own? Taüt was sitting at the end of the bed. He lifted his talon and saluted me. He was completely calm.

"Taüt," I said. "Who can bear a pointless torment?"

The bird opened his beak.

"The heart of the future is ancient," he said.

"Indeed," I said. "Indeed it is."

Then I thought, what am I going to do with the abyss — incalculably large — I have found myself in? This abyss into which I have leapt only to come out the other end more mired in shit than I had been in to begin with? I stared at the ceiling until I drifted off to sleep again.

Hours later, in the silence of the night, I sat bolt upright in bed. Camus's words were swimming around the labyrinthine corridors of my mind: *Everything is strange to me, everything, without a single person who belongs to me, with no place to heal this wound . . . I am not from here — not from anywhere else either. And the world has become merely an unknown landscape where my heart can lean on nothing.* I got up and paced the corridor. Taüt, loyal companion, hopped off the bed and walked at my heels.

A week passed during which I could not sleep. Each night, I paced the corridor. My emotions surged and retreated. I was walking through the shallows and profundities of my mind. One moment I was downtrodden, grief-stricken; the next, restless, enraged. But, irrespective of the highs and lows of my mood, one question looped through my mind, a question with roots: What had the pilgrimages exposed? Finally, one day, in the feeble light of dawn, while Agatha and Fernando were asleep in their room, I heard: *my total inadequacy in the face of life.* I felt struck by the lacerating precision of those words. Who had written them? Benjamin, Levi, Unamuno? That's when it hit me: I couldn't believe Ludo was gone.

I walked into his room. I dragged my sick hand across the yellow walls, the surface of his desk, the rug on his floor. I opened his closet and smelled his clothes. I went through his drawers and his books. I found a note in his handwriting, which was timeless, elegant, floral. I recognized the words.

The note contained a transcription of the sentence the elder Nietzsche had used to criticize the work of his youth: *badly written, ponderous, embarrassing . . . uneven in tempo, without the will to logical cleanliness, very convinced and therefore disdainful of proof.*

Had Ludo been keeping a philological commentary on the record of my suffering? I wondered. For a moment, I felt indignant, inflamed. I rolled those words off my tongue: *badly written, ponderous, embarrassing!* In that bitter heat, I remembered Nietzsche's other words: *equality before the enemy: the first supposition of an honest duel.*

But as soon as I retreated to the corridor, I felt confused. Who was the enemy? And where did the enemy lay hiding? Was the enemy manifest, like death, within me? There was no way of knowing. I sat on the floor next to the busts of Agatha and wept uncontrollably. I was in the hollows again. No one was home. Taüt ambled down the corridor and nudged my sick hand. I lifted it to pet him. He had picked up new habits from the dog. He cooed and cawed in response to my touch, and I heard that bass voice of his come at me as if from across a great distance. I was exhausted. I felt as though I was outside this world looking in — already dead and yet still slogging through, dragging my ignorance behind me. What parts of my mind had I fed? I wondered, as I stroked the bird's wings. What parts had I starved? I had been faithfully devoted to the person who had set off on the Grand Tour of Exile, but that person no longer existed. I had been reborn in the pile of ruins like a phoenix, that pile to which I had added my own cold cruelty, my own wretchedness.

After that, I slept for days. In the limpid light of sleep, the questions metamorphosed; they blended together and took on dramatic proportions. One afternoon, while I was aimlessly walking through the verdant hills and valleys of Sant Daniel, I thought: What does equality consist of in a case where it remains unclear who the enemy is? I flipped through the possible candidates — Ludo Bembo, the knotted and knobby paths of my ill-fated life, the world's leading dictators who have acted upon it ruthlessly — and again felt my sadness give way to rage. My anger became focused. I felt irate at this bloodthirsty, disordered universe, disgusted for being a part of it. My thoughts spooled and spun. I wondered: What would the greatest revenge be? I scanned the limpid, wind-polished sky. I saw the answer, which had presented itself to me in so many forms and facets throughout the Grand Tour of Exile and against which I, fearful and uncertain, had repeatedly thrown myself only to be repelled, as if it had been written across that sky in ink. The greatest revenge, I saw, lay in the simplest revenge of all: to love against all odds, to prevail, to persist in a world that fought tooth and nail to eliminate me. That's all there was. That's all there ever had been. I stood there utterly dumbfounded. How stupid, I thought, how utterly simple. I felt a fool. I picked up a rock as if I were picking up that word: *love.* I put that rock in my mouth and sucked on it. It was unyielding, hard, an object I could not metabolize or break into parts. I returned home terrified, confused, and yet somehow resolved, determined to pursue Ludo, to draw a new path of exile across the map of my ill-fated life. I sucked on that rock the whole way back to his apartment. It left a mineral taste in my mouth.

The next day, I packed my things. I was done in no time. I didn't have very much. I had Taüt, my notebook, the rock, the clothes on my back. I had lost everything. I had very little money left; the objects of my past were long lost. I had no identity and yet, I thought, I was infinite, multiple. Like a blank page, I can be whatever I want. I heard Agatha moving around in

the living room. A copper light was filtering through the window. It cast
the room in an amber glow. I watched her silently for a moment. She was
hovering over the aquarium. She had combed her hair to one side; it was
dangling over her shoulder. I could see the fish darting across the tank
through the gaps between the thick strands of her hair.

"I'm leaving," I announced. "I can't bear the thought of Ludo's abandoning me like this, hanging by a thread like a piece of laundry."

"Where to?" she asked.

She turned around. Her face caught the golden light. She looked serene, pale, tranquil. If there is anyone to whom I can speak the truth, it's
her, I thought to myself.

"I'm going to pursue Ludo," I said.

"How?"

"On the next ship," I declared. "I am going to cross the waters of the
Mediterranean, Sea of Sunken Hopes."

She looked at me, stunned. Her jaw had dropped slightly, enough for
me to see that the corners of her mouth had grown wet. "Shouldn't you
give things a rest for a while?"

Her tone was somber, as if a tide of worry had risen and drowned her
voice. She regarded me with a look that betrayed feelings of pity, confusion, fear. It was as if by addressing me, her mind had come into contact
with something rough, incoherent, disturbed. That expression seemed
to be everywhere lately, superimposed on the faces of people I knew and
strangers. As soon as people looked at me, their faces would collapse. It
was as if they could see through me to the shattered bits of my father and
mother that had drifted in my void like tumbleweeds in a drafty desert. I,
a perpetual stranger in every city. Was I subverting its norms from the inside? I had no idea. I had no idea about anything. It had been so long since
I had looked in the mirror.

That evening, I boarded the ship to Genoa with Taüt on my shoulder. I retreated to my cabin. It would take seventeen and a half hours to cross the
Mediterranean to Italy. In Genoa, I would walk to Terminal Traghetti and
board a train to Genova Brignole station. From there, I would transfer to a
train headed for Florence. I was sure Ludo would be waiting for me in the
geometric city that had produced him. I closed my eyes. I imagined knock-

ing on his door. He would open it, and through the slit, I would see his father, defeated, old, frail, lying supine on a bed in front of the television in the living room. Ludo hadn't lied after all. I imagined the blue glow of the television screen giving him a pasty, ghostly look. I imagined he would be tense at first. He would stand rigidly before me. He would try to forbid me from coming in. I would remind him that my father had died many deaths; I would tell him that I had watched my father's face transform in life and in death and that each time I had to sever my attachment to him. I would tell him I know what it means to enter the uncharted waters of grief. I would tell him that I could be a mountain of wisdom for him to lean on, that our long macabre dance had whittled down to this moment, this simple gesture of making sure he would not be pacing alone in the shadow of his father's imminent death. His lips would tremble. His father would turn his leathery face to look in our direction. His eyes would be puffy, small, and watery, but his gaze would be conclusive, determined, the gaze of a man aware that he is standing on the verge of his own death. He would say something, a quick protest about the draft we were letting in through the open door, and Ludo would let me in. He would shut the door behind me. We would stand in the foyer contemplating each other in silence, considering each other's faces, the many selves we had either silenced or resurrected within each other. I would be the first to speak. After all, it was I who had come all this way after him. What choice did I have? My father had vanished from my void. So had my mother. They had joined the residue of the world. They were everywhere. They were in the very air I breathed. They existed in my inky veins as knowledge. What did it matter what streets I walked on? What did it matter where I sank my anchor when the whole world was a single surface, an infinitely unreeling roll of paper?

"Ah, Ludo," I would say. "What a tragedy. What a drama. Once again, the world as we know it is coming to an end. Is this what it means to be human?"

Ludo would stagger toward me in the dark. Without saying a word, he would reach out and grab my hand; he would pull me into his embrace, and we would cry together. That night, we would lie motionless on his bed, our eyes open in the dark, the colossal weight of the tragedy of our young century hovering over us, the television still on in the living room, the patter of his father rising from his bed, reaching for his walker, rolling his way to the bathroom, remorseless words floating up from the set, congealing in the air, taking on enormous proportions: "suicide bombings," "air raids," "mass death," "dearth of food, of water, of justice," "severed limbs of children," "buildings covered in soot."

After a prolonged silence, Ludo would utter into the air: "We need the rest of our lives to untangle the toxic knots of our childhoods."

I saw then that he understood why I had eaten the mud. We were on the cusp of recognition. Soon, half the world would be rising up in revolt. Half the world would be eating dirt. I closed my eyes. I saw blurry shadows, eddies, trenches, craggy mountains, the endless black waters of the seas and oceans. I raised my hand and waved it in the air.

"War is a contagious affair. Sooner or later this violence will spill over. We will all be drawn into it. This is the beginning of another end," I would say. "We are all poor. We are all starved. We are all persecuted."

"Yes," Ludo would say. "If one of us is persecuted, we all are." He would roll over and climb on top of me. His cheeks would be wet with tears. We would make love. Then, panting, weary, exhausted, I imagined that he would say: "I don't know what it means to be human. I thought I knew, but that, too, has been undone along with everything else."

We had been warned the sea was high. A storm was brewing. I sat in a windowless cabin. The ship pitched precariously in the inky waters. I could hear rain falling. A heavy, warm rain. It was the last storm of the year. I could hear the waves rising up to scrape the underbelly of the damp sky. Restless bodies moved impatiently outside my cabin door. Dante's voice came at my side: *For the straightforward pathway had been lost.*

"Lost," I mumbled into the vaporous air. The Grand Tour of Exile had come to an abrupt end. No, not an abrupt end. Like the many faces of my father, the Grand Tour of Exile had reproduced itself. It had acquired a second and third and fourth face; it had metamorphosed, acquired digressions. A new phase of exile awaited me in Florence. A new living death in that rational city with its open piazzas, its Haussmann-inspired boulevards, its bloody history, the Arno that floods its ochre banks every hundred years. In my mind's eye, I saw the image of a bull plowing the earth with its horns, exhuming the dead. I said quietly to myself: "I am a patient born into an inhospitable world, an outsider, a spectator, a painmonger, a nonmember." Words spooled through my mind. An alien, a fugitive, a castaway, a boat person.

Taüt nervously paced my shoulders. The sea was threatening to swallow us whole, as if enough people hadn't already drowned in its brackish waters. The bird intermittently hooked his beak to my ear. I felt my stomach float up into my throat. I belched. I emptied myself out. Then I sniffed the acerbic, briny air.

It had been hours. We had likely passed Montpellier, Marseille, Cannes. The ship rocked and rolled in the violent waters. I nursed Taüt. I held steady through the night. I fell asleep a few times. I dreamt Ludo and I were raking the depths of the sea, gathering the bodies of the dead, resurfacing with them one by one. I was holding my notebook in one hand and scraping the seabed with the other. We walked in silence until we came across a sunken warplane. The rusted fuselage was covered with algae, barnacles, starfish, shrimp. Schools of tropical fish were moving through it. Ludo kept a certain distance from me as we examined the wreckage. He seemed rather suspicious of my presence. I climbed onto the blunted nose of the plane. I opened my notebook; it had acquired a prophetic aura underwater. In an oratorical tone, I declared: *"The process of decay is at the same time a process of crystallization.* Arendt on Benjamin through Shakespeare."

Ludo considered my words. He had a pensive expression on his face. He dragged his nimble hands across the tendrils of algae. Those hands had tried to nourish me. I climbed back down and stood on the seabed next to him. We were moving with such grace underwater. He stared at me in silence for a long time. He opened and closed his mouth in rapid succession. When he finally spoke, his words were rich and strange.

"Crystallization," he declared, "is *that action of the mind that discovers fresh perfections in its beloved at every turn of events.* From the commentary on your notebook," he admitted.

"Ah, Stendhal," I muttered forgivingly, content that our notebooks had multiplied and merged. "Sentimental weasel, doppelgänger to Marie-Henri Beyle."

A monkfish swam by. I stared at its huge mouth, its depressed head, its inwardly inclined fangs. It had been camouflaging itself in the sand.

"*Lophius piscatorius*," Ludo said. Then he asked: "Where should we eat this evening?" We were getting along swimmingly.

I laughed, and replied: "*Lophius piscatorius* swims through the liquid continent, the great green, the inner sea, the corrupting sea, the bitter sea, but, most important, the Sea of Sunken Hopes, the sea of refugees."

My words cut the jovial mood. Ludo's eyes swept through the waters. He took a few steps back. He regarded me anxiously. He was preparing to ask the most conclusive question of all. "More important, when will you say *the great and coherent yes to life?*"

A deep silence ensued. In that chasm, I heard Nietzsche: *A soul that knows it is loved but does not itself love betrays its sediment: what is at the bottom comes up.*

Ludo, having posed his question, leaned against the engine of the plane. A school of pink fish swam through the gaps between the blades. His blond curls were floating in the saline water. He looked at me in that special way of his, with a petulant pout; he was sulking again.

"Ludo," I protested. "We have to keep walking. We have to keep raking the bed of this inner sea." But he refused to move.

"Then why not bring it all to an end?" he asked reluctantly. "Why this obstinate perseverance to live a life you are not committed to?"

The monkfish swam over the wings of the plane. I watched it pump the water out of its gills and carve its way through the water in sections. We can only conquer life a little at a time, I considered. There will always be a remainder out of reach. We have to make our peace with that. Would I make my peace? Would I conquer? I wanted to dig my head in the sand.

Suddenly, as I looked at Ludo, I realized he was upset with himself for loving someone who hadn't yet managed to land on earth. To cheer him up, I swam over and perched on the nose of the plane. I said: "Ludovico Bembo, I came down to this earth through the same canal as everyone else: my mother's vagina. In that regard, I am like everyone else. But in other respects, I am unique. I arrived physically, but there was a part of me that lingered behind. My descent was incomplete. This incompleteness, this gap, was widened by the cruel facts of my life, its elusive calamity, the cultural assassination of my ancestors, the psychological massacre of exile, the physical and transcendental homelessness that has marked my life. But don't worry, I am an irregular genius who is in the process of synchronizing her multiple minds in order to acquire the privilege to rise in the morning and say *a great and coherent yes to life."*

I expected him to come back with a rebuttal, but he just tossed his head back and laughed. We walked side by side through the seabed, raking the void.

I woke up hours later sweating, panting, out of breath. What did I see when I opened my eyes? The bloated waterfowl of Lake Urmia. The craggy flanks of Mount Sahand. The date palms of the Caspian. Will I ever return home? I turned that word — *home* — around in my mouth. It tasted like dust, ash, decomposed corpses, and simultaneously, like fresh mulberries, cherries ripened in the sun, rose water, pulverized saffron, dates.

There was a swell. The ship rose, then leveled again. A body moving through the corridor slammed into the wall and then began to vomit. Everyone was emptying their stomachs. The stench of death was everywhere. It was wafting up through the porous waters of the sea. I reached for my notebook. Had I been waiting in vain for my life to become legible in it? I flipped through it, browsed sentence after sentence. *Cut them and a viscous fluid will pour*, I heard.

I fell asleep again. In my dream, I walked up the narrow spiraling staircase of the double-helix dome of Santa Maria del Fiore in Florence. It was night. There was no one else there. The baked red bricks of the dome looked like they had been soaked in blood. There was something organic, anatomical, about that labyrinthine staircase. I felt as though I were walking the pathway of my converged brains, as if all my selves had overlapped into this radiant and strange structure. At the top of the staircase, I climbed through a small opening and stood on the terrace overlooking Florence that wraps around the dome like a belt. In the quiet air of the night, I had the sense that the baked stones of the city were breathing, that the city was alive with all its deaths, that everything it has ever been, everything it will ever be, was always already here.

I opened my notebook one last time. I read: *My formula for greatness in a human being is amor fati, that one wants nothing to be different, not forward, not backward, not in all eternity.*

I stood there attempting to cultivate undying love for everything that had happened to me: my mother's untimely death, my father's near blindness and ultimate death, my subsequent entanglement with Ludo. But I came up short.

As soon as I thought of him, Ludo manifested. He was standing next to me, staring out at the city of his childhood. He had demolished the obstinate walls of his character. We had been transformed by our own narrative.

"What is wrong with us?" he asked tenderly.

I told him that I didn't know, that I couldn't be certain. I told him the only thing I knew was that I had tried to keep my love for him locked down, because if I projected it onto him, invited him into love's sweet glow, I knew that he, too, would inevitably disappear. That is my belief, I told him, distorted and delusional, but so far unchallenged by the strange and staggering events of my ill-fated life.

There was a knock on my door. I woke up. The sea had calmed. The ship was sailing smoothly. There was a vague buzzing in the margins of the universe. It was the sound of the residue of the dead. It was beautiful. I lay there listening to its music. I didn't bother to open the door.

At midday, I walked out onto the deck with Taüt. He was happy to get some air. He spread his wings. He stretched his talons. He fanned his crest. I sucked on that rock. There were whole families sitting on the orange plastic chairs fixed into the deck. The sea was clear. The sun was hanging low. The waters parted for our ship to pass. In the distance, the sky looked as if it could catch on fire at any moment; the horizon was tinged with sparkling embers. I turned around and looked at the faces of the other passengers. They seemed so safe, as if they had been ensured against any and all potential losses, their lives saccharine, punctuated by beach vacations, lobster bisque, freshly folded laundry, pool parties, champagne toasts. Everything regulated, balanced, even pain and suffering delivered in measured blows designed never to overwhelm the recipient whose emotional life was protected by vast and sturdy guardrails.

I turned back to the sea. I imagined swimming in those open waters with Ludo, hundreds of feet from the shore. A golden light fell across the water. The eddies sparkled. The water foamed up against the sides of the ship. I stood there under the broad dome of the midday sky, and as seagulls flew through it and the rugged coast of Italy came into view, I thought to myself, reality is either liquid, or it consists of nothing at all. One moment we are here, and the next we are elsewhere and everything we thought we knew dissolves. Memories we have eschewed are awakened. They rise and beckon us to realign our multiple selves again and again. Even if I turn out to be a lone voice in the dark night, I thought inwardly, I will not lose conviction. I am unafraid to admit that the world we live in is violent, obtuse; that a gulf, once opened, is not easily sealed; that one does not drink from the waters of death and go on living disaffected, untouched. And what, I wondered, does it mean to love in the midst of such shifting shores? Love, I thought, a provisional remedy to decrease our suffering, which will be infinite and self-perpetuating as long as we flock back to this meager universe. Love, like death and literature and liberty, is everywhere and nowhere at once. It is nothingness itself — only I hadn't seen it as such before, and even if I had, how would I have known to recognize it or welcome it when the ill-fated are only ever given the most infertile fields to plant our lot in? I sucked on my rock some more. I had been sucking on it intermittently since I had found it. It had grown smooth. I removed it from my mouth and cast it into the great green sea, into the Sea of Sunken Hopes, thinking to myself, it's just a word. And yet, I considered, it is the greatest key and the greatest riddle.

We were approaching land. The banks of Italy were brilliant ochre. I scanned the black water of the coves, the white sand, the crescent-shaped beaches. On the coast, Genoa — sooty, industrial, sinister, hemmed in by mountains — seemed perfectly lovable. Those mountains were the bones of the sea, the fangs of the earth. I stood there staring at the land. I thought of the Matrix of Literature. I thought of all the black holes and crevices. I thought of the Pyramid of Exile. I thought of my sick hand. I thought of the mind of the universe. I heard the voices of the writers of the void speak to me in a calm susurrus. *The air*, I thought, remembering, *is full of noises.*